SOME OF US ARE REAL

Some Of Us Are Real

Are Real

Alexander P. Sigrist

Dedication

Dedication 1 (July 2021)

There are many things that would need to be said and I am probably forgetting most of them. So, for starters, just let me say: Thank you. Thank you to all the real people who have been part of this journey in some way or other:

Foremost, of course, thank you to those people that have allowed me to peek inside their minds and write a story about what I have found in there. Yes, some people in this novel are real. I hope I have done them right.

Second, my thanks go to everyone who had to listen to me talk about this novel for the past few years. I know I can get obsessive about this shit, so I appreciate your patience.

Dedication 2 (February 2022)

Is anyone out there?

Dedication 3 (July 2022)

As we are closing in on the end, there are some questions that remain:

1. Will anyone want to read this?
2. Why the fuck am I doing this?
3. What is this monster I have created?

Like Frankenstein, I look at the thing in front of me, stitched together from many parts and ideas and words, words, so many words. But unlike Frankenstein, I hope, the monster will walk away from me and find a life of its own.

I have people to thank – in no particular order: The people who have read the monster and who have given me feedback. Could not do it without you. Second, the people who have stayed close to me and who have fuelled my creativity. Could not do it without you. Third, my editor, Phil Brunner, most definitely could not have done this without you. The Caretakers. You have indulged my outburst for years and I would not be the writer I am without you. Simon H. for your mentorship, support and unwavering criticism. Simon Z. for being my closest friend, through good and bad. Tanja W. and Simon R. for letting me part of your family. And, finally, my family for driving me mad and keeping me sane.

And anyone I should have mentioned but forgot.

Dedication 4 (November 2022) - Final Dedication (?)

We are closing in on the end - so this last one goes to the readers. I had the opportunity to attend a lecture by Prof. James Phelan the other day, in which he described the act of writing and reading as a dance between the author and the reader (I am completely unfamiliar with his work, so please forgive me, Prof. Phelan, if I am misrepresenting your theory). It was one of those rare moments when I felt like the speaker was talking directly to me, to what I'd been attempting all along with my writing. Writing is a dance, and it demands an exchange, a dialogue, a collaboration between the writer and those who read. So, please, dear readers, do not be afraid to take the lead from time to time. This novel is meant to engage you. It will demand you to work as well. I think that is just fair retribution for all the time I have put into it. It is *our* novel now. Let your imagination roam free.

Contents

Part I: I   1

Five out of Ten Hours   2

Part II: Dog is Dead   31

Tokyo / Runners   32

Yamadera / Dance, Destroy, Die / Yonezawa   83

Yokohama / The Old Mill   121

A Tale of Two Girls / Nara 1   168

Part III: You   201

Poppy Field   202

Some of Us Are Real   241

Part IV: The Human Angle   277

Nara 2 / Osaka / Tesseract and Post-Apocalyptic Blues   278

Hiroshima / Point of Convergence   321

Fukuoka / Amelie   358

Onomichi / The Things we Pass on / Tokyo Fox Story   409

Part V: From Here on Out 453

God is Dead 454

My Friend's Wedding 468

The Ghosts of Other People 486

Vickie 504

Some of Us 515

Part I: I

Five out of Ten Hours

It was five out of ten hours into my flight from Frankfurt to Tokyo when I realised that I would die alone.

I did the math: I was thirty-five years old and maybe half my life was already over. Maybe only a bit more than a third if I was lucky. And even though the math and the probability were not correct, it seemed to me endlessly more likely that I would die alone than finding that special someone we were all looking for (Were we all, though? Did I really speak for all of humanity?).

It was a terrible flight from there on out. I wanted to cry, couldn't, and even if I had cried, I would only have done so hoping someone would see my tears, my diamond tears, my crystal-clear tears, and come over to me and hug me, find it impressive I had emotions, kiss me, and hold my hand. And have wild sex with me on the airplane toilet.

My entertainment system didn't function properly (the screen had a terrible green tint), so while everyone else was watching some movie, all I could do was sit there and listen to a podcast on my phone about some serial killing maniac. I felt sick, not because of the podcast, but because of the two glasses of acidic red wine I'd drunk before getting onto the plane. It didn't help that the air inside the plane smelt rancid, maybe caused by the older man two rows in front of me who'd taken off his socks, or maybe it smelled bad in general, and the air condition-ing seemed not to work properly, alternating between spitting out icy breaths and fiery farts. I had decided to wear jeans, which certainly had been the fashionable choice, but after some hours of travel, they'd become uncomfortable, most likely thanks to the fact I'd pulled them up too far after I'd been to the toilet, and it now felt like they were strangling my privates. Also, I was sweating. Not profusely, still enough to make me feel disgusting.

The flight attendant came by and offered me a glass of water. Bless her soul, always smiling at me. Yet, I knew she didn't like me. My large body ever-so-slightly leaned into the aisle, and she constantly bumped into my right knee when walking by. On the seat next to me, there was an Asian guy, tall and quite muscular. He seemed unhappy about having me and my oversized belly next to him. I'd tried to talk to him before we'd left, say a few words about the weather, but he'd looked at me with an annoyed look and hadn't replied. Maybe he just had nothing to say about the weather. Instead of talking to me, he'd taken a small silver case out of his rucksack, opened it to reveal a Polaroid showing the photo of a woman. He'd looked at it for a long time. His girlfriend, I decided. Very romantic gesture.

I liked Polaroid. Back to-the-roots photography. You snap a photo and there is no way of correcting it. No digital non-sense between the act of taking it and the result. That is why every single Polaroid photo looks good. Because it is a singular, frozen moment in time, not reproducible, only destroyable. The only thing that troubled me about Polaroid was the fact that people had that urge to shake the photo as soon as it came out of the camera, like little monkeys, not knowing that there was no use in that. Quite the contrary, the vigorous, masturbatory shaking could damage the photo. Everyone who buys a Polaroid camera should know this: you do not shake it like a Polaroid picture.

The girl in the photo had looked nice. Friendly. Not beautiful, but good-spirited. I envied him. Maybe that envy had got me in a bad mood.

I remembered having a crush in kindergarten. Being in love. It had been an unshakeable feeling, a certainty pulsating inside me every time I'd seen her. Unfortunately, with the same certainty as I knew I was in love, I knew she'd not love me. Love was doom.

I didn't have any memories from the time before kindergarten. Cue to music, flashback to my first memory: I was engaged in some game at kindergarten that required skill and precision and while playing that game, my brain, my being, slowly cut through the veil of existence, and started to think consciously. I looked up and from one moment to the next realised that I was. That I existed. Fucking kindergarten Descartes toddler. I knew in that moment, for the first time, that I was a being. A person. And that I was in for a long and shitty ride.

The seatbelt sign came on. The plane began to rattle, jump up and down like a kid on their first day of school. The tall, muscular Asian guy next to me continued to sleep and didn't notice. I assumed his seatbelt was closed – after all, they tell you to keep it fastened whenever you are sitting on your bum, whether the sign is on or not. Interestingly enough, they don't tell you it's an obligation or a law, they just recommend it "as turbulences can occur without warning." And that was why we all obediently put it on as soon as we sat down. Sheep with belts around their furry bellies. For a moment I hated that thought, I felt a punk attitude rise within, wanted to fight the law (which wasn't even a law, but just a recommendation), finger raised to the plane authorities, and take that fucking belt off whenever and however I pleased.

Sure, they tell you it is for your own safety. But then, it's not. It is just about the airline not wanting to clean up the mess you'd make if a turbulence ejected you from your seat and you'd bump into the ceiling and fall back onto the floor, hit your head against the armrest of the tall, muscular Asian guy, and start bleeding all over the cheap, plastic meals you get on planes these days, those pretentious meals that are designed by some famous chef, but taste as shitty as any old microwave dish you can get for a few bucks in the supermarket, those dishes you know you shouldn't eat when buying them and you feel real bad when the cashier takes your money and you give her a look somewhere between consternation and torture, a look to let her know you know you shouldn't eat that microwave dish, but you have no choice, because you are a busy man, and by the way, what's your name, madame cashier lady, and what's your phone number, shall we chat for a bit, and you think to yourself, as she takes the money, maybe you should make a joke, maybe you should just say something funny and eloquent, but you pay your sad microwave dish and you go home and you put the sad microwave dish in the microwave and it tastes just like a shitty meal you get on any old airplane.

"As you can see, the pilot just turned on the seatbelt sign," the Maître de Cabine rudely interrupted my train of thought. "We are expecting a bit of rough weather and turbulences ahead. Nothing to worry about and we should make it out of the harsh-weather-zone in about half an hour. We'll start serving dinner right after the pilot turns the seatbelt sign off again."

I was getting hungry. I looked for the menu card the attendant had handed out at the beginning of the flight to check what shitty meal I had to look forward to, but I couldn't find it. Maybe she'd taken it away while I had my eyes closed, because she thought I was sleeping, and that a menu card in the seat pocket in front of me somehow disturbed my sleep.

Most people seemed to sleep around me or had their TV on, and the flight attendant was hustling around in the little kitchen area at the end of the aisle. Doesn't look like we are expecting bad turbulences, I calmed my nerves, otherwise she'd have sat down as well. She was completely carefree. I wondered whether flight attendants got special training in quickly grabbing hold of something to prevent themselves from falling. The flight attendant special school of not falling. I could see myself, in an alternate universe, as a flight attendant, hustling around in the kitchen, quietly laughing to myself because all the stupid passengers had got their asses glued to their seats by the seatbelt sign, when, suddenly, the plane is thrown about by turbulences, and I grab the first thing I can get a hold of and it's a hot kettle of hot coffee and, despite my best efforts, I fall and I spill the hot coffee over an old lady in the first row and her face gets burnt badly. And she spends the rest of her life seeking revenge against me. What is even worse, I must clean all the coffee stains on the seats after the plane's arrival. And all the others, my so-called colleagues, laugh and leave the plane, laugh at me, little Cinderella-girl, because I still have to clean the mess, while they already head out of the airport, walking the professional flight attendant walk, the walk only flight attendants can do, always a group of them, two in front, three behind them, another two behind them, walking briskly, but relaxed, always smiling their perfect flight attendant smiles, because they do not hire you if you don't have that perfect, white-teeth smile. But not I. I stopped smiling the moment I spilled coffee over the old lady, because I knew I would have to spend the rest of my life on the run from her.

Maybe I should run. Maybe just not return home from my holiday. Two weeks of holiday, of getting away, of being someone else. Two weeks of pretending I was who I wanted to be, a glorious writer, an amazing talent, ready to be discovered. "I am working on a novel," I'd tell everyone who wanted or didn't want to know, "it is going to be big. Important. It will be about people. I am interested in whether there is something that... [dramatic pause] ...holds us together. That unites us. As people." I'd started telling this to people three years ago. That I would *author* a novel. For a year, I didn't write a word. Then, for another year, I tried to find the right sentence to begin my book with. And then, in the time-span of yet another year, I wrote five pages. Five pages of internal monologue, of vomiting my guts out, about the hate we accumulate over the years, concluding that this hate, this feeling of having OD'ed on this fucking planet and its people, is the only thing that brings us together.

The seatbelt sign came off. "This is the pilot again. We just switched the seatbelt sign off," – no shit –, "and the cabin crew will begin serving dinner. The rest of the flight should be quiet, otherwise, you'll hear from me."

What did pilots talk about during the flight? Did they talk at all? They were in that little cockpit for twelve hours, holding a plane in the air with hundreds of people under their wings. Did they even think about that? If I had to take on that kind of responsibility, I would go crazy. Maybe I could handle fifty people, yes, but hundreds? Think of all the years of life, the stories, the egos, the love and hate assembled on one plane. If I walked through the plane right now, it seemed likely that I'd find someone I truly liked, a new friend, a sympathetic soul, and it was equally likely that I would find someone who was so different I would instantly hate that person, couldn't stand to be in the same room, in fact, one of us would have to leave the plane, take a chute and jump, otherwise we'd start killing each other.

"Beef or vegetarian?" The flight attendant had magically appeared next to me with the food trolley. "Sorry, what was that?" I replied, dumbfounded, mouth open. I'd understood her question, but I needed more time to think my options through, although I already knew what I would order. I rarely ate vegetarian if meat was an option, yet I felt like I needed those few seconds of consideration to see whether I'd changed and whether I unexpectedly had become someone who preferred vegetarian. "Beef or vegetarian?" she repeated, and I promptly said "Beef." Looked like I hadn't changed. She put the plastic tray in front of me and I looked around to see whether the drink trolley was close, only to find that the attendant was still five or six rows away and only making her way towards me slowly.

I opened the small box that was the centrepiece of the meal and found that the beef option was a Korean-style-readymade-microwave-bulgogi-kind-of... *thing*. I found it somewhat funny, getting a Korean dish, considering we were flying towards Japan, and wondered how the big, tall Asian (presumably Japanese) guy next to me would react when he'd see they served him a Korean bulgogi. Maybe he would take out his samurai sword and slash the entire crew for insulting his tastebuds by serving this bullshit, beef-shit. Then, I felt disgusted by myself for thinking about someone committing a massacre on a plane that was based on taking the piss out of complicated historic incidents between Korea and Japan that were much too serious to make fun of.

Well, maybe he'd just commit suicide when he tasted the food, I thought when I took my first bite, which faintly tasted of beef and carried a hint of Asian spices, but, apart from that, bore little resemblance to edible food. Maybe it would have been a decent meal if it were three o'clock in the morning and I'd been completely drunk, yes, under these circumstances, this could have been the best beef ever, but for now, it was a tasteless piece of chunk with the consistency of melted plastic.

I let my eyes travel across the tray to check what else I'd got. There was a small piece of bread, which probably was so dry it would suck up whatever little spit I had left in my mouth – the drink-trolley-attendant was still three rows away from me –, but I felt relieved I had also got a small piece of butter. Then, some fruits and a yoghurt. Korean beef, canned fruits, yoghurt, dry bread – a meal as if the West and the East had had hate-sex in a dirty kitchen.

I took the yoghurt container in hand. It kept getting worse. Strawberry-yoghurt. The food-equivalent to a person you know, but don't really know, because it is the most normal person in the world, a person truly with no depth, like Jim from the office, Jim who is nice and friendly, but when you leave the office, you've already forgotten he exists, Jim, the strawberry-yoghurt of people. If there was one thing I hated...

"Something to drink?"

"A coke," I said. Finally.

I hated yoghurt. No, I didn't hate it. I did not understand its existence. I did not understand why anyone would peer into the fridge and see a ton of good things, like bacon and cheese, only to go: "Oh, there is a yoghurt here, I really want to eat that, because yoghurts, wow, they are delicious." No, they were not. They were fucking flavoured milk-mushes, as if someone had taken real food and punched any kind of realness out of it, punching so hard that anything that was ever real about it evaporated from the present and disappeared backwards through the past, so far back in time that even dinosaurs would have vomited strawberries backwards.

I took a sip from my coke and wondered why I hadn't ordered a beer. I was a big guy, so I shouldn't really drink alcohol on a long-distance flight because of thrombosis and whatnot, but then, did one beer really matter? And what was that with the idea of you only live once, anyway? Yet, it would be a damn shame of a way to go, killed because of thrombosis because of that beer he drank on that flight to

Japan, killed by an aneurism that travelled from his leg to his brain. He just fell on the floor in a sushi bar, they'd say, as he got up after a most amazing sushi-meal, he got up, he fell, he was dead and the papers got it all wrong and said that the chef had poisoned him because the chef used to be a spy and he'd thought that this guy was an assassin sent to kill him.

I turned around, halfway, awkwardly in my seat, to look after the lady with the drink-trolley and I considered whether I should get up and ask her for a beer, only to reject the idea. I didn't know whether a second drink was included in my super-cheap-super-saver-if-you-try-to-change-the-flight-we-will-send-Satan-after-you economy ticket and didn't want to ask. Instead, I resorted to finishing the rest of the hate-bulgogi and the fuck-yoghurt. As much as I hated the meal, the thought of wasting food disgusted me more. While I was finishing the piece of cardboard-bread, I tapped the screen in front of me again. The menu showed up, but the screen's primary colour was still green. Maybe I should watch the Avengers, just for the fun of every character looking like the Hulk, but then, I didn't really see the sense in watching an action movie on a tiny, low-resolution screen.

Maybe I should watch a rom-com instead. Julia R. and Hugh G. fresh in green. But then, I hated rom-coms. At least, that was what I would tell everyone who asked me about my taste in movies. Hated them because they were worthless. The truth was, I didn't hate them. I was ashamed by how much I liked them. How much I liked the warm feeling they gave me, that promise that even after you royally fucked things up and your love is leaving the country, you can still rush to the airport and the security guard, who sees your struggle, lets you go through the gate, and you can stand there, in front of the plane's doors, and tell your love how much you love her and/or how big an idiot you were and she will decide that she'll stay and love you and happily ever after bullshit.

Rom-coms omitted the actual ending. Because we do not live happily ever after. We will fuck up again, make the same mistakes again, try again to rush after our love and give our speech at the gate again, but our love will be our ex-love now and she will say fuck you and leave for Spain to live with Juan, the guy she met on that trip with some friends, Juan, that fucker. She will leave you, because you fucked up, and she also fucked up, and the security guard is not nice anymore, he spots you at the gate and he beats you up and bans you from the airport for life, which takes away any chance of you going to Spain and give another speech to your ex-love (or exact revenge on your ex-love and Juan, which could be a hilarious comedy movie).

I wanted to go to the bathroom. Not because I needed to pee, but because I wanted to get up, wanted to stretch my legs, walk around for a bit, as if that would get me to Japan faster. But the tray with the now-empty dishes was still in front of me and the trash trolley was half-a-plane away. I could try to get past the tray – which would most likely result in an undignified embarrassment, me trying to balance the tray in my hands to allow my big belly to make it past the little plastic table, trying to get up, hands holding the tray shakingly, lifting myself up to get past the armrest, all hands and limbs engaged in the task, my jeans would slip downwards, not far, still far enough for the top of my ass to show and people would gasp in shock seeing my hairy behind. The last thing I wanted to do was moonlight a plane full of people.

The Asian guy finished his meal and leaned back again to close his eyes. His reaction to the food had been less agitated than I'd imagined. He'd pulled back the thick tinfoil from the main dish, looked at it for a couple of seconds, ate it and that was that. No sigh, no angry breathing, nothing. He hadn't touched the yoghurt, though, which filled me with a jolt of sympathy. It also made me feel bad because I'd eaten mine. I should have followed suit, should have shown my contempt for the yoghurt by not touching it.

The trash bin attendant stepped up to me – I hadn't expected her so soon, so I wasn't ready to give her my tray. Helpful as I wanted to be, I quickly fumbled, trying to hand it to her, yet was too slow. To compensate for my sluggish movements, her hand reached forward, which made me want to move faster, lifting the tray too fast now, gravity doing its thing, the yoghurt container wobbling dangerously. For an endless split-second, I saw how it tipped over, as if life was going on in slow-motion, and I knew I could still catch it, but decided not to, I just froze in shock and awe, unwilling to prevent the catastrophe of the yoghurt container falling into the abyss between my legs and the seat in front of me. It left a thick smear of strawberry yoghurt on my left knee and disappeared somewhere on the floor, out of sight.

"I am sorry..." I mumbled.

"Don't worry. We'll get it later," the flight attendant said, took the Asian guy's tray next to me and moved on. I turned halfway around to the Asian guy and mouthed the words "I am sorry," but he had not opened his eyes. He didn't care. Or maybe he hated me.

But at least the tray was gone. I got up, pulled my jeans up, and looked down at the floor. The strawberry yoghurt container had rolled over and was now lying next to the tall and muscular Asian guy's right foot. I knew that the right thing to do was to get down on my knees and try to reach for the container, but I was afraid that I might touch the Asian guy's foot or that he'd think I was trying to pray or wanting to give him a blowjob, so I let it be and left for the toilet.

I entered the small toilet cabin, squeezed in, squeezed out of the way of the door to close it. I felt like a blob in a shoe box. I pulled my trousers down and sat on the toilet to see whether I had to pee. I sat there. No real purpose. No-smoking sign in front of my eyes. Toilet paper on the wash basin.

Shit, I wanted this flight to be over.

Steal the toilet paper. Just for the sake of adventure.

My brain was full of shit thoughts.

I remained sitting on the toilet for a few good minutes, too tired to get up. It had turned out I didn't have to pee. After a few more minutes, I finally stood up, pulled my trousers up and, this time, tried not to pull them too far, did anyway, because I was afraid my ass would show, washed my hands, and made my way back to the seat. The tall and muscular Asian guy was still sleeping, or at least had his eyes closed, but the yoghurt container on the floor had disappeared. Probably, the flight attendant had made good on her promise and picked it up. Or maybe, as soon as I'd left for the toilet, the Asian guy had opened his eyes, picked the container up, thrown it across the room while spurting insults about this European foreigner, this clumsy individual that was me, and everyone on the plane agreed, nodding their heads fervently.

I sat down.

I thought about continuing listening to my podcast, but my ears hurt from the earphones. Maybe I should say something about my entertainment system to the flight attendant, complain, and maybe that would be my ticket to first-class. You unfortunate thing, the flight attendant would say, no TV? Here, sit in the first class, watch some first-class TV, and drink some champagne. But then, it was more likely she'd ask why I had said nothing six hours ago, when we took off. I survived thus far, she would add, so I could survive another four hours. Four hours. Four hours didn't seem like a long time. You could watch two movies in that time and that'd be it. Or you could try to sleep, maybe that'd be a good idea, because it is going to be lunchtime when you arrive in Tokyo, so for you, it is night now, so you should sleep, and I put my earphones in and put some music on and closed my eyes and tried to sleep.

...

....

I tried to sleep.

I had a headache.

...

Maybe I should get some water. Or orange juice.

Why do they always serve orange juice on flights? Is it because of the vitamin C? Because you are flying in a cylinder filled with germs emanating from your fellow passengers, eating, sweating, sleeping, drooling, snoring, farting, taking their shoes off, sometimes even taking their socks off, people in comfortable trousers that almost look like pyjamas, as if the plane was their living room, and I missed those glory times when people still put on a suit to go on a flight, had a smoke on the plane, made some flirtatious remarks to the flight attendant and she laughed and it was a mad world for mad men. I wished I were one of those mad men, sometimes, I wished I had the charm to say something

SOME OF US ARE REAL | 13

smooth, the self-security to be charming, the looks to be secure. The plane, everything, all drenched in glorious black and white and there is smoke in the cabin, I am smoking a cigarette, Gauloise, French, and the flight attendant, in a blue mini-skirt would come by and say to me: "You are smoking Gauloise. They are my favourite." And I nod, puff the smoke towards the ceiling and offer her a cigarette, and she says she can't, because she is working and they may not smoke when they work, so I say maybe we could have a cigarette after work and she laughs and smiles and I smile, faintly.

I was craving a smoke.

I didn't smoke. But then, I did. I would occasionally buy a pack, just the one, but then I'd buy another one. Stopping smoking is easy, someone said, he did it a million times, he said. Someone famous said. Or maybe it was just the internet claiming that someone famous said it, when in fact it had been made up by a guy at his computer. People say all kinds of things on the internet with no one actually knowing who said what and when. I could pretend to be your aunt Marta sending you a picture and a good luck note for your university exam and you would have no idea that it was not Marta, that Marta didn't care about you, that she'd forgotten about your entry exams. But I'd pretend to be Marta, and I'd be nice, so at the next family reunion you'd be nice to her and have a wonderful day and you'd talk quite a lot and she'd say to her husband Frank that she never knew you had turned into this charming young man and that they should see you more often and you'd become good friends, you and Marta and Frank, kinda, but he doesn't talk a lot, usually he goes for a walk with the dog when you come around, but Marta bakes for you, her chocolate cake, even though you don't really like chocolate, but you eat it anyway, and she is happy and you are happy and Frank is happy, kinda, and the dog is happy, because now he gets to go outside more often, and when she dies, Marta, years after you've finished university, you inherit her car, she doesn't have anything else, since she had to pay for the care of Frank, who'd had Alzheimer's, so you get the car, and you sell it for five thousand bucks, not much, but it pays for a nice holiday for you and your girlfriend and you have a great time together in Southern France and Italy and Eastern Europe, and you and your girlfriend are happy, you get married, you have two kids, good kids, they are happy, and you are happy, kinda, a bit of midlife crisis, a bit of too-much-work, a bit of a nagging wife and annoying kids, but whenever things get too much, you remember Frank and take your dog for a walk and you are happy and the dog is happy and you secretly smoke a cigarette on your walk and life is...

Bullshit.

Life is bullshit. We are covered in bruises when we are born, the obvious ones heal quickly. Then, we spend the rest of our life accumulating new bruises, only, they are not obvious anymore. And our friends tell us that everything is going to be fine, and time heals all wounds, but time only makes us forget that we have wounds, until we end up opening the same old wounds again and we bleed the same blood and cry the same tears. A cat on the hot stove. It touches the stove, it burns, it will never touch the stove again. But we are more stupid than a cat.

What was I thinking about? What stove? What was the connection between stove and life? Food. Food was life. I loved food, going to good restaurants, discover the latest best-restaurants-in-the-world-trends. But how do you know you are eating good food? Amazing food, like those Instagram bloggers? Who is the authority on that? Who decides what's good and what's bad? Why was I not an expert at anything? I should dedicate myself to something. Study something hard, spend years of my life perfecting it. And people would turn to me for my opinion. And my opinion would be good. Gentle, but also harsh, direct. I would have a long beard and look like a wise man, sitting on the floor behind a small table, with a stern look on my face and people would come to me and sit down on the floor on the other side of the table, and they'd be nervous. And I would look at them, but suddenly, I would burst into laughter, and they'd ease up and ask their question. And I would get serious and give them my advice. And they would thank me, and I would thank them.

I was thirty-five years old. I should have been an expert at something by now. Thirty-five years was a long time. You could learn how to play the guitar in that time. Or how to write wonderful poems. Or how to be an amazing chef. I was not an expert at any of these things. A master of none. A jack of all trades.

I was lacking the connection to find the ambition to be great at something.

Where did that sentence come from?

It should be easy these days to connect, no? Turn on the internet, find someone. Just any kind of connection. Anything to make you feel less lonely. I tried. I checked websites with people who have the same interests. I tried dating apps. I used Instagram, WhatsApp, Twitter, I was on Facebook, and I looked at the pictures of people and imagined how it would be if we connected and what we'd talk about, but I never sent a single message to anyone. I just stared at their pictures. Creepy fucking creep.

We are all creeps.

Creeping each other out.

Blaming each other for our mistakes.

Fuck.

The world is a mess.

Baby boomers busy complaining they made too many babies, complaining how the babies have all grown up and how they must now watch their former babies fall to pieces, babies going through a perpetual state of midlife crisis before they even turn thirty, those freaking millennials, a generation of self-entitled shitheads that think the world owes them everything. And the millennials open their apps and they snapchat with bunny ears and dog eyes and click and click and burn themselves out because the internet never stops, it keeps on generating likes and you have to post, next photo, next video, don't forget to like your best friend's photo, or maybe you should comment, a smiley maybe a XOXO, RR, LOL, ROFL, LU and every second you miss is a second you miss, maybe you miss something, the FUCKING FEAR OF MISSING OUT THAT KEEPS THE WORLD TURNING THE GEARS ROLLING THE COGS CLICKING CLICK CLICK CLICK CLICK CLICK CLICK THE plane had become quiet. The music I'd been listening to had finished, and I heard the dead sound of the earphones in my ear. I was breathing.

What is this?
Have I fallen asleep?
Is this what sleeping feels like?

I was not scared of missing out. I was scared I'd already missed out. That I'd come home to my apartment, and I live alone, and I wish there was someone in the bed next to me. I wish the roof above our heads was gone and we could see the stars and count them. The universe is endless. It is expanding. The endlessness of the universe is getting bigger. What is in the space that is not universe (yet)? Or does the universe expand into itself, growing like a Moebius band, like that snake that will eat itself at the end of days? What would I do if this were the end of days? If I came home from a gruelling day of work to my empty and lonely apartment and I'd go into the living room and turn on the TV and it's the news and I would turn up the volume, so I can go to the toilet, and hear the TV from the toilet, I'd leave the door open because I live alone, and I hear the newscaster say:

"This is the end of days. We have two hours to go."

And she'd explain why and give some scientific reason and the science is sound and I almost fall off the toilet and I hurry back into the living room, and I change the channel, but the newscaster is on all channels, repeating the same message over and over again. This is the end of days. Two hours to go. What would I do? What would we do? Would we stand together like a group of school children and sing a song boldly facing the end that is nigh? Or would we turn our phones on and text our loved ones and post to our followers hashtagthelast-supper and look at this picture of the most amazing ramen I cooked, although it's just instant noodle soup and it doesn't taste as good as it looks and you take a photo and smile because it is a nice photo, then you sit there, alone, eating your soup while the world nears its end. Two hours. Two hours is not enough. Not for all the things I'd want to do before I die. So, I'd just sit there and think about the things I'd want to do and wait for the lights to go out. And the rest is silence. Silence seemed to make so much more sense than talking. What did we even talk about when we talked? Why could we talk about things that did not relate to our current surroundings? What was it good for that we could talk about abstract concepts, think about our existence, our existential nihilism? Abstract thought only leads to depression.

I opened my eyes. The noise of the plane came back to me. The tall, muscular Asian guy sleeping next to me. Many TVs turned off. I slowly got up and turned around to go to the bathroom. I didn't need to go, yet it was the only thing to do. I'd have preferred to go up to the hatch, open it and just leave this goddam plane. I could see myself stepping past the flight attendant, and she'd look at me with a questioning look, not understanding what I was about to do. I'd step to the door and grab the handle and I hear the flight attendant yell something, but it is too late. I glance back and I smile, and I open the door and the cold air, the wind, surrounds me. I can see lights of the world below, behind a thick veil of clouds. I step outside, I see the stars above. The plane vanishes from sight quickly. I float there for a moment and look at the world above the planet. A lot of stars, the moon somewhere off in the distance. Then I turn around and start falling. Towards earth. Clouds embrace me, disappear, the city lights below getting closer. I fall faster, the air is frosty, my lips frozen. I fall onto a city, some nondescript city in Russia, I destroy half of it as I crash, a gigantic explosion of ice and my body, I leave a crater behind. I step out of the crater and get arrested by the police, they call my falling a terrorist attack and I am thrown into jail. They send me to Siberia and my government tries half-heartedly to get me back, but they don't want me back, so I'm to work in Siberia, and I become one with the cold and I drink vodka and learn Russian, and I meet Dimitri and together, we write an epic novel about wars and people and life. People take the ideas in the novel seriously, as if it were a religion, and they march to Siberia, millions of them, and they free me, sadly, Dimitri has already died, eaten by a polar bear, they set me free, and I lead the rebellion and we overthrow all dictatorships on Earth and we dissolve all nation states. The people have become one under my teachings and we all learn my language and kids have to read my book in school and Dimitri has become a footnote in my life, his name disappeared from the cover of the book, and I am a benign king, I rule with and through love. Everyone is happy. The few who are not I send to prison, lock them away, until, one day, two of those prisoners write a novel about life and war and everything in between and people read that book in secret, even though I have banned it, and they take the ideas of the book seriously and they free the two of them and they overthrow me, I get killed, shot, my head chopped off, but that is fine, I had a good life. I give way to the next one who will be a benign king, until, one day, he will not be so anymore.

"Do you need anything?"

Someone rudely awakened me from my thoughts. I was standing in the galley. How long had I been standing here?

"Water?"

The flight attendant who shared the small space with me handed me a cup of water, turned around and left, walking down the aisle towards the front of the plane. I stood there with the cup. I was not thirsty. I felt sick. The bulgogi lay heavy in my stomach, but hydrating seemed like a clever idea, so I drank the water.

And then? Go back to my seat? Go to the toilet? Try to have a chat with the pilot? All options seemed shitty. The hatch was right in front of me.

Unlock the true potential within, it whispered to me.

Free your mind. Free.

Weren't all our lives prisons? Get on a train between seven and eight in the morning and meet the endless number of people, commuters, all the same, all with their ties and their little suitcases, off to their offices, to the small desks they have, dreaming of earning money to buy a house, have kids, steady, steady, a steady dream of life within the confines of the small dreams they have. Adult dreams are small. Kids want to become astronauts. They want to become archaeologists and discover new dinosaurs. They want to become pilots. They want to be bus drivers. They want to be endless. They want to have fun. They want to ride rollercoasters, they want to fall in love for the first time, want to have their first drink with their friends before they are allowed to drink legally, they want to run across the motorway, not afraid of death, because their hearts are full with *Weltschmerz*, the pain they have inherited from their parents who had to abandon their big dreams and before they know it, the kids have to decide what they want to do next, playtime is over, and they go learn a job or they go to university and step by step they realise they will not be a famous actor, a famous writer, they will never discover a new dinosaur, they won't fly a plane, they will work in an office, get a tiny desk next to other tiny desks and will be a good part of the system, typing their shit away at a computer, printing, stapling, filing the big dreams in grey cabinets, while the creative cells in their brains get drunk, not good-drunk, but depressive-drunk and the cells commit suicide, one after the other, until the world is empty and they come home and their freaking kids have left all their toys in the kitchen and they pick the toys up and they hit their head against the kitchen cupboard and blood runs down their forehead and they realise they don't hate the cupboard, they don't hate the toy, they don't even hate their kids, but they hate their entire fucking life.

I returned to my seat. The tall, muscular Asian guy still seemed to sleep, so I tried to slip into my seat without waking him. I asked myself why I was trying to be considerate when the tall, muscular Asian guy next to me had taken possession of the entire armrest for the entire flight. In fact, I should tell him to go fuck himself or push his arm off the armrest and pretend I was sleeping when he'd wake up all puzzled, trying to figure out why he'd woken up. However, maybe he'd know it had been me pushing him off the armrest, because I couldn't keep the chuckle in and would start laughing. He'd get up and tell me to go fuck myself and beat the living shit out of me. And I would try to defend myself with a plastic fork and the flight attendant would come running and tell us to calm down, but together we'd tell her to go fuck herself and she'd yell "Excuse me!?" and we'd laugh, tell everyone it had been a joke, would order sake, tell the plane to redirect to Hanoi, Vietnam, land like two fire starters, crush the city, go drinking, become friends, go back to the Vietnam War and win it, not for anyone but ourselves, we'd have a party with everyone there, a party that would last five days and six nights, before we pass out and wake up with the worst hangover ever, not remembering what we had done and, most of all, why.

When had I last been at a party? A proper party. Not the parties you partake in when you are past thirty, when you meet at someone's house and cook a nice dinner with your friends, discuss the merits of locally produced food and everyone drinks the wine you've brought and pretends you made an excellent choice. Everyone knows you know nothing about wine, and you brought a cheap one with a nice-looking label, because you are a cheap bastard and who the fuck likes wine, anyway? Maybe you and your friends are still into craft beer, beer bearing names that sound like some marketing experts vomited all over a dictionary, "Your Grandmother's Strawberry Octopus Black Amber IPA," which tastes like something died in the tank when they made the beer, but you like it, because normal beer is for clean-shaved suckers.

I scratched my face. My beard had grown and was itchy. I wondered what I looked like. Of course, I knew what I looked like, I'd seen myself in mirrors and photos, but did one really know what one looked like? What one looked like to other people? When we see someone, we instantly have prejudices in our head based on the first thing we perceive about that person.

What prejudices did people have about me? A not-tall, heavy guy with a scruffy beard and glasses and no logical sense of fashion? *An overstuffed teddy that tries to be a hipster, yet fails.* The thought hurt. I liked it. I continued: *He tries to be a hipster, only he has not enough money or courage to join the army of zombies that dress in overpriced woodchoppers' shirts and skinny jeans and his ass is too big for skinny jeans, so you should be glad he doesn't try, otherwise you'd see his big white behind every time he bends over and you don't want to see that.*

The socially accepted discourse is that we don't want to see a fat person naked. We don't even want to think about a fat person naked. It's *disgusting.* We are okay with models in bikinis and shorts and six-packs and tanned bodies, they are everywhere, on every ad, on TV, in every superhero movie (except for Kung Fu Panda) but as soon as there is a fat guy naked on a screen, it is for shock, or it is played as a joke. Naked man with flabby man-tits? Funny.

I was no different. I didn't want to see myself naked. I was okay with slim hips and female belly buttons framed by flat bellies. I also enjoyed a Ryan-Gosling-six-pack. I did not want the see the barren pudding that was my body.

I couldn't sleep. Hadn't I fallen asleep before? Why had I woken up? Was it the tall, muscular Asian guy next to me? Had he moved? Or maybe the flight attendant had bumped into my knee. I looked around. Some of the other passengers didn't sleep, either, were still watching movies. Touching the touch screens with their fatty fingers, leaving fingerprints everywhere. Did they use planes as training grounds for CSI agents? Maybe that could be a business model. The plane lands, gets rented out to CSI schools, the students come onto the plane and collect as many fingerprints as possible, profile the fingerprints, determine that right here, where I was sitting, there had been a guy with a beard thinking about the un-aesthetics of his body.

How many people on this plane were thinking about their body? About their most private parts? I could do a survey. Get up, walk around and ask people: "Sorry, Sir/Madam, at this very moment, are you thinking about your genitalia?" I would have to be careful and make sure no one overhears the question, otherwise I'd create a pink elephant and suddenly everyone'd think about genitalia.

I quietly laughed to myself at the thought of a plane full of people thinking about privates, everyone trying to remember what theirs looked like, some of them sneaking off to the bathroom to check in the mirror, making sure it was still where it was supposed to be. That would be hilarious, a hilarious Judd Apatow-comedy about genitalia on a plane. Hardy har har.

Har. Har.

I was stuck on this plane. And time kept dragging on. But the plane kept on flying all the way down to Tokyo. Lucy in the sky with diamonds zoomed past outside the windows. I imagined what it would feel like flying through a thunderstorm. Rain falling against the windows. The turbines howling against the storm. The pilots trying to stay calm. One passenger saying to another not to worry, this is normal, there are a lot of thunderstorms, and the pilots know what they are doing. I wasn't afraid of flying, never had been. I was only afraid of crashing. I wondered what I'd think about if we crashed. Would I think about all the things I regretted? Or would I think about mundane things, about the fact that my bank account would automatically transfer my rent money to my landlord? If I died on this flight, my bank account would continue to transfer the money until it would be empty. How many months of rent were in my bank account? Five, maybe six? How long would my employer still transfer my salary before realising I hadn't returned? Would I still be entitled to my holiday days if I were dead? Or would they go with me, leave this earth with me? If there is no one there to take leave days, do the leave days exist at all? Or do they turn into normal days, Monday, Tuesday, Wednesday, Thursday, Friday, Saturday, Sunday? Why did we agree we should work for five days a week and only get two days off?

Seriously, who had come up with that stupid idea? Whoever got up one morning in a bygone, pre-work era and said: "I think it would be a clever idea if we worked five days a week and got two days off." Why didn't the other people beat the living daylights out of that guy and his stupid idea? Why didn't they say: ""Jim, this is the stupidest thing we ever heard. Now, put this sock in your mouth and shut up."

And you never actually get two days off. Because on the weekend you have to do things, take care of things, clean your apartment, mown the lawn, and meet friends, see your family, be social, dress nicely, shower, dress comfortably and then turn on the TV, because you missed out on the last episode of fucking whatever series everyone is watching right now, you have to catch up, otherwise the internet is going to spoil you with all its memes of Sean Bean dying and fuck you, Jim, for posting that fucking meme on your fucking Facebook timeline.

I hadn't had time to clean my apartment before I'd left. Which meant I would have to clean it when I'd come back. Dust. Dust everywhere. We are dust. We shed skin and hair and they become dust on the furniture around us. When we dust, we do nothing else than picking up dead pieces of ourselves, removing the traces of our past. Which meant, if we got lucky, by dusting, we might delete our past mistakes and regrets. Those regrets that come back when you are lying in bed and you are about to fall asleep and suddenly, shit, think about that time you told someone you liked her, but in a weird way, you told her she's an interesting person, and you'd like to get to know her better and she says that is nice and it would be nice to get to know each other better, and you tell her she should email you and arrange a meeting for beers and a talk.

You fucking told her to email you.

You should have looked her in the eyes and told her: I love you and I want to run away with you. You should have come riding in on your horse, your long hair flowing in the wind, the hair on your chest a sign of your sensitivity and ride off with her into the sunset.

I needed to sleep. I would arrive in Japan at lunchtime local time. I needed to sleep now. At least two, maybe three hours. I was jealous of the people on this plane who were sleeping. How did the bastards do that? Maybe they'd taken some pills. I should have taken some pills. I never did, because the thought of going to a pharmacy to ask for sleeping pills made me nervous. The asking was not the problem, but the barrage of questions I would have to answer. Do you take any other medication? No. Do you have any health problems? No. Have you taken sleeping pills before? No. What do you need these for then? None of your fucking business. Do you have heart problems? Are we talking about my actual heart or the figurative heart? Cue to sad music. I hop onto my horse, my long hair flowing in the wind, my chest hair a sign of the hurt I have seen in my life. I ride off into the sunset, without the sleeping pills, alone, ready to ride to the next town, shoot some bad guys, and expose the sheriff for the corrupt slime bag he is and when that is done, I ride off again until the sequel.

Stop imagining things, brain. Let me sleep.

Maybe we were living inside a Truman show. And we got on planes, and they convinced us we were travelling. But the time we spent on a plane was just the time needed to prepare the new set, rehearse the lines, make sure everything was on point, and wait for Truman's arrival. The main character. Everyone loves him / her, watches, as fate hovers above, not God, but the show runner, the game master, the guy who invented Truman's world and who makes sure Truman will never stray outside the world that has been given to him / her. I turned to the imaginary camera next to me...

"Orange juice?" The flight attendant had stepped up to my seat with a tray of orange juice and water cups, had seen I was not sleeping and concluded that I was in need of a refreshing beverage.

"Yes, please," I said. I was in need of a refreshing beverage. I took one. Reality check: Kicking a stone and seeing it fly away was enough proof that the world around you was real. Action, reaction. Therefore, taking a plastic cup of orange juice should be enough proof that I was real. That the world was real. I drink orange juice, therefore, I am.

Maybe we should just stop thinking. Have a switch in our brain to turn it off. Do you want to go to sleep without being haunted by that embarrassing thing you did when you were twelve years old? Sure, just flip the switch. You don't want to listen to your grandmother's knitting club adventures? Flip the switch and get the luxury of experiencing a fake lobotomy for the next two hours. Then you come back, surface, the brain kicks back in and you are ready to think, to interact. But even if you are not ready, just flip the switch again and return later. Flip, lobotomy, resurface, things are still shit, flip, lobotomy, resurface, shit, flip, gone, sleep, back, shit, flip, gone. It is like suicide in easy instalments.

When had life become so complicated? Had it ever been easier? Maybe I'd been born in the wrong times. Medieval times. I could see myself there. Just without all the plague and the shit everywhere and the smell. But I could see myself, a brave knight, without my belly, because there was less food in those times, and it was healthier food. And I would have time to train, because there was no TV, and I would be good with the sword. And I would ride into battle on a gigantic horse and people would whisper my name. I'd slay my enemies, battle after battle, my sword drenched in blood. But now, I'm already past thirty, I'm getting old. My horse is getting old. We ride home, tired from all the battles, back to my castle. It is a gracious building, impressive. It stands on a hill, the sun sets behind it as I arrive. However, it's cold inside. No one is there to get a fire going. I sit in the big living room, the wolves howl outside. I'm alone. All the battles, all the blood, I've never had the time to accomplish other things. I'm ruling my castle, but there are no citizens to rule. I love, but there is no one to love. I've become the freaking knight of depression supreme. And all the while I sit in my palatial room, before the cold fire, pondering my misery, I do not realise that my enemies have plotted against me. In the morning, as the sun rises, they have surrounded my castle. I put on my armour, I take my sword, but they don't want to fight. They have blocked my drawbridge. They know they will not win in a fight. Even if they are a thousand men strong. I would slay them all. They just keep me inside and starve me to death. And it doesn't take long. So many battles, I never had the time to stock up my food storage. I die within a week. And they leave. And the castle falls apart. I return to ashes.

Why was I thinking about death again?

What was death if not... No, wait. What was death?

What was life? Was it the experience of waking up without ever having gone to sleep? I thought of my funeral and how I would give a speech at my funeral, and I knew the thought made no sense, but I didn't care, and I said I was a good man, I said those things I should have said while I was still alive like...

...send me an email. If you find time.

Fuck that. Just kiss the girl. Fuck.

Kissing someone. The weirdest thing.

Why did we do that? Whoever had the brilliant idea of pressing lips against each other? Must have been Jim. Brilliant idea, Jim. Post it on your Facebook page.

We will follow.

Follow me, please. Look at my pictures. Aren't they wonderful? Aren't they deep? Don't they say something about the state of humanity? But no one cares. Ten likes. Twenty on a good day.

I wanted likes. If people pressed the digital representation of a heart, that would mean they liked me. They thought about me. I wanted someone to wake up some morning, and I wanted them to feel like shit because I was the one who was not lying next to them, because I'd be gone, far away, I'd have travelled to South America and I'm now in a temple, in a city, an alleyway, I'm living my life and I want them all to know I'm happy, fulfilled, I am fucking Buddha on a trip to enlightenment, like a star, the cold neon lights of the plane, and I closed my eyes, I opened them and I wondered whether this was what it felt like this feeling of forgetting yourself of stepping outside your body and forgetting that you smell of cold sweat and forgetting that you should sleep that you should arrive soon like a star like the cold lights of the city in the mirror in the rain on the street the asphalt steaming after the sunny day of the heat of the summer of the winter snow of ski I don't ski of heights of being afraid of heights of being afraid of feeling eternity of feeling you have become part of a story that is bigger than you that is like a movie like a legend like an epic and like the lights of the plane like the lights like the lights of the plane of the plane the plane the plane the plane I'm sitting in my back hurts and I. I. Me. I. I wake up. Breathing.

They have turned the lights of the plane back on. The cold, un-friendly simulation of morning.

I checked the time. We would land soon. In two hours soon. They would serve breakfast soon. It was nearly over.

People around me were getting up, making their way to the bath-room. I could get up as well, brush my teeth, what was the point in that, though? Maybe after breakfast, but, at that time, even more people would have the same idea, and I would have to stand in line in front of the bathroom, that awkward situation when you stand silently in a group of people, cooped up in the same place without saying a word, as if you were all in the same twelve-hour elevator to hell. And someone farted.

The tall, muscular Asian guy next to me still had his eyes closed, either still asleep, or maybe, dead.

Down the aisle, the attendants had begun to distribute breakfast. I considered whether I should order coffee when they came round to me. Caffeine, yes. Disgusting airplane coffee, no.

I felt tired. I felt sad. I felt empty. The realisation that had hit me was slowly wearing off, it was still there, though, lingering in my thoughts like an empty stomach. I would die alone. At some stage. If the nearing end of this flight was anything to go by, it wouldn't be today, we wouldn't crash like a fireball, but some day. Someday, we all would die.

"Asian or continental?" There it was. There was another choice to be made among the living. Life choices, live your choices. "Asian," I said, and the flight attendant put down a plastic tray in front of me, which carried a little bowl of rice and a bigger container housing the freak child of a French omelette and a Japanese tamagoyaki. The flight attendant seemed unsure whether to wake the tall, muscular Asian guy, decided against it and moved on. No breakfast for you, armrest-thief. Maybe *dead* armrest-thief.

I inspected the tamagoyaki-French-omelette-thing, which had obviously been cooked by someone who felt like s/he did not get paid enough for this shit. At least, they served the abomination with a small package of salt, so I did the sensible thing and drowned the tamagomelette in salt, then ate the sucker. Plane food was delicious. Said no one ever. Still, I diligently ate it all.

What now? Wait for them to collect the tray? Or try to get up, brush my teeth? Waiting seemed the better possibility, let them remove the tray, be patient. Maybe lean back again, try to go back to sleep for the last ninety minutes of the flight. Rest your head, your brain, your eyes, dream of all the things you would do once you arrive in Japan. Eat ramen. Go to a bar, have a drink. A cold drink. Have more drinks. Until you are drunk.

Was I drinking too much? Was I thinking about getting drunk too much? Why was it that getting drunk alone was pathetic, while getting drunk with friends was a party? Sometimes I wished I'd take drugs. Drink a dash of absinthe, like Goethe, like Shakespeare, write, let the green fairy be your muse, stop thinking whether the words you lined up next to each other like pearls on a string made any sense at all, trust in the fairy, because she is going to unlock all the secrets, and you'll write them down. She will unlock the lock to your soul. Didn't they say that a soul weighed 21 grams? Those 21 grams that just disappeared after someone died, unaccounted for, gone, metaphysical proof for the existence of the soul? Probably just hot air, a fart of a dead corpse, gas disappearing from the body, gone to fuse with the air molecules around. Maybe that was what the soul was, 21 grams of fart. By the smell of it, there was an entire congregation of souls in the air of the plane around us.

The flight attendant came by and collected my tray. I stretched my legs, got up, forgot to unfasten my seatbelt, got stuck, opened it, got up again, took my toothbrush, and made my way to the bathroom. I stood in line for a long five minutes, pretending I was in no hurry, thinking about peeing, hoping I would make it to the bathroom before the seatbelt sign came on. I arrived at the front of the line, stepped inside one of the small, tiny bathrooms. It smelt of a night of people, of sweat, of spit and toothpaste. I closed the door behind me and took my tooth-...

The seatbelt sign came on. "Ladies and gentlemen. We have begun our descent..." I started to brush my teeth. Looked at myself in the mirror. I looked tired. "...and we will land in Tokyo in about half an hour."

About fucking time.

Part II: Dog is Dead

Tokyo / Runners

Clearing immigration took less time than feared at first sight. If found myself in a long queue in a room that seemed straight from the 60s, a wide hall with a disgusting, brown carpet floor. However, the line moved fast, and I soon faced the immigration agent for a brief exchange of words (he: "Tourism?" I: "Yes, tourism."), fingerprints and a photo.

I was never sure how to look at the camera for those immigration photos. To smile? Not to smile? Serious look? Friendly? Dignified? Maybe no one knew that. We all probably just looked tired and sleepless, an endless collection of awful photos kept by the authorities, sleepy tourists, people looking their worst after hours on a plane. The face of humanity.

My suitcase arrived soon at the belt and, together, me and the suitcase, we made our way through the airport, following the signs to the subway. The suitcase felt heavier than when I'd left, which I attributed to my tiredness. Unless some airport worker had stashed his dirty underwear inside, which seemed unlikely.

Getting into Tokyo was easy, especially since I had booked a room in a hostel in Asakusa. There was a direct subway train from the airport to that part of town, so all I had to do was find a machine to charge the Suica prepaid card I had bought from a travel agent in Switzerland, charge said card and find the right train.

Luckily, all signs were in English. I couldn't read Japanese and only spoke a few words. Maybe enough to order a beer – birru o-kudasai –, that was about it. I wondered how it must have been, back in the day, when the world hadn't been ruled by the economics of tourism and English, when all the signs must have been solely in Japanese. How did one travel to Japan back then? How did the foreigners back then find their way to Asakusa?

The train was on time, clean and terribly old-fashioned. A moving museum piece that raced down the tracks with me inside. I stood in a corner, holding my oversized suitcase, and wondered why I didn't feel tired anymore. Before I could find an answer, the city came into view, houses that seemed familiar in their architecture, yet foreign enough to remind me I had travelled halfway around the world. The sun stood bright in the sky, but there were clouds approaching and I remembered checking the weather app before I had left, which had told me that there would be rain today.

The train drove into a tunnel, heading underground, stopping at stations whose names sounded familiar. People entered and left, Japanese office workers in their uniforms of white shirts and black or blue trousers, with their briefcases and their well-groomed hair and tourists, a lot of tourists, all with that wide-eyed expression on their face, that realisation that they were in a foreign place whose real meaning would forever remain lost in that unbridgeable gap between cultures.

I thought about getting my earphones from my bag and listen to music, finding that perfect Tokyo soundtrack when the train, unexpectedly soon, pulled into Asakusa Station and I hurried to get off with my oversized luggage, which had become too heavy for my arms. I made my way towards exit 5, as had been recommended on my hostel's website, and overground. It rained. I had packed an umbrella, yet it was lying somewhere at the bottom of my suitcase. So close, yet so unattainably far away.

I followed the road, past a 7/11, turned right into smaller alley. A swarm of traffic guards stood around a construction site and directed me to the other side of the road, making sure I wouldn't get too close to the construction, lest some falling debris should hit me or I should get construction site dust onto my trousers. I obliged with a smile and a "konichiwa," yet was afraid that my pronunciation was off, so I whispered the word so quietly that I might just as well have said "ass-hole" under my breath and the traffic guard would have understood the same thing, i.e., nothing.

The hostel looked nice. They had a bar on the ground level, serving craft beer and coffee – the main reason I had chosen this hostel, next to its relative cheapness. I made my way through the bar and followed the signs to the reception on the second floor, lugging my luggage, which seemed to get heavier and bigger by the minute, up a narrow staircase. The reception on the second floor (I was breathing heavily when arriving there and my lungs sounded like a dying bagpipe) was a small table in a corner manned by a cool-looking, younger dude. He looked up from his laptop and greeted me in Japanese. I nodded, sat down on the chair in front of the table, and caught my breath. I wondered how bad I smelt. I could feel my sweaty armpits and wished for a fresh t-shirt.

"Do you have a reservation?" the cool-looking, non-sweaty Japanese receptionist asked me with a thick Japanese accent. I nodded and told him my name, which he did not understand, so I spelt it to him, which he still didn't understand, so I spelt it a couple times more.

"Will you be staying in a dorm?" he asked as we finally agreed on the spelling of my name.

"No." I was too old for a dorm. "I have a double room."

"Ah." He found my reservation. "But you will stay here alone?"

"Yes. I booked it for single use." Rub it in, man.

"And you will stay two nights?"

"Yes, until Wednesday."

"Can you pay now? Cash only."

I had come prepared and handed over a swat of clean-looking yen bills, feeling like a drug dealer. He explained that the room would only be ready after four o'clock and that I could leave my luggage with him. I got a fresh t-shirt from my suitcase before I left it in his good care, got changed in the toilet, and left the hostel.

This was the start of my holiday.

My bloody veins were thirsting for alcohol, fun, and sun. My first journey took me along Sumida River and over a bridge. I turned away from the river and headed towards the thin needle of the Tokyo Skytree looming in the distance, like a modern version of Sauron's tower, looking down at me. I stopped at a random ramen restaurant and was proud of myself for being able to use the vending machine at the restaurant's entrance where I purchased a ticket for a bowl of ramen (I hoped) and a beer (I was sure of that as the button displayed the Asahi logo). These ticket vending machines had always amazed me. No human interaction necessary. Push the buttons, get the ticket, hand it over at the counter, wait for the bowl.

I gave my two tickets to the older woman behind the counter and took up a seat. The lady bowed, smiled gently, and disappeared between stacks of plates and bowls, only to re-emerge on the other side of the counter a second later, where she opened a fridge behind me to get my beer. I assumed that, normally, customers would get their beer themselves, yet with me not speaking Japanese and her correctly assuming this was the case, she must have decided to just bring me my beer instead of trying to explain to me how to get it myself. I felt bad for making her do extra work and wondered whether the Japanese got annoyed by tourists, those non-Japanese speakers not understanding their culture and customs. I felt out of place.

She put the beer in front of me and I stammered an arigato, asking myself whether I was using the right term. Was it domo? Arigato Gozaimas? Maybe I shouldn't even try. Just go full foreigner, say thank you, dankeschön, merci und auf wiedersehen.

The lady disappeared again. At the far end of the counter, there was a man slurping down on a bowl of his own. He looked like he was around forty. He was not wearing your typical salary man attire, but a black shirt and cargo-trousers with side-pockets like an unfashionable blast from the nineties. On my other side, three barstools away, there was an old woman who had just finished her bowl of ramen. In front of her, there was an entire array of crumpled, used napkins, an unholy mess I did not know the Japanese were capable of making. She was sipping from a glass of beer when she looked up and saw me looking at her. She smiled a short and bewildering smile, that kind of demeaning,

motherly smile only old people could make, and raised her glass to me.
I smiled as well, quickly, insecurely, and raised my glass, too. We both
drank a couple of short sips before she looked ahead again, and I did
the same – just in time to see the ramen-woman reappearing between
stacks of glasses and plates with a steaming bowl in her hands. She put
it down in front of me and the overpowering hot steam-smell of ramen
hit me like a train.

I dipped my spoon in the soup and tried the broth.

There it was, the feeling I had been waiting for, rising inside as the
strong umami of the ramen hit my palate. It felt like coming home,
your home away from home, the place where you were meant to be.

(Do not read this)

She checks her watch as she passes the second mark. Two seconds
better than last round. Maybe just a statistical anomaly, not the new
normal. She runs on along the track. Trying to maintain the speed.
Stay ahead of the two seconds.

It is a frosty morning. The sky is grey, the air feels wet. A patch of
mist is crawling down the hill in the distance. Her lungs hurt.

Faster, she yells at herself in her head. She tastes blood in her mouth.
There is still room for improvement. There are still ways to go faster.
Do not lose the two seconds.

She reaches the mark again. Checks the watch. The two seconds
improvement has increased to four. Good. Now, keep it that way.
There is no going slower.

She enters the gym and goes to the dressing room, she takes a shower
and gets ready for school. Half an hour before most students arrive.

"You have been running again?" She passes the gym teacher on her
way out.

"Like every morning," she replies.

"You make the track team look bad."

"I am not stopping them from training more," she replies, and the
teacher laughs a big, hearty laugh.

"You should join the team."

"I run better alone."

"Let me sign you up for some solo competitions, then."

"Nah, I am good. Thanks."

"Let me know if you change your mind."

"You got it, coach."

She makes her way across the campus. The mist has crawled down and is engulfing the houses on the other side of the road. It is colder than she expected. She should have brought her coat, not the spring jacket. No time to get sick.

She is sitting in the classroom before the first bell rings and the other students pour into the room. Some of them nod at her and she nods back. Most of them don't acknowledge her.

She is not looking forward to the first period – math – but she does not mind it, either. She is not particularly good at it, just good enough to get by – which is the case in most subjects. She is what one of her teachers called her at a parent-teacher-evening years ago: unproblematic. The teacher felt bad for calling her that afterwards and apologised, but the term stuck. To this day, her grandmother would occasionally call her "my unproblematic one" (heck of a snappy nickname). But only rarely these days.

She hears her name being called and, inside, curses at herself for not having listened to the teacher. She fumbles an answer, which the teacher comments with a "yes, good, but not quite. You have to consider…" So much for being the unproblematic one. Someone in the back laughs quietly, and she feels a shiver crawling on her spine.

She goes for another run during lunch and then eats an apple and a salad. "You should eat something proper," her grandmother would tell her when she sees her packing her lunch. I will buy a sandwich, she always replies. She suspects her grandmother suspects it is a lie.

Her grandmother picks her up after school in her beige 1976 Toyota Hilux. "How was school?" she asks her.

"Unproblematic," she replies. They both laugh.

"I will do some shopping on the way home. I was thinking stew for dinner. Okay?"

"Sounds good."

"Do you want to go by the graveyard?"

"Another day. I am tired."

Lucy, her grandmother's Australian shepherd, comes running out of the house the moment they drive up. The dog jumps up to her, and she bends down to pet her.

"I will go for a walk with Lucy."

"Be back before six. It is going to rain."

"Sure."

"Don't go to the lake."

"I won't."

The lake lies quiet in the setting sun. It is a short walk up to it, just off the small road leading past the house, through the forest, up a hill and out into a clearing. Lucy is standing at the water's edge, sniffing the air.

"Don't go in," she tells the dog, "Grandma is going to kill us." As if she understood her words, Lucy comes back to her, eyes her, expecting her to play with her. She picks up a stick and throws it alongside the lake. Lucy dashes off in chase of the stick. The dog picks it up and comes running back, drops the stick at her feet.

"Let's run together," she says, throws the stick. Both give chase, but Lucy, naturally, is faster. The dog catches the stick, and, adapting to the new game, does not turn around to give it back to her, but continues running, running away from her, protecting her treasured stick.

They are tired and sweaty when they return to the house. Her grandmother is still in the kitchen, putting the finishing touches on her stew.

"I will have a shower and then I am ready for dinner," she tells her grandmother. Lucy walks into the kitchen to observe her grandmother working, waiting for her turn to be fed.

The phone rings halfway through dinner. "I'll get it," she says and picks it up.

"Hello..." It is her father's voice. There is a moment of silence, almost as if he changed his mind and hung up. "What's up?" she says, trying to sound way too cool.

"I just wanted to check on you. See how you are doing."

"Who is it?" her grandmother yells from the dining table.

"Peter," she tells her grandmother. "We are doing fine," she tells her father.

"Good."

"Are you still off the coast of Iceland?"

"Nah, we are heading South now. No point in waiting. We gotta deliver what we have. It is a shame we had to depart with a half-empty ship, but it is what it is."

"How is the weather?"

"Rough when we left, and we got into a storm." She imagined her father's ship crawling up and down waves, a big, misshapen metal heap that had no business floating. "Now, it's quiet. But you know what I say when it's quiet."

"Calm before the storm?"

"Yes."

"I'm fairly sure the saying is not exclusive to you."

"How is school?"

"Good. I've been running a lot."

"Have you joined the track team?"

"No."

"You should. You're good at it. I always said it's your thing, running and all. You should make something of it."

"Yeah."

A moment of silence.

"I gotta get back to work. Say hi to your grandma for me."

"Don't you wanna talk to her?"

"Just say I said hi."

She wants to say something like "I love you" but it seems silly, and he's already hung up.

"Is he doing fine?" her grandmother yells from the kitchen. She's started to wash the dishes.

"Yes."

"What did he want?"

"Just see how we are doing."

Lucy approaches her. She pets the dog's head. Lucy nudges her hand with her cold, wet nose when she stops petting her. "I will do my homework. And then head to bed."

The sky is clear the next morning, the air feels even colder than yesterday, though. Her lungs hurt after the fifth or sixth lap, she continues to run. Her time is not as good as yesterday. Four seconds lost again. She pushes hard, feels her body getting slower. She is annoyed with herself. Go faster.

"Running again? How many shoes do you go through a week?" the coach asks her in front of the dressing room.

"Will the school buy me shoes if I go to competitions?"

"I think I could arrange that."

"Then I'll go. Solo competition."

"I'll sign you up. There's one on Friday morning. I can get you dispensation from your classes. Do you have someone who can drive you?"

"I'll ask my grandma."

"I'll sign you up. I will give you more info tomorrow."

"You know where to find me."

She goes to the classroom. She waits for the bell. She sees a flock of birds circling the trees outside and wonders how they manage not to crash into each other while flying.

Her grandmother is waiting for her in her Toyota after school. How was it, her grandmother asks, good, she replies. There are dark clouds off in the distance, she spots them from the car while driving home. There is going to be a thunderstorm.

Lucy comes running down the lawn towards the car. "I'm taking her for a walk," she says. "That would be nice," her grandmother replies.

She turns away to leave. "Don't go to the lake," her grandmother says. "I won't."

She play-chases Lucy along the lake, the dog still faster than her, when Lucy spots a group of ducks minding their business in the lake. She yells "don't, Lucy, heel," the dog does not listen, sprints into the lake. Water sprays up. She does not think, heads in after Lucy, as if to save the dog, or maybe save a duck from the dog, she does not know.

She gets hold of Lucy's back at the same moment as the ducks take flight. The water is cold and Lucy, now mortified by the sudden hand grabbing her neck, howls, turns around, catches her hand with her teeth, bites down, she screams in pain and shock, gets hit by Lucy's kicking back legs, loses her footing in the water, sinks down, swims up, holding the dog, pulling the poor animal under water as well. Lucy struggles and bends, a fight against what must seem certain death to her, uncertain why her friend is trying to kill her, howling, and barking in panic, her, with a bloody hand, pain, and cold water in her mouth, dragging the dog back to the edge of the water, lifting her out, lifting herself out, lying on her back, laughing, Lucy licking her face.

"You bit my hand," she says and hugs the dog and then, somebody approaching her, alarmed by the noise they'd been making, her looking up and seeing her grandmother, her face red with anger.

"What are you doing?"

She pulls herself up, trying to hide her hand.

"I... Lucy went in..."

"I told you not to go here." Her grandmother's voice is not much more than a whisper.

"I'm sorry."

"Go home." Her grandmother grabs Lucy by the collar, the dog whining in shock because of the violent grasp. "Did she bite you?" Her grandmother has spotted the bloody hand.

"It was not her fault."

"Go home." She complies, walks away, tears on her face. Lucy pulling against the grip on the collar, trying to go home with her.

At home, she cleans and bandages her hand. Her grandmother comes back a little while later.

"Where is Lucy?"

"In the shed. Show me your hand." She takes the bandage off.

"Does not look too bad."

"It was not her fault."

"If she does it again, we will have to put her down."

"I am sorry."

Her grandmother does not reply, only brings her a plate of soup from the kitchen. She sits and eats in silence. Her grandmother sits at the other end of the table, looking into the distance.

"No mother should bury her child," her grandmother says, that's all she says, and gets up and goes to another room. She finishes the soup and goes upstairs to do her homework. Outside, she can hear Lucy scratching against the shed's door.

She must train more, she decides. She is not fast enough to be ready for Friday. In the morning, she asks her grandmother to drive her to school even earlier to run on the track. Lucy has snuck back into the house and sleeps under the dining room table.

"How is the hand?"

"It is just a scratch."

The hand hurts going into the fifth lap. She ignores it. Her lungs hurt soon after. She ignores that, too. It starts raining during her next lap, she continues. Her time is bad. She hears her voice yelling at herself in her head. You are a runner, she tells herself, yells at herself, and that's what you do. You run. You do not stop.

She falls going into the next lap. She must have slipped. The rain made the track slippery, surely. Her shoes are old. It happens. It does not look graceful. She goes for a shower.

The coach greets her outside the dressing room, handing her a bag with shoes. "Try them on tomorrow. See whether you can run in them."

"Thank you."

"You okay?"

"Yes. Fine."

"Is your hand bleeding?"

"It is just a scratch."

She sits in class looking out of the window. Her left knee hurts and she misses a question the teacher asks her, and she does not know what to say. Someone sniggers behind her back.

She sits in her grandmother's car on the way home, mindlessly scratching her left hand with her right until she feels blood under her fingernails. She covers the hand with the sleeve of her jumper.

Lucy comes running out when they park in the driveway. She bends down to pet her, and Lucy wags her tail. She mouths the words "I'm sorry" even though she knows the dog cannot understand her.

"You gonna take her for a walk?" her grandmother asks.

"If it is okay."

"She needs a walk. Don't go to the lake."

"I won't. I promise."

"Good."

She and Lucy walk down the road, alongside the forest. There is a field further down that way, a good place for Lucy to run after a stick. She passes the driveway leading to the house closest to theirs – too far away from their home to consider the people living there neighbours. She's never met them.

It's an old house. The facade needs a fresh coat of paint, the veranda looks like they have not used it in years. She almost bumps into Lucy, who suddenly stops dead in her tracks.

"What's wrong, girl?"

A cat emerges from the bushes alongside the other side of the road. The cat looks at Lucy and at her, showing no signs of fear or aggression. The feline creature seems so self-assured that Lucy forgets her basic dog instincts and just stares at the cat crossing the road. It prances past a few meters in front of them like a four-legged fashion model and strolls alongside the driveway up to the house. As the cat approaches the building, the screen door opens and a girl, maybe her age, greets the animal, who strolls into the house without showing much interest in anything.

Before she closes the door, the girl spots her and spots Lucy and all of them just stand there and stare at each other. Then the girl waves. She awkwardly waves back. Lucy wags her tail.

"Let's go," she says to Lucy, and they continue on the road and arrive on the field. On the way, she picks up a stick for Lucy to catch. Today, she does not chase the dog, does not run with her. She feels too tired.

The shoes are a good fit, her time does not improve, though. She pushes harder. Her hand hurts, but it's just superficial pain. She scratched the wound open on the drive to school. She must go faster. Her lungs hurt. Her left knee hurts. She feels the familiar taste of blood on her tongue.

She takes Lucy for a walk after school, down to the field. She does not encounter the cat, nor the girl on the way. The old house lies silent, not a single light on. Maybe they are out. She wonders whether the girl goes to the same school as she does.

She play-chases Lucy across the field. It looks like there'll be another thunderstorm tonight. Clouds cover the sky.

Thursday comes around. Last day to train. On the way to school, she scratches her hand again until she bleeds, hides the hand in her sleeve. "Have a good day," her grandmother tells her.

Her time does not improve. The voice in her head yells at her. Her scratching her hand under the shower. Blood mixing with water, pink, bright pink.

"Are you ready for tomorrow?" the coach asks her outside the changing room.

"Yes," she lies.

"Good. When you get there, ask for Tim. He's a friend of mine. He'll show you around."

"Thanks."

She goes for another run during her lunch break. "How was school?" her grandmother asks her on the drive home. "Unproblematic."

Lucy comes running out of the house.

"I'll take her for a walk."

"Don't go to the lake."

"I promise."

Past the house. No cat, no girl. To the field. She throws a stick for Lucy, chases her, she feels slow. Go faster, she tells herself.

"Let's run home," she tells Lucy. Her body hurts. The final bit of training. Running home. She checks her stopwatch. Too slow. Faster. Almost at the house now, almost in the driveway. Lucy in front, four legs faster than two.

Then, her left knee lets go. There are surges of pain pulsating through her body. She can't run anymore. She can't stand. She falls. Tumbles. Red pain in her leg, up into her belly. Lucy stops, comes running back to her. She is crying now, on the floor, rolling, in pain. Lucy pushes her wet nose against her face, turns away, runs away, like in a movie, in search of help. Comes back with her grandmother only minutes later.

"The ligaments are torn," the doctor tells her. "In your left knee." It is hard to hear his voice through the pain killers. The medication makes her feel safe and warm.

"The doctor has said you should move as little as possible for the next couple of weeks," her grandmother reminds her, helping her into the house and onto the sofa. "No going up the stairs. You will sleep on the sofa." No going to school for two weeks either, the doctor had decided.

She takes another pill. Safe and warm. She does not protest. She will stay on the sofa. Lucy lies on the floor next to her.

"She is watching over you," her grandmother says. "She is a good dog."

"I have the competition tomorrow," she says, half-delirious because of the medication.

"I'll call the coach. You won't be running. Not for a long time."

Not. For. A. Long. Time.

The echo in her head.

The echo makes her feel dizzy.

She closes her eyes. Mind gone. In her sleep, she is falling, deeper and deeper asleep, into a black hole. She wonders how both can be the same, the falling deeper into a hole and the falling deeper asleep, but there is no time to find an answer.

She wakes up, red pain pulsating through her body. Her knee hurting. She must have moved in her sleep.

And her hand is bleeding.

She sits up. Lucy, in front of the sofa, wakes up, jumps up, looks at her, wags her tail, then puts her snout and head on the sofa next to her, ready to be petted.

She reaches for her crutches and slowly gets up, which sends another surge of pain through her body. That would be normal, the doctor said. It is just a waiting game now. Wait for your body to heal. Give it as much rest as possible. She limps into the bathroom to pee, then into the kitchen for a glass of water and pain killers. Take one in the morning, one at lunch, one in the evening. Three more during the day as needed. She takes a pill, a sip of water, then another one and the rest of the water.

She sits at the kitchen table, waiting for the pain to subside. Falling. Asleep.

The noise of her grandmother walking heavily down the stairs wakes her. She startles, looks up. It is not day outside. Dawn, maybe. All grey and unclear.

"What's wrong?" she asks when she sees the expression on her grandmother's face.

"Tom just called." Her grandmother's sister's husband. She is surprised she didn't hear the phone ring. "They brought May to the hospital." Her grandmother's sister.

"What's wrong?"

"They are not sure yet. Maybe an attack. Or a stroke. She wasn't feeling well and got up at night and then just fell over." Falling. Her grandmother sighs a heavy sigh. "When it rains, it pours." She gets the coffee machine ready, carefully puts in a filter and five, six spoons of coffee. Without saying a word, she fills the water and turns on the machine. "Making coffee," she says, superfluously. "Tom will call as soon as he knows more. How are you feeling? Have you been sleeping at the table?"

"No, erm... I was in pain, so I took a painkiller."

"Better now?"

"Better now."

Steam rises from the machine and the first drops of black coffee fall into the container below. The smell of freshly brewed coffee.

"I'll go by the school and talk to your teachers. They'll need someone to bring you schoolwork for the next two weeks." Two weeks. Seems like a long time. "Coffee?"

"Yes, please."

She heads back to the couch and falls asleep again, the dog on the floor in front of her.

When her grandmother comes back from school, she wakes up. Her grandmother looks tired. "All sorted with the teachers. Another student lives close-by, she'll bring you the homework. She'll come by tomorrow." The phone rings. Her grandmother talks quietly in the hallway. She can't make out the words.

Her grandmother hangs up the phone and sits down on the armchair opposite of the sofa. It is the first time she sees her grandmother sitting there. There is a moment of silence. Small needles of pain in her knee. Her not trying to twist the knee when she sits up.

"Tom," she tells her. "May, she is... they are not sure... she is not doing good."

Another moment of silence.

"We are getting older." It is the first time in a long time she sees that pain in her grandmother's eyes. That pain that leaves emptiness behind. It reminds her of her mother's funeral.

"You should go to her," she says, her voice and mind blurry. Say goodbye. Get a chance to say goodbye.

"I can't," her grandmother gets up. "I have to look after you."

"I'll be fine," she replies, feebly, unconvincingly, feeling the urge to pee, but being afraid to get up and move her knee.

"No, you won't. I have to go shopping," her grandmother says and leaves the house.

She takes a pain killer. She is not sure how many pills she's taken today. Finally, she gets up to pee and back to the couch. She is useless. Maybe she could take a few steps, get out of the house.

She is out of breath just from her trip to the bathroom. She lies down on the couch, unable to sleep. She just lies there and listens to the ticking of the clock on the wall.

A little while later, her grandmother returns with two shopping bags and a girl. The girl looks vaguely familiar.

"This is Olivia," her grandmother says. "She's the neighbour's daughter." She has seen her before. The girl with the cat.

"She'll be bringing your homework as of tomorrow. And..." Her grandmother sits down on the armchair again. Olivia pulling up a chair and sitting next to her grandmother, as if rehearsed, a tribunal of bad news. "I talked to her mother. Olivia will come by every day and check on you."

"Why?"

"I have to see May." A ten-hour drive. "I have to make sure she is getting the help she needs."

"Hi," Olivia finally says and smiles, out of place and out of timing. Still, she returns the smile, the warmth of the most recent pain killer making her feel friendly.

"Okay?" her grandmother demanding everyone's approval. She nods, so does Olivia, who explains that she'll put a note with her home's phone number next to their phone and that she should call any time she needs something.

"Thanks," she says. Lucy gets up from her spot in front of the couch and lets Olivia pet her. She feels a surge of envy.

Her grandmother spends the rest of the evening cooking and filling food into plastic containers. "It's a good thing I bought these containers from Elvira," she says from the kitchen while she pours the carrot soup into a container. Her knee hurts, but not as bad as before. Nevertheless, she is thinking about taking another pill, just to be safe. She sits on the sofa and sees the outside through the window. A flock of birds is passing over the nearby trees.

Her grandmother leaves at 4 the next morning. She is already up, awaken again by a surge of pain in her knee. And bloody skin under her fingernails.

"Drive safely," she tells her grandmother.

"I'll call you when I arrive."

"Okay." Lucy follows her grandmother to the door and watches her leave. Then, the dog comes back to the living room. She can feel the warmth of the pill rising in her body, taking the pain away. Time to sleep.

She wakes up to silence a few hours later. She grabs her crutches and limps to the door to let Lucy out into the garden. The dog dashes past her, thrilled by the prospect of being outside. She watches Lucy for a moment running up and down, chasing imaginary ghosts, leaves the door ajar and heads into the kitchen. She prepares coffee, a piece of bread and another pain killer.

What day is it today? Isn't her competition supposed to be today?

She limps out onto the veranda and sits on the stairs. Lucy spots her and presents her with a stick she has found on the lawn. She throws the stick, Lucy runs after it, brings it back, she throws it again, Lucy catches it. An endless circle.

She eats lunch, another pill, water. Lucy now sleeping under the kitchen table. She sits on the couch, falls asleep again. Her hand is bleeding. A pill. She eats an apple. Is it too early for her grandmother to call?

Suddenly, late afternoon, Lucy darts up and runs to the door. Then a knock. "It's Olivia," a voice says through the door. Lucy wags her tail.

"Come in."

Olivia puts a stack of papers on the dining table. "That's your homework. But your teachers told me to tell you that you should get some rest first and not worry too much about it."

"Are you in the same year as me?"

"Parallel class, yes."

"Thanks for bringing the stuff."

Olivia sits down on the armchair opposite the sofa. Lucy puts her head against Olivia's knee, asking to be petted.

"You have a nice dog." Olivia puts her hand on Lucy's head. "How are you feeling?"

"Tired. And it hurts."

"What happened?"

"I... I fell. I ran, and I fell."

"I am sorry."

"You have a cat, right?" She remembers the cat prancing across the street.

"Percival? Right, he walked past you the other day."

"Percival?"

"My brother's idea. What's her name?" Pointing to Lucy.

"Lucy."

"Hi Lucy," Olivia says, and Lucy wags her tail in response.

They sit in silence for a bit. Occasionally, they talk about something, exploring the terrible little they have in shared experiences. That time the water fountain was leaking at school, the time that teacher disappeared, allegedly having run away with the wife of his neighbour, nothing of any importance, but it feels good enough to have someone in the house.

The phone rings. Olivia jumps up and picks it up. "It's your grandma," she informs her. Olivia puts the phone down and helps her onto her feet, limp to the phone. "I am leaving. I'll see you tomorrow," Olivia whispers. Lucy follows her to the door.

"I have arrived safely."

"How is May?"

"Still in the hospital. We'll talk to the doctor tomorrow."

"Good."

"How are you?"

"Fine."

"Good."

The silence feels heavy after the call and Olivia's departure. She heats carrot soup and eats in silence. She turns on the radio, but there are only angry people talking to each other about their ideas of how other people should behave.

She takes a pill and sits out on the porch, watches Lucy run across the lawn, who presents her again with her trusted stick. She thinks about running along the lake up in the clearing in the forest.

She stands up, leaning on her crutches, and takes a few steps out onto the lawn. Maybe if she could just get to the mailbox. She walks – it is fine. Maybe if she could just put a bit more pressure onto the knee, walk faster. She takes a step, shifting her weight away from the crutches and onto the knee.

She stumbles as the knee offers no backup and she steps down too hard, which sends the familiar red pain through her leg.

She holds onto the crutches, panting heavily.

"Fuck," she says. Her grandmother would not approve of her swearing. She goes back inside. It takes forever.

She allows Lucy to jump onto the sofa and lie next to her. Another thing her grandmother would not approve of.

"Update: all teachers want you to know that it is not urgent, but they still gave you tons of homework," says Olivia, putting down a second stack of papers next to the first one from yesterday (which has not been touched since then). "How are you feeling?"

"Okay."

"Good." Olivia sits down in the armchair. Lucy next to her.

"Have you heard from your grandmother?"

"She called. They have talked to the doctors, but they cannot quite figure out what's wrong. She, my grandaunt, May, has a high fever, and she's weak. She has trouble breathing."

"Is she going to be alright?"

"She couldn't say."

"I'm sorry." There is a pause. "My mother asked me to ask you whether you needed anything from the pharmacy?"

"Oh. Yes... Erm, my grandma forgot to get my medication. The prescription is on the table."

Olivia gets the note from the table.

"I can never tell what these doctors write. What's that, a three or a nine?"

She feels a flash of pain growing down her spine. "Nine," she replies, which triples the amount. Ninety-something.

"My mom will get it tomorrow."

"Thank you."

Night. Heading into the next day. Pain in the knee. Pill. Getting to the door, letting Lucy out. The dog running in the garden, standing still, looking at her with that unspoken accusation that she is not running with her.

She should try again to go to the mailbox. She feels too tired. She should sit down and do her homework. She is too tired. A pain pill. She sits at the kitchen table, scratching her hand. She should drink more. Lucy comes in and sits next to her, looks at her with those fake-puppy eyes. Then she remembers she should feed the dog. That she should eat herself. She staggers to the couch. She needs to lie down. She feels light-headed.

"You okay?" Olivia's big face in front of hers, concerned look. She startles. Lucy standing there, wagging her tail. Pain.

"I... what time is it?"

"It is four. In the afternoon."

"Shit. I fell asleep." She sits up. The world is in a spin.

"Can you feed Lucy? I have... have not. Forgotten to give her food." Her words barely form a string of sense.

"I'll go for a walk with her first, okay?"

"Yes. That would be good." Don't go to the lake. No, wait – that's what her grandmother would say. She watches the two of them leave,

Lucy jumping up and down, wagging her tail in happiness. She gets another pill.

She is woken by Olivia coming back. Olivia brings Lucy to the kitchen, feeds her. "I'll heat something up for you, okay?"

A little while later, Olivia brings her a plate of some stew. Maybe Irish stew. She cannot discern the taste. "This will do you some good. You need food."

She needs to move. She needs to burn the calories. She feels sick. She eats. "My mother has been to the pharmacy. I left the pills in the kitchen," Olivia informs her. She has nothing to reply, except for a nod. "You have to stop scratching your hand." It is bleeding.

Three days pass. Sofa. Kitchen. Pills. Lucy's big puppy eyes. Olivia's concerned eyes. Another pill. Stew. Soup. Her feeling sick. Her eating. Then, the third evening, her throwing up. The moment she puts the first spoon into her mouth, her entire body rebelling. There is nothing much to puke except for bile and blood, and it is the most exhausting thing she has ever done. Onto the carpet. Her stomach a hateful knot of cramps and pain.

Olivia jumps up. Brings water. Cleans.

"I am sorry."

"Drink," she says.

Olivia brings a suitcase the next day. "I have convinced the teachers and my mother that you need help to move around the house. I'll stay with you. I just have to swing by school every day to get our homework. Also, my mom gave me some money, so we'll order pizza tonight. But first things first – you really need to take a shower."

Olivia helps her to get to the bathroom and inside. "I'll get you fresh clothes from your room. Upstairs, right?"

"Yes. To the left."

Her undressing in the bathroom, slowly, cautiously, as not to move her knee too much. She steps under the shower. Then she cries, silently. The water is cold. Blood running from the back of her hand.

"There you go. You look like a human being again."

She sits down heavily at the kitchen table. Lucy in the corner, eating from her bowl. "Did you go for a walk with her?"

"Yes. Actually, Lucy went for a run, and I tried to keep up. She likes to run, doesn't she?"

"Yes, she does."

"What pizza would you like?"

"Salami, I guess."

"Excellent choice." Olivia gets up to go to the phone to order food, stops. "Hey... erm... you are scratching your hand again."

She looks down at her hand. Blood under her fingernails. She stops. She reaches for a pill from the bottle on the table while Olivia orders the pizza.

They sit there, her on the sofa, Olivia on the armchair, eating their pizzas from the box, not talking much. It feels nice.

Olivia makes breakfast the next morning. And coffee. It feels good to drink coffee. She takes a pill and, on Olivia's insistence, gets out onto the porch. Olivia empties the mailbox and then they sit down at the kitchen table to work on the homework. In the evening, Olivia opens another plastic box with stew inside.

"So, let me guess, your grandma really likes stew."

"She enjoys making them. She actually doesn't like them too much," she replies.

"More for you, I guess. Why do you live with your grandmother, anyway?" Olivia asks while inspecting the stew.

"My father works on a ship. Container ship. I see him only every few months. But he never really lived with us. Not even back when..." she stops, stuck in a memory.

"Back when?"

"Before my mother died."

"I'm sorry."

"They split before she died."

"My parents separated as well. Not that that's a bad thing. You're scratching your hand again."

"Fuck."

After dinner, she takes another pill and Olivia disinfects and bandages her hand. It burns. They sit outside on the porch, watching the sun settle past the trees in the distance. There is endless silence between the two of them, their shoulders touching as they sit on the steps. She asks Olivia at one point why she is helping her. Olivia takes her time before she replies. "Because you needed help," she simply says.

The smell of coffee wakes her the next morning. She reaches for the crutches and heads into the kitchen. Olivia is not there, though. Steam is rising from the coffee drip. She sits down at the table and reaches for the pill bottle. A moment later, the door to the bathroom across the hallway opens and Olivia steps out, wet, a towel wrapped around her body, held by her bare arms.

The arms are a landscape of small scars, remnants of countless minor cuts of some unspoken yesterday.

"Hey," Olivia says, clutching the towel, quickly disappearing up the stairs. Her knee hurts. She takes another pill.

They walk to the mailbox together. It takes forever. And back to the porch. Then, sitting on the porch, she is out of breath, the voice inside mocking her for being so slow. She wants to run away.

"It'll take time," Olivia tries to comfort her. Her face turns red. She feels a sting of pride, of embarrassment.

"How would you know?" she snaps. Then apologises. It's fine, Olivia replies and goes to the kitchen. "Time for homework."

Later that day, Olivia heads into town on her bike, to pick up more homework and to buy food. "I'll be back in a few hours. Have to see my mother as well," she says and disappears, leaving the house silent. Lucy is sleeping under the kitchen table, tired from the walk with Olivia. How she wishes she could walk with the dog – walk up to the lake – run along the water's edge.

Fuck, she thinks.

Fuck.

Takes a pill. Opens her grandmother's cabinet with the alcohol inside. Port. She doesn't even like wine, but the sweetness of the port makes her forget she's drinking alcohol. Just a glass. Just until she feels that drowsiness in her head. Make the pill work faster.

Dusk has settled when Olivia returns.

"You okay? You look terrible."

"I've fallen asleep."

"Hmm." Olivia puts down a bag of groceries on the kitchen table, moving aside the pill bottle, holding it a bit too long, looking at it, frowning for a second. She fights the urge to get up and take it out of Olivia's hands.

"It's spaghetti tonight."

"Nice."

"With homemade sauce. Family recipe."

"Even better."

"You can chop the vegetables." Olivia puts a chopping board on the kitchen table and hands her a knife.

She sits there at the table, diligently chopping the vegetables, while Olivia is working the stove. Her hands are shaking. Soon, a homely smell of cooking food fills the room.

"That's what my grandmother used to cook. Italian," Olivia tells her while watching her cut the carrots for the salad.

"Is she Italian?"

"Yeah. My father's family is from Italy."

"Are you close?"

"I haven't seen her in years. I don't know whether she is still alive, to be honest. Can you chop them smaller?"

"Sure." Pause. She feels bad. "I am sorry I snapped at you earlier." She puts the knife down.

"It's fine. Just don't do it again."

After dinner, they sit outside and watch Lucy run up and down the lawn. "You wanna walk to the mailbox?" Olivia asks her.

"Nah, I'm fine." Lucy catches the stick Olivia throws for her, an elegant jump into the air. "I've always liked to run with Lucy. Up at the lake. She's fast," she says, not taking her eyes off the dog.

"Well, she is a dog. The extra legs gotta be good for something. Humans have not been made for running. Trotting, yes. Strolling. Running sucks."

"Hmm."

"Sorry. You are a runner, I know. You will run again. It takes time. You'll be fine."

"I don't know. It sucks." She swallows. She thinks about the pills on the table. The bottle in the cupboard. Run, run, run.

"You have to take care of yourself." Olivia gets up and leans against the railing of the porch, the sun colouring the sky in bright pink and purple.

"Have you been up to the lake? With Lucy?" she asks Olivia. She does not know why. She remembers her mother. Her grandmother telling her not to go there. Her going there anyway. Like an open wound that refuses to close. She thinks about the scars on Olivia's arms.

"Yes. It's nice." Olivia responds. Envy.

"My grandmother doesn't want me to go there." Her voice trembling more than she would like to admit.

"Why?"

"My mother drowned there."

"Drowned? In the lake?"

"Yes." Long pause. Purple and pink sky getting darker. Thoughts lost in the past.

Finally, she continues: "We moved in with my grandmother after... when my mother wasn't feeling well. My father was useless. He left to work on his fucking ship. He couldn't cope with it. With her... moods." Lucy now lying in the grass, tongue out, looking at the coloured sky as well. Wind coming up. "One day, my mother went for a walk with Lucy. She said she'd be back soon. Up to the lake. She didn't come back." She doesn't even talk to Olivia. She talks to no one. She talks to herself. "We found Lucy sitting at the edge of the water some time later.

Gazing out onto the lake. Where my mother had disappeared." Where my mother had killed herself, she should have said. She couldn't.

They sit in silence for a long time.
"Let's go inside. I need to bandage your hand."
"Yes."
Lucy follows them quietly.

She has this dream. Seeing her mother disappear into the forest with Lucy. Not looking back. And her running after her. The lake is too far to reach. Her legs too short.

Her father telling her mother this is what she does. Run away. Not really. But inside. Her father's voice telling her on the phone this is what she does. Running.

She wakes up, drenched in sweat. The pulsating pain in her knee is back. She must have twisted it in her sleep. She gets up. Lucy wakes up, looks at her quickly, puts her head back down to sleep. All is fine, the dog thinks.

"Nothing is fine, Lucy," she says, goes to the kitchen and takes a pill. It is medicine. It is good for her. She swallows it with a jug from the bottle. She needs that drowsiness. She needs to sleep. Outside, there is the cry of an owl. The pill doesn't work. The pills will, she is sure. Somehow or other. Once the pain is gone, she will be fine.

Olivia finds her passed out on the kitchen floor in the morning. She helps her up, sits her down on a chair. Olivia yells at her in shock, but she can barely understand the words. Words, so loud, coming out of Olivia's mouth.

"Shut up," she finally whispers, just to make Olivia stop.
"I'm calling an ambulance," Olivia replies.
"No, I'm fine." Her brain goes into defensive mode. Panic. No doctors. No adults. Don't tell my grandmother. I don't need help.
"You need help." No. Back off. I need to run away.
"I fell. It's nothing. Don't be dramatic." She wants to punch her.
"Have you looked at yourself?"

Olivia does not wait for an answer, takes the pill bottle.

"I will flush these down. You are killing yourself." I need them.

"I need them."

"No, you don't." Olivia turns to the bathroom.

She gets up, forgetting all about her knee and the crutches, and, for a second, it is fine, almost like a miracle, but then, she takes a step forward, putting her weight on the damaged knee, and she stumbles, and she falls. On the floor again. Olivia drops the pills, hands outstretched, trying to catch her, she can't, she can't reach that far. Time freezes: Olivia standing there, eyes wide open. The pill bottle on the floor popped open, pills scattered all about. The empty port bottle on the kitchen table. Lucy, hiding in the hallway, away from the loud voices, away from the human problems. She on the floor wincing in pain.

"I'm sorry..." Olivia stammers, as if it is her fault, takes a step forward to bend down and help her up. She doesn't want to be helped. She hits Olivia's hand. Pain turns into rage.

"Get lost," she says.

"You need help," Olivia says. Help to get up. Help.

"Leave me alone," she yells, an angry little child, sits up, crawls backward on her bum. "Go home," louder, tears streaming down her face. Olivia takes a step back, holds her hand, the one she just hit. Olivia whispers, talking to herself, shaking her head, "I'm not doing this again," Olivia says, "not again," clutches her arms.

"I don't need you," she says.

"Stop it!" Olivia now yells, the yell of a small child fighting against a world crumbling apart, a fight so deeply ingrained in her being, it has defined her, shaped her, and will destroy her.

"Just go home." She leans on her arm, sits up. Her knee screaming in rage, in pain, in rage-pain. "Don't play the good Samaritan. I haven't asked you for this."

This is where Olivia's heart breaks. At the sheer destruction coming in her direction. Olivia has seen that kind of destruction before. She has felt it. She, on the floor, can see it in Olivia's eyes, the pain, but Olivia's vulnerability only makes her lash out more. She wants to crush her like a small animal, wants to feel that power. She tells Olivia to run home and cry, accuses her of covering up her own problems by helping her, the scars on her arms, her silly, unhappy existence, says so, so many things that cannot be unspoken. She grabs the pill bottle and throws it, throws it at Olivia. "You want my pills? Take them. Take them and get lost."

Olivia does not reply. She does not react. She is empty now.

Olivia turns to leave. And leaves. Out the door. Leaves. And she is alone. She lies on the floor and cries quietly until her head hurts because of the dehydration.

She finally crawls up, collects the pills, puts them into the bottle. She drinks water in the kitchen. Stands at the window, hoping she'd see Olivia out there, playing with Lucy.

This is when she realises Lucy is nowhere to be seen. Olivia's bike is still standing in front of the porch. Olivia is gone, though. Lucy is gone. Her body trembles.

They find Lucy at the lake some time later, sitting at the water's edge, gazing into the distance.

#

I paid for my ramen and left, filled, happy, looking forward to my next meal. I turned to walk towards Tokyo Skytree.

I was heading in the general direction of the touristy landmark, not because I was planning on ascending the tower but because I had a coffee shop close to the tower marked on my map. I was craving a coffee and a good one at that. A friend of mine had told me about the place and I trusted his judgment.

I walked down a busy street, cars zipping past me. The rain had disappeared, and the sun was up in the sky. It was getting hot. I still smelt of airplane. I wasn't tired, which surprised me. By all laws of my body's biology, the jet lag should have been hitting me hard. It would, eventually, and I was intent on making the most of my first day in Tokyo before that was the case.

At the same time as I arrived at the coffee shop, some people dressed up as Nintendo characters drove past me in go-karts. I had to smile to myself seeing them go by, because of the sheer cliché of it. People dressed up as Peach, Yoshi and Luigi playing real life Super Mario Kart, where else would you see that but in Tokyo (until, of course, Nintendo would decide to put an end to it)?

I entered the coffee shop. It looked like your dime a dozen third-wave-coffee-shop, wooden-metallic interior, a big bar to the one side, the smell of coffee in the air, a big, handwritten sign behind the counter announcing today's roasts, a big, shiny coffee machine on the counter, some shelves on the other side with bean bags, French presses, filters, and slow drips on sale. For all the celebration of individuality the third wave of coffee had been built upon, it was amazing how similar these shops all looked. I should've hated them for their pretentiousness, their fake coolness. The problem was that, if you got lucky, they made a damn good coffee. And I was ready to forgive almost anything for a good cup of coffee, even general hipster posturing. At least the guy behind the counter wasn't dressed in a flannel shirt and didn't wear black-rimmed glasses.

"A flat white, please," I mumbled in the man's general direction. He smiled and handed me a piece of paper which detailed the choice of beans suitable for a flat white. I went for the Guatemalan beans, which promised a strong flavour with a hint of berries and flowers. Flowers, of course. I should have asked him to specify the type of flower, dandelion or chrysanthemum, or daffodils.

The guy nodded at my order and told me – in English – to have a seat. He would bring the coffee to me. He went to work behind the machine, got the espresso shot for the flat white ready. Then, he steamed the milk in a metallic container, and I was pleased seeing the gentleness he put into his work, heating the milk slowly, carefully. Many people didn't realise that the magic of the flat white did not just lie in the espresso shot, but also in how the milk was treated. Get it warm, build a nice, strong foam, but don't make it too hot. Don't boil the fucking milk. Any coffee beverage containing milk should be at a temperature that is instantly drinkable. If you burn your tongue taking the first sip, they overheated the milk.

If the milk is heated right, then its general sweetness complements the coffee shot's taste, enables the coffee to develop a slightly bitter undercurrent, mixed with, in the best cases, some acidity and a hint of berries, or some other well-rounded fruit (or, of course, chocolate if you want to go old-fashioned).

The first sip of the perfect flat white should make you close your eyes, sigh, and crave for the next sip. You should be done with the flat white within instants, wanting to order the next one.

The guy arrived at my table. He put down a cup in front of me, which contained a small amount of coffee. He had also brought the metallic container with the milk. He explained to me they poured the milk at the table, so that the customer could watch and enjoy the texture of the milk.

I smiled and nodded. I would enjoy.

He took the cup in his left hand, held it at an angle, and started pouring. The pristine whiteness of the milk mixed with the dark coffee, the colours melted into each other, a swirling of movement and smell and I forgot how silly the moment was, me watching the man pouring the milk as if he were performing a feat of wizardry in front of my eyes. He created a perfectly shaped image of a leaf on top of the milky foam and put the cup down in front of me, gently, smiled and I smiled back, and I smelt the coffee and put the spoon into the foam, tasted it (perfect texture) and lifted the cup to my mouth and drank a small sip. The coffee's temperature was perfect. The sweetness of the milk mixed with bitterness, berry, lemons. I closed my eyes and sighed. The day kept getting better.

I threw myself into the Skytree building soon after, walked into the tower's entrance hall, marvelling at the lines of people waiting to take the elevator to the top. A Japanese employee headed towards me, most likely wanting to help me queue in the correct lane (there was one for Japanese citizens, one for tourists without a ticket, one for tourists who had bought a ticket online and a fast lane selling more expensive tickets with the promise of getting you to the top faster), but I shook my head and smiled (never forget to smile in Japan). I had no intention of wasting a couple of hours and yen just to be herded into an elevator together with an endless stream of other bodies.

I passed the hall and, at its end, took an escalator to the second floor, where I found the building's shops and restaurants. I found a Pokémon store and lamented the fact that I wasn't a huge fan of the pocket monsters and couldn't obsess over the many plushemons and pikachudons on sale. I walked some time, mostly aimlessly, then exited the building, following a sign for a smoker's corner, which was hidden behind a couple of vending machines. I leaned against the wall back there and lit a cigarette, mapping out my next steps before my inner eye. There was a metro stop around the corner which I could use to head to Shibuya. I checked a map on my phone. Shibuya didn't look too far away. Maybe twenty minutes with the subway. I could go for beers and dinner there.

On the metro, I fell asleep. I'd been thinking about listening to music, but I was afraid to miss the announcement for my stop. The train was crowded, but not as crowded as those videos on the internet suggested, those videos of people pushing other people into full train cars like sardines upon sardines. The train I was in had enough space to enter comfortably and even enough space to find a seat upon one I'd placed myself. Sitting down had been a mistake, I thought, as I nodded off, eyes heavy and my brain filled with those weird thoughts, images, and conclusions you have when you're just about to fall asleep, that line between thinking, daydreaming, and handing over control to the subconscious part of your brain. I saw lights in my metro-dreams and realised that my fridge at home was empty, and I'd have to go shopping or I could order pizza and I wondered whether I'd turned off the stove before I'd left. For a moment, voices filled my head, Japanese voices. I opened my eyes, pulled myself back into consciousness, to realise that it was eerily silent. People did not talk. They did not make phone calls. You couldn't even hear music from headphones.

We were seven stops out from Shibuya. I'd been on this train for over half an hour and had passed only five stops so far. It seemed Shibuya was not as close as the map had promised me. Or maybe I sucked at reading maps.

Still, I made it. Subway cars are always bound to arrive at some point. Not like us poor, wandering souls.

If you've ever wondered how many people live on this planet, Shibuya was a good place to figure out that it was a freaking lot. I stood on a viewing platform at the train station and looked down at the crossing, the famous one, the one everyone knew from movies and Insta-videos. I watched the people walk when the lights turned green. There wasn't even a word for it. A mass of people? A pile of people? A never-ending procession of person after person, a sudden explosion of ant-people, as if a giant had vomited them onto the world, a sudden eruption of individuals, all of them with the same intention of crossing the street.

Shibuya crossing was a scramble crossing (I'd read the crossing's Wikipedia page back at home), or X crossing or an exclusive pedestrian interval crossing, which means all pedestrian lights turn green at the same time and all vehicular traffic is stopped at the same time. So, all pedestrians walk together, no matter where they come from or in which direction they go. Every two minutes they walk. Every two minutes, up to 2,500 people cross the street. That is more people than I would ever know or meet in my lifetime. That is 12,500 people in twenty minutes. 37,500 people in an hour. 900,000 over twenty-four hours. And within eight or nine days, the entirety of Switzerland would have walked across the crossing. Funny thing was, it would take more time for the entire population of Tokyo to cross the intersection than it would take to send every person living in Switzerland across, since there were more people living in Tokyo than in all of Switzerland. Which also meant that if, for some strange reason, everyone in Tokyo should die and Switzerland, for the same or another strange reason, should become uninhabitable, you could move everyone from

Switzerland to Tokyo and they could live comfortably within the city. In fact, they would even have a few million empty apartments and houses. The Swiss would probably miss their cheese and the mountains and the chocolate, but slowly they would get used to Japanese dishes and would fuse them with their own, would put grated cheese on top of sushi and would think they just invented the next big thing in international cuisine.

Looking at the crossing made my head spin. Or maybe it was the jet lag. Maybe I was craving a beer. I wanted to get drunk, but I was afraid to do so, because I was alone and it was a long way back to my hostel, which seemed a lifetime away, even though only a few hours had passed since I'd dropped off my luggage. I turned away from my vantage point, made my way out of the station, paid my respect to the statue of the dog whose name I had forgotten, and walked across the crossing myself, joining the thousands of ants looking for the green light.

The rest was the opposite of silence, it was a cacophony of sound and lights, of drunk people yelling, talking, laughing. I crossed a huge building, presumably a concert venue, and watched the people standing in line, waiting for a concert to start and I saw big posters plastered on the side of the building, showing me a Japanese girl group in short skirts, knee and thighs barred, big breasts in tight blouses, their faces framed by blushy make-up and girly smiles, a sight that both disturbed and aroused me.

I walked through the noise, the people, wishing I could join the parade of young Japanese men, them taking me in as one of their own, bringing me to bars I did not know about, speaking a mix of English, Japanese and sign languages, yelling names of famous Japanese bands at each other trying to find common ground between us.

I consulted my map on my phone. I was heading towards a restaurant I had read about, an Izakaya serving Japanese-European fusion dishes somewhere in a side alley. I found it and checked the time. It was shortly before six – I believed the restaurant would officially open at six, but surely, they'd already be open, waiting for the first early guests to arrive. I didn't have a reservation and was eager to get a spot.

I entered the place. The floor of the entrance was made of stone, ending at an elevated platform made of wood. I approached the wooden elevation. I knew I was supposed to take my shoes off before stepping onto it. I had come prepared and was only wearing summer slippers which I could easily slip in and out of, saving myself from the humility of having to tie and untie shoelaces while someone from the staff would watch me, patiently waiting for my clumsy fingers to finish fiddling with my shoes. Before I could take them off, however, a server, a huge Japanese lady, came around the corner, looked at me, smiled, stopped smiling and told me, in broken English, that they weren't open yet (3 more minutes!, I gathered from glancing at my phone). "Wait, please," she said and disappeared again. So, I stood there in the stony entranceway, ready to take my shoes off in 3... 2 and a half minutes.

There was a row of milky windows to my left, through which I could see the blurred image of the dining room. I spotted several people, probably the staff, gathered in the middle of the room, around a long countertop. Group meeting. Discuss the menu for today. Some motivational words. I felt bad for disturbing them. For being that kind of Swiss person who was three minutes early. One of them yelled something (the owner?) and the staff replied with what I assumed was a fixed sentence. I imagined something like: "This will be a glorious night. Give it all you got!" – "Yes, it will be! We will give it all we got." But what did I know?

Not five seconds later, the Japanese woman came around the corner again, gestured me to take off my shoes (I slipped out of them rather smoothly) and led me into the dining room. She pointed to a spot at the long counter from where I could overlook the cooking area, which was situated just behind the counter. Show-cooking. I liked the idea. The lady gave me an English-language menu, and I mapped out my food orderings for the evening. As a first round, I ordered a glass of the sake of the day ("Craaazyyy-sake" the huge lady called it and smiled at me) and a traditional Japanese stew.

Delicious.

Next, I moved to the tuna-avocado tartare, served with baguette, which brought tears to my eyes. Yes, I was crying because the food was so good.

I continued with the mackerel, which they roasted right in front of me with a torch blow. The food didn't stop to amaze me. I was getting slightly drunk, which lowered my inhibitions not to get completely drunk, so I ordered a shochu highball.

Then, I ordered the fried prawns with chilli-mayo and, when I took the first bite, contemplated ordering a second serving.

The lady passed by and smiled at me. Maybe because she saw the glow of happiness around me. I felt like a child, fingers sticky from the food, mayo all across my face.

I asked for another highball and decided to have one last dish. The fries seasoned with cod roe. For a second, I felt bad for ordering such a mundane, non-Japanese dish (fries, what the fuck?), but when I put the first fry in my mouth, I forgot any regrets. My senses were overrun as the tastes of salty cod roe and the savoury fried potatoes exploded in my mouth, covering my palate. My stomach, revolting against the over-abundance of food, gave in, cried for more while I stuffed my mouth with the fries.

For a long time, I thought about ordering another dish, another drink. But it was a long way back to the hostel, I was on my own, I didn't want to get lost, I didn't want to get sick on the subway.

So, instead, I paid my bill and left. Shibuya had turned to night and got dark when I emerged from the restaurant. No, not dark, the daylight might have left, but the city was still bright and alight, aflame with thousands of lights, the neon-city in all its beauty, a Gibsonesque fever-dream. Thousands of people crossed my way, me trying to get back to the subway station, getting lost time and time again, passing bars that seemed more than questionable, places guarded by tall and muscular Asian bouncers. I turned my phone's GPS on, but it seemed confused by all the people and lights and it took me another good half an hour before I finally found the station and got onto a train carrying me back to Asakusa.

The streets back in that neighbourhood were empty and sleepy, a stark contrast to the place I'd just been to. Hard to believe I was still in the same city. My tiredness had disappeared by the time I was back at the hostel, left behind in the busy streets of Shibuya.

To my surprise, the bar on the ground floor of my hostel was still well-occupied. I checked the time to find out that it was only nine. My body and brain felt like the middle of the night. It seemed I had left the hostel this afternoon a decade ago. The people behind the bar greeted me in Japanese with what I assumed was a fixed phrase, and I regretted not knowing the fixed answer to give.

On the second floor, behind the door to my room, my suitcase was already expecting me. It was a small, empty room. A two-story bed to the left, for people who didn't travel alone, some space to the right, barely enough to fit my suitcase, and a small table in the back, which I used for the coins that had accumulated in my trouser pockets over the day. I sat down on the small stool next to the table. I should go for a shower, I thought. I smelt like shit. Sweat. Plane-sweat. People-sweat, walking-sweat, drinking-sweat, food-sweat, travel-sweat.

I could also go for a shower in the morning. There was no one to smell me till the next day. I stood up, undressed down to my boxers, and lay down on the bed. Sleep did not come for a while. I closed my eyes and saw the lights of Shibuya. The people. So many faces. I wondered what they were doing, all these people. All of them. Together. Right now.

...

I woke up earlier than expected. I'd set my alarm clock for 8:35, which seemed like a sensible time, but I turned around and looked at the digital clock on my mobile when it was shortly past seven. Still, I remained in bed and thought about trying to go back to sleep. Get fit and ready for a long day.

Or, I thought, I could get up and get my guidebook to plot out my schedule for the day. My brain felt weary of planning, though. My brain needed coffee first. Problem was, the bar downstairs, which doubled as a café during the day, would not open before eight o'clock.

So many choices to make. So many problems to overcome. So much time. I settled the problem by staying in bed, drifting away, thinking, daydreaming, until my mobile informed me it was now indeed 8:35.

After a long shower, which helped to make me feel human again, I stumbled downstairs, ordered a coffee (flat white made with the help of a professional looking Italian coffee machine, not the best coffee on the planet, but decent enough), drank said coffee in front of the hostel while I smoked a cigarette and tried to decide which way to go.

I settled on remaining in the neighbourhood of Asakusa first, walking up to the Sensō-ji temple, which would take me a good twenty minutes. On the way, I stopped at a café, which offered a spacious smoking room overlooking the river, and had, weirdly enough, a French name, even though neither the coffee, nor the food on the menu (curry and pasta) were French. I drank another coffee and took a couple of pictures of the river from the restaurant's windows, which would make an excellent post on Instagram (hashtag amazing hashtag tokyolife hashtag coffeewithaview), before I continued to the temple.

I soon crossed the first red gate leading me into the street leading up to the temple. The place was filled with people, many of them your obvious tourists carrying oversized cameras (I was no exception).

There were market stands on either side of the street offering the usual tourist kitsch, just like anywhere else in the world on a street leading up to a famous landmark, but I had to give it to the Japanese for making even their tourist crap look good, artsy, well-crafted. Closer to the temple, there was a small stand offering Buddhist blessing charms, charms for good health, or for passing an exam, succeeding at the driver's test and, even, to find one's soulmate. The monk sitting at the stand quickly glanced at me and smiled, inviting me to have a look at the blessings. I stepped closer and feigned interest as not to seem rude.

Did the Buddhist belief assume that every person on the planet had a soulmate? If so, what if there were an odd number of people on the planet? Did that mean that someone's soulmate was yet still to be born? Or did that mean that someone's soulmate had, tragically, died early in a fateful accident? If you'd be the one having lost your soulmate in that tragic accident, would you get your money back if you bought the blessing? Did the blessing come with a guaranteed time-limit within which you'd find your soulmate? What about reincarnation? Did the blessing carry over into the next life if it didn't work out in this one? What if you were reborn a pig, whereas your soulmate was a fly? Or did one get a new soulmate in every life? Did that mean that your soul changed when you were reborn? Because, surely, as long as you had the same soul and as long as your soulmate had the same soul, there was no way you could change your soulmate. If we had a soul, that was. 21 grams of fart to determine who we'd be with. Your fart-mate.

I turned away. I had been staring at the monk's blessing stand for far too long. I walked towards a square at the end of the street, smaller temple buildings on either side, countless people milling about, covering the place in people-noise. At the end of the square, there was the main temple, people lining up at the stairs leading up to the shrine, where they would throw coins into the altar, to pray for good luck, or children or happiness or that stupid soulmate. Or maybe just for fun. Oh, Buddha, all I wanna have is some fun.

I took my camera out in order not to look too lost and snapped pictures of the temple, the people about, used my zoom lens to get a few shots of the individuals lining up for the shrine.

Fifteen pictures later, I left the temple area, feeling overwhelmed by the heat (even though it was October), the number of visitors and the noise. I turned into an alley, which ended at a small mall selling Japanese craft items. I spent a good hour browsing the stores, with no intention of buying anything at this point. Most of my journey was still ahead of me, there was no point in lugging souvenirs around Japan. I could always come back here when I'd be back in Tokyo in a few weeks. Long-term planning. How terribly fucking Swiss of me.

I found a smoker's room inside the mall. It was the one thing I had always liked about Japanese malls: they usually had a dark, crusty, dingy looking smoker's room somewhere. You'd never have to smoke in front of the building, like you'd do in Switzerland, and garner the evil looks of the people who'd have to walk through your smoke to enter the building. There was always a smoker's room somewhere in Japan, complete with at least two vending machines, a room where the last remaining smokers congregated to slowly kill themselves.

I contemplated my next steps, while I blew grey smoke towards the fan hidden in the ceiling. Maybe I should just turn the GPS on my phone off, forget about all the restaurants and places I had saved on my map and meander the streets aimlessly, get lost until I'd find something I hadn't known I was looking for. But then, maybe I wouldn't find anything, would get increasingly lost on my journey until I'd forget who I was and why I'd come here. I needed an aim. And I was hungry. I checked the map on my phone.

A short ride with the metro later, I arrived at Tokyo station. Not because I would have wanted to take a train somewhere (that would be tomorrow), but because I had read about a ramen street somewhere in the bowels of the station.

There were only three things one needed to know about ramen streets:

- First, definitions: a ramen street was a conglomeration of many small ramen restaurants in close proximity to each other, and they were a thing in many cities all over Japan. Many of these ramen streets had grown organically, over time, like the famous ones in Sapporo. Some of them, however, were entirely artificial, planned, like the one in Tokyo station.
- Second, selecting the right restaurant: usually, the restaurant with the longest line was the best one. However, and this was the...
- ...third thing to know: if you felt impatient and didn't want to join the queue, you had to find that one small ramen shop located somewhere in a sidearm of the ramen street, away from the promises and colours of the bigger restaurants, a place you'd just have to take an extra step to reach. Usually, you'd find such a side-alley without a problem, only to face yet another issue:

○ There were two restaurants back there, two small ramen bars in that side-alley, each of them with only two or three seats left unoccupied, and you couldn't decide which one to take. This would be when you should look at their ticket vending machines in front of the entrance and go for the one that has no English text on the buttons, no translation. Of course, you'd feel like an idiot trying to figure out with your translation app on your phone which button would get you what kind of ramen, and you'd end up pressing the one on the top left and there would be one with a picture of gyoza, you press that, and one with the Asahi logo, you press that, and you'd proudly present your tickets to the owner inside, smiling like a monkey who feels like he has achieved something only humans can do.

○ Then, you'd sit there, eager for your meal, eager to find out what exactly you have ordered, and you think about everything you might have missed because you couldn't read the other buttons. No egg for you. No extra ham. No extra spiciness. And all the other ramen magic you would never know.

You have some, you lose some. The ramen was excellent. The cold, early lunch-beer reminded me I was on holiday.

Still, I remained restless. I continued my odyssey through the bowels of the station, past shops selling every aspect of Japanese culture, whether it be traditional or pop or post-modern, past people buying their last few souvenirs before heading home or visiting family, past people hurrying towards their train platform having grossly underestimated the sheer size of the station, past everything and everyone, so many of us, and I wondered, statistically, how many soulmates met every day at this station.

Imagine:

There is this young guy from somewhere outside the big city, from a small village, having just arrived in Tokyo to look for a flat, because he's been accepted by Tokyo university, and he's stressed by all the people at the train station and he doesn't know where to go, he buys a coffee at the Starbucks and he takes the plastic cup, and thank god, he has bought an iced coffee, because, you'll see, in a second, he turns around and—

—bumps into *her*.

Coffee, ice cold, milky-brown coffee splattered all over her top. She jumps backwards, a sudden, jerking movement and crashes against the sideboard which carries the milk and sugar and wooden spoon-sticks and they fall, she, the sideboard and he, all of them, to the floor, one of the milk containers pops open and milk sprays all over, over the middle-aged American couple that sits at a table close-by and she, the soulmate-to-be, now sits on the floor in a puddle of milk and he, the country-boy, is horrified by what he has done and there is this moment, endless, precious, awkward, thunderous moment of silence and she looks at him, her gentle features not featuring a single trace of anger and suddenly bursts out laughing and he laughs shyly, only the American husband who has been sprayed with milk is cursing in fucking fuck fuck English and demands a towel from the Starbucks workers, who themselves have frozen in astonishment over the display of gravity, fate and chance that has just revealed itself to them.

Reality kicks back in. Country-boy moves, lost, dumbfounded, torn between helping soulmate-to-be back to her feet or getting some towels to clean the mess, like a light particle that can't decide whether it should turn into a wave. Finally, he apologises profoundly, and she makes her way back onto her feet by herself and smiles and says she didn't want to go to the office today anyway and that she would now go and buy new clothes. He makes the offer to come along and pay for them. That is the least he could do, he says. There is no trace of ulterior motive in his offer since he is a sweet, innocent country-boy, so she says yes and they leave, leaving behind the puddle of milk and coffee and the speechless staff and the American husband who has stopped cursing, mouth wide open, watching country-boy and soulmate-to-be leave without looking back.

I hoped they would find happiness.

I walked a little while longer through the artificial tunnels of the train station before climbing back to the surface, into the sunlight. It was warm, for a guy from Central Europe, warm and humid. I checked my GPS and figured that I could walk to Akihabara, which should take me not much longer than half an hour. I could also take the subway, but walking there would offer me a good sense of the flow in which Tokyo's neighbourhoods connected.

I arrived in Akihabara, sweat flowing down my back, silently cursing at myself for not taking the subway. I felt disgusting and envied the fact that Japanese people never seemed to sweat, whether they were wearing t-shirts or shorts or whether they donned full business attires with ties, shirts, trousers, and jackets.

Were they just used to the climate? Did they have no pores? Was I just over-sweating?

I tried to get lost in the electric town, amidst the sound of plastic techno J-pop, women in skirts handing out flyers for nearby maid cafés, and the vanishing daylight, which was fast being replaced by the artificial neon lights of Akihabara. Akihabara, the place for lovers of nerd culture, electronics, and computer games. The artificial lights turned the city into the cliché of Tokyo people knew from films and postcards. I walked to famous Mandarake, supplier of everything remotely connected to Japanese anime and manga culture, where I slowly travelled from the top floor to the bottom, browsing bookshelves, DVDs, scantily clad figurines, being surprised by the fact I couldn't seem to find a single book nor comic in English. On the third floor, I walked down an aisle filled with manga on either side, where I noticed a small passage leading to a side room. The entrance to the passage was covered with pink curtains and I wondered whether only staff was allowed past this point, just as a tall Japanese man in a long, black trench coat emerged from the curtain, giving me a view of the room behind. The room, considering from the quick glance I had got, seemed to be the same as the one I was standing in now. Just another room filled with walls stacked with shelves full of books.

The adult section, most likely. Hence the curtain, to keep prying eyes and minors out.

I felt my heartbeat speed up just ever so slightly as I stepped through the curtain – not because I felt aroused by the idea of comic porn, just because I had this image in my head of someone watching me going into the porn section, the security guard observing me on the CCTV camera, thinking of me as yet just another Western pervert who had spent hours learning Japanese so he could read all the Japanese hentai comics, because "it is not porn," the pervert would tell his friends, "but art, story-driven, handcrafted art. It takes skill to draw boobs and vaginas." I was not that pervert. I was just curious.

I'd read that apparently no one batted an eye at hentai in Japan, that people even read it on the subway. Looking at one book from the shelves, I found it hard to believe that anyone would show this in public. The page I'd openend displayed a comic girl in a short skirt surrounded by a multitude of faceless tentacles that seemed to be attached to a gigantic alien octopus sitting somewhere outside the frame, stretching its rubbery limps at angles and in ways that made me wonder whether it was just one alien octopus or rather several that worked together to – well, to do what they were about to do underneath the girl's skirt.

I put the book back. I had nothing against manga porn, hentai, or anything Japanese. In fact, I could see a certain appeal in it, the innocence of the endless return of the short skirt, the relative absence of the male genitalia through the tentacle substitution. I got the point on an intellectual level. My sexual arousal did not agree, though. But then, maybe, my view on Japanese sex comics was one-dimensional, as, to my surprise, I also found non-schoolgirl-non-tentacle-porn: There were comics with men as the main act (ha!), muscular men, feminine men, men whose gender was not clearly defined, and there were also women that seemed more dominant, dressed in tight leather or business clothes. If nothing else, one could at least be impressed by the thematic spread the Japanese hentai imagination seemed to have.

I had spent way too much time in the adult section.

I left the small room through the curtain, hoping that no one would see me (no one did), walked back through the long alley of non-hentai, past a vitrine of figurines, the most expensive of which cost several thousand Swiss francs, and, finally, exited the shop. I had seen enough for one day.

Night was closing in. I found myself on another illuminated, neon-dream road. Unseen ghosts made of sounds and beats filled the area. There weren't as many people as expected, only a few lonely wanderers. Most of the girls handing out flyers had vanished, probably taking a break before Akihabara would come back with a vengeance, at around nine or then, when people would flood the streets, looking for the town's very own brand of craziness and diversion.

Diversion.

What were we trying not to see?

My feet felt sore, and my head was still bouncing with the image of nude comic girls, so I headed to the nearest metro station to get back to Asakusa, my trusted part of the city, small-Tokyo, quiet Tokyo. I followed the GPS on my phone to find the nearest subway, but a gigantic crane-truck that was lifting heavy crates into the windows of an office building soon brought my journey along the map to a halt. The metro entrance was on the other side, past the truck. Unfortunately, they had blocked off the street with a plastic railing. There was a construction worker, impeccably dressed in a yellow helmet and white gloves, apologising to people, and pointing them into a side alley. I approached the construction site, and he promptly waved at me as well and gestured into the alley, offering it as an alternative route. I smiled (never forget to smile), murmured my usual arigato and stepped into the alley. It was barely two people wide and weirdly darker than the world I had just come from. I walked on, passing by closed doors, most of them unlabelled, and a cat ran past me, zooming off into the distance, chasing or being chased by imaginary ghosts. A few steps ahead of me, suddenly, I heard a sliding door being opened and a Japanese man came out of what must have been a bar (I gathered from a sign atop the door). He was obviously drunk, yelled something at a person inside, before he turned away and walked in the same direction I was walking, a few steps ahead of me.

I wondered whether his tone had been aggressive. Maybe he'd been telling a joke just as he'd been leaving. Or maybe not. I passed the bar and couldn't help but turn my head to the right, so I could get an innocent peek into the room that was beyond. The sliding doors were still open, and I saw a small room with a counter. The lights were on and there was a smoking cigarette in an ashtray on the counter, a whiskey bottle, and several glasses. Apart from that, the room was empty. I walked on, not wanting to stop in front of the bar, not wasting too many thoughts on who the drunken man had spoken to. Yelled at. Told a joke to.

He disappeared from my view soon afterwards at the end of the alley. By the time I was in the same spot, he had dissolved into a thick crowd of people flowing in and out of the metro station entrance that was right in front of me.

Back in Asakusa, I continued to walk the streets, going through my schedule and departure time for tomorrow in my head. I was planning on taking a nine o'clock Shinkansen in the morning, which would bring me to Yamagata, from where I would take a regular commuter train bound for Yamadera. Nine o'clock meant I probably would have to leave the hostel at around seven, allowing myself more than enough time to take a subway and get into Tokyo station. All was planned, all was good.

I checked my GPS to see whether I was close to any restaurants or bars on my list. There was nothing, though. I was hungry and felt the existential emptiness of not knowing where to eat.

I continued my journey (idle walking in this case) for a while until I passed a place with a display of plastic sushi next to its entrance. It looked cute, the plastic sushi, more real, vivid than the real thing. A quick peek through the windows revealed one of the more traditional-looking places, with some tables off to the side and a big counter behind which a sushi-cook was assembling the fish and rice. Maybe this was the place.

Maybe not. I did not enter. Instead, I resumed my way down the street to see whether there were any other places that looked interesting, and because I felt nervous about entering the restaurant. Sushi in such a place always seemed like a formal affair and I did not know whether they had an English menu. I felt insufficient for not knowing enough Japanese to feel confident to navigate such a restaurant.

However, I couldn't find another place close-by, so I walked past the sushi restaurant again, slowly working up the courage to enter. I felt like a tiger circling its prey, a weird, awkward tiger going in circles. Probably, the chef inside had already seen me and wondered why the heck I was sneaking around his restaurant.

The tiger knew he had already made up his mind and that he would enter the sushi bar eventually, still he continued to walk up and down the street, entering smaller alleys, backstreets, turning left or right, heading up and down other roads that crossed his way, always walking maybe six minutes in one direction, before heading back towards the sushi place, the watering hole, his destiny.

Then, the tiger finally gave in.

I entered the place. The taisho behind the counter greeted me and gestured towards an empty seat at the counter. I complied and sat down. He handed me a menu the size of an A4-paper which had several pictures of individual sushi pieces on them, but also a small selection of fixed sushi menus. I pondered whether it would be possible to arrange my own set, combine my favourite sushi into one amazing plate, but as I looked up and saw the taisho, who looked at me with a mix of friendliness and suspicion, I realised there was no way on this planet I could ever explain my wishes to him. So, I ordered one of the set menus. The easy way. He nodded, a pleased look in the corner of his mouth, which turned into delight when I also ordered a sake from the menu.

Should one even drink sake with sushi?

I looked to my right where the only other two patrons were sitting, a couple maybe in their early forties, one of those hip-looking Japanese couples, him with the faint shadow of a beard, glasses, and a turtleneck sweater, her with a white sweater and brown dungarees. They were drinking beer.

Soon after, the chef put a wooden plate down in front of me with salmon eggs, eel, salmon, tuna (of the chutoro variant), albacore, shrimp, and a piece of tamago, all artfully arranged on beds of shari. All pieces were seasoned nicely with a trace of wasabi in between the neta and the rice.

The sushi plate was very good, not outstanding, simply good, I thought to myself, just as someone else entered the small restaurant. Interestingly enough, the person did not come through the same door I had, but entered the room from the other side. I leaned backwards to get a better look, to see where the second entrance was coming from, and realised the truth about this place, looking through the door that now stood open. The door led into a mall. We were inside a mall.

It was a mall sushiya.

A restaurant in a mall.

Two doors, one from the outside, the other one from the mall.

Fuck.

Normally, every ounce in my body would be horrified by the thought of eating in a mall restaurant. After all, from my experience travelling other countries, mall restaurants were the places where you got your fix of cheap, greasy food that made you feel disgusting, that made you hate yourself and made you want to run a few exercise laps to get rid of the calories (not that I would ever have done that). Mall restaurants were the hell-place of cheap ingredients and chefs who had given up on life. They were the places of food-poisoning and premature death.

But then, this place...

I tried to compute this. My sushi had been good. There were only two likely explanations: either sushi in Japan was generally good, no matter where you ate it, or I had found that one mall-sushi-place that still cared about quality.

The more interesting question would be, the oracle from the Matrix would now say: if I had known that this place was in a mall, would I still have liked the sushi? Or would I have looked for the bad in it, that tiny discolouration on the salmon that would have made me think it'd been outside the fridge for a bit too long? Maybe I'd have thought that the wasabi was not strong enough, the fish not fishy enough, the shari not sticky enough, would have dipped that shit in as much soy sauce as possible, drowning out all other tastes with the sheer explosion of salty soy umami.

The taisho smiled at me when I stood up, went to the front of the restaurant, and paid my bill at the registry, where an older woman was waiting for any patrons to finish their meal and pay. I thanked her for the meal and headed past her into the mall. A clean, nice mall with shops selling tight jeans and uni-coloured t-shirts.

There was nothing else to do. I felt tired. I walked back to the hostel, which was not far away. On the way, I picked up some drinks, shochu highballs and Santori-cokes from a convenience store. There were still a fair amount of people in the bar at the hostel, but I didn't feel like trying to get into a conversation with any of them. I walked past everyone, not greeting, not being greeted, up to the second floor, back into my room.

I would have to pack before going to bed, I thought to myself. Early morning tomorrow. I opened one can I had bought from the store. I felt like getting drunk, yet what was the point? I didn't want to wake up with a headache. I'd become prone to those ever since I had turned thirty. Drink too much alcohol, wake up with a headache. Fucking old man. Fuck an old man.

Early start tomorrow. I took a sip from my can and got started:

Pack.

Count the money.

Consider whether you must go to an ATM in the morning.

Check the train schedule.

Check the time it takes to get to Tokyo station.

Continue to pack.

Finish packing.

Check everything again.

Re-check train schedule, maybe I have made a mistake.

Still the same.

Have another sip.

Check one last time.

Check the time it takes to get to the train station.

Think about sending someone a text, send a few texts to friends, hey it's great, here are photos of food. Hashtag great sushi. I am doing great. Time of my life. The people are so friendly here.

Check train timetable one more time.

Brush your teeth.

Finish the can.

Realise you should brush your teeth again.

Think about masturbating.

Only shared bathrooms, don't want to masturbate into a sock in my room like a teenager.

Don't do it.

Check time. Getting late.

Lie down. It's hot.

Listen to music.

Check whether you have set the alarm clock.

Turn off music. Roll over. Die.

Sleep. I meant sleep.

Often, when I dream, things are in disarray. Pictures flow into each other. People become other people. I dreamt of a person who was both a friend and another friend. I dreamt of flying to Japan. Two-hundred years on a plane. I lived there. Lived there. My room, my apartment, was on the plane. And people came and people went. We were flying. I was talking. To myself.

Then, there was a dream about you.

Yamadera / Dance, Destroy, Die / Yonezawa

Once again, I woke up before the alarm clock. I took a shower, got dressed, checked my luggage one more time. All packed, all still there. No sneaky leprechaun had snuck into my room to steal my washed-out Star Wars t-shirt. I went downstairs to check out and learnt with some pleasure that the bar was already serving coffee. Flat white it was.

I left the hostel and got to the subway station. I was nervous. It was still quite early, and I remembered those videos on YouTube showing the rush hour in Tokyo, people crammed into the subway trains like cattle or sardines, cattle-sardines. Too close for my comfort. Too many people for my comfort. Also, I had my oversized suitcase with me.

There was a decent amount of people at my station, yet I was relieved when the first train came in. There were a lot of passengers, sure, but nothing even close to the videos. Me and my suitcase entered easily, stood in the back, and smiled at each other. This was fine.

Little did I know that my luck shouldn't last long.

Little did I know was the worst phrase in literary history. I didn't even know little, I knew nothing. I had a vague premonition, sure, a flat feeling in my stomach, but I didn't know. There was no knowledge that could have prepared me for the madness to come.

My train leisurely arrived at the next bigger station, an intersection point, where I would have to change lines. Naïve me, silly me, made his way past platforms and down stairs and up escalators. Bilbo Baggins excitedly shouting in my head that he was going on an adventure.

Then, the mother-fucking hobbit had to face Mount fucking Doom (yes, I knew I was mixing up hobbits).

I made it to my Mount Doom, i.e., the platform for my next subway ride. And arrived in a sea of thousands of people. Shibuya, at its busiest times, would have been a cakewalk. I passed them, so freaking many of them, walked to the end of the platform, shivering like a frightened animal. Dodging bodies left and right. A uniformed monster in business attire.

The first train arrived. People stood inside, pressed against the windows, their stares hollow. The doors opened. Barely anyone stepped out, even though the car looked like a popcorn bag about to explode. One false move from anyone in the car and all the people would just pop out, like rag dolls, devoid of motion, pushed forward, through the open doors, and down by the laws of gravity. And then lie there, unmoving, until the caretaker would come and sweep them away.

Unfazed by the mass of people in each car, the people outside walked up to the open doors, turned around and ever so gently moved backwards, pushing in, step by step, until they were inside, and the doors closed. No one spoke. No one complained. It just happened. And I stood there, mouth wide open.

How would I ever, a large, sweaty European tourist with a ridiculously enormous suitcase, make it into one of those trains? I moved towards the back wall, out of the sea of people who had started anew to pour down from the escalator. I'd just stand back and wait for a later train, I told myself. Rush hour must be over soon. There was enough time to catch my Shinkansen.

The next train arrived. People, people, people.
The next train arrived. The same.

The next train arrived. Silence. People. As if the crossing in Shibuya had sent them all away, all at once, all in the same direction, all on these trains. Where were they all going? To work? Offices? How many of them, almost the same suit, women dressed in business skirts, men with their white shirts and ties? What was their goal? What would they do? What people were they?

I' stood there, in the corner, for half an hour, watching train after train after train. I had to take the next one. I had to get to Tokyo station, onto the Shinkansen. Otherwise, all my plans, those I had so painstakingly devised before I'd come to Japan, would have been for naught. I would miss the train, arrive later, not see the things I wanted to see. The next one, I told myself, a man talking to a child, giving the child courage. The man and the child watched the next train leave as well. The next one. I walked up to the tracks. Stepped away. Too many people. The next one. Now or never. The train stopped. I turned around to walk in backwards like everyone else, saw with horror that more people had lined up behind me, had also turned around, and now pushed up to me, I pushed backwards, they pushed, slowly, surgically, I could feel the touch of bodies everywhere and wanted to apologise for my suitcase, yet no one spoke, no one even acknowledged the existence of anyone else. The doors closed and—

—there was a bit of space opening up. Like an animal breathing out, the doors closed, and the people in front of me took that tiny step forward, pushing themselves as close to the closed doors as possible. The train left the station.

A young woman to my left was reading a book, and I admired her calm demeanour. I clutched my suitcase. Only two stops. Only two stops. Make sure you do not touch anyone. Resist the urge to check whether your wallet is still in your pocket. No one is going to steal it, not in Japan. If you try to slide your hand into your pocket now, that other woman to your right would notice your movement and would think you are trying to slide your dirty fingers down her butt. Just be like everyone else. Calm demeanour. Pretend you are alone. Pretend you do not mind. Pretend you are not thinking about what would happen if the metro car suddenly stopped, if there was a power outage, if there was panic, if someone farted. You wonder how they managed not to smell of sweat as sweat is running down your forehead. You wonder how they managed not to look at each other.

You wonder how you managed to survive two stops as you arrive at Tokyo station. But survive you do.

After some searching, I found the ticket counter where I could reserve a seat for the Shinkansen, which would take me up north. Then, I had the choice of trying to find something to eat for the train ride or go to the smoker's room. I decided on the latter. There would be enough time to catch lunch when I'd arrive.

After two cigarettes, I found myself inside the train, found the seat assigned to my butt, heaved my luggage onto the compartment above (the compartment was much too small, so that at least a third of my suitcase stuck out and I spent most of the train ride worrying it would fall onto the old lady next to me and kill her), sat down, and waited for the train to depart.

There was a map of the train in front of me, which informed me that there was a smoking room on this train only a few cars down. Looked like I'd have had time to buy something to eat – which would have been a good thing, considering the fact I was feeling hungry. And I was craving a drink. Even though it wasn't even lunchtime yet.

 # (Stop right here)

She imagined she was floating in the ocean. Like a dead body carried by the waves, the sun hot and burning above her in the sky. Underneath her, the sea promised an endless abyss. She imagined she'd close her eyes and just let herself drift, be alone with the sea and herself, lost in random thoughts, big and small. She imagined laying all still until the surrounding fish would not realise that she was alive and swim close to her, touch her outstretched fingers.

She opened her eyes and saw the grey ceiling of her apartment's bathroom. The water in her bathtub was getting cold. Her ears were under water. She could hear the dripping of the drops falling from the faucet like distant thunder. And there were other sounds, too, sounds from people moving in other apartments, enhanced and echoed by the pipes running through the building and amplified by the bathtub.

She should get up, she thought, and get out of the tub before she'd catch a cold.

Huddled up in a blanket and her PJs, she sat on the sofa watching a documentary about forests and monkeys when her phone beeped to inform her that her delivery was on the way. The drone was coming in fast, her phone told her, it was only five minutes out. With some urgency, the screen showed her the little dot zooming across the map, asking her to open a window to receive the noodle soup from the busy drone. It felt somewhat patronising. Maybe she shouldn't get up, rebel against her phone's nagging, and pretend she knew nothing about the drone.

Suddenly, the dot stopped on the map. Immediately, she felt bad for her thoughts, feeling as if the drone had heard them and was hurt, and had decided not to bring her food.

Maybe the map was frozen. She checked her internet connection, which was fine. She closed the page and reloaded the map. The drone did not move. The little red dot stared at her from a few blocks away, unwilling to deliver her food. She hit the reload button five, six, seven times, the map disappeared, appeared, disappeared, appeared, disappeared, yet there was no movement. Reload. The map disappeared again, but, this time, did not re-appear. In its stead, a notification popped open on her phone, informing her that "we have noticed irregularities in your connection. You either have a problem with your internet or pressed the reload button too many times..." ...well, no shit... "please contact support if you are experiencing problems." And below that, there was a button to start a call. Call support? Was that a thing people still did?

She pressed the phone symbol and her phone called a – blocked – number. After the second ring, someone answered.

"Hello. Support. How can we be of help today?"

"Oh. Yes. Hello."

"Hello."

"I... erm..."

"I see you ordered food via our drone service."

"Yes."

"And there seem to be irregularities with the live tracking."

"Ah... yes... there..."

"Let me see..."

"I reloaded the map a few times because..."

"Your drone does not seem to move."

"Yes."

"Let me first express my apologies. As ours is a relatively new service, there might be some technical glitches. Some growing pains. We would like to offer a voucher for your troubles."

"Oh. Thank you."

"Sure."

"And..."

"And?"

"What about my food?"

"Ah. Yes. The drone seems to be stuck."

"Yes."

"Could you do me a favour? Could you look out of the window to check whether you can see the drone?"

"Sure."

She stepped to the window, but there was no...

"No, the other window. The one facing east... sorry, I am tracking your location."

"Ah. Sure."

She stepped to the other window.

"And?"

"I cannot see a drone."

"Ah."

There was silence on the other end of the phone.

"And?" she asked.

"I am running diagnostics. Hmm. The drone seems to be fine. No error messages. And you are sure there is no drone in sight?"

"No," she said, slightly irritated.

"Let me offer you another voucher," the support-person said, noticing her growing irritation.

"I don't want a freaking voucher. I want my food."

The person on the other end didn't seem to listen. Instead, she could hear the clicking of a keyboard.

"This is weird," the support person said.

"What's weird?"

"I have never..." And: "There is no..." And: "I need someone from IT to help me with this."

"Hello?"

"Ah. Yes. Excuse me. We'll have to check on this."

"But..."

"Could you do me another favour?"

"What?"

"The last confirmed location of the drone is not too far from your apartment. Could you go over there and check on her?"

"But..."

"I would go myself. But I am in Ireland."

"But..."

"Thank you. We will call you back in a few minutes."

The support person hung up.

What the?

What the fuck?

What the actual fuck?

Did the support person actually expect her to go outside and check on their fucking drone? She threw her phone on the sofa. She would not check on their drone. This was their job. It wasn't her fault that their support centre was in Ireland.

But then. She was hungry. She picked up her phone and opened the map. The drone was still immobile. It wasn't too far away. Maybe five minutes' walk. She could go, get her food, and wait for the vouchers that had been promised to her. Maybe demand a third one. Have free food for a week.

She put on trousers, a coat, and her shoes, put the phone in her pocket. She left her apartment, took the elevator down, and stepped outside. The noise of the city welcomed her. Cars zipped by on the busy road right outside her building. Somewhere, the screeching tires of a car, the sound of horns, someone yelling an insult. Home, sweet home. What a shit place. She took the phone out of her pocket and checked the map. To the right. Walk between the two high-rise buildings housing the fancier apartments. Those she'd never be able to afford.

She walked down the street and into a smaller alley behind the tall buildings. The unpleasant smell of sewage and trash hit her. It seemed darker here, the sunlight blocked by the buildings surrounding her. Somewhere from above, from an open window, she could hear music, the sound of a saxophone and some drums in the background. The pavement was wet, even though it had not rained in months.

She followed the alley, out onto a bigger street, down to a crossing. She waited at the crossing for the lights to turn green. Then across the street, past a shopping mall whose bright lights glowed in the expectation of the coming dusk. To the right again and into another side-street behind the mall. Two shop assistants on a break were smoking cigarettes without taking notice of her.

Her phone rang. A blocked number.

"Hello?"

"Ah. Yes. I see you are getting closer."

"So I am."

"You are coming up to a fence and a gateway on your left."

She did. There was a fence blocking people from entering a construction site. She tried to open the gate, only to find it locked by a keypad.

"Let me just..." the support person said, "the code is... 1234."

"Are you sure I am allowed to enter?"

"Yes."

"Is it legal?"

"Don't worry. We will take care of it." Not exactly the answer she'd hoped for. Still, she entered the passcode, 1234, and with a click, the door opened. She walked into an enormous construction site, to her right the looming shadows of big vehicles and to the left a skeleton of a half-finished building, a car-park-to-be.

"Ah, okay. Continue to the right and the drone should be about 200 meters in front of you."

"Yeah. There is a car park in the way."

"I see. It must be on top of the building. You'll find a construction elevator straight ahead."

What kind of goose chase had this become? All she'd wanted was a meal and a sofa and some stupid series on stream.

She walked towards the car park, which seemed to become bigger with every step. There was an elevator, as promised.

"Let me just call the elevator for you..."

With the sound of an extinct animal coming back to life, the elevator moved above her head. She would have asked the phone support being how he managed to call the elevator, but she was tired of talking. She wanted to get this behind her and go home. A few seconds later, the elevator door opened, and obediently, she stepped inside. The door closed, and the elevator rattled upwards.

"At the top, you just step out of the elevator, and you should be able to see the drone."

"Sure," she replied in a tone she wasn't sure was supposed to be defiant or compliant. The elevator's doors opened again. It was almost dark now. From the building's roof, she could see the lights of the city burning brighter with every second and even though the car park could not have been taller than all the high-rises around, it felt as if she were looking down at the city.

"I cannot see anything," she informed the person on the phone.

"I will send an impulse to the drone. You should see a blinking light. Here we go."

There it was, in the middle of the roof. A faint, blue light, helplessly blinking. She couldn't help but feel pity for the drone that had stranded up here.

"And?"

"I can see it."

"Good. If you could walk towards it."

"That's what I am doing."

"Very good. Again, we apologise for any inconvenience we have caused. If your food is cold now, we'd be happy to..."

"That's weird."

"Sorry?"

"The blue light..."

"Yes, that's because of the impulse I have sent..."

"No, it's growing larger."

"Interesting."

"It's warm. And bright."

"Are you still walking towards it?"

"Yes. It's growing."

"Maybe you should turn around."

"It's like cold energy. Like it's alive."

"I think we will send in a support team."

"I think I can touch it."

"I've just dispatched a new drone to your place with fresh food. You shouldn't concern yourself..."

"It is touching me. My fingers. Hand. Arms. Shoulders."

"That's just a hallucination."

"I... it's everywhere now."

And the blue light was everywhere.

Through the blue light, she saw herself and everything, and the rest of the world. She saw cars, billions of them, their sounds, the clouds of dust and dirt they produced and honking and people, people, billions of them, and she saw they were nothing but dust, dust and dirt, and she saw them talking, chatting, making so many of those weird sounds by moving their tongues and teeth and pressing air from their lungs through their throats, and it all had become quite senseless by that point, and she heard walking, saw things walking back and forth from here to there and back again, and she saw herself amidst that chaos, she'd turned into the blue light, a mother working hard to give them purpose, some comfort, some love, fear also, and despair, just to keep them in their place.

"You just *had* to touch it."

"Excuse me?"

"I said: You just had to touch it." The voice seemed to come from everywhere. She wasn't sure whether it belonged to a human being or a machine.

The blue light disappeared, and she found herself in a big, almost empty room. There were no windows, only orange lights hanging from the ceiling. The room reminded her of an office with its greyish, nondescript carpet and a yellow-white, creamy wall. In the middle of the room, lost amidst the size of the room, was a single desk. A person sat at that desk, back turned to her.

"Did you talk to me?" she asked.

"Obviously."

"Are you... the support person?"

"No. That would be silly. That person is in Ireland."

"But... where am I?"

"Not in Ireland."

Slowly, the person turned around in her chair. It was a woman, maybe in her late forties, a normal looking, every day, late-forties woman in a grey business suit.

"Now, since you are here, you might as well help me." The woman took out a binder from one drawer in her desk.

"No. I have to get home. Where am I?"

"Really? You want to go home? Back to that... what did you call it the other day?" The woman opened the binder and flipped through some pages. "Ah, yeah, a shit city filled with hipsters running after the latest coffee-macchiato-ginger-spiced-pumpkin-fuck and assholes that stick a knife in your back motherfucking American psycho-style." The woman looked up from the binder. "You should really work on your language."

"How do you know I said that?"

"I'll make you a deal. You help me and I let you know."

"You let me know how you know?"

"Yes. Deal?"

"Deal."

"Good. We secured the drone, so your dinner is waiting for you in the mess hall. I suggest you eat, relax for a bit, and then get changed. Meet me back here when you are ready."

She complied.

The noodles were cold now. Still, she ate them silently, sitting in the enormous mess hall, rows after rows of metal tables around her. At least it was warm in here. It made her feel safe, despite being all alone. Warm and safe. It made her think about visiting the Scorched Earth once. On a trip with her mother. It had been warm and safe in the car. They'd been driving for hours to get out of the city, and her mother refused to tell her where they were going. First, there'd been villages, smaller houses. They were empty, falling apart. Then there was nothing. Only the Scorched Earth they had told her about in school. The black earth, burned and empty, a wasteland that had died with both a whimper and a bang.

"What happened here?" she had asked her mother, even though she knew the answer.

"People happened," her mother said. And that was all she said about it. Her mother turned on the radio playing a song by the Beatles, Here Comes the Sun. She soon fell asleep in the passenger's seat. It was funny how she could remember that part of the journey but had no recollection of what happened after. When she closed her eyes to remember the trip, she could see the car before her inner eye, the old blue Citroen, she could see the Scorched Earth pass by outside, she could see her mother driving – even though her mother's face was a blur – and that was it.

She went to the room that had been prepared for her, a small metallic room with a niche for sleeping in the corner and a desk on the other side, and put on the clothes that had been laid out for her. A brown shirt, trousers of a darker brown tone, sturdy shoes, and a hat. She looked like a mix between a safari tourist and a delivery person.

Back in the vast office room, the woman behind the desk informed her she needed her to count elephants.

"But they are all dead," she replied.

"We will send someone to meet you. He knows places where a few are left. I need you to count them, note how many you have counted, and report back to me. Understood?"

"Sure."

She wanted to ask the woman where to go, yet before she could say anything, the woman pointed to the left where a door had appeared, suspended in the middle of the air. Obediently, she stepped through. A green light surrounded her, forcing her to close her eyes. When she opened them again, she'd left the room behind and found herself on a wide, green pasture on top of a small hill that bent gently down and then upwards again onto another hill. The world was filled with colours, green grass, yellow dandelions, blue sky, white clouds. A flourish of smells overran her senses and an accumulation of tiny sounds, birds and bees and a creek somewhere off in the distance blinded her ears. She let herself fall into the grass, which was so much softer than she'd ever expected, and prayed that this moment was real and not a dream and not a memory that was not hers.

"We have little time." A man stood above her, only a dark form against the bright light of the sky. "The door will not be around for long. And this world won't be here for long."

"Who are you?"

"I am Nobo. I am here to help you count the elephants."

"Ah. Yes."

"I felt the same way the first time I came here," Nobo told her, having noticed the smile on her face, lying in the grass, unwilling to get up, "but you can't stay, trust me. You will always return to where you came from. The question is just how painful you want it to be." Reluctantly, she got up.

They walked down the hill, Nobo a few steps ahead of her. The ground underneath her feet felt soft, and she took off her shoes and socks to feel the grass against her naked soles. Nobo stopped as she did this and eyed her carefully without saying a word. Maybe there was a twinkle of amusement in the corner of his lips or a hint of disapproval in his eyes. She cared neither way. The sun stood high in the sky but did not burn on her face. There were a few clouds scattered above. None of them felt threatening, though, no rain in sight.

"It has not rained in a long time," Nobo told her, as if he'd read her mind.

"Does it rain often here? Normally?"

"A few times a month. More in fall and spring."

"Is it summer?"

"Early summer."

They approached a small forest. Nobo told her to put her shoes back on. She wanted to protest, but saw the logic in his request. Walking barefoot in an unknown forest sounded like a wonderful and stupid idea. She could get hurt by sticks and stones hiding beneath the fallen leaves. She obliged.

"There is a clearing in the forest half a mile down the road," Nobo told her. "They usually gather around there."

The light was muted inside the forest. It was green, yellowish, bouncing off the trees and their leaves. She could hear small animal feet running through the branches above their heads, yet could not spy any squirrels or birds. While they walked, she stretched out her arms to touch the barks of the trees to the left and right, feeling their hard skin, the age of hundreds of years. She felt like a child, an urge to run as fast as she could, to get lost in the forest. She felt like an old woman, the urge to sit down underneath the oldest tree and reminiscence about her life, she felt the urge to be alone, to cry just for herself and then to fade away, to become a tree herself.

She followed Nobo through the forest. There was no path, yet Nobo walked securely, as if he'd gone this way a thousand times.

"Do you come here often?"

"Every time they want a count of the elephants."

"Do they count them often?"

"Not as much as they used to."

"How many did you count the last time?"

"Maybe five. Or seven."

"Oh." She had expected more.

The forest opened in front of them, and they stepped out into the clearing. Nobo gave her a sign to be quiet. There was a pond in front of them, and at the far end, there they stood. Elephants.

The beasts had gathered at the edge of the pond. One of them was drinking water through his trunk, most of the others stood quietly. A smaller elephant had got into the pond and seemed to have fun splashing around in the water.

"Can we get closer?" Her voice was but a whisper, so quiet, she wasn't sure whether she'd actually said the words.

"You can. I'll wait here. Just walk slowly around the pond. Don't scare them off."

She nodded and started walking. She resisted the urge to walk faster, tried to walk as consciously, as non-threateningly as she could. As soon as she got close to the pond, two of the elephants raised their heads and observed her. They did not move, and she saw this as permission to come closer. She continued her path along the water's edge. The two elephants were still watching her. Two other elephants had turned around and were approaching the forest, not to get away, only to get some food off a tree. The small elephant stopped his playing in the water. It looked at her as well and, suddenly, charged out of the pond and in her direction. She was scared that it would attack her, stopped, unsure whether to turn and run away. She looked back to where she'd left Nobo, but he was lying in the shade of a tree and did not take notice of what was happening.

The small elephant still came closer fast, yet also slowing down. He was not charging to attack. He just wanted to say hello. The small elephant stopped at an arm's length in front of her. It was barely tall enough to reach her chest. Excitedly, the elephant stepped up and rubbed its head against her body and she stroked the animal as if it were a cat or a dog. The elephant wrapped his trunk around her wrist and pulled her toward the other elephants. They, too, had started to walk towards her. Before she knew it, she found herself in front of the biggest elephant. It was a beautiful animal. Her skin wrinkled, of a strong grey colour, her big ears flapping to chase away flies. Her left tusk had broken off, but the right one was big and beautiful, pristinely white. She lifted her hand to touch the elephant. She was not sure whether she should. Before she could decide whether to go ahead or to pull her hand back, the elephant reached out with its trunk and touched her hand, slowly, gently, and she could feel tears shooting into her eyes and running down her cheeks. The elephant looked at her, at the tears. Next to her, the small elephant leaned against her hip. In the back, the other elephants had gathered and were observing the scene.

The elephant retracted its trunk, and she could feel the small elephant next to her stepping backwards. Slowly, all of them turned around and walked into the forest, not making a single sound. And then they were gone.

She was crying. Why had we killed them?

"Because stupid men fight," Nobo said. He'd appeared behind her. Quickly, she swept the tears off her face. "It's okay. I cried the first time I saw them."

"Can we go after them?"

"No. They are gone. Did you count them?"

"Oh... I... I... No. I forgot."

"I counted five. Or seven. Make it six. Five big ones and one small one."

"Six. Sounds good."

"Right. I better bring you back to the door."

Back in the other place, she went to her tiny room, changed out of her safari clothes, and put on her old ones. Then she sat down in the mess hall, where they had put out a bowl of noodles for her. They were not cold, the noodles, but also not quite warm. Just kinda off. Which reminded her of her mother again, the lukewarm noodles. The luke-warm air from the air conditioning in the car. She remembered asking her mother, when they drove through the Scorched Earth, whether they could stop, have a look at the world outside the car. Touch it. Her mother said no, vehemently, and told her it was dangerous. She looked through the car's windows and wondered how something so empty could be dangerous.

A voice over the intercom cut her thoughts short: "I am ready for you. Please come over."

The woman was sitting behind the desk, her back, as usual, turned towards her.

"How many did you count?" the woman asked her as she arrived at the desk.

"Five big ones and one small one."

"So, that's...?"

"Six."

"Good. Less than we hoped for, but what can we do?"

"Why do we count them? Why... are they... where are they?"

"Outside. Somewhere behind the door." The woman sighed and, for the first time since she had come into the room, looked up and directly at her. "Did you cry?"

"Yes."

The woman behind the desk scribbled something down on a piece of paper. "Very good. We have one more task for you. But I suggest you get some sleep first."

She left the room, through the empty mess hall, through another door, and down a corridor leading her to her small room and her bed.

She took off the shoes and tucked herself in. She felt the presence of something or someone, but she was too tired to care and fell asleep fast, breathing quietly, slowly, lightly, as if she was floating on water.

She imagined she was floating on water. In the ocean, far, far out. The illusion did not last for long. She opened her eyes and saw the grey, boring ceiling of her bathroom. The water had got cold, so she got up, dried herself with a towel, put on her PJs and sat down on the couch. She didn't feel hungry. She just lay on the couch, watching TV until she felt it was late enough to go to bed.

The red light from a billboard advertising outside the window illuminated her bedroom. It did not bother her. She had got used to it and felt quite safe being bathed in the red light.

Her alarm clock woke her up, like every morning, at 6:43 and, as usual, she put it on snooze until 6:52. She got up, went to the bathroom, peed, washed herself, brushed her teeth, took off her PJs, went back to the bedroom, put on her clothes, went back to the bathroom, checked her face, put on some make-up, went to the kitchen, ate some bread and fruit, brushed her teeth again, put on her shoes, left the apartment and made her way to the café. She put on an apron and got to work. She served 312 drinks during the day, plus 56 slices of pie and an assortment of brownies she was too lazy to count. She talked to Linda, who worked the morning shift with her, and learnt that Linda had been on a date the other day but was unsure whether something more would come of it. She left the café at five, walked along one of the busy shopping streets, and decided not to buy new shoes just yet. She came home, prepared herself some noodles for dinner, watched TV and, when she felt it was late enough, she took a bath and went to bed.

She dreamed she was floating on water. Lightning above her head in the endless sky. There was a group of elephants walking across the sea, their vast bodies' shadows only briefly illuminated by the sharp lights that ran across the sky. The lightning looked like trees with forked branches making their way through an impenetrable darkness. She traced the way of the lightning and saw that its branches were people, decisions, pathways.

As every morning, her alarm clock woke her up at 6:43, but she just lay there, cursing the morning. The noise of a nearby construction site hammered into her head. Finally, at something after seven, she got up and went to the bathroom. She sat on the toilet for a long time, long time after she'd finished peeing, looking at her mobile. She put on her clothes, looked at her face in the mirror, hated it, put on some makeup, and left the house on the way to the café. There were people in the streets, all walking, somewhere to go. The noises of their voices and footsteps and the cars made her feel nauseated. She looked up to remind herself what colour the sky was, yet she couldn't see it, the huge skyscrapers that stood around her blocked it. She put on an apron and served the customers. She got into a fight with one of them because he said she was unfriendly. She listened to Linda, half-heartedly, she was not interested in Linda's date and she wanted to smack Linda's face and she left work when she was done, the drinks and cakes and brownies uncounted, and she went into a shop to buy shoes she would never wear and she went home, bought fries on her way home and watched mindless TV about stupid people and she went to bed to sleep, unable to do so and there stood a small elephant in the corner of her room, just looking at her. She knew the elephant was there to accuse her of being miserable, so she shooed it away and it was dark, all dark, in her dreams.

Her alarm clock rang at 6:43 but did not wake her up. She was already wide-awake, reading a book, startled by the sudden noise of the alarm. She turned it off and got up and went to the bathroom, put on some music, and listened to the radio while she was peeing and brushed her teeth and took a shower. She sang along when Maniac came on, almost slipped, and fell out of the shower, which made her laugh and she put on her clothes and put on some makeup, some rouge for her cheeks, which she found quite beautiful today. On the way to the café, she stopped at a shop to buy comfortable shoes and she was running late for work, Linda had already opened the café. She laughed and apologised, and Linda said it was fine. She served customers and the radio in the café was playing pleasant songs and she caught herself singing along, which made the customers smile and give her tips. She wished they all would burst into song, a song about sunrises, and everyone would dance, and suddenly, she would catch a glance of a group of elephants in suits dancing in the back, tap-dancing and holding canes, all proper-looking. She listened to Linda and agreed to come on a double date that evening. They went to a restaurant and had tasty food and they went to a bar and they got drunk. She and her date did not kiss, still she gave him her number and maybe they would meet again, and she went home and had a bath and went to bed.

As usual, her alarm clock woke her up at 6:43, and she was sad. She got up and peed and brushed her teeth and put on clothes and looked at her face and wondered whether there was someone out there she should look nice for. Her eyes were empty mirrors. She left her apartment. People seemed to walk into her, not looking left or right, and she stopped and cursed at someone. She made it to the café and Linda was out sick and people were lining up, complaining that she was opening late. She cursed at them, and someone wrote a negative review of the café online and she spilled coffee, and someone said he wouldn't pay for the cake since it tasted off and a kid made a mess and, suddenly, an elephant entered the café and no one took notice, despite the elephant crashing into the furniture and trampling someone to death. The elephant arrived at the counter, and it was only then that she saw that there was someone sitting on its back.

"I am sorry. You'll have to leave your pet outside."

"Oh, he is not a pet. He is my friend," the man sitting on the elephant said.

"It is still an animal."

"Aren't we all?"

"Of course. But your fucking elephant is too big for the shop."

"Really?" the man asked, skidding down from the elephant. Suddenly, the animal stood on the counter, only marginally bigger than a normal-sized cat, and then it was as small as a hand, a finger, a nail. The man opened his wallet, and the elephant gracefully jumped into the wallet. The man put the wallet away.

"Better?"

"Sure." She didn't like him. "What do you want?"

The man turned around as if to get a good look at what everyone in the café was drinking. Most people, though, had left, except for the one who had been killed. Most chairs and tables were broken, and coffee had been spilled everywhere. A window was shattered.

"You should take better care of your establishment," he said.

"Fuck you. Thanks to you, I'll spend hours cleaning tonight."

"My name is Nobo," the man said.

"So?"

"So, what would you say if I gave you power over everything?"

"What?"

"I'll turn you into a goddess. You could do whatever you want."

"Sure. I'll take it."

"Okay. You are a goddess now."

Like a fork of lightning, we see the things we can do: we could mend the broken windows and chairs and bring the dead guy back to life. We could make excellent coffee and cake and meet people. Or we could just leave this place and curl up in our home. Or we could burn everything down, the skyscrapers and cars, make them all go away. We could fly to the Scorched Earth and make it live again. We could watch the trees grow and take Nobo's little elephant and make a home for her. We could burn everyone who tries to build another house, who speaks, who makes noise, who drives a car.

We could dance, destroy, or die.

The goddess remembers seeing the Scorched Earth once. On a drive with her mother. Her mother had had a fight with her father, they'd been screaming at each other for hours and she'd been in her room, hearing the muffled voices. Suddenly, her mother barged in and took her by the hand and put her in the car. They left the city and drove into the Scorched Earth. Her mother drove off the barely paved road, onto gravel and sand. After hours, she stopped the car in the shade of a burned-out skyscraper. She left the car, saying she'd be back soon. The shade of the skyscraper disappeared, and it was getting hot in the car. She was sweating, little child she was, clutching a stuffed animal to her chest.

They found her unconscious, just before the end. They never found her mother, and she never saw her father again.

She woke up in a hospital. Someone had propped up her stuffed animal next to her pillow. "He is a good friend," the nurse said, pointing at the little stuffed animal. She took it in her hands.

"Does he have a name?"

"Nobo," she said.

"That's a funny name. For an elephant."

The little girl started crying, quietly, all the pain washing down her cheeks.

"Shh. It's all right." The nurse held her hand and gave her the stuffed elephant to hold. "Have you ever seen a real elephant?"

The girl shook her head.

"You should someday. They are quite beautiful."

#

After somewhat over two hours, I arrived in Yamagata, where I had nine minutes to catch a commuter train to get to Yamadera. For most, there would be terrible little reason to visit the small town of Yamadera. I had found myself two: first, there was a temple up on a hill. So-and-so many steps would bring me to the top, where I'd have a view of the valley below and, hopefully, find enlightenment on the way up. Second, the region and the town were famous for their udon noodles. Climb a mountain and eat some noodles. Easy going.

I arrived and then promptly left the train station (which, to my delight, had lockers big enough to fit my comically large suitcase) and headed into the village. My GPS told me that the ascend to the mountain temple would begin at the other end of town, which was, despite its relative smallness, buzzing with people, many of whom seemed to be travellers like me, people who had found at least one of my two reasons compelling enough to come here. Not far from the train station, I stepped into a small restaurant, where an old lady welcomed me enthusiastically, uttering a slur of Japanese sentences which I didn't understand. She motioned me to sit at a table and handed me the menu, which, not shockingly, was only in Japanese. However, the fact that this place's menu, like in many other Japanese restaurants, had photos of their food items next to the items' names saved my Japano-dyslexic ass. I decided on a blurry photo (it looked like they actually had taken pictures on film, developed them, and glued the photos onto the menu) of something that vaguely looked like a bowl of udon. I also mumbled "birru" when the lady took my order. She smiled and replied again with a cascade of Japanese words, and I smiled and nodded. She seemed contempt with my reaction, disappeared into the kitchen (not without mumbling more friendly sounding Japanese sounds to herself), only to come back seconds later with a bottle of beer and a glass. "Arigato gozaimas," I said as she put both down in front of me and she replied with a drawn out "Aaaah, ooh" and more things, which, again, I couldn't understand.

The udon followed soon after.

The interesting thing about a bowl of udon is that the dish is all about the noodles, nothing else. Compare that to a bowl of ramen, which is mostly about the broth. Of course, ramen noodles are important, and they are delicious, yet they are primarily a vehicle to transport the liquid from the bowl to your mouth. The ramen broth, no matter which variation you go for, is the rock star of the Japanese cuisine, loud and edgy, cooked, in the best case, for days, bearing a truckload of flavours that hit you like a slap in the face.

Udon is much gentler, the classically trained little brother of the rock star, the gentle soul. The clear broth is a background player, the string section playing to the solo artist in all the best ways. The solo artist, of course, being the udon noodle. The first bite of said solo artist makes you think of worms, since the noodles are thick and strong and a bit squidgy against your teeth, tongue, and palate. As you chew, however, you notice how well-balanced this noodle is, a balance of wheat, flour and the (hopefully non-literal) sweat of hours of work in the kitchen. If ramen was the heavy, flaming truck of Japanese cuisine, then udon was the slick family car. Not nice to look at, not loud, not edgy, yet always reliable and smartly designed in ways most people wouldn't realise.

Maybe I felt a certain kinship with the udon noodle. I was smartly designed in ways people did not understand. Maybe. Maybe not.

Fully filled, I paid and left, happy, ready for the second reason of my being here. According to my GPS, the ascend of the mountain wouldn't take long, maybe an hour.

Oh, little did I know...

An hour later, I had ascended maybe a third of the mountain. Sweat was dripping down my forehead. Despite it being overcast and not too hot, I felt like my lungs were on their last legs and my legs on their last... lung...? ...breath? They hurt, that was the thing. It must be the humidity, I thought to myself, taking step after step, up and up, ready to jump off the mountain to end my misery. Other people overtook me at a constant pace, people for whom the ascend seemed to be a leisurely Sunday stroll. Nothing about this felt leisurely. And it wasn't Sunday. I wanted to smoke a cigarette. If my lungs were about to give out, I could at least give them a reason to.

The path led mostly through a forest, so I could neither see how far above the village I'd risen, nor how far above the top of the mountain was. Locational nothingness inside a forest. I occasionally stopped to take pictures of trees or the forest or some religious shrines or small stone statues that stood along the path. Not because any of it had been nice to look at, but because it gave me a reason to give my legs and lungs a break without having to acknowledge openly to the people overtaking me that I was fucking out of shape.

I had to do more sports. When I'd get back home. At least once a week. Train those legs. Get rid of the belly. And lose the double-chin behind my thick beard. Look presentable.

There was nothing forcing me to continue up the mountain. Except myself. Except the ancient Buddhist promise one might find enlightenment on the way up.

I'd followed up a set of makeshift steps that were particularly unforgiving when a group of people coming down crossed me. I stepped aside to let them pass, wiping off at least some of the sweat on my forehead with my bare hands. A woman of the group, she herself also heavy-set and quite out of breath, shortly smiled at me and said: "gambate." She said it with purpose, seriousness and friendliness, a tone which caught me off-guard and made me smile at her. I knew what the word meant from my years of watching anime with English subtitles downloaded from the internet. Gambate. You can do it. Give your best. You will get into Tokyo University. You will find the girl. Happy ending.

No gambate for me. Knowing my luck, I would die on this mountain. Still, her gesture moved me, and it upset me not knowing the appropriate expression to reply.

Gambate. I walked on. I did not die. I made it.

I learned two things: first, I did not find enlightenment. My mind seemed the same after arriving at the top. Second, even Buddhist temples needed upkeep. So, it came that the temple on the top was covered in scaffolding and closed to the public. And instead of serenity and peace, the sound of hammers and drills greeted me. It was the way that counted, I told myself, and turned around to see the view of the valley. Enlightenment my ass. Way my ass. The sky was grey, and it looked like rain was coming. My gaze searched for something below that would catch my eyes as beautiful, giving me a reason to have come up here. I could spot the train tracks, the small village of Yamadera, another small village in the distance, hills on the other side. Sure, I would find something nice to look at, I would take some photos and put some online. It had all been worth it. Right? RIGHT?

What the fuck was I doing? Had I really expected I would find something else than sour muscles?

I leaned against the railing, right at the edge, the path below me, and I wondered how far the drop was. I had to think of this film where the heroine at the end jumped off a mountain, in the hope she would find something she'd been wishing for at the bottom, and you see her, in the movie, sail through the grey clouds, same grey clouds as today. I wished there was someone next to me, someone who wouldn't make me feel ashamed for being as exhausted as I was, and I would tell her about that movie, but the person would shush me and point to the side, where soulmate-to-be and country-boy would stand and the two of them would tell each other about their childhood and all the things that fucked them up, for him, his father, an old, conservative man living on his farm, expecting his son to take over the family duties, only to see his son leave for Tokyo, what a disappointment. And for her, her parents, too. Not the fact that they expected too much, though, but that they gave her no direction at all. No one ever told her whether what she was doing was good or whether she was good at anything, she just tried out stuff to see what would happen, only to have that feeling grow inside that nothing she did mattered. She is wearing the dress he has bought for her, and she looks beautiful, and he is wearing his old country-boy uniform, a chequered shirt and jeans, which, as it happens, is quite hip in Tokyo, all the city-boys wanna look like a country-boy. Except for his shoes, he is wearing his trekking shoes, functional, not fashionable. But his feet don't hurt. And that is all that counts. If necessary, he'd be able to run up and down the mountain all day with his trekking shoes.

But there is no need for that, they know and smile and hold each other's hands. I turned around and left them alone. It was too private a moment for me to stare.

I found an ashtray next to two vending machines hidden behind a hut. I bought myself some water and a Boss coffee and enjoyed a cigarette.

Getting down from the hill was easier than going up and I felt the urge to tell someone on my way down, someone who looked as miserable as I had, that they could make it and it would be all worth it, eventually.

Back at the train station, I reclaimed my luggage, had another smoke, and waited for the train that would bring me to Yonezawa, which was in the opposite direction from where I'd come from. I had booked a hotel there and a seat in a restaurant because I'd read they were selling their very own local variation of wagyu beef.

The train journey took me past more small villages. People entered the train and left. One time, a horde of school children, all dressed neatly in the same uniform, boarded the train, filling almost every seat and every corner, and I did my best not to take up too much space with my over-sized luggage and body.

I wondered what life must be out here, living in a small town in Japan. Was it vastly different from living in a small town in Switzerland? The school kids would get up in the morning, walk to the station, take a train, go to school, and go home again in the evening, taking the train in the opposite direction. The parents, maybe one of them, maybe both, would go to work, return in the evening, have dinner, maybe have a family argument, do homework and housework, and then sleep. In summer, they fall asleep to the sound of the crickets, that stereotypical arr-arr sound you hear in every Japanese anime. That was a sound we did not have in Switzerland. However, I remembered that flock of sheep on a meadow close to the house I'd grown up in, I remembered them keeping me up all night with their ceaseless bleating.

Yonezawa and its train station felt like a place most people only passed through. The station was small, offering little more than a single ticket counter, a tiny shop selling a selection of stationary items, train food and local goods, and a bathing house attached to the train station. Probably for people who waited for their train. Case in point. No one stayed in Yonezawa.

Except for me. I had a room in a business hotel, one night in a small hotel room, no breakfast, no luxury.

The staff of my hotel only spoke little English and seemed apologetic about it. No need to feel bad, I wanted to tell them, because I am the idiot with no knowledge of Japanese. Sure, I could order a beer, but that was not a useful skill to check into a hotel. Unless you wanted a beer upon check-in. Excuse me, I'll have birru with that roomu.

Despite the language barrier, the woman found my reservation, after looking at my passport and looking at the computer screen and looking at my passport again and looking at the computer screen, putting my name into the computer, keystroke after keystroke. She handed me a plastic card-key, and she also informed me that the "TV... erm... for free." I nodded and smiled. I had always assumed that TV was for free in hotels.

She hadn't meant just any regular TV channels, I learned in my room while I lit a cigarette (yes, I had booked a smoker's room - not because I absolutely needed to smoke in my room but because I wanted to have the experience before they banned all smoking in hotels everywhere around the world), turned on my TV and faced an impressive selection of Japanese porn movies for no extra charge. I wondered what chain of events had led to the hotel deciding that the adult section should be available without charge for all guests. Maybe the hotel saw it as a selling point, an extra thing for free, that criterion that made people book a room here instead of at the next-closest hotel. Here is some free slippers, here is free breakfast, here is porn. Fuck, yeah. Yeah, fuck.

I sat down in front of the TV and took a drag of my cigarette. I knew nothing about Japanese culture, I thought, looking at the movies' titles in badly translated English. I wondered how many men my age, in midi-expensive suits, sitting in hotel rooms, in town for a work trip, were doing the same, browsing through the porn, because that was what they did, in their home away from home.

Salary men, they called those men in suits. People who worked for a salary in faceless offices for big companies.

The name of this one was Ryu, and I met him at a bar. I'd been smoking outside and got talking to some people who were smoking, too. After some chatting, they asked me to join their group for some drinks at their table and, since I was alone, I agreed. The group was a peculiar mix of locals and travellers who had come together in this bar at this table, Ryu among them. They introduced me and there was a chair free next to him, so that's where I sat down. We talked, he asked me where I was from ("Switzerland. Nice! I want to visit.") and he told me he had grown up in Hiroshima, actually in a smaller suburb just outside the city, and that he had lived his entire life in different places within the city limits.

"What do you do?" I asked him.

"I work in an office," he replied. He was hard to understand, not because his English had been bad, but because of the music inside the bar, which was much too loud for my taste. "I am... erm... salary man."

I nodded. I'd heard the term before. "But I don't want to do this forever," he continued, without me having asked. I nodded again, he didn't offer any additional information, though. He took another large sip of his whiskey-cola and smiled. "What do you do?" he asked me. "I work in an office as well." "So, salary man?" "Yes. Kinda. I am also an artist, though. A writer. Kinda." "Ahh..." "I have written several short stories," I hastily added, eager to prove my credentials. "Ah, interesting!"

This is where our conversation ended. We listened for a while to the other people at the table, who were talking about places where you could get cheap shots and talk with Japanese women (only talk, no touching!). One guy, a chap from Belgium, told us he had, by chance, met a famous Sumo ringer in the streets earlier that day. The Sumo invited the Belgium guy to dinner, and I wondered if his story was true.

Ryu thought little of the evening or me after he left. He went back to work the next day, after only four hours of sleep and still half-drunk. He bought a bottle of Pocari Sweat on his way to the office, which helped to lift most of the fog in his brain. At work, his boss told him he would have to go to Yonezawa next week, Monday through Friday, to visit the company's branch in the small town and meet with the local manager. His task would be to make sure everything was in line with HQ regulations. All the communications. All items on sale. The shop. The branding. The way the items were on display. It was standard procedure. Every year, HQ sent out hundreds of workers across the country to check on the local branches. It was a boring but not meaningless task, and Ryu was thankful for the opportunity. After all, it would give him the chance to show he could carry out an important task on his own, despite him only being 25 years old.

Ryu had never been to Yonezawa before. In fact, he'd seen little of Japan outside of Hiroshima. Work kept him busy. Arriving in Yonezawa, the small town didn't look like much to him at first, neither did the hotel.

At the desk of his hotel, the receptionist informed him about the local attractions (if he found time to visit them), breakfast time, that there was a public bath on the eight floor (in fact two of them, one for men, one for women) and that a certain section of the TV program was for free. Ryu tried hard not to blush when she told him, took his key, went up to the sixth floor to his room. He lit a cigarette in his room.

He went to the bath on the eighth floor, which was almost empty, except for two older guys who were silently soaking in the hot water. He did the same for about half an hour until he felt the tense muscles in his back and neck relax. He went back to his room and went to bed.

The local branch manager was an asshole. There was no other way to put it. He was Ryu's senior in years, yet not in rank. Still, he refused to comply with any of the suggestions Ryu made. He had to re-organise the storefront completely, Ryu told him, to make sure the first item customers saw were the company's products, not the local products. Sure, it was a good thing to sell local products in the store as well, to show the company's support for small producers, but the main thing people had to see was the company's items, the familiar logo, the familiar branding. This was the case for every branch, from Sapporo to Kagoshima. The manager only sneered at the suggestion and mumbled a non-committal "sure, sure" before disappearing into the warehouse next door not to be seen again before lunch.

At least the shop's younger employee was nice, a guy, maybe twenty-one, twenty-two years old, whom Ryu found an instant connection to. In between the long breaks, when he had to wait for the manager to come back from the warehouse, they talked. The employee told him about his life, growing up in the small city of Yonezawa and about working with the asshole manager ("I just nod and smile and do what he tells me," the employee told Ryu). Of course, that was not an option for Ryu. He needed the *manager* to nod and smile and do what Ryu told *him* to do.

The employee had long hair. Much too long for a man, completely out of fashion in bigger cities such as Hiroshima. There, they preferred short or half-long hair, cleanly cut, not like the employee's hair, which flowed freely down to his shoulders. He didn't have a beard, but wasn't clean-shaven, either. He had small shoulders, almost too small for his age, yet the store uniform nicely framed and complemented his hips and his buttocks. Ryu realised this as he observed the employee filling up shelves.

In the evening, Ryu went back to the hotel, took another bath, and thought about ways he could convince the manager to cooperate. The easiest way, of course, would be to call HQ and have his boss talk to the manager, order him to listen to Ryu. However, he didn't want to involve HQ. Maybe he should try to appeal to the manager's sense of obligation for the company. Remind him of the long history of the company, its role in the development of Japan in the past 60 years and remind the manager that it was his duty to uphold and continue this long tradition.

Ryu had to think of the employee. Where did he live? Maybe his house was close-by. Maybe just down the street. Did he live with his parents? Or did he have his own house? Ryu lit a cigarette and sat down in front of the TV and scrolled through the videos on offer, not finding anything that appealed to him. His mind was preoccupied with the manager and with the next day.

The employee greeted him with a hot cup of coffee as he arrived at the store shortly after eight. He saw with some pleasure that some of the company items had been moved to the front and some other items, the local ones, had been moved to the further corners of the shop. Sure, there was still a lot of work to be done, yet, maybe, this day wouldn't be as hard as he had feared it would be.

"I thought I'd help you a bit," the employee told Ryu, seeing that he was eyeing the items that had been moved, "the manager came in five minutes ago, yelled at me when he saw what I'd done, and then stormed off to the warehouse."

Maybe the day would be exactly as hard as he'd feared. Luckily, he had come up with a strategy: first, let the manager sulk in the warehouse, leave him alone. Second, do not make any further changes in the store for now. Just let the situation develop.

Ryu sat down on a stool in a corner of the shop and observed. The employee was doing his job, Ryu watched him going back and forth, talk to the occasional customer and take phone calls. He had a pleasant voice for phone calls, Ryu thought, a smooth and friendly voice he could have listened to for hours. From time to time, the employee smiled at him and asked Ryu whether he needed water or anything else. Every time, Ryu would smile back, but shake his head.

His strategy progressed to the next phase when the manager, shortly before lunchtime, left the warehouse and came to the store. He frowned when he saw Ryu, but Ryu immediately jumped to his feet and apologised. Yesterday, he was too demanding with his, erm, demands, he explained to the manager, when he should have first listened to the manager's perspective and profit from his many years of experience. The manager raised his left eyebrow when he heard this, which Ryu interpreted as a sign to continue. To mend the situation and to get a grasp on the manager's needs, he wanted to invite him for dinner. There was a local restaurant in town which he had heard made the best Yonezawa beef and he asked the manager whether he'd give him the honour to allow him to invite him for dinner there.

There was a moment of silence. No one moved, not even the employee, until, suddenly, the phone rang. The employee took the call with his sweet voice and then, after another second or so, the manager nodded and said he would accept Ryu's apology and invitation. He would also need to invite his wife and his employee. After all, this was a business dinner. Ryu was delighted to comply.

The manager left for lunch (a small one, he said, he wanted to make sure he was sufficiently hungry for dinner). Ryu was pleased with himself. He looked at the employee, smiled. The employee did not smile back, though. He seemed like he was about to say something, but a customer entering the shop stopped him from doing so.

Ryu met the employee again shortly before seven at the restaurant. He'd reserved a private room offering enough space for twice as many people as they were – on purpose, to show off the company's generosity for loyal employees. He had also instructed the staff to keep the sake flowing, to bring meat and rice until everyone was completely stuffed and not to hold back on sweets for dessert. He'd heard that the restaurant's crème brûlée was excellent. With such a feast, he hoped to remind the manager that the company took care of its people.

"Thank you for inviting me as well," the employee said to Ryu as they sat down in the dining room, waiting for the manager and his wife to arrive.

"I am happy you are here," Ryu replied. "You'll make it far in the company if you continue your good work."

"Thank you," the employee said. "However, I am not sure I would want to—"

This was when the manager and his wife entered. Both Ryu and the employee jumped to their feet and greeted them. Soon after, their glasses had been filled with sake and they toasted. Three or four glasses later, the manager even cracked a smile when raising his glass and by the time the beef arrived, he loudly told jokes – which were exceptionally unfunny.

The meat was as excellent as the reviews on the internet had suggested. The wagyu beef was riddled with strains of fat, giving it an extraordinary juicy taste. It was cooked perfectly, and Ryu felt waves of relief washing over him. The evening was going well. Not only was the manager sufficiently drunk, he'd also become emotional, thanked Ryu repeatedly for the wonderful invitation and seemed even apologetic for his behaviour during the previous two days. Ryu gave his speech on the generosity of the company and the importance of everyone working together to achieve a common goal. The manager grew silent after Ryu's speech, looked at him, looked at his wife, at his employee and then, ever-so-slightly nodded, took the sake bottle and filled Ryu's glass. Ryu then did the same for the manager's glass. They toasted and Ryu called for the staff to bring them another bottle of sake and, heck, another round of meat as well. The servers made a sound of astonishment, everyone else laughed, except the employee who had been mostly silent, silently smiling.

Ryu could barely walk when he got up to go to the restroom an hour later. He left the private room and put his shoes on. He turned left in the bathroom's direction, walked down a long corridor with smaller private rooms on each side. One door was open. Ryu peeked in while walking by and he saw a man sitting there, alone, back to him. Clearly not Japanese. A foreigner, heavy-built, sitting behind an empty plate of what must have been beef, a glass of sake next to him. For a second, he wondered what a foreigner was doing alone in this restaurant in this town in the middle of nowhere-special.

The thought passed.

After midnight, the manager and his wife left, leaving Ryu and the employee alone. "Did you like the food?" Ryu asked him. He was surprised by how difficult it'd become to speak.

"Yes, very much," the employee said. He didn't seem drunk at all. There was silence. The employee smiled. "I better leave as well," he said after a moment.

"Yes. Let me go and pay. I'll leave with you."

"Sure."

Ryu went to pay with his credit card. The entire evening had cost close to 100,000 yen. It had been worth it.

"Is that the company's credit card?" Ryu hadn't realised that the employee had followed him and now peered over his shoulder.

"No... no..." Ryu said quickly. "I'll... get reimbursed."

"Better take the receipt then."

"Oh, yes. Sure."

They both left the restaurant. It was a warm night.

"Thank you very much," the employee said once more and turned to leave.

"I could walk you home," Ryu said suddenly, surprising himself.

The employee turned back around and smiled at him. "No, that would be a detour for you. Your hotel is on the other side of the station. I live that way." Pointing down the road.

"Ah. Yes. Good night, then."

The employee turned around to leave again, took a few steps. Unexpectedly, he turned around to Ryu one more (last?) time. His smile had vanished.

"You are not the first one they've sent. You know that, right?"

"What?"

"They send someone every year. To fix the manager's shop. To fix his attitude. And these people, like you, are always eager to change him, hopeful, motivated, always invite him for dinner or give him gifts, complement his years of service."

"What?"

"It's always the same. Tomorrow, he will be friendly and will do anything you ask of him. And he means it at that moment. But after a week or two, he will send a nasty letter to your boss, complaining about your rudeness and will rearrange the store as he likes it. Your boss will reprimand you, and you will have to apologise formally. And they let the manager do his thing, pretend he is not there, the Yonezawa branch is not that important, anyway. A year later, some new hotshot manager will try again and send a young salary man to Yonezawa to fix things."

At first, Ryu did not know what to say. Finally, he only asked the one question that probably was least helpful to solve his problem: "How long have you been working at the store?"

The employee laughed. "How old do you think I am?"

There was a moment of silence until the employee turned around again and disappeared into the night. Ryu walked the other way, not sure whether the last conversation had really happened or whether it had been an alcohol-induced hallucination.

He made it to his hotel room, where he vomited, turned on the TV, scrolled through the adult video section, before he fell asleep, naked on his bed, dreaming of things he would not remember the next morning, of pain and shouting and then also a soft touch, like a whisper in his ear.

The sound of his phone woke him. The receptionist informed him it was half past seven, and he'd asked last night, when he'd returned from dinner, for a wake-up call. At least his drunk self was reliable, Ryu thought to himself.

When Ryu arrived at the store an hour later, the manager was already fast at work, rearranging shelves. He greeted Ryu and, at once, bombarded him with questions on whether the canned goods should be on the top of the shelf or rather at the bottom.

Ryu gave precise answers, yet his mind felt distracted. "The employee not working today?" he finally asked.

"Who?"

"The employee."

"Ah. No."

Only a few hours after, they had rearranged the store. The company's signature items were at the front now. They'd moved the local products off to a corner in the back. Ryu went through his company checklist but couldn't find anything else that would need to be changed. So, he bid farewell to the manager, who still was in an exceptionally good mood, and promised him to send a set of new uniforms for him and the employee. The employee should contact him, he said, to tell him his size. Sure, the manager said, and gave Ryu his best wishes from his wife, who more than enjoyed the evening.

The sun had started to set, and the day was growing colder. Behind him, the manager turned off the lights of the store. The rearrangement had taken the entire day. Ryu was happy with his work. Surely, the manager was genuinely happy, too. Surely, the employee's words had never happened.

He wondered where he lived, the employee. Why he hadn't told Ryu that he'd taken the day off.

Then, rain set in. Ryu didn't have an umbrella, so he ran to the hotel. He was completely soaked by the time he made it back. In his room, he took a warm shower, sat down on the chair in his room, naked. Surely, the manager would not send an angry letter to his boss. Even if the employee's words had happened, this time would have to be different. Ryu had given his best. Gambate.

He wondered why the employee had even told him these things. Had he lied? Or was it he cared about Ryu? But then, why hadn't he told him he wouldn't be at work today? Ryu tried to remember the employee's soft voice and toyed with the thought of calling the store tomorrow to hear it. He lit a cigarette, naked in his room, dripping wet from the shower. He turned on the TV and browsed through the films. He selected one movie, a cigarette in his left hand, his penis in his other. There was a girl walking down a road when a car next to her stopped. Inside, a man, his face blurred. Gently, the man spoke to the girl, offered her to pick her up, bring her to the next town. She agreed and after a brief ride, he told her she was beautiful and asked her whether she wanted to do *something*. She agreed, and they went to a barn, where he undressed her, his face still blurred. Ryu wondered what he looked like, that man, underneath that blur, as the man gently, softly, smoothly kissed the girl's breast and legs.

It would all be fine at one point. This life. Smoking the cigarette. Naked. Looking to be someone else, that person on TV, seeking that human touch. That thing that would give you reassurance that you existed and that someone outside of you, in this endless, barren world, existed as well.

I turned off the TV. I felt dissatisfied with the evening. The Yonezawa beef had been good, sure, but worth the trip? Maybe I had misunderstood it, hadn't done enough research on Wagyu beef to really appreciate it.

I had already packed my suitcase. There was nothing else to do.

I put my earplugs in, listened to some music. Johnny Cash. I See Darkness. It felt right. After all, it had become dark outside. I sent some messages to people I knew, pictures of the beef, of the temple. Hashtag bestlife.

I had another smoke, disgusted by it, disgusted by the heavy cloud of smoke that had formed in my room. I'd placed my clothes for to-morrow as far away as possible, hoping they wouldn't pick up the smell. Then, I went to bed. No dreams. Just darkness I saw.

Yokohama / The Old Mill

It is funny how travelling on a train can make you feel like you do not exist at all. You exist as an entity, but it isn't you who takes the train. It is another you, an adventurous you, someone who will have a lot of stories to tell their grandchildren.

I sat there, notebook on my lap, pen in my hand, on my train ride from Yonezawa back to Tokyo, from where I would take a limited express train (whatever that was) to Yokohama, and tried to write about that other me, the adventurer-me, only to find that my brain felt out of ideas. It probably was the holiday mood. The brain needed to relax first and have the grandiose ideas later.

So, all I did on my journey, which took a bit over two hours, was listen to music and watch the world go by outside the window. I felt sonder. A beautiful word swimming around in my brain. Sonder. There was an entire world filled with people out there, living their lives, and I would never know about most of them.

"But that is not the problem, is it?" you said. "The problem is that you would want them to know about *you*, no?" I smiled and nodded. Yes, that was the problem.

I arrived in Tokyo on time, of course. Best train system in the world. As a Swiss person, I had the power to bestow that victory on the Japanese.

I didn't have a lot of time, so I hurried off in search of the platform for my next train – which wasn't as easy as I had imagined. I hurried

121

through halls and hallways, looking for the elusive platform number 32, feeling like Harry Potter not finding that semi-permeable wall. I got stuck at a turnstile, which demanded I swiped my Suica metro card, yet refused to let me through. An attentive station attendant helped me (she re-swiped the card until it worked) and I bowed to thank her, wondering whether it was okay for me to bow or whether that was cultural appropriation.

I found platform 32 without running through any magic walls and, looking at my phone, realised with pleasure that I still could make my train (easily).

The half an hour train ride to Yokohama felt like never leaving Tokyo. There was no space in-between, just city merging into city. I wondered whether I should just have stayed in Tokyo and visited Yokohama during a day trip, but then, I had booked a night boat trip of the factories and port facilities surrounding the city, to see the lights of the big factories in the dark. Easier with accommodation in Yokohama.

I had reserved a hotel room in Minato Mirai, a big district of Yokohama right at the seafront, originally an accumulation of factories and warehouses with zero tourist appeal, until they rebuilt into the "port of the future," a place now consisting of malls, shopping, parties, and friendly bars. Thank you, guidebook, for enlightening me.

Sometime later, I marvelled, having arrived in my hotel room, at the view from the window, the open sea in the distance and a Ferris wheel to my right, which seemed to be the centrepiece of a small amusement park. Right in front of me, there was a major shopping centre. People ebbed and flowed on the streets below.

The city felt decidedly different from Tokyo. I walked along the pier, heading towards Chinatown. Yokohama seemed strangely more international than the big T., as it not only featured a Chinatown but also many English- and German-looking bars. Probably because it was a port-town, a place for international trading and goods. My impression of internationality was enforced when I turned a corner and heard German Volksmusik off in the distance. I drew closer and found several open tents filled with wooden benches and people. A sign informed me that there was an Oktoberfest taking place, complete with a fake-German folk band (I decided that the singer of the band, who spoke in English after he'd finished a song, must have been Dutch, judging from his accent) and licensed (Hofbraeu!) German beer. I toyed with the idea of checking it out more closely, however, found that the entrance fee was 1,000 yen. Not a huge amount, yet, since I was neither too fond of German beer, nor German music, nor Asians that ran around in lederhosen (or maybe I was?), I decided to invest my ten francs into something that would bring me more pleasure. A craft beer somewhere. Or some cheap 7/11 highballs.

I continued my way to Chinatown. It seemed silly to visit a Chinatown in a Japanese city, but then I wanted to find out, having already seen Chinatowns in Europe and the U.S. of A, whether the one in Yokohama was different.

It wasn't. It seemed remarkably identical to the Chinatowns I'd been to, offering the same selection of knick-knack shops and Chinese restaurants. I bought a steam bun from a street stand and sat down on a stool the vendor had set up in a side alley next to the shop. The next ten minutes I spent blowing gently against the bun, trying to get it to cool down, yet still burned my mouth as I took my first bite. The first bite is the hottest.

I observed a young Asian couple buying a (one) steam bun as well and then wandering off down the street. I wondered whether only one of them was hungry or whether they intended to share the bun. If so, the question was how they could ever tear it in half. I looked at the steaming, mushy mass in my hand. Not only was it much too hot to be split by hand, but the wet dough also seemed impossible to tear apart. The bun would just extend, stretch, until the meat filling in the middle would drop to the floor. Their steam bun was doomed. I felt sorry for it. I took another small bite of my bun. It was edible now. Still hot, though. I was glad I had no one to share it with.

I wandered the city for a while and the day passed. Yokohama was less bustling, less neon-lit than Tokyo. Still, the enormous Ferris wheel in Minato Mirai drenched the night in all kinds of neon, as the lights mounted on its spikes kept changed colours in different rhythms. It was a comforting view, since I knew my hotel was right next to it, a tower of light always reminding me of the way home.

Home?

Enjoy your home away from home. A hotel room. A different ceiling to look at when you wake up. A weird carpet, one that must have been in fashion once, dark colours, so that no one can see the stains made by people eating the food from room service, because people eat like swines when they are alone in their hotel rooms. In underpants, dirty t-shirt, sauce dripping onto the floor. The TV shouting Japanese words beyond comprehension.

But not me. It wasn't time to return yet. I would not eat like a swine in my room. Maybe get drunk, yes, but later. I continued to walk down the harbour, marvelled at the big cruise ships waiting for passengers to board. They looked like floating buildings. How many people fit on one of these ships? How many of these ships were out in the ocean at this very moment? How fucking big was this planet?

I passed by the tents again where the Oktoberfest was still in full swing. The German Volksmusik hurt my ears, people seemed to have fun. A girl with an oversized Bavarian-style hat stood in line to get a bratwurst, holding a big plastic cup of beer in her hand.

I, once more, toyed with the idea of putting up the ten francs and going in, chat up some Japanese people, have a beer with them, teach them some German. Only I was scared I would have to admit at one point I was not from Germany and that we didn't have an Oktoberfest in Switzerland, which would certainly kill the mood and make me seem like an imposter.

Instead of the Oktoberfest, I entered a building close-by. I had read about the place online. It was a peculiar mix of shopping mall and fusion-restaurants in what used to be a warehouse a long time ago. The architecture differed completely from your usual mall, no bright lights, no endless halls. More narrow passages and confusing walkways. There were no big-brand stores. It felt like walking through an upscale, local in-door market, all remotely genuine, all quite hipsteric. It was like a shopping mall for people who said they didn't like capitalism, yet still wanted to be part of it.

I ascended to the top floor, where I entered a restaurant offering a fusion of Chinese, Western and Japanese cuisine and was ushered to a table.

Looking at the menu, I found they had a decent collection of wine. I considered ordering a glass of red, classy as I was. Then, after spotting the wine prices on the menu, I opted for a bottle of local craft beer, a dark, chocolaty beer, as the description told me. Also, I ordered a noodle dish with chicken, some Italian-Chinese fusion thing.

The dish, nor the beer, were by no means bad, yet I missed the magic, the revelation that had accompanied many of my meals in Tokyo and, to a lesser degree, the one in Yonezawa. Maybe that was what life was. Not everything could be a revelation, not everything could be magic. Sometimes, you just had to hold your head down and run, make it through the day, until you'd reach the next sunset.

There were plenty of people in the restaurant and a big row of windows offered a beautiful view of the harbour and the world outside. The surrounding people were deeply lost in conversation, some of which seemed to be funny, people laughing, some of them drifting into serious conversations, judging from the concentrated looks on people's faces. What were they talking about? What did one talk about in such a bar? In Japan? What would I talk about if there was someone sitting next to me?

(Why are you here?)

Imagine life condensed into one place. This is what the Old Mill is. A place filled with tragedy and comedy and sounds and people. And music. Despite its name, the place has never been a mill, but a huge factory where they built ships a long time ago. After that, it had been empty for a while, until two guys, who had made a fortune with a chain of Hawaiian burger joints, bought the place, and turned it into the Old Mill.

You enter the Old Mill on the shorter side of the former factory, through an immense door. Once inside, you pay your entrance fee, and you are on your merry way. You can turn left, through a doorway, where you end up in a bar modelled after a turn-of-the-century English pub with cold beer on tap and classic cocktails. This is where the older crowd hangs out to complain about the dropping quality of bands playing at the Mill.

Or you can go straight ahead, down a wide staircase and into a vast hall that takes up the rest of the building's ground floor. This is where the headliner bands or DJs play, the famous names, crowd-pleasers. The hall is equipped with a state-of-the-art sound and light system, as well as wind machines and an air conditioning system that could cool the place down to below-zero temperatures.

If you are looking for a more intimate setting, you turn right and take a flight of stairs up. The second floor is separated into two areas: to the North side of the building, there is The Mill Lounge (not a highly creative name) which is a spacious room with couches and tables and comfy chairs scattered about. Hip DJs put on smooth post-Jazz and elevator-lounge here, music that lulls you in, makes you feel nice and relaxed and crave another drink. Bills and taps run high here.

On the South side, there is another concert venue, smaller than the one downstairs, where non-mainstream bands play dark and heavy and death metal, or dream pop and a good serving of 90s trance and hardcore techno. If that is not your fancy, you can follow the stairs up to the third and fourth floors. On the third floor, there is the Play Zone, hallway after hallway leading to smaller rooms where you can sing karaoke or just sit in quiet and talk to your friends. Or make out. No one is watching. On the fourth floor, there is the Disco Maze, a Labyrinthian system of corridors and rooms, music emanating from every corner. It is a popular place to get lost, to find new things and to do drugs (but management, officially, does not condone the last bit).

Our man is in the main concert hall. There is a band playing, their retro-inspired sound from the speakers a mix of real guitars and digital synthesisers. He does not care about the music too much, though. His

SOME OF US ARE REAL | 127

fascination is reserved for the lights, how they have been synched to fit the music perfectly. There is a guy behind a lighting desk on an elevated platform in the middle of the room, calmly pushing buttons and moving regulators. He admires the guy's posture, how his fingers glide across the desk, how he is unfazed by the loud music and the countless people dancing. None of them realises, he thinks, how important the lights are, how empty the music would be without the dance of the spotlights and without the colours, how the lights trick their brains into thinking that they've entered some other-worldly location outside of the laws of time and place.

He stays for a little longer until he fancies a beer. He leaves the concert venue, crosses through the entrance hall (there is a huge line of people waiting outside and he is happy he came early) and into the faux-English pub. The barkeeper greets him as he comes in. They know each other, not privately, but from this very setting. Without a word, the barkeeper pulls a dark beer for him and puts it on the counter. Without a word, our man takes the glass and drinks. It is nice and cold. He'll pay later.

He crosses the pub, arrives at a glass door at the far end and goes into the smoking room. He sits down in one of the comfy chairs and lights a cigarette. The smoky taste of the tobacco melts with the bitterness of the beer in his throat and he enjoys the mix of unpleasant tastes. It is only after his fifth or sixth sip he notices he is not alone in the room. There is a girl sitting in another big chair across the room, her ear pressed against a smartphone in her hand. She is listening attentively, a blank stare in her eyes.

She is attractive, our man thinks. Her hair is red, long, divided into two braids falling from her head over her shoulders and going down almost all the way to her breasts. She is wearing a black shirt and dark, skinny jeans. The shirt is just tight enough to make her breasts seem bigger than they are, give them a perfect round shape. A bit of her hip and her belly are showing in the crevice between her jeans and the shirt. Her eyes are big and green, and she is looking right at him.

He takes his male gaze off her and looks at his beer, hoping that she has not registered his staring at her and her clothes and her breasts and the crevice between her jeans and her shirt.

After a while, he looks up again, maybe to get another look or maybe to see whether she is still looking at him. She is not, she is still listening to the phone. There is a single tear coming forth from her left, green, big eye and rolling down her left, pale cheek. "I see you upstairs," she says to her phone, before she puts it down on the table next to her chair. She looks at our man, gets up and says, "What's your problem?" And her tone hurts or embarrasses our man, while she bolts past him and leaves the room.

She is long gone by the time he sees she has left her phone behind. It is still there on the table. Not my problem, he tells himself. Especially not after her unfriendly tone.

But then. He could pick it up and at least give it to the bartender. Not be an asshole. Her conversation on the phone had obviously upset her, hence the unfriendly tone. And he had been staring at her. Gotta make up for that.

He remembers the crevice between her jeans and her shirt. And the braids falling onto her breasts. He gets up and picks up the phone. She said she'd go upstairs. He would go after her and give her the phone back. Maybe apologise. Say that he'd not been looking at her, he'd been lost in thought. See whether she is alright. Maybe strike up a conversation. Maybe not be lonely tonight.

He leaves the smoking room, goes to the bar to pay for his beer – the bartender just nods when he puts the money down – and leaves for the entry hall. He can hear the music coming from the main hall of the still-ongoing concert. There are several groups of people milling around. He takes up a flight of stairs and arrives on the second floor. Where would she have gone? The phone call had sounded serious. She'd be meeting the other person on the phone for a serious talk. He can hear a dark, droning bass loop coming from the second-floor concert hall. A darkwave-industrial-gothic band reminiscent of the sound of the early Nine Inch Nails is performing. Certainly not a good choice for a serious talk. She must have gone to the lounge on the other side, so this is where he goes to.

The place is filled with people, but not packed. A smooth mixture of slow-tempo house and lounge beats engulfs the room, and he thinks he should come here more often. He stands in a corner close to the bar, observing the people, trying to find her two red braids.

There is a commotion at the far end of the room, two guys yelling at each other. Suddenly one of them jumps up and knocks over a couple of beer bottles, which roll off the table and onto the floor. Almost immediately, the guy he has been yelling at gets up, too, and they beat their chests, hurling insults at each other.

"Like a pack of dogs," someone says in his general direction. A person sitting at the bar a couple of feet away from him.

"Excuse me?

"Like a pack of dogs."

It looks like at least one guy is ready to let his fists do the talking, when a third guy, another member of their group, calmly gets up, puts his arm around one hothead and pulls him aside. The situation deflates. The other chest-beating guy, now left alone in his anger, seems to be unsure what to do. Flight it is: he spins around, takes his jacket and leaves. The calm guy and the now-former hothead take no notice and are aside, whispering to each other.

"I said: like a pack of dogs."

"What do you mean?"

"Those guys. Maybe more like a pack of wolves. Alpha versus alpha, that sort of thing. Manly manliness."

"What were they arguing about?"

"A woman. Sort of. On the surface. If you look past that, it turns into a much more complex story. You see, the two guys that were going at each other – Alpha One and Alpha Two –, they've known each other since kindergarten. Best friends, that sort of thing. But it all changed when Alpha Two started seeing a girl..."

130 | ALEXANDER P. SIGRIST

"...and Alpha One wants the same girl?"

"What a cliche. No, in this case, One thinks the girl is taking advantage of Two. That she is just after his... what do young people call it these days... after his fame."

"Fame?"

"Two is the leader of the group. Being with him is like being the queen. Alpha One thinks she is only after that and keeps telling Two that his girl is no good."

"Which has upset Two and led to the outburst?"

"No, it gets even more complicated than that. Because, you see, there is this other girl, and One has set his eyes on her."

"Jesus..."

"Two thinks this girl is completely out of One's league. Until just before, he has kept this thought to himself, though. Being a good friend and all. But tonight, tired of the relentless criticism from One, Two has lashed out. At least I have a girl and at least I know what league I am playing in, he has said to One, or something along these lines. Which almost led to the fistfight we've witnessed just now."

"And how do you know all of this?"

"Oh, I sit here and observe. Just like you."

"Me?"

"Watching people. No?"

"I am looking for someone."

"For whom?"

"Someone... she left her phone downstairs. I am trying to give it back to her."

"What does she look like?"

"Red hair. Braids. Not too tall. Black shirt."

"Hmm. Haven't seen her. Do you know her name?"

"No."

"The knight in shining armour on the quest for the anonymous damsel in distress."

He turns to walk away. He has seen – and heard – enough. Maybe the braided lady is in the concert hall after all. Maybe she went further upstairs.

"Don't get me wrong," the person at the bar says, seeing him turn away, "I like it." The person gets up. "Let me help you."

"That's fine."

"It's not like you can stop me. I can always try to find her first and tell her you've stolen her phone."

"Wow. Nice." What has he got himself into?

"Come on. Cheer up. It is going to be fun. On our merry quest, we will uncover many secrets, find untold stories, we will bond, and we will argue. Like Shrek and Donkey."

He looks at her as they leave the lounge and tries to discern whether she is serious. She seems pleased about the whole endeavour. Is she bored? Who is she?

"I am Lake," she says, as if she has read his mind. "Nice to meet you," she adds when he doesn't reply. "And I will call you the elusive man," she concludes, since he still doesn't offer his name. Together, they walk into the concert hall on the other side of the second floor.

The not-Nine Inch Nails are playing a slow, rumbling string of different drones laid atop of each other. People are not as much dancing as they are just bobbing back and forth in the non-rhythm of the music. Occasionally, the singer – if one can call him that – whispers words into the microphone. Stuff like death, darkness, blood, heart, love, and tears.

"Terribly edgy. Pretentious shit," Lake comments on the music. He could not agree more, but he likes the lighting the band has chosen. A string of red and blue spotlights for atmosphere, the spots moving across their faces and bodies. To add to the mysterious ambience, they are using a dark-orange back light that turns their bodies into silhouettes.

"They seem decent enough," he says in the band's defence. "I have seen worse," he specifies.

"Seen. But heard?"

He ignores her quip.

"I can't see her," he says instead.

"Me neither."

"It is terribly dark in here. Maybe we should ask them to turn on the lights."

He cannot help but smirk at the thought of how everything would look silly if the lights would suddenly shine at full brightness.

"Ah. So, he can laugh."

"I only smirked," he retorts.

"Smirk. Laugh. It is a linear progression of intensities. Smirk long enough and eventually people will think you are laughing."

"You are full of wise words."

"And you sound like Shakespeare."

She turns around to leave the hall. "Come on," she says. "She is not here."

"How do you know?"

"Woman's intuition. We can feel each other's presence."

"You are full of shit."

"And you are not very nice."

She holds out her hand as if to pull him out of the room. After a second, he grabs it. It is nice, soft, and warm. "Your hands are dry, man," she informs him. "You'll need some moisturiser."

They leave the drone-sounds and the lights behind and return to the hallway.

"Uh, it's like zombies in there. Is that what this kind of music does to you?"

"I don't mind it. The music."

"Neither do they!" She laughs a clear and beautiful, heartfelt laugh, but then realises that he is not in on the joke. "Because they are zombies. No brains, no minds." Pause, no reaction from him. She continues: "Ah, it is not a good joke if I have to explain it. Not that you'd mind that, either, right?"

"What is that supposed to mean?"

"It is all a bit undercooked with you. Not liking the music, not minding it either. Running after a girl with her phone, but not actually taking any genuine effort. That kind of thing."

"You are full of shit."

"Don't be an asshole."

He deflates, feels bad. His tone has been harsh. She only tried to be funny.

"I am sorry. Don't mean to be rude, but you... I just want to get rid of this phone and then go home."

"Sure. You'll probably find her upstairs. Check the Play Zone. You could ask at the reception whether they've seen her."

"Don't... you... want to come along?"

"Nah, this is where I step off. I have a drink waiting for me in the lounge. Still, this has been fun."

"Yeah. Yeah. Sure." Not a hint of sarcasm in his voice. Rather: Confusion. Regret. He should be glad to get rid of her. He isn't.

"Alright then, see you."

She turns around and disappears into the lounge. Maybe he should go after her. Maybe ask her to come along, help him get rid of the phone and then have a drink with him.

He turns towards the stairs. He feels tired, out-of-place. Instead of heading upstairs, he takes the flight leading down. He needs a drink. A cigarette. New plan of attack.

What's her name? Lake? He enters the pub on the ground floor and orders a beer. What's her deal? Who is she? He gets a beer and goes to the smoking room.

Maybe he shouldn't have said that she was full of shit. He feels bad about it. He could go upstairs and apologise.

No, keep your head in the game, man. The phone. He must find the girl with the braids and the crevice between her shirt and her jeans. The nicely formed breasts. Why is he thinking about her breasts? This is just about the phone. Not about her belly, bellybutton or breasts or braids or hair, or about her jeans or t-shirt. This is about a good deed and nothing else.

He'll just give the phone to the bartender. That's it. And then go upstairs and apologise to Lake and that's that. And then go home and that's the evening done. Time to grow up, man. Time to do the right thing.

He takes a drag of the cigarette. Feels a vibration in his left trouser pocket. His phone is in his right pocket. It is *her* phone vibrating. He gets it out and, with a swipe to the right, answers.

"Hello?"

"You fucking asshole. Where is my phone?" A female voice.

"Ah. Oh. Sorry. I was looking for you. I have it."

"I know you have it. You answered it. Where is it? I am calling the cops on you." Seems drastic.

"No, I wanted to bring it to you. You left it in the smoking-room downstairs. But I couldn't find you."

"Don't bullshit me. I have my boyfriend kick yer ass."

Boyfriend?

"No, seriously. I found it here."

"Why didn't you just give it to the bartender?"

"I... erm... wanted to be nice..."

"You are a fucking prick, that's what you are."

"No, I'll prove it. I'll bring you your phone. Where are you?"

There is a moment of silence. Then he can hear muffled voices speaking in the background.

"Ten minutes. Room 237," she finally says.

"In the Play Zone?"

"Yes, where else, dumbass?"

She hangs up. He looks at the screen of the phone, which shows a picture of the redhead in the arms of a big, bully, Asian guy. The before-mentioned boyfriend, most likely.

Time to do the right thing. Bring the phone back, show them he is not a thief, then go home. Fuck this.

He finishes his beer in one big gulp, puts out his cigarette. He pays for his beer at the counter and leaves the pub. Up the stairs he goes, past the second floor, the lounge, and the smaller concert hall, and on to the third floor to the Play Zone. He arrives in a big reception area, a thick, fluffy, red carpet on the floor. There is a counter opposite, two hallways leading to more hallways and rooms on either side.

"Can I help you?" the guy behind the counter addresses him.

"Yeah. I am looking for room 237."

The guy checks the computer screen in front of him.

"Yeah. That one is occupied at the moment."

"I know. I am meeting someone there."

"Who?"

"I... erm... what? Erm... a girl. With red braids."

"Ah. Anne. You a friend of hers?"

"No. Yes. No. I have something for her."

"She comes here often. I think I know all her friends."

"I... I have her mobile. She lost it."

"Oh. I am sure she will be happy to get it back."

The guy returns to his computer screen, not taking further notice of our man.

"Erm... where is it? Room 237?"

"Oh. Yes." The guy pulls up a map on his computer screen. "Okay, you take the left hallway. All the way down. Then turn right and left at the second opening. It is right next to room 144."

Next to room 144?

He enters the left corridor, goes past several doors, all numbered in no discernible fashion. The corridor ends at two new corridors leading off to the right and left. He turns left, walks on. He hears faint music and singing, bad, bad singing from behind some doors, and some shouting, almost sounding like an argument and there is laughing and, occasionally, a door opens, and someone steps out, walks past him in the entrance's direction.

The corridor branches off again, one corridor leading to the left and another to the right. He is almost sure he has to turn right and will find his destination down that corridor. That's what he does.

It is not there, though.

He turns around and walks back. A woman with a trolley carrying drinks passes him by, but by the time he realises he could ask her for directions, she is too far away. He goes back to the last intersection and walks down the hallway he has not come from, still unable to find the room he is looking for. He turns left, right, and around again, walking back towards the entrance, or at least he thinks that's the direction he is heading in, past room 111 and 891 and 654 and other rooms, room after room after room like walking down his own personal nightmare. Maybe he should knock at one door. Someone must know the way back, the way out, and he feels panic swelling up and down his throat. Who the fuck designed this fucking place?

He stops at a, any, door – room 321 – and raises his hand to knock, as he hears a voice singing behind the door. He knows this voice. It is quite beautiful. He imagines this voice on a big stage singing a mid-tempo version of The Killers' When You Were Young, imagines her engulfed in the flames of yellow and red spotlights, lights swirling around her like fireflies, behind her the giant projection of a night sky with shooting stars, the stage surrounded by hundreds of people holding coloured glowing sticks up, battling the darkness of the night, all together, swaying on the wings of this voice, like a single organism that lives now, yesterday and tomorrow.

The singing stops in the middle of the song. The low-quality, midi rendering of the music is still playing, now empty without the voice. Before he can turn away, the door opens.

"There you are."

She grabs him by the shoulders and pulls him into the room. She puts a shot of something alcoholic in his hand and cheers with him. Before he knows it and can ask what is happening, he knocks it back and feels the comfortable, sticky warmth of cheap whiskey trickling down his throat. He looks at Lake.

"What are you doing here?" our man says.

"It's nice to see you. Or: Hey, so cool you are here. Wow, you have been waiting for me. Or: You look gorgeous, Lake. That would be great conversation starters."

"Oh... I am sorry."

"No, you are not. You are just saying you are sorry because it is the easy way out." Silence. "Ah, come on, man, I am just pulling your leg. Here, have another." She puts another shot of whiskey in his hand. "And then let me introduce you to my friends."

It is only now that he realises they are not alone in this room. On a long, plastic-looking sofa taking up the entire wall to his left, there are several people. An enormous window showing him the city at night takes up the wall on the other side of the room.

"So, these are..." He does not listen. He walks towards the big window and takes in the city and its skyline, which is illuminated by countless lights radiating out of windows and from streetlamps and enormous billboards. He can see the street below, people walking and cars driving, it is all quiet, not a trace of sound pouring through the window. "...I met them in the bar, and we started drinking and, hey, we thought, it is time for a bit of karaoke before it is time to go home, right, friends?"

They all agree. The view still transfixes our man. He doesn't respond, he's lost in the sights outside.

"It is beautiful, isn't it?" Her tone has changed. She has stepped up to him and is looking out as well. Her voice reminds him of her singing, a silk tone that crawls into his ears like an embrace.

"Yes. It is," he replies.

"Glad you found something you like."

"What do you mean?"

"Here. Time for a song." She hands him the microphone. Her friends are sitting on the long sofa, whispering, not taking much notice of them. Someone pours fresh shots of whiskey.

"I can't. I have to bring back the phone."

"Come on, don't be an asshole. Sing."

"That's exactly what I am trying not to be."

He gives the microphone back to her.

"You can spend all night running after her and look for her and hope for something good to come out of that, or you can just settle for what you have now, and sing and drink with us. Forget the phone. Just leave it at the counter when you leave. Easy as that."

"Easy as that?"

"Yes."

She picks up another microphone and puts it into his hands. She still holds the one he gave back to her. "Let's sing together. One song and then you can decide. One song and two to three shots of whiskey."

Alright.

His life turns into a whirlwind for a moment, from the first note he bellows out, way too loud, way off key, but it makes everyone cheer and someone gives him something to drink while he's singing, and he almost suffocates trying to do both, drinking and singing, and Lake laughs and they sing together and it sounds awful, yet it is loud and it is fun and it is good. They sing through a selection of Linkin Park, Aretha Franklin, some more of The Killers, followed by Blink-182 and The Offspring, and then, the Grand Finale with Meat Loaf, Bat Out of Hell, until Lake, suddenly, stops the music and stops singing to look at her mobile.

"Somebody's calling me." She picks it up and listens. "Really?" She asks and: "Okay, thanks for letting me know, Amato." She turns to him: "They are on their way."

"Who?"

"We gotta dash." She turns to the people sitting on the sofa. "My friends, it was my pleasure. Unfortunately, me and him will have to run for our dear lives now. We have neglected our duties and have to pay the price."

"What are you talking about?"

"Check the phone."

He takes out his phone.

"No. *Her* phone."

He takes out *her* phone. Twelve missed calls. They've been trying to reach him. Probably thought he'd skipped town.

She peers over his shoulder at the screen. "Uh, they left a voice message. Play it." She touches the command on the phone.

A male voice: "You fucking asshole. I'll find you. I'll kill you. You thief. You bastard." The message goes on, repeating the same unkind words over and over. Probably her boyfriend.

She grabs his hand and leads him out of the room, into the hallway, where she stops and bends over to tie her shoelaces. "Amato from the reception called to let me know her boyfriend is looking for you and that he told him where you are, because he is a friend of theirs," she says. "Good thing that Amato is also a friend of mine, so he warned me. Double-play, man. And now, he is watching everything on the security cameras. Us escaping. The boyfriend approaching. Apparently, they have bets going at the reception. Most people think he'll catch and crush you. Most people don't know I am a master of escape."

"What the fuck are you talking about?"

"Okay. Plain and simple: big boyfriend is coming to destroy you. We have to run."

She grabs his hand again and starts running down the hallway, he after her, stumbling like a confused millennial on his first day of work. They have only taken a few steps when they see a big, lurking shadow coming around the corner at the far end of a corridor to their right. A belching monster of a man, tall, muscular, terrifying, shouting things that sound like a James Bond henchman: "There you are! I am going to destroy you! Give me the phone back!"

She pulls our man to the left and runs down another hallway. He can't see her face, he can't see much of anything, but he's got that feeling that she is smiling, that she is enjoying this. The pleasure of being hunted. He is not of such good spirits. A tall, muscular Asian guy is after him, after a not-stolen phone, after his neglect of not returning it in time, and after a big, monumental, silly, stupid misunderstanding.

He stops. That is what it is. Easy as that. A misunderstanding. She almost falls over as she loses the grip on his arm because of his sudden stopping.

"What are you doing?" she yells at him.

"I'll just give the phone to him. Easy as that."

"Oh, right. Dude, it is never that easy."

He turns around. The big, muscular guy is storming down the hallway like a steaming locomotive that will stop at nothing. But stopping is what the Asian man does, seeing our man here holding up the braided woman's phone like an offering of peace. They look at each other. Both panting.

"What's that?" the boyfriend asks in a deep, god-like voice.

"The phone. I wanted to bring it back, but I got lost."

The big, tall, muscular Asian guy takes the phone – it seems much too small for his hand – and puts it into his pocket.

"So, we're good."

"No. We are not good." The big, tall, muscular Asian man closes his big, left paw to a fist, which comes running at our man like a cannonball. It probably would have killed him, if Lake wouldn't have pulled him back in the last second. He can feel the fist going past his face and thinks that this would be a suitable moment to have a flashback of his life.

"Man, I gave you the phone! I am sorry," he yells desperately.

"This is not about the phone..." The tall man's voice turns into a bear's roar. Lake swirls past our man and he hears the swooshing sound of a pressurised can being emptied.

"...it is about the principle, yadayayda," she mocks the guy who is now squirming in pain, holding his hands in front of his eyes, where the content of the can hit him.

"Pepper spray," she says, seeing our man's confused look. "Never leave the house without it, unfortunately. Now, can we proceed running?"

Yes! They run past the big, screaming, muscular dude, down the hallway. Some doors have opened, people standing in the doorways, wide-eyed, trying to figure out what's going on. Our man glances back, just for a second or two, and sees how someone approaches the big guy to help, but the big guy, in his rage, strikes him down (with furious anger). It won't be long before he continues his chase.

"It won't be long before he continues to chase us," Lake confirms his thoughts. They turn round the corner, another corner, and out into the reception hall. The guy he has met before is still there – probably Amato, both the red woman's and Lake's friend, caught in the middle of a battle for the ages.

Then, things get worse: At the reception, her back turned to our running couple, stands the woman with the braids.

Multiple things happen:

1. Lake: "A little help here, Amato!"
2. Amato freezes for a split second, only to come back to life instantly and open a door behind the reception.
3. The big, tall, muscular dude is yelling in the hallway behind them, screaming, furiously coming closer.
4. The red woman turns around and: "What the fuck?" Plus:
    1. Lake and our man jump across the reception and into the hallway behind the now-open door.
    2. Our guy yelling in slow-motion: "I am sorry!" to the red woman.
5. Amato shuts the door close.

They catch their breath. Behind the door, they can hear the woman and the tall guy yelling at Amato, who tries to calm them down and promises that he will sort this out and then, a heavy thump and silence.

"What just happened?"

"Up or down?" Lake asks him, not answering his question.

"Down and out," he replies.

"No, that's what they'd expect us to do. I say: Never go to the same place twice. Let's go up."

"To the labyrinth?"

"They'll never find us there."

"We have to leave the building at some point."

"He'll never give up. We live here now."

And without another word, she storms up the stairs. It is eerily quiet behind the door. Maybe the tall guy has given up. He has got the phone back. Our guy has done his good deed. Story is over. He should just check. They'd have a merry laugh and a drink and clear this up. Or maybe the big guy would strangle him. Bash his head in. Also, a way to end this story.

"What are you waiting for?"

He springs into action and runs up the stairs behind her. This must be the stairwell for the staff. It smells of old, is small and badly lit. Unlike the other areas of the Old Mill, this staircase lacks any kind of presentation or enactment. It is a real, no-bullshit set of stairs. It is like coming back to the real world.

They make it to the next floor and end up at another door. Lake knocks three times, and not a second later, a person opens it.

"Lake?"

"No time to explain. Have you seen a scary dude on a rage trip?"

"Oh. That one. Amato warned us. He is not here. I think he went downstairs. Hopefully, he'll get kicked out by security."

"See, told you they'd look for us downstairs."

"You wanna hide in the labyrinth?" the person says.

"Yes, please."

They step into a reception hall, which is the exact copy of the one downstairs. A big counter, dark, carpeted floor, two hallways leading off on either side.

"That will be ten bucks each. Sorry, I have to collect the admission, even from fugitives."

"Sure." Lake pulls out a ten-buck bill from her pocket. He reaches for his wallet, but it is not where it should be. Nor in any other pocket.

"Fuck. I lost my wallet."

"Jesus, man. You are terrible at fleeing." Lake reaches for another bill.

"I tell you what: Just tell me you are a couple and I give you the couple-discount. That would be another five."

"Yes, sure. We are a couple," Lake says. He feels uncomfortable with her saying that. Just because he's not sure whether to take it seriously. Lake hands over fifteen bucks.

"Alright. I recommend you go right and then head straight for one of the hidden backrooms. I can give you a map."

"I know the way."

"Sure you do."

They turn to head into the corridor on the right when the woman behind the reception produces a loud "ha" sound.

"What is it?" Lake says.

"Have a look at the surveillance feed." The woman behind the reception turns the computer screen around. "Your friend is tearing through security downstairs." On the screen, the tall, muscular Asian is in a fight with five or six security guards. He, unarmed, against five proper blokes equipped with batons. Still, it looks like they are losing. His left and right fists fly through the air and connect to faces, chins, noses. "Somebody should call the police," our man says. "They won't come," the receptionist answers, "that's the deal they have with the owners. They won't raid the place for drugs, they won't help when there are problems. Meaning, guys, you are on your own. And you better go fast. Big dude here is down at two guards standing. Won't be long before he realises you went upstairs." Our man's eyes rest on the screen. In the image's corner, he can see the woman with the red braids standing, watching in shock. Then, she turns around and hurries upstairs, now on the run herself in the face of the violence her boyfriend is producing tonight.

"Maybe we should help her."

"Not our problem," Lake replies. She takes his hand for the umpteenth time tonight and pulls him into the right corridor. A maze of mirrors and hallways opens up. Lake does not stop to consider the way, turns right, left, straight, right, left, left, right without hesitation. "We'll have to go through the beach of mist," she informs him. He does not know what she is talking about.

"Don't you think we should see whether she's alright?"

"Who?"

They walk on briskly. He frees his arm from her grasp.

"The woman I took the phone of."

"That's a complicated sentence."

"I am serious."

With a fast movement, Lake swirls around, facing him.

"Why do you always act as if you want to help people, while not being helpful at all? Pick up the phone and give it to the bartender. That's it. That's helpful. But no, go on this insane quest to find someone in this madhouse."

"I just..."

"...wanted to do the right thing? Man, spare me. You did not. You were after her boobs and hoped you would fuck her tonight. Talk about a damsel in distress complex."

"Fuck you. I did not ask you to help me. You can leave."

"No, I can't."

"Why not?"

"Because I sprayed our friend with pepper spray?"

There is a moment of silence.

"Why did you even help me? It makes no sense," he says.

"You seemed lost, so..."

"Maybe *you* just wanted to fuck *me*."

She does not reply for a while. They walk on.

She finally speaks: "I was alone. You were alone. So, maybe, yes, I thought he does not look half-bad, and I like his expression and... but then, you drag me into your mess."

"I think we both did the dragging."

"Quiet."

He wants to protest, but they turn a corner and the corridor in front of them opens into an immense room. Instead of a ceiling, he can see the stars above – or something that looks like stars, most likely LED-lamps positioned against a dark ceiling. He feels sand underneath his shoes and hears the ocean off in the distance. In front of them, there lies a vast beach, or a simulacrum thereof. Mist is rolling in and out where the ocean should be, masking the fact that there is no actual water. A long pier leads out into the mist and connects to several yachts wobbling gently up and down. She was not kidding when she called this place the beach of mist.

"We have to be quiet now." Her voice a whisper. "We don't want to end up at a frat-party. They will drug us and take our stuff. Or worse."

"What do you mean...?"

She looks at him, briefly only, still, long enough for him to see a new expression on her face. Pain, maybe. Or resignation. The look of bad memories. She walks in front of him, out onto the pier, onto the beach of mist.

He can hear music and laughing from the yachts. Behind and above them, half in the mist, there is the moon, unnaturally big and looming. He can even smell the breeze of the ocean and when he licks his lips, they are salty.

What are we that we have to escape from reality and create a new one?

"Over there," she whispers and points ahead. He thinks he can see the dark shade of a passage leading out, away from the beach, in a wall only a hundred meters away. He reaches for her hand, he grabs it, and it feels warm. He only now realises that her skin is soft and alive.

And then, they hear a voice hollering from one yacht. Startled, they turn around and see a guy, only dressed in a (unfastened) silk robe, standing on deck.

"Hey, you guys, what are you up to? Have you seen Jim? Hey, Tim," he yells into the belly of the yacht, "are we expecting anyone else?" To them: "Hey, you guys have some weed on you? Jesus, man, I am pissed." He slurs the words.

"Don't run," she whispers to our man. "Hey! No, we've been to Carol's. You know, down the crazy alleyway. We are just off to the other castle."

"Right on. What you gonna do there? And if you see Jim there, tell him: What the fuck, dude?" The man in the silk robe jumps onto the pier. "You sure I don't know you? You remind me of someone. What, Alice, right, Alice, that's your name."

"No. That's not me." She stumbles backwards, gently, trying not to betray the feeling of rising panic our man feels coming off her. Her hand in his hand shakes ever so slightly.

"You sure? I *have* seen you before." The man stumbles along the pier towards them. "Hey, Tim, can you get the flashlight?"

"We gotta go," Lake says.

"Why?"

Lake, quickly, rehearsed: "We are off for a shag."

"Right on. Right on." The man stops. "First time?"

"Yes. For me. He said he would... you know... be gentle."

The man laughs a dirty, male, manly laugh of approval. "Right on, right on. Lucky bastard." He licks his lips.

"We gotta go before I have second thoughts," Lake says, her voice the voice of a rabbit in the headlights.

"Right on. Wouldn't want to impede that." The man in the robe turns around to stumble back towards the yacht. Lake and our man turn around to head for the corridor. "Oh, silent man!" the man in the robe yells. They freeze. "Get me some pictures, m'kay?" The man in the silk robe laughs his dirty laugh and climbs back onto the yacht. They head for the corridor. She frees her hand from his. "You are hurting me." "I am sorry. I just wanted to help." She sighs. After a while, she says: "I know." She walks faster, a few paces ahead of him, and they head through the passage away from the beach.

Silently, they walk down dimly lit hallways, another dark, twisted labyrinth. Occasionally, a wall makes space for a window looking into a room. They walk past many windows and see many rooms.

They see a group of people arguing. They see a family celebrating Christmas. A mother abandoning her child. Lovers embracing for the first time. An old couple of friends playing squash. A person standing in the rain, just standing, while artificial rain drops from the ceiling. A writer writing a book. A songstress singing a silent song. A lonely person pretending to cuddle a cat that is not there.

"The hidden rooms are just back there," Lake informs him when they arrive at a dead end. Before he can figure out where to go, Lake puts her hand on the wall to press a hidden button. The wall glides aside and opens to another corridor.

"What's the plan?" our man asks.

"I don't know."

They follow the hidden corridor around a bend and end up in a circular room whose walls are taken up by doors of various colours, sizes, and shapes.

In the middle of the room, the lady with the red braids is waiting for them. The escape has ended. There is no escape. They have failed. He braces himself. The Asian guy can't be far.

Lake takes a step towards the red woman and greets her.

"Hey, Anne. Nice to see you," Lake says.

The woman with the braids does not return the greeting. Her furious eyes meet our man. "Where is my phone, you fucking thief?" He does not respond to the question, the only thing he manages to say is: "Wait, what, you know each other?"

"Hmhm," Lake affirms his question. He tries to say something else while the braid-woman comes towards him, half-yelling and half-whispering insults and threats, until Lake stops her: "He doesn't have it anymore. Your phone. Gave it to Mark." Mark, the Asian-looking guy? "Don't fuck with me." "I am not. You know me. I am telling the truth." Our man is still stuck: "How do you guys know each other?" "Doesn't matter," Lake replies, then addresses the braid-girl again: "Anne, it was a misunderstanding. He meant well." "Meant well does not mean shit. Mark is somewhere in the Mill tearing the place apart because of him," braid-girl retorts. "Not your problem. Mark is your boyfriend." "Not anymore," Anne says, not a trace of emotion in her voice. "Oh... I am sorry." Lake seems taken aback.

"Don't be. Fuck off." Anne steps past them to leave the way they came from. Our man still does not know what to say. Lake steps towards one door on the other end of the room and starts entering a code into the keypad.

Then, Anne, just before she steps into the corridor, delivers her last words: "You know, he will not stop until he finds you, right? And he will find you, eventually. He always does."

Lake: "We'll keep it in mind." The door in front of her opens with a loud whoosh. Lake and our man step into the room, and Anne disappears in the corridor on the other side. Lake closes the door. The room they are in is modelled after the space-room in 2001 – A Space Odyssey, where the astronaut spends the last act of his life before being reborn into the next step of evolution. It feels cold, the bland, white furniture, the stone floor. Our guy sits down heavily on the white sofa that is even harder than it looks.

"How do you know her?"
"We're old friends?"
"Why didn't you tell me?"
"That's my business."

And now he explodes, all bottled up, all confusion and anger: "Your business? Screw me, Lake. You could have ended this just like that. Just by calling her and explaining the situation. Instead, you conjure doomsday upon us!"

"A little dramatic, no?"
"No! You lied to me."
"I did not tell you the entire truth. That's not a lie."
"Ah, come on. Not telling the truth, lying, that's the same."
"Semantics, my friend."

"I am not your friend!"

Silence. He gets up, walks up and down in the space-room. No drinks, no nothing in here? Could he at least have a smoke? It seems ages to him since he had his last cigarette.

"We are all liars." Lake has sat down on the sofa. Her voice is low, almost as if she is talking to herself. "Everyone lies."

"Speak for yourself," he retorts. Lake looks up and he can see that look on her face. That look of anger and disappointment, of sadness and helplessness.

She speaks: "We are all liars. We are all assholes. We are always an asshole in someone's story. Whether we want to or not. And you can't deny that." He wants to say something, only to be cut off by her. "And don't bore me with your good intentions. Good intentions are just a lie we tell ourselves to make our mistakes weigh a little less heavy. Why didn't I tell you I knew Anne? Well, because first, this seemed like fun. And then it would have got weird if I had told you. And then it was too late." No reply from our man. She sighs, says nothing for a moment. "Why did you have to pick up that stupid phone?"

A long, long silence. He sits down on the couch.

"Because she caught me staring at her and I knew that she knew that I'd been staring at her because I thought she was hot. So, I wanted to prove to her I am not an asshole... and I wanted to see her again... and I wanted to feel less lonely..."

Somewhere in the bowels of the Old Mill, a tall, muscular guy is raging. People have fled. Only a few security guards are left, pursuing their duty, calling for backup. Our man closes his eyes, and he thinks he can feel the music that has gone silent and the lights that are off now. It is as if the Mill itself is dying.

"What now?" Lake asks him. "We cannot grow old here."

He nods without knowing what to say. They could try to leave, but the muscular guy might catch them. Or even if they got out, he would follow them. Chase them across the planet.

"We could get up to the roof," Lake says, "and jump to the next building. We could escape that way."

"He would still try to find us. We'd be on the run. Can't escape the past."

Silence.

Then: "What if we burned the place down?" Lake says.
"What?"
"We start a fire and escape via the roof. He'll think we died."
"But how?"
"We short-circuit the lights."
"Again: how?"

Without another word, Lake steps past him and to the wall at the far end of the space-room. He wants to quip that the door is on the other side, but she's already found yet another hidden panel. With the press of her fingers, a secret door opens next to her. He can see a steep stairway leading up.

"How do you know this place so well?"
"I dated the architect." She steps into the stairway and up.
"Really?"
"Don't be weird about it."

They make their way up into another set of corridors on the top-most hidden floor. Without hesitation or thought, Lake walks ahead and opens another door, which leads them into a cold, neutral, grey office. A series of screens and computers takes up the wall opposite of the entrance, making the room look like the mission control for a spaceflight to mars. "You can control everything up here," Lake tells him. On a screen, they can see the tall Asian guy fighting a couple of guards.

"They must have evacuated the place. We can still sound the fire alarm, just to be on the safe side." She presses a few buttons on the keyboard. Almost immediately, all the rooms on all screens are bathed in red lights and they can hear a high-pitched siren bellowing from the innermost of the Old Mill.

"And now for my masterpiece..." Lake continues to press buttons. "Did you know that they have a state-of-the-art lighting system?" Yes, he knows that. "It's actually pretty cool. You don't have to program anything. There is an algorithm that listens to the music and directs the lights in real time. Lots of computing power. In fact, every light is its own mini-computer. Downside is that computers produce a lot of heat. Needs a lot of cooling. To get the job done, the complete system is water-cooled. Tons of water running from two tanks in the cellar to every single light and back. All fine and dandy. Only gets difficult when there is an emergency that forces the tanks to empty. For example, an earthquake. In that case, the cellar gets flooded, and the cooling does not function anymore, which would lead to the lights overheating in a matter of seconds. To prevent that, there is a shutdown process in place that turns all lights off," she dramatically pushes a final button, "but I just disabled said shutdown process. Would you press the big blue button over there?"

There is a big blue button on a console to his right. Obediently, he presses it.

"You just emptied the tanks. And..." she points to the screen showing the big concert hall, "the lights have already caught fire. Time for our exit."

He follows her out of the control room, down the hallway and through another door. She leads them onto the roof of the Old Mill. He can already smell the smoke of the fires below. Still, the night is frosty and the stars above are beautiful.

Lake tells him to grab a ladder that leans against the wall next to the entrance and to bring it to the edge of the building. The next-closest building stands less tall than the Old Mill and is maybe ten, fifteen meters away. Lake grabs the ladder off our man and extends it.

He helps her to lower it to the roof of the other building, building an improvised bridge. They get lucky and the ladder locks against a small smoke chimney protruding from the flat roof on the other side. They test the ladder, it seems to hold. Slowly, they crawl across, away from the Mill.

On the new building, they finally get a second to catch their breath. He looks at the scenery below. People are running back and forth, yet no one seems to have a plan for what to do. He can hear sirens of the incoming fire fighters, far off in the distance. It will be too late by the time they get here.

Lake sits down at the edge of the roof and silently watches the flames now leaking from the windows of the Old Mill. Only seconds later, the roof where they just stood collapses. The ladder slips off the roof and falls towards the ground. People below run away screaming. He thinks he can see a tall, muscular Asian dude pacing up and down the streets, trying to find their faces in the crowd. If they get lucky, he will truly think they are dead.

"Are you going to sit down?" Lake asks him. He does so. Together and silently, they watch the mill burn, not close enough to each other to touch, still, close enough that he can feel her.

"I am glad we burned it down," she says after a while.

"What are you going to do now?" he asks her.

"Shower, sleep." She gets up. "You can come to my place if you want to. You don't have to."

He shrugs. He doesn't know what he wants anymore.

#

I honestly didn't know. I honestly didn't know what I'd say if you sat down next to me and asked me what I wanted to talk about. Yes, I was on holiday, I was doing things and I felt the pressure of having to accumulate experiences which I could tell people about back home, yet, what had I been doing, truly? Going from restaurant to restaurant? Eating? Looking at sights? What was the story? Where was the narration?

I paid my bill, left, left the place of talking people, wondering where my foul mood had come from. No, not bad mood, tired, sad mood, that mood that questions your existence, as you walk down that road, take a picture of the lights, because they look beautiful, continue towards the Ferris wheel that glows in the dark, because it is only shortly after eight and it's too early to go back to the hotel room, because you still have to experience something today, something that counts, but what the fuck counts? What the fuck is the purpose? What the fuck is pushing you away from yourself, why the fuck is no one in your hotel room you could talk to right now and tell them you feel... feel... feel something? Or nothing. Or anything.

Words. Words. Words.
Thoughts.

Finally, you have pity on yourself and make your way back to your room. Get some sleep. It must be the jet lag. The tiredness. Buy some booze on the way back, have a pleasant drink in your room. Listen to some music. Maybe write something. Maybe send some messages.

And then, sleep. Sleep all the maybes away. Awake a fresh man. It has been a false start. New day in Yokohama tomorrow.

A man needed a schedule to follow on his new day. I woke up and set my plan. First, I would walk to a pin on my map marking a coffee shop. Afterwards, there was a model train museum close-by – it was raining, so a museum seemed an excellent choice. I wasn't a big fan of model trains, but it seemed peculiar enough to make people giggle when I'd tell them about it. Then, lunch. I had read about a good tonkatsu restaurant in the vicinity. Later in the day, back to the port for the night boat tour I had booked. And then, my mind was set, this man would join the Oktoberfest. I would try to find a group of Japanese people I could impress by being from Europe. Even if I wasn't from Germany.

It was a grey day. Rain hovered in the air like mist. My GPS guided me along streets and past the small amusement park housing the enormous Ferris wheel. The park, despite the terrible weather, was open, and, to my surprise, didn't ask for an entrance fee. There were a few people milling about, yet most of the handful of rides were closed because of the weather. Split-second decision, addition to my plan: I entered the amusement park.

Exciting. Unplanned. Spontaneous.

I thought about taking a turn on the Ferris wheel, which was one of the few open rides, but decided against it. I remembered being on the famous Ferris wheel in Vienna and that feeling of claustrophobia mixed with vertigo when I'd been in the gondola. That thought that had crept into my mind: what if one screw came loose? What if the gondola became detached? What if I fell? Died?

I walked through the small amusement park, snapping pictures of closed rides, the empty spaces, the lack of people. I entered a bigger building on the far side of the park, a multilevel mix of shops, a restaurant and booths selling tickets for the rides. A family with a small child stood in front of the only open booth, buying a ticket for the wheel. On the top floor, I found a room filled to the brim with arcade machines. The machines produced an unholy accumulation of sounds coming from hundreds of loudspeakers, gunfire, voices, beeping, and others, unintelligible sounds that filled the room like an intangible, vibrating carpet. I snapped some pictures of the room, which was devoid of humans, only the machines talking to each other, begging each other to use a coin to give them some meaning. It almost felt like I was not supposed to be there, like no one was, as if the empty arcade was preparing for the coming apocalypse.

I was happy with my pictures (hashtag nopeople, hashtag apocalypse), so I left the park to continue my way to the coffee shop. It was still raining and my feet, thanks to my sneakers, which clearly were not made for rainy weather, were wet.

The coffee shop turned out to be some kind of co-working space-plus-coffee, not only offering the dark beverage of gods but also rooms for rent. After stumbling around the space for a while, feeling out-of-place, I found a counter down a hallway in a communal area and approached the woman behind it.

"Sorry... is it okay for just coffee?" I asked the woman behind the counter, trying to make it clear I was not here to rent an office room. I am not working, lady. I am just here to enjoy your amazing third-wave-coffee.

"Yes, yes," she replied. There was a moment of silence until I realised she was expecting my order. Brain slow, caveman.

"Oh. Ah. A flat white."

"Sure. To drink here or to go?"

"Here," I said. She motioned me to have a seat at one table, which I did, and went to work. I observed her, trying not to be too obvious. The gentleness she put into steaming the milk, heating it carefully and slow-enough not to burn it, pleased me. She made the espresso and slowly poured the milk into the cup before placing it on the counter.

There was another moment of awkward silence until I realised I was supposed to get up and get the cup.

Which I did, quickly. Hastily. Hurriedly.

She had formed a perfect-looking leaf on top and I marvelled at the texture of the steamed milk, trying not to destroy it as I carried the full cup to my table. I tasted the foam, which was firm and sweet. Very good. Next, I carefully took a sip of the coffee. Perfect temperature. The espresso maybe was missing the gentle aftertaste of berries and/or acidity, but was strong, earthly, and offered a good counter-taste to the sweetness of the milk. I should get up, I thought to myself, and ask her where the beans came from and what kind of roast it was, show her I was a connoisseur of all things coffee, strike up a conversation about the mysteries of the magic beverage, but she was working behind the counter, cleaning, rearranging things, and I didn't want to disturb her.

I finished my coffee in silence, paid, and left for the model train museum. I followed my trusted map, crossed the (real) train station, the bus station and headed towards a major office building, which belonged to a famous Japanese manufacturer of cars and, according to my GPS, offered a shortcut to the other side of the block. I felt nervous about walking into an office building, walking like I belonged, yet there was a sign outside which invited the public to step in and have a look at an exhibition of the manufacturer's most popular cars on the ground level. Not surprisingly then, I found myself inside confronted with a selection of polished cars, expensive and clean-looking. Men in business suits mingled in-between the cars, talking important talks, walking important walks and I felt, once again, out of place in my dirty, wet sneakers, my t-shirt (with a Marvel print, no less. Nerd much?) and my camera dangling from my neck. I tried not to show it. Walk like I was supposed to walk through the hall, up an escalator and along a gallery towards the high-ground exit in the back.

The gallery offered an unobstructed view of the entire hall, the cars, the people. There was no need to feel out of place, I told myself, there were plenty of other tourists and "normal" people about. A guy with an oversized rucksack, or a travelling family looking at the cars, the father standing next to a vehicle, smiling, the mother snapping a picture of the father. They dream of the day when they would have important walks to walk, important talks to talk, expensive cars to buy, however, their children are getting restless, so they leave before the children can damage any of the cars and the family gets slapped with a bill from the famous Japanese manufacturer of cars and they beg their rich aunt to lend them money, but he, the father, can't take the shame, so he starts drinking and, eventually, the mother leaves with the kids, leaves for a small town somewhere up north, where she can both work and take care of the kids, it's a hard life, and he does what he does, can't take the shame and drinks and drinks and drinks, cursing at the empty sky, and people avoid him at work, even his boss does, and, eventually, he doesn't show up anymore and they send him a letter, wish him all the best and let him go, he lets himself go, but she works and works and works and hopes for her children to grow up strong, tries to be a mother, tries to leave the past behind and, hopefully, become something more than a mother again someday, something more than a role, something akin to a whole person.

I stand on the gallery, the exit behind me. I look at the car exhibition below and look at the family taking the picture. I feel bad for them. I feel bad for not knowing their story, yet still making one up in my head. A story that brings them many hardships, many tears. A story that would end with the inevitable: their death in a sea of unfulfilled dreams. Because that is what we are. Sea urchins in a sea of unfulfillment. Blind and ugly. But delicious.

I left the building and arrived at the model train museum soon after. I spent the next hour and a half walking through big and small rooms, most of them lighted by cold neon lights, looking at glass vitrine after glass vitrine filled with detailed models of trains. It was what it was. Small trains from around the world. What had I been expecting to find in a model train museum?

I looked at the brochure that I had got at the entrance. The train models had been brought together by a private collector who had found his passion for trains and models while travelling the world, had centred his travels around them, to see the real ones, buy models everywhere, assemble them or to build models from scratch. There were trains from the USA, China, Russia, Germany, Italy, Brazil, Australia, Chile, and many others, yes, among them, also, of course, Swiss trains. I felt a sting of national pride when I found the first model of an SBB train, a recent and pretty common one. I wanted to turn around and tell the people in the museum that I knew this train and had seen it many times in person, in real, in big. That pre-Baudrillardian thing when you didn't just know the copy, but the original.

I wondered where that feeling of national pride came from – I certainly never felt it when I was back in Switzerland. In fact, I belonged to those Swiss people whose favourite pastime was to complain about the Swiss and their shortcomings. Their unfriendliness. Their relative coldness. How they went ape-shit when someone put out the trash a day early. About the look they gave you when you did something wrong in public. THE LOOK! About how they'd rather ignore you than ask you whether they could help you, how unfriendly they treated you in stores and restaurants and how fucking boring everything in Switzerland was.

Maybe that was what made me Swiss. That complaining, complaining, quietly complaining without taking any action. That was what we Swiss people did – we complained about each other behind our backs, yet, when we saw each other, we smiled and we shook each other's hand and we said "Jo, Greetli, schön dich wieder mol zgseh, wie gohts dir?", even though Greetli can go and get kicked by a donkey. Fuck that shit.

Still, we had excellent trains. One had to give us that.

My tour of the museum ended in a spacious room which was taken up by a huge model train set. Trains were running on the tracks, and, to my amusement, there was a train schedule announcing when which train would pass by the main station in the middle of the set. Just in case you had a favourite train you wanted to see – unfortunately, I had just missed the Swiss train.

I marvelled at the details of the model, the huge train station as its centrepiece, the little plastic people running towards it, trying to catch their train, even though they'd been frozen in time and space and their rushing was pointless. I walked to one of the farther corners, where I found a small model village, vintage cars, and more people. They seemed more relaxed over here, mingling in town, shopping at a farmer's market, looking for fresh plastic produce. There was a tiny train station up on a mountain above the village. Some people sat on a bench, waiting for a train. But none of the trains I watched driving up the mountain stopped at the tiny station, and I had the distinct feeling that they would have to wait for a long time. There were some plastic people having a picnic close to a lake at the edge of the model. The end of the world of the plastic people. There was a girl taking a photo of her parents sitting at a picnic table. Everything seemed perfect, frozen in eternal happiness – but one had to wonder what was happening inside the small houses, behind those windows, the curtains.

I'd seen enough trains. Enough plastic people.

I left the museum and followed my GPS to my next destination: the tonkatsu restaurant.

Tonkatsu is an easy food, but, if done right, utterly delicious. In many places, you have the choice between two cuts of pork – either a lean cut or a piece of meat that is fattier, heartier. Always go for the second one. Don't mind the fat, it will not kill you. If you are lucky, you end up sitting at a counter with the kitchen area right in front of you and you can see the magic happen. You can see them take the meat, drop it in flour, egg and panko and fry it. Fast, perfected movements of deliciousness. The tonkatsu is served with tons of rice and cabbage, simple in their taste, nothing to steal the thunder from the main act, the meat, and its wonderful fried goodness – the only competition for the juicy meat is the sauce. The dark-brown, sticky tonkatsu sauce. The dish comes with buckets of that sauce, which you can use to your content. And you will use it, on the meat, on the cabbage on the rice, everything will taste of that sauce, but here is the thing: the sauce plays along, despite being strong and flavourful, it doesn't rob your food of its taste, doesn't overshadow the pork and panko, but adds complexity, like a party in your mouth full of countless voices all speaking at the same time, a wonderful chaos of cacophonous unity. Let's zoom in on that: imagine how you put a piece of tonkatsu into your mouth. You feel the acidity and sweetness of the sauce against your tongue and palate, and you close your mouth and chew. Your teeth wander through the crispy outer layer of the tonkatsu, meet the meat, which would be quite dry if it weren't for the fat's juiciness. The components mix and it all comes together: sour, sweet, strong, crispy, some hints of spices, pepper, salt, and the meat, fatty, juicy, you bite, chew, mix, swallow. You try the cabbage next. You taste the freshness of the vegetable playfully fighting against the heavy thickness of the sauce. The rice, as many times, is only an addition, something to make sure your stomach is full. Still, you gobble it up, every grain.

Fully satisfied, I paid my bill and left, leaving the small, yet still somewhat posh-looking restaurant behind. There was still plenty of time until I would have to go to the pier for my night boat trip, so I walked back to the hotel, to maybe have a little rest, stretch the old legs for a bit.

While laying on my bed, through the window of my room, I could see the day change. That moment when the natural light of the sun vanishes and makes space for that zone of dim greyness, which, suddenly, gets replaced by humanity's artificial lights, emanating from the mall across the street, from the hotel, from the coloured lights on the Ferris wheel to my left.

Around an hour later, I stood in line for the boat that would carry me on my night tour of the factories surrounding Yokohama. I eyed the mix of people waiting with me. An older couple in front of me – the man, just like me, had his camera ready and was nervously waiting for the boat to arrive – behind me, a group of young men in business suits, and a little further in the back, a group of about five men and the equal number of women. Probably some kind of group dating situation.

Our cruise ship was a small boat with benches in the back that offered just enough space for everyone to sit. I chose a good seat close to the left edge of the boat. Next to me, the older couple sat down, the man holding his camera like a dressed animal, ready for its duty. I quickly nodded to greet them, but they didn't seem to notice me. As soon as everyone had taken a seat (myself, the businessmen, the group dates, and the older couple had been joined by a family of a man, a woman and four kids, some more businesspeople and two or three couples in their twenties), a middle-aged woman appeared in front of the benches. She said something into a microphone, cheeringly, and some people seemed to reply something. She continued talking and wouldn't stop doing so for the entire trip. Breathlessly, she would say things I didn't understand, maybe about the things we were seeing, sometimes she said words in a tone that sounded like she was trying to animate the group, she would continue to talk, whether or not people were listening. She talked and talked and talked without stopping.

Thus, we drove (floated?) through the night, through the industrial areas of Yokohama, accompanied by the relentless chatter of the woman. It was dark now, and the factories were lit up by dim neon lights, smoke rising from their chimneys towards the sky. If there was ever a reality that could represent the fever dreams of Blade Runner or Final Fantasy 7, this was it. I took some photos, trying to balance the harsh difference between the darkness of night and the lights from the factories with a 50mm pancake lens. It wasn't the most expensive piece of equipment, still it seemed to do a decent job in the dark conditions around us.

Sometimes, the boat stopped, and the woman seemed to narrate something particular about a factory building we were looking at, or the area, or anything, but I, of course, continued not to understand what she was saying. I wondered what she must have been thinking, seeing me, a foreigner, the only foreigner on this boat, sitting there, occasionally nodding, a reflex, an innate human movement to show her I was listening. Did she think I understood Japanese? Or did she suspect I did not understand one word of her memorised and carefully rehearsed speech? Did she find it funny that a foreigner had found his way onto this cruise? Or was it annoying I was there? Me sticking out like a sore thumb?

"Neither of these," she'd tell me later. She stopped me just as I was about to exit the boat. I had waited for everyone else to get off, no hurry, no rush for me. I had got up, the last person on the boat to do so, wanted to step back onto the pier, as she appeared next to me and uttered the words above.

"Sorry?" I said.

"Neither of these," she repeated. "In fact, I didn't care you were here. I was just doing my job."

"Sure," I said. "I was just thinking..."

I looked at her. And then it hit me. It was *her*. Soulmate-to-be. The one I had invented in Tokyo. Why was she in Yokohama?

Country-boy was still studying. Studying hard. And she wanted to support him. And he wanted to support her. So, he worked in a factory on the weekends, loading and unloading trucks. And to be close to each other, even when they were working, she'd taken up a job on the night cruise. Narrating the same story time and time again. Trying to see his silhouette against the darkness when her boat floated by his factory.

"That's life, isn't it?" I heard myself say without thinking about the impact my words might have on soulmate-to-be. I saw the hurt in her eyes only a split-second later and knew it would only be of little solace if I told her that my statement had not been directed at her and her story, but at myself, at what I was doing in my head, a purely selfish statement.

"I am sorry," I said. She only shook her head, brushing my statement away. We should have a drink, she told me then, talk about more pleasurable things. She knew nothing about me and wanted to know whether I had a family or a dog, a sister, or brothers or a pet parrot.

She became a different person almost instantly, and we walked off the boat. She was bubbly, made jokes, walking, almost skipping, always a few paces ahead of me. Together, we walked past the pier, and she explained many things I didn't understand about this country. We finally made it to the Oktoberfest and paid the entrance fee and had some bratwurst, and there were some friends of hers, amazed by the fact that I came from Europe, and we talked. And drank.

Even the music seemed better compared to yesterday, a jazzier version of the insufferable German folk songs, played at full speed, trumpets, big band style. Suddenly, people danced on the table, and I moved aside. I didn't want to join them. I was afraid that the table would collapse under me.

"What are you afraid of?" someone asked me, "nothing can happen here."

I wanted to say something smart, couldn't. "You don't have to say something smart," someone else told me, "just say something funny." I turned halfway around to see who was talking to me, however, the flow of people made it hard to discern. I saw former soulmate-to-be dancing on one table, singing a rendition of the Killers' Somebody Told Me and I asked her whether country-boy would come by.

"Yes," she said, "he should be here soon. Or maybe he already is. Somewhere in the crowd."

We soon left the place, though. Country-boy hadn't shown up. Former soulmate-to-be told me not to worry, he would be here soon. We hit Yokohama hard, went to a pub. The beer flowed freely, and I wondered who was footing the bill. I tried to order some more beer for the group and pay for it, but couldn't find the counter. Again, former soulmate-to-be told me not to worry. She was dancing again, this time singing the song of Oasis I hated so much, yet, somehow, she made even that one sound good. Soon, we left the bar, off to an arcade, where we played shooting games, killing zombies, saving the world. The graphics were old, the game must have been from the early 2000s, but I was impressed by how well the plastic gun handled. We competed against two Japanese gamers, we were no match for them. Still, they congratulated us for our spirit, we left, off to a karaoke joint to sing, mostly songs I hated, some I liked, I sang songs in Japanese and wondered whether my pronunciation had improved, or whether the alcohol gave me the feeling it had. In the meantime, our group had expanded to about ten people, all of them students of Tokyo University, and we saw the sun rise from the windows of our karaoke room.

"Have a good night," soulmate-to-be said when she saw me off at the hotel. Her group of friends were standing in the background, smoking cigarettes, looking tired, hungover.

"We never met country-boy," I replied.

He is working hard, soulmate-to-be explained to me. Besides, you never really wanted to meet him, no?

"I wanted to apologise to him," I replied. "I made some mistakes. I am sure we could improve the story."

Things don't want to be improved. Otherwise, where is the tension? You can only improve them by the end. Or send them down the drain. Whatever you prefer.

"What do you prefer?" she asked me.

The philosophical question seemed out of place, out of character. So, I deleted the story in my mind.

I bid my farewell and stepped off the boat. The night cruise had taken the better part of two hours and I felt tiredness setting in. Still, the night felt young. And I felt hungry. For many things.

Most of the people had already left the boat and stood scattered along the pier. Some were taking photos of themselves in front of the dark sea, the light of the factories behind them. I also took some last photos before I made my way back along the seaside. The narrating lady had disappeared.

The night was quiet. The waves crashed against the land as I walked. The sound of crickets occasionally filled the dark when there was a burst of wind coming in from the sea. It was like walking in twilight, the warm air from the city on one side of my body, the cold air from the sea on the other.

I crossed a bridge to get back to Minato Mirai and soon could spot the tents of the Oktoberfest in the distance. To my dismay, the place looked darker than before, quieter, and sure enough, I learnt as I approached, it was closed now. Some stragglers were still tumbling through the streets close-by, laughing, wearing fake lederhosen and German hats. I strolled along the fence of the fest, the smell of wurst and fries and beer still heavy in the air. There were a few lonely Japanese people armed with brooms walking between the tables, collecting trash. On the far end of the biggest tent, I spotted the stage where the probably-Dutch German folk band had been playing. Most of the food trucks next to the tent had their fronts closed and a small group of people wearing dirty aprons had gathered in front of them, sitting on the floor, eating sausages or noodles, talking to each other. The owners and workers taking a well-deserved rest after the craziness was over. It reminded me of the time I had waited tables. That moment when the last customer finally had left, and the tables were clean, and we'd sit down and realise that our feet hurt. If you were lucky, the last customer had been a friendly family or a middle-aged couple and they'd been happy with your service and thanked you when they paid, giving you a generous tip. If you'd been unlucky, you had a young couple on a date, one party trying to impress the other party, usually by showing superiority over the server, making stupid jokes at your expense.

I realised I had to find a different place to eat something, since the Oktoberfest was closed. I had no interesting restaurant close by on my map and I didn't feel like walking back to downtown Yokohama, so I instead turned to check out the mall in the port's heart across from my hotel.

Most of the shops were already closed or in the process of doing so. So were the restaurants. Nothing struck my fancy. Aimlessly, I left the mall and headed down the street. The Ferris wheel glowed in front of me, but the amusement park was closed as well. I wondered again whether I should have taken a ride on the wheel. It was too late now. I would leave tomorrow. Southbound. The thought reminded me I would have to pack tonight.

No one would miss me. No one in Yokohama would remember much of me.

I found a famous fast-food chain restaurant on the side of the mall. It was okay to get a fast food meal from that specific chain in Japan, I told myself. Because they had a teriyaki burger, a burger you couldn't get anywhere else. The excuse helped me not to feel too bad about my visit, even though I should have, for eating a fatty piece of burger on my travels while there were so many better options out there. I swatted the bad feeling aside, ordered my burger (by pointing at the picture. I didn't even try to speak Japanese), received it and sat down, unpacked said burger and—

In true fast food tradition, the teriyaki burger was an ugly piece of shit. They had smeared sauce in abundance all over the burger, the bun resembled a crushed car crash of bread that had been handled with a sledgehammer, and the meat looked lost and lonely amidst the chaos of sauce and bread and garnish. I guessed some things were universal, and even if it was just the ugliness of burgers in fast-food chain restaurants.

Still, I thought, taking a bite, feeling the umami of the teriyaki sauce tingling my tongue, it was delicious. It had no right to be, yet it was.

The bread was soft, almost sweet, the meat dark, slightly smoky, and then, there was the heavy saltiness, soy-ness of the teriyaki that filled my heart with joy. And if this were a story, the moral would be: don't judge a book by its cover. Or: we can move beyond what we look like and be so much more. Urgh.

The rest of the evening passed by with some drinks I bought from a 7/11, packing, unpacking, checking, and packing my suitcase, some music and then sleep. Heavy emptiness swatting the thoughts in my brain away.

No dreams. Or none I could recall in the morning.

The next day didn't start too early. I had enough time to stop at a 7/11 and withdraw some money from an ATM. Then, I continued to the subway stop close to Minato Mirai, leaving the port of the future bound for shin-Yokohama, where I would catch my Shinkansen.

I got some snacks at the train station. I didn't feel too hungry today, so I only bought something small. Also, I was planning on visiting a small restaurant in Nara, my destination, a restaurant that specialised in eel. I hadn't had eel yet on my trip, even though it was one of my favourite fish, so I felt that feeling of cuisinal anticipation in my guts.

I left shin-Yokohama with the Shinkansen heading towards Kyoto. The train was filled to the brim with tourists and their suitcases (I was one of them) and I felt overwhelmed by the sudden fact that I could understand the surrounding conversations. In front of me, there was a trio of Australian travellers discussing the many marvels of Japanese culture and comparing it to the other countries they'd been to. One of them lamented the fact that, while he liked Japan and all the beautiful vistas and people very much, travelling here didn't feel like an adventure, unlike Myanmar or Vietnam. It was too ordered and all a bit boring, he said. I wondered what someone who'd grown up and lived in Vietnam or Myanmar would think of his statement. What it felt like, to them, to live in an adventure-country.

Behind me, there were a couple of British travellers and in the row behind them another couple that, judging by the conversation going on, was travelling with them. I couldn't place the second couple's accent, the only thing I could discern was that their native tongue was not English. The four of them spoke loudly and enthusiastically about some sort of outlandish party they'd been to when visiting Jerusalem a year ago. I had problems following the exact thread of the story, yet it seemed to involve a lot of alcohol and general craziness on everyone's part. One of them, the non-British guy, hogged most of the conversation, speaking in a tone and volume that made me feel uncomfortable. I felt it disrespectful to speak and laugh that loudly on a train in Japan, in a culture that seemed to have been largely built on the division between noise and silence, where it was your duty to know where one and where the other belonged. Whereas places like downtown Tokyo were a place of noise, coming from every mouth and every loudspeaker, there were places of silence, like modern-day temples, the Shinkansen one of them. You do not speak loudly on a train in Japan. That was the unspoken rule. I felt the urge to get up and ask the non-British tourist to respect this and apologise to the Japanese people who sat in the same car and must have been annoyed by the noisy tourist, even though they'd never admit this.

But then – was it really that wrong to talk on a train, to have a little fun, to connect with one's fellow travellers? Shake up the crusted parts of this culture that demanded cold, pervasive grace and churchish silence, funeral-like behaviour on a train, a silly, unreasonable demand to anyone who wanted to live a little?

Maybe it was all in my head, anyway. Maybe none of the Japanese passengers was annoyed, maybe they simply didn't care. Let them speak. Let me be silent. No one cares what anyone does, and it wasn't my business to decide otherwise.

A Tale of Two Girls / Nara 1

The 1970s Ford Coupe purred like a kitten on the highway. Her father was driving, as usual, her mother adjusting her makeup next to him, and she was in the back, stretched out on the bench, pretending to be asleep. On the radio, some singer begged her not to be cruel, and she had no intention whatsoever to be so.

"Can we stop at the gas station?" her mother asked her father.

"We will be at the hotel in an hour."

"I need the ladies' room. And I am sure B. would not mind either, would you, darling?"

"She is sleeping," her father replied in her stead.

"No, she is not. She is just pretending."

"Is she now?" Her father laughed. "Cheeky, little girl."

She was not little and almost no girl anymore. She was seventeen, going on eighteen. But she did not protest. She kept her eyes closed and enjoyed being called little girl by her father.

They stopped at the gas station, and she remembered Billy from when they stopped at the same gas station a year ago. He was her age and was working there during the summer. He waved as they arrived and opened the car door for her.

"Hey, Billy, how are you doing?"

"Hey, B., I am doing mighty fine. Are you driving to the resort?"

"We sure are, Billy." She got out of the car. She was wearing a beautiful summer dress, and she knew that all the men at the resort would turn their head when she walked by, even though they really should not.

"It is a wonderful place for a holiday, isn't it?" Billy asked.

"It sure is, Billy," she replied.

"Can I get you something from the shop, B.?"

"A soda and chewing gums would be nice, Billy."

Billy disappeared into the shop. Her father was talking to Mr Emmett, who owned the gas station, while another station attendant was filling the tank of the coupe. Her mother left for the restroom. The sun stood high, and it was a bright and warm day. She felt like hopping in the sun, twirling her dress, she felt like talking to Billy and she was looking forward to dinner at the resort.

Billy soon returned with the soda and the chewing gum. "How much do I owe ya?" she asked him, but she knew well before she asked that he'd say it was a gift and that her father would look up from his conversation with Mr Emmett and protest and tell Billy that naturally he'd pay for it, which he would, giving Billy a very generous tip. Then, they would return to the car, her chewing a gum, sipping from her soda, would wave Billy and Mr Emmett goodbye and drive up to the resort.

The resort had been built twenty years ago, after the war, and had quickly become a popular holiday spot for families from all over the country. It had something for everyone: good food, music, beautiful rooms, and the owner made everyone feel welcome. Of course, like everyone else, he'd always been fond of B. Little did B. know that this would all change this year and that it would be her last stay at the resort. Or anyone's last stay.

Slowly, her father drove the car up the mountain road until the view opened on the left, and they could see the resort in the valley below. The main building, beautiful in its pastel-coloured state, in the middle, the bungalows, five of them, to the left, a four-story building to the right offering smaller apartments. And behind them all, the crowning achievement, a huge, long construct, a hall, which functioned as an extension to the main building with a stage, a dining hall, a bar and a smoking room – the last of which her father's favourite room where he could spend hours in deep political conversation with other guests and the owner. B., when she'd been younger, would sneak into the room in the evening after dinner and listen to the conversation while sitting on the floor until she'd fall asleep on the carpet like a cat in front of the fire. "Look at that, B. has fallen asleep," she remembered Mr Barnflat exclaim one evening (she was not really sleeping, only pretending), a chuckle in his voice. He was a rotund man with a bushy moustache, wearing small-rimmed glasses and smoking a cigar that smelled of herbs and moss. Soon after that, everyone at the resort would jokingly say that her father was paying too much, since B. didn't need a bed and felt comfortable sleeping just about anywhere.

They drove down the winding road towards the resort. It seemed to B. she could already smell the food that was being cooked in the kitchen, a roast or maybe fish, salmon, rice, and spinach, maybe they would have goulash tonight or, sometimes, if the weather was as nice as today, there would be a barbecue with burgers and potatoes and salad.

Her father parked the car in their usual spot. Before they even got out, the owner hurriedly emerged from the main building and walked towards them to greet them at the car. He shook their hand, her mother's like a gentleman, her father's like an old friend and her hand like someone who was not sure whether he should shake it like an adult's or just hold it and give her a pat on the head because he'd known her since she'd been a child.

"It is so nice to have you back," he said, "just leave the luggage in the car. I will have them brought to your rooms right after."

"Rooms?" her father asked. Usually, they were staying together in an apartment.

"Yes. We had an accident in your usual apartment – a pipe broke and flooded the entire bathroom. We will have to rebuild the entire room. But it will be a marvellous chance to refurbish everything. Make it a bit more modern."

"So, what do you have for us?" her mother said.

"Well, I figured let's do something new. The two of you will stay in a bungalow. It is down the road, a little walk of a couple of minutes. It offers the most spectacular view of the lake."

"That sounds nice," her mother said, taking her father's arm.

"And B. will get her own room on the second floor of the main building. An exceptionally beautiful room with a king-sized bed. Not that you would need it," he laughed, and so did her father and her mother and herself.

Her parents went to their bungalow. She saw them walking away like a couple in love, holding hands, an employee from the resort behind them carrying their luggage. She followed the owner to the reception, where he handed her a key to her room on the second floor. She made her way upstairs – she'd never been up here, so she felt a faint hint of excitement – and to room 234, her room, which was a small suite that offered a living area with a sofa and a state-of-the-art TV set with a VHS player, a bathroom with a luxurious bathtub and a bedroom with an enormous bed. Her suitcase arrived a few minutes after her and she put it on the bed and started to unpack her things. Suddenly, she heard a noise from outside. The window was open, and there were voices coming from the parking lot down below. She stood in front of the window to look outside. The sun had begun to set over the trees to her left. It was a gorgeous sight.

In the parking lot, there was the owner, talking to the employee who had brought her parents' luggage to their bungalow. The owner seemed agitated, almost nervous, she could not tell why. He was talking to the server as if giving him orders. The employee wanted to reply, but the owner shushed him, as a car pulled into the parking lot and into the space next to her father's car. The employee rushed up to the automobile and opened the front and the back door on the passenger's side, whereas the owner stood on the driver's side. He greeted the man that exited from the driver's seat with a warm handshake. On the passenger side, a woman, the wife, B. assumed, and a younger woman, the daughter, she assumed, emerged from the car. The younger woman – girl? – was maybe her own age wearing a slight smile on her face, determined features, something that struck B. She wore black trousers and a loose sitting shirt, her face and lips pronounced by a hint of make-up. The owner turned around and shook the daughter's hand, then the wife's. They exchanged some words, which B. could not understand, before the owner led the parents towards the hotel. The daughter followed them, paused, and looked up towards the window where B. was standing. B.'s heart skipped a beat, and she quickly pulled out of view, hiding behind the curtain.

A little while later, the phone in her room rang. It was her father telling her they would meet in half an hour at the bar and then go for dinner. It all seemed overly exciting, she thought to herself, as if she were travelling alone and meeting people she did not know yet. She put on her flowery dress and thought about the images she had seen in magazines of women in beautiful, long dresses with velvet gloves and cigarette holders. She made her way downstairs and into the bar. Her mother and father were already at the counter, each holding a drink with a tiny umbrella in hand, talking to someone. She recognised the man they were talking to. It was the father who she'd seen emerging from the car a little while ago. She turned her head to see whether she could spot the mother or the daughter somewhere, yet they were nowhere to be seen.

"Ah, that must be your B.," the man said when she approached the three of them. "Your parents have told me about you. In fact, everyone at the resort told me about you. My daughter absolutely has to meet B., they said."

"Nice to make your acquaintance, Mr...?" she replied shily.

"Call me Jim. Or John. Whatever you prefer." He was wearing a colourful Hawaiian shirt, and it felt difficult to take her eyes off the blue-green-red-yellow imprint that seemed to yell at her. "Nice to meet you... John," she said. "You have a daughter?" "Yes. Bella. I have no idea where she is. But I am sure you'll meet her at some point." "Maybe over dinner?" The man roared with laughter. "Bella never eats dinner with us. I think she usually hangs out with the kids at the river."

Kids at the river?

She'd never heard of them. She had been to the river, sure, yet had only seen families there with children, walking along the banks or sitting in the sun or sometimes swimming if the water was warm enough. Before she could ask John for more information, he had turned around to greet his wife, who had entered the bar. Her parents shook hands with her, and B. introduced herself. The wife, Francis, repeated John's statement that B. absolutely had to meet Bella at one point. Then, she listened to her parents, Francis and John talk a little while about the resort and the many times they had stayed here (Francis and John were also regulars of many years, but this was the first year they were all vacationing at the same time. Her parents and B. always stayed at the resort in September or October, while Francis, John and Bella preferred the height of summer in July or August. This year, however, Bella had to retake some exams at school to get her diploma, so they had to move their holiday to September. "Not much of a problem for me," said John, "I work in technology, I can take holiday whenever." "Ah, technology," her father replied, "what kind of technology? Surely not those computers?").

One of the staff members from the restaurant interrupted the discussion, informing her parents that their table was ready. "We must eat dinner together next time," Francis suggested, and her mother agreed. She would talk to the staff right after dinner to get a table for all of them tomorrow. What time should they have dinner? Six-thirty, they all agreed, and B. expressed hope that Bella would join them. Both Francis and John laughed as if she had said something extremely silly.

She and her parents had dinner at their usual table, in one corner of the restaurant. A guitar player sang Spanish songs while the waiters hurried back and forth from the kitchen to the tables. The thick, red carpet covering the entire floor of the restaurant muffled their fast footsteps. She had always liked the carpet, it made the room feel cosy.

The owner stood at the other end of the restaurant, at Francis' and John's table, talking to them for a long time. After dinner, her father smoked a cigar in the smoker's lounge, while B. joined her mother for a walk outside. They walked all the way to the bungalows, and B. had a look at the one her parents were staying in. It was a spacious two-room bungalow that offered an immense bed in one room, a sofa, a TV, and a kitchenette in the other. "Your father can cook something if he gets hungry at night," her mother said jokingly. "And if I feel lonely, I can come and sleep on the couch." "Sure you won't," her mother replied. They both laughed and left the bungalow to walk back to the main building. Outside, B. heard music, the faint melody of a rock song from somewhere not too far off. Probably from the river. She had to think of Bella, the girl she had yet to meet. She seemed like the type of person who would listen to that kind of music, rude music with guitars and drums and male singers with long hair.

After walking back to the hotel, she and her mother went to the restaurant for a coffee and dessert. Her mother talked to Ms Cunningham for some time, the head of staff. Ms Cunningham complained that the quality of the personnel was declining, that very few of them had a proper education. Sure, many were young and eager to work during the summer, but to them, this was only a temporary job on the way to somewhere else.

After listening a while to Ms Cunningham's complaining, B. got bored and excused herself. She went to check on her father in the smoker's room, who was in an intense conversation with someone about the state of the Middle East. "We should have grabbed them by the balls when we had the chance," her father's conversation partner said, and B. blushed and excused herself. She went outside and wandered around the parking lot for a bit. She could not hear the rock music from the river anymore. B. left the parking lot, crossed the street, and walked onto a small hill that stood opposite of the resort. She climbed the hill, hoping it would offer a pleasant view of the resort and the stars up above that stood against the darkening sky – which it did. She took in the chilly evening air on the hill and tried to figure out which of the windows belonged to her room, when she saw somebody appear from the woods next to the parking lot down below. It turned out to be a couple of shadows, two people. She squinted her eyes, and she thought to recognise Bella as one of them. The other one she did not know, a boy maybe her age, maybe older. Bella walked briskly, smoking a cigarette, the young man a few steps behind. He was talking to her, intently, she threw the cigarette to the ground, turned around, faced him. B. could not discern her expression. Then, Bella leaned in, kissed the boy, he stopped dead in his tracks. B. felt the warmth in her cheeks as she blushed for the second time this evening. Bella let the young man's lips go and B. could see her smile with a cheeky expression in her eyes. After two seconds, she turned around and, with a few quick steps, disappeared into the main building. The man remained in the parking lot for a little longer, like a rabbit facing the headlights of an oncoming truck, before he finally unfroze and trotted along the parking lot to enter the building through the staff entrance on the side of the house. B. remained on her hill until she was sure there was no one else coming from the woods, walked back down, across the parking lot, into the main building through the main entrance and up to her room.

She had slept a dreamless sleep when a knock on the door woke her. She put on her dressing gown and went to open it, only to find a young server with a serving cart outside. "Your breakfast, Ma'am," the server informed her. "Oh, I have ordered nothing," she replied. "You haven't? Shit. Oh, excuse me. Excuse my language. I did not want to bother you – I must have written down the wrong room number. Shit. Ms Cunningham is going to kill me." B. laughed. "What's so funny?" "Oh, I am sorry. I just can't see Ms Cunningham going after you with a knife or something, that's all." "Oh, she does not need a knife. She'll strangle me with her bare hands." They both laughed.

"I hope she won't," B. said, trying to put on an earnest tone. "We'll see. If I am nowhere to be found tomorrow, call the police and have them search the garden for my body." The server turned around to leave, but stopped. "You staying by yourself?"

"Yes," she replied. It was amazing how easily the lie came across her lips.

"You should join us. We usually have a drink and listen to music down at the river in the evening."

"I am not sure...," B. replied.

"Just meet me at the staff entrance at eight-thirty," the server said, turned around again and pushed the trolley with the homeless breakfast down the hallway. "Be there or be square. You don't want to be a square."

B. looked after the server for a while until she realised she was running late. She got dressed – a blue dress with a white collar – and met her parents downstairs for breakfast. "She gets her own room, and she already oversleeps," her father said, with a smile on his face. "Maybe she fell asleep in the smoker's lounge," the owner said, approaching the table with a glass of orange juice for B. In the back, as if on cue, the door to the smoker's lounge opened, and out stepped Bella, the girl B. had never met. Bella hurried across the dining room and disappeared out of view.

"Croissant, jam and an apple?" the owner asked B., citing her usual breakfast routine. She smiled at him and nodded. "How have you slept?" her mother asked her. "Good," she replied. Her father smiled at her. It was the first time she noticed, looking at him in this moment in the restaurant in the resort, that the hair on her father's temples had turned grey. And for the first time that she thought the wrinkles around her mother's eyes were growing deeper. She wondered how much she resembled her mother.

The owner brought her food and stood next to the table to talk to her father. About the changes he intended to make to the resort, the old and the new carpet, the same discussion they seemed to have every year. B. felt bored.

"Is something the matter, B.?" her mother asked her. No, B. replied. All was fine.

After breakfast, she drove to the nearby town with her parents for a stroll along the main street and some window shopping. Her mother suggested they return another day to buy a nice dress for B., maybe the day after tomorrow, when her husband would play chess with Mr Rogers. B. agreed and said she loved the idea. They walked along the lake and had a late lunch at a fish restaurant. B. did not like fish, so she just ordered some salad and fries, watching in disgust as her father got served an entire cod, head, and eyes and all. To make up for it, her father bought her mother and B. ice-cream. Then they went back to the car and drove back to the resort. B. went back to her room to get changed, back down again to the bar for a coke before dinner, then dinner, this time together with Bella's parents. They told B. again she absolutely had to meet their daughter. They did not know where she was, though.

"Doesn't she ever get hungry?"

"She most likely does," Francis said, "but I think she has befriended some of the kitchen staff and eats with them. Or down at the river. They are grilling sausages over the fire down there."

"You should go to the river," John told B., "that's where the cool people hang out. Not like us old farts."

B.'s mother cleared her throat.

"Not like us old-timers," John corrected himself.

"I actually talked to a server earlier who offered to take me."

"I think it would be sensible to be accompanied by someone if you want to go," her mother said, adding: "Have we met her?"

"Who?"

"The server."

"Oh, no, you haven't met *him*."

"Oh," her mother said.

"We can ask Billy (the owner) if one of the girls could take you," her father offered.

"That would be nice," B. said. "Or maybe I can go with Bella?"

"If you can find her, sure!" John said, laughing.

"I tell you what: I'll check whether she is in the apartment after dinner and let you know if she is there, okay? We can ask her to take you," Francis said. B. nodded. The main course arrived. John ordered some wine. Her parents, uncharacteristically, shared a bottle with them. They talked about politics and that tech company everyone was investing in. Francis cut off her father at one point, telling him that, whether or not he liked it, tech was the future. He insisted some things would never be replaced, when, suddenly, her mother burst out: "If you ask me – and no one does – all that computer stuff – to me, it is complete bull.... crap. Bullcrap."

There was a moment of silence. Then, her parents, John, Francis burst out laughing. People at the other tables turned their head and B. blushed.

"Another bottle of wine," John yelled into the room. Her mother nodded and her father jokingly: "Sure, darling?" "Oh, I am only getting started," her mother said, imitating the voice of a character from a TV sitcom. "Look at us," Francis added, "all getting tipsy and the only reasonable person at the table is the teenager." *Who?* "B., you really have to head down to the river. Go party. Have fun." "But...," a feeble-sounding protest from B. "Just knock on our apartment. Maybe Bella is there. She will go with you. Or find your servant d'amour." B. blushed. Her mother giggled, her father was about to say something... "Relax," John interrupted him, "we're in paradise here. Nothing happening, nothing bad at least." The second bottle of wine arrived. "Go, B.," Francis told her, a smile on her face. Her parents smiling, nodding, filling the glasses, B. getting up, walking across the room, in a weird way, like walking a across room she'd never walked across.

She left the main building, realising that she was still wearing the cute dress, and she wondered whether she should get changed, wear jeans. She liked the dress, though. The parking lot lay silently in front of her. She wanted to head towards the apartments to find Bella, but was stopped dead in her tracks by a figure coming around the corner from where the staff entrance was.

"There you are!" It was the server from this morning. "I was thinking you wouldn't come."

"Oh. Of course, I came. I am not a square." He laughed, and she appreciated that. "Also, I am looking for a... friend."

"You do not have friends. You have me. Let's go." He turned around and headed towards the forest on the far side of the parking lot. He was carrying a bag and B. heard the clinking of bottles. "What's that?" she asked. "Beer. Stolen from the kitchen." "Really?" "Do I look like a thief? Uh, that sounds like the beginning of a bad pickup line." B. blushed AGAIN! She felt thankful that he was walking briskly in front of her and couldn't see her face. They reached the forest. Far off, B. could hear music. There was a path leading down a small slope until the forest disappeared and the path led them out onto the riverbank. The music got louder, coming from a transistor radio, loud rock'n'roll. There were people swimming in the river and people hanging out at the river's edge. Many people, many more than she'd expected. B. felt shy, silently followed the server, who greeted people sitting around a campfire. "That's...," he started to introduce B., stopped when realising he didn't know her name. "B.," B. introduced herself. "She is staying at the resort. So be nice. She is paying your bills," he finished her introduction. "Hi," a South American-looking woman, a server she recognised from the dining hall, greeted her. "I've seen you before. You are here with your parents. Sit down." She offered B. a seat on the log next to her and B. complied. She did not recognise most of the other faces.

"It's actually good that we finally have a guest joining us," a guy said to her. He was sitting across from B. "We had an argument earlier about the following question: why the hell do people stay at the resort?"

"Mark!" The South American woman retorted. "She is a guest."

"Yeah, but she's chosen to sit with the common people. So, she needs to answer."

"Oh...," B. stammered.

"You are making her feel uncomfortable."

"I am actually here because of my parents...," B. answered.

"But you would go somewhere else if you could?"

"I guess so."

"Imagine, people could be at the beach in Santa Michaela, or have drinks at the Mill, but up here? Nothing ever happens."

"I am telling you," a woman on the other side of the fire said, "once this generation dies, they'll have to close the resort. There is nothing here for young people."

"We have the river," the boy-server said next to her, opening a beer, "and we have the old radio with the latest rock tunes. Beer?" he said to B., offering her a bottle. She did not know what to reply. "I am fairly sure she is not allowed to drink yet," the South American woman said. "Well, the good thing about being a place where nothing happens is there are no police." "Give her a coke." Someone gave her a coke. B. felt overwhelmed – but in a good way – by the people chatting away around her, talking about the state of the resort and life and happiness, asking her for her opinion occasionally, as if she was an expert on anything. After a while, the sun was already setting behind the trees behind their back, she realised that the boy-server who had brought her here had disappeared. She hadn't noticed him getting up, walking away. Her eyes wandered across the bank of the river, trying to find out where he'd gone. There were some people sitting closer to the river, smoking cigarettes. There were some people on a makeshift wooden platform, dancing to music B. could not quite hear, the wood creaking underneath their feet. Then, she realised that the group around her had got silent.

"B.?" the South American lady addressed her. "You have not been listening to a word we have been saying, have you?" The fire was burning brighter, and the flow of the river got louder. The coke in the bottle in B.'s hands tasted funny. "No, no, I haven't," B. admitted. She felt like getting into the river, but the South American lady told her that was probably not a clever idea. It was too cold. The fire was getting dimmer now. The South American lady was silent. B. felt it was time for her to get up and walk back to her room, get some sleep. She saw the shades of the people dancing on the platform.

Then she saw *her*.

Bella dancing, dancing with a server from the resort, her hands on him, his hands on the long of her leg which was half-exposed below her short skirt, and then, the server, her server, kissing, his lips sweet, his sweet lips, dancing together on the platform.

...

B. woke up to a knock on her door. She crawled out of bed, put on a robe, and went to open it. It was a girl, one of the staff from the kitchen. "Ahem, I am sorry. Ms Cunningham has sent me. She asked me to tell you that your parents called to let you know they were running late for breakfast. You should have breakfast alone or wait for them, whichever you prefer."

"Oh, thank you," B. replied. The girl turned around to go off, but B.: "Excuse me, what time is it?" "It is 10:35."

B. went back to her room, showered, put on a clean dress with a flower print, combed her hair and went downstairs. Having a late breakfast, the owner asked her jokingly and brought her to a table. Her parents were nowhere to be seen, she only found John and Francis sitting at there.

"Hey, B., sleep well?" Francis asked her. B. told her that yes, she had slept well and was hungry. They ate breakfast in silence for a while, before, about half an hour later, her parents joined them. They seemed all smiles and giggles this morning and told B. that they'd decided to head over to town to visit a nice restaurant close to the lake for lunch together with Francis and John. "And this time, Bella will join us for sure," John promised. This was when B. excused herself to go to the bathroom to throw up. She told her parents afterwards she was not feeling well and that she might have caught a cold at the river last night. The owner, who was standing next to their table to talk to John and her father, was worried she might have been allergic to something in the food and said he would investigate in the kitchen. Maybe it was a woman thing, Francis said to her, and she nodded. She needed a lie-down but convinced her parents to go with John and Francis to have lunch. She would join them again in the evening for dinner and, hopefully, Bella would do so, too.

B. went to her room and threw up again, this time only acid coming from her empty stomach. She lay on the bed until a knock on the door forced her back to her feet. She went to open it and recognised the boy-server from yesterday. "Ms Cunningham has sent me with some tea. Heard you were sick." She saw the snuck smile on his face as he pushed the trolley carrying the tea into the room. "You look like you can hardly stand," he said. "Yeah. Not very graceful, I know," she replied. "You are full of grace. We learnt that yesterday." "Did we?" He poured tea and put the cup on the coffee table in front of the sofa. Next to it, he placed a pack of cigarettes. It looked hideous, the sofa, B. realised. It made her wanna throw up again. "Hope I see you tonight?" he said, pushing the trolley towards the door. "Sure. Hey, you forgot your cigarettes," she replied. "They are yours." And then he left the room. B. took the cup and sat down on the sofa. Slowly, she sipped the tea. She felt better, surely. Surely, she would feel better soon. She lay down on the sofa. And fell asleep.

It was afternoon when she woke up again. The room felt stuffy, and she opened a window. The sound of faint music was reaching her from the outside. She took a shower, got changed into her jeans and a shirt, left her room. The hallway lay silent, so the downstairs. A single concierge stood behind the reception, but she did not recognise him, and he did not take notice of her. She went outside to the parking lot to see whether she could spot their parents' car – she couldn't. She walked across the parking lot and into the forest, down the path to the river. The seats around the campfire from last night were empty, the only people around were a group dancing orderly on the makeshift platform. A dancing class, she figured. B. sat down on the log she'd been sitting on yesterday and watched the group for a while, thinking about asking them whether she could join.

Slowly, the sun travelled across the sky and B. entered a dream-like state. She felt tired, felt her mind falling asleep while she watched the group dance, repeat the same steps over and over, the instructor showing them how to move their legs and arms. It was getting colder, and B. wished she'd brought a jacket. Or the cigarettes she'd got from... she didn't even know his name. She'd never asked him. Or maybe she had and forgot.

"Ah, you are already here!" the South American lady she had met last night woke her from her reverie. "I brought beers," the lady said with a heavy sigh and sat down on the floor next to her. "You want one?" "Sure," B. said and took the bottle the lady offered. "Did you enjoy yourself last night?" "I did," B. replied. "Looked like it," the lady said, laughing, and B. wondered what she meant exactly. "Listen, a group of us is heading into town tomorrow after lunch. We'll have a party at the beach. I could take you. If your parents allow it, that is." "I am sure they will. If not, I'll just go." "Rebellious spark. I like it."

The place slowly filled with people. Some she'd met yesterday, bringing firewood to start a fire. The group on the makeshift platform had changed. The dancing class had disappeared, replaced by the rowdy crowd from yesterday, and B. was sure she could spot Bella among them, dancing like a whirlwind between boys and girls, touching everyone she wanted to touch, dancing with everyone she wanted to dance with. If Bella had been in town with her parents and was now here, that meant that her parents were back as well. They would have dinner soon.

"B., you are alive!" The server, her boy-server, sitting down next to her. "Do you need food?" Without waiting for her answer, he passed her a sandwich, which she ate up quickly. "You looked a little cheesy this morning. Pale. Looked like death warmed up. Partying does not become you." B. blushed. "I vomited," she admitted quietly, "in the toilet next to the dining hall." "That was you!" the South American lady yelled, "I had to clean it up!"

Everyone, including B., laughed. B. finished her beer. Then she got up. The server looked at her. "I'm gonna dance. Do you want to join me?" she said in his direction. He said yes and got up, too.

…

She woke up to a knock at the door. She crawled out of bed and yelled: "Whoisit?" on her way to the door, not getting a reply. She opened the door and found an abandoned serving trolley carrying a steaming cup of coffee. She grabbed the cup and closed the door. Her head felt stuffy, luckily not as bad as yesterday, though. She sat down on the couch and sipped the coffee. The server's pack of cigarettes, which she hadn't touched yesterday, had disappeared – shame, she thought to herself, otherwise she could smoke one of them while standing at the open window.

She finished the coffee, got dressed (jeans and a shirt) and headed downstairs. Francis and John were sitting at the table having breakfast and she joined them. "How was your evening?" Francis addressed B. Good, she replied, "I was at the river." "We had dinner and stayed up for quite a while. You should have joined us," John said. "Maybe tonight?" Francis added. "I can't," B. replied, "I am heading into town with some of the staff." "Ah. Oh," Francis said, a tone in her voice that struck B. as sounding like disappointment. Or disapproval. Or anything she could not quite place. After breakfast, B. headed over to the bunga-lows to see whether her parents were up. No one answered her knocks on the door, so she left a note on the door informing her parents that she was going into town, and they should have dinner without her.

She returned to the main building and waited in the alley in front of the staff entrance for the South American lady – Luz. There was a window into the kitchen next to the entrance, and she could see the staff hustle and bustle about inside. A dance of work and life, of food being brought back and forth, of people almost colliding, talking, yelling, laughing.

Then she saw *him*. The boy-server, hurrying past the window, talking to someone behind him. Then *she* appeared. Bella. Of course. Always Bella, the girl she would never meet. For a brief second, B. envied her for being in the kitchen, a place where she should not be, Bella being a guest, not a member of staff. Bella and the server were talking to each other. It almost looked like an argument. Suddenly, he stopped and stepped towards her and... kissed her. She kissed him back, pulling him closer, touching the back of his head, holding his hair. The kiss ended, and she looked at his eyes for five, ten seconds, turned around and disappeared out of sight without saying another word. No one else of the staff had taken notice of the scene. B. turned around and sat down against the wall. Her chest hurt. She watched a flock of birds circling in the sky above, up and down and back and forth.

Luz appeared around half an hour later – not that B. would have noticed, since she'd fallen asleep.

"So, the stories about you are true," Luz said as B. woke up.

"Yes, I can fall asleep anytime and anywhere."

"Don't be so defensive about it. One day you'll realise that is the greatest skill of them all. Shall we?"

They walked across the parking lot. With amazement, B. watched Luz not go to a car, but to a Vespa, where she took out two helmets from under the seat, gave one to B., put the other one on herself.

"Are we heading into town with... this?"

"Don't you like it?"

"Are you kidding me? I love it!"

The Vespa purred under her bum like a content cat as they headed out of the parking lot and up the mountain road. The resort disappeared behind and underneath them. On her left, the mountain rose like an unclimbable, towering wall, to her right, the valley grew larger and larger. She felt like stretching her arms out and screaming, like an eagle, so she did, and Luz almost lost control over the Vespa, startled by her scream. They reached the top of a mountain plateau, and the resort was only an infinitesimal speck behind them. In front of them, down below, she could see the sea and the small seaside town they were heading to. The wind hit her face thanks to the Vespa gaining speed down the mountain road, and she could feel her pulse speeding up.

"What did you argue with Eric about?" she heard Luz yell in front of her.

"Who?" she yelled back.

"Eric!" Her boy-server.

"We did not argue," she replied, but was not sure whether Luz had heard her. And to be honest, she did not care all that much. She'd rather take in the scenery while they descended the mountain and drove into the port town. It was like stepping into a different world, something from a movie, something quiet, something that would never change, not in a million years.

"A movie set!" she cried out. Luz was decelerating, looking for a spot to park the Vespa.

"What was that?"

"This place looks like a movie set," she repeated. Luz laughed and took a right into a parking lot. "We can walk along the pier from here. Let's have lunch in town. And then off to the beach."

"Sounds like a plan," B. said.

They walked along the pier, then to the left into town. Luz led B. down a row of small houses, little more than shacks, each of them operating a grill with fish and meats of various kinds. Luz bought her a mixed skewer, and they sat down on a rock, eating, and looking at the sea, the waves crashing in and out.

"When are you heading home?"

"Tomorrow."

"You looking forward to it?"

"Being home with my parents? Sure. They are perfect."

"They seem nice."

"They are."

"For me, it is a couple more months in the kitchen. Then the season is over."

The waves kept crashing.

"And then?"

"I'll look for another job. Maybe head north, maybe try to work in a winter resort. Travel with the season."

"When is the last time you have been home? South America?"

"I haven't been. Not since I left."

"Don't you miss it?"

"Some of it. My parents. My brother. But I had to leave to find a job. I am trying to save money to visit. Flights are expensive."

"I have never been on an airplane."

"You should tell your parents you'd wanna go to Italy for your next holiday or something. I am sure they would take you. Also, the resort must be getting old for you."

Luz bought her ice cream at another shack, and they walked along the seaside of the town. The wind had picked up. B. was glad she had brought a jacket. Luz bought some cans of beer at a small shop, and they walked further along, between the sea and the houses and then onto the sand of a stretched-out beach. They found other staff members from the resort there, sitting around a fire, watching the sun, which had begun its slow descent towards the horizon. The server, her boy-server, was already there. Luz and B. distributed the beer among the people. A guy with a guitar was playing a famous song and some of the staff were singing along. The wind grew ever stronger, which made it difficult to understand what they were singing.

"I guess this is our only chance to get into the water. Before it gets too cold," Luz next to her said, taking off her top.

"I did not bring a swimsuit," B. said.

"You are wearing a bra and underwear, no?"

She hesitated. Then exclaimed: "Oh my god...," and took off her top and jeans. "No one look!" She was wearing a matching turquoise panty and bra. She felt naked.

"Can I come as well?" the boy-server.

"You pervert," Luz said half-jokingly.

"It is a free world," B. said.

Luz grabbed her hand and, together, they ran towards the water and into the sea. It was cold and harsh, the waves crashed against her ankles, legs, then her entire body as they both dived in. She dipped her head under water and the wind became quiet for a moment. Only a few meters behind them, the server had followed, wearing only boxers, now also diving into the sea. He came up just in front of B. and she splashed him with water. He splashed back. The game went on for a while, the server, B., and Luz splashing each other with cold, salty sea-water and laughing like little children.

Then, they just floated in the ocean, watching the sun march towards the horizon. The colour of the world changed from harsh and bright to something more soothing and warmer. "I am getting cold. I am going out," Luz said and swam towards the shore. "We should get out as well," B. said. She turned her body around, treading water, holding her head above. Her wet hair stuck to her face and her cheeks had taken on a pink colour. The server turned around as well to look at her. For a long, long, long time.

"I don't get you," he said.

"What is not to get?" B. said.

"Do you want to kiss?"

"No."

"You are leaving tomorrow."

"Yes."

"We might never see each other again."

"I know."

"I want to see you again."

"I know."

"Let's get out of here. Let's go for a walk and talk. Let's make out in an alleyway," he said, almost pleading. And then, he added:

"B., I love you."

That felt good. It felt good to hear these words. She looked at him, struggling to stay above water, struggling against the waves. She looked at the guy and his teary eyes, his pleading look, his small shoulders, and thin arms. He was just a boy, afraid of losing his favourite toy. He'd find a new one.

"Eric... it was fun. But we gotta move on. I have moved on. You will move on."

He did not reply. She tasted the salt on her lips.

"I'll go back to the others."

She swam to the shore and re-joined the group. Luz gave her a big towel which she wrapped around herself. Someone gave her a beer.

They grilled meat over the fire. They talked about the state of the world and this place. About how everyone hoped not to be back at the resort for the next summer season.

...

A knock on the door woke her up the next morning. She got up and yelled something through the door without opening it. "Excuse me," replied an unknown voice, "your parents asked me to let you know you will leave in an hour. If you want breakfast, you should join them now." "Please tell them I will meet them at the car." "Sure."

She showered, got dressed, packed her bag, moved her bag down to the reception. Then she went into the kitchen, hoping to find Luz to say goodbye, but she was nowhere to be seen. On the way out, she grabbed two slices of toast and a green apple.

She went outside into the parking lot, where she sat on the hood of their parent's car and ate her improvised breakfast. A little while later, her parents appeared from the building.

"How was your evening?" her father asked her.

"It was great, actually. We went to the village."

"Cool. Did you have dinner?"

"We had barbecue. Like the wilder people."

"They served roast again last night."

"Was it good?"

"It was okay, I guess," her mother replied. "The food here seems to get worse."

"I have been saying we should go somewhere else," she replied.

"And miss out on all the fun up here?" her father/John said. She was not sure whether he meant it as a joke. They got into the car. "This car is getting old," she commented on the creaking of the back bench. John turned on the radio. A rock'n'roll song came on. "Louder," she yelled from the backseat. "Ah, what terrible noise," her mother/Frances said with a smile on her face.

#

We arrived in Kyoto and, like all the other tourists, I took my heavy suitcase and left the train. Unlike most of the tourists, though, I had not arrived at my final destination. I stumbled through the train station, following the signs to the train that was bound for Nara – for most only a day trip during their stay in Kyoto, for me, an overnight trip, off the beaten path kind of thing. I arrived at the designated platform and saw with some surprise that the departure time on the sign did not match the time I had looked up yesterday evening on my phone. But the train in front of me was Nara-bound.

Was this a different train? Wrong time? My mistake? I entered the car. The direction was right.

What was the worst that could happen?

In the grand scheme of things, it wasn't the worst, yet bad enough to send my plans into turmoil. I had caught a train that stopped at every station, every small, tiny station, edging forward at a snail's pace. The other train, the fast one, the one I had intended to take, soon zoomed past us, a strike of lightning, a bullet. Through the windows of my slow train, it seemed, I saw people in the other train looking at me with glee, mocking me for my mistake.

My plan had been to arrive in Nara just around lunchtime, take a taxi to my hostel, which was located somewhat outside town, and then walk back into town for a late lunch at around 2 o'clock. I had marked a restaurant serving eel on my map. If this train would continue as slow as it was – my estimate was that it would take us another forty minutes to arrive in Nara – I might make dinner.

But I was hungry now. And in a foul mood now. I shouldn't have been so stressed out about this. Dude, you are on holiday. Be the dude. Go with the flow, I told myself. Fuck you, I told myself.

Backup plan. I would leave my luggage in a locker at the train station, head on out to the restaurant, eat, make my way back to the train station, pick up my luggage and head to the hostel for an early night in. Easy. Stress level decreased. New plan. Good plan.

One and a half eternities later, we arrived in Nara, where I promptly encountered a fresh problem: there were no lockers at the train station. Dismay. Doom. I walked the length of the station, losing more precious time, but couldn't find any lockers.

Backup plan addendum: I found a tourist information centre that doubled as a luggage holding facility. It cost me 700 yen – which seemed like a steep price – yet the thought of a traditional restaurant serving traditional eel seemed to be worth it. What was 7 bucks in the grand scheme of eel?

Of course, a second problem followed soon after: the restaurant was further away from the train station than I'd expected. My phone's map told me it shouldn't be further than ten minutes. However, the time estimate on my phone did not change after walking ten minutes. Technology had failed me.

Backup plan addendum number two: I kept going. My stomach a loud, growling monster. Eel we come.

My mood hung by a thread when I finally reached the location of the pin on my map (25 minutes!) and, you could not make this shit up, encountered a third problem: the pin was not accurate. Or the restaurant was not in the street where it was supposed to be. I walked the entirety of the narrow road twice, unable to find it.

Backup plan, final addendum: I kept walking up and down the road, then switched to another minor road running parallel to it, alas, to no avail. I cursed the gods, the old and the new, fate and all eel in the world, until, by chance, my angry-hungry eyes spotted the smallest, silliest passageway between two houses leading into yet-another, even smaller road running between the two small roads I'd been pacing for the better part of twenty minutes. On that third road, the tiny-tiniest road, I found a doorway that looked like it could be the entrance of a restaurant – or not. I stood there for another eternity, working up the courage to open the door and stepping on through. For all I knew, I could be walking into someone's private home.

Ah, eel it.

My heart was beating disproportionately fast as I finally stepped through the door.

Only two minutes later, I was sitting on the tatami floor at a small table and had ordered my eel-meal. And felt annoyed at myself for having turned this into such a huge deal. Eel-deal. I had found the restaurant, my luggage was safe, I would get my eel. Life was good.

I ordered some sake, for good measure, to calm down, which arrived promptly. Taking a sip, I wondered whether I should learn more about sake, the different tastes, the different regions it came from. I could do so right now, on my phone, educate myself, if I had mobile data in Japan, or had a mobile Wi-Fi-thing. I had neither, so all I could do was sit, wait, and take a mental note to look the topic up later in the hostel. And forget said mental note.

The eel, eel of eels, what an eeling, arrived. It was exactly what I had imagined it to be. The fish was covered in a dark, thick Teriyaki-like sauce and lay on a bed of pristine white rice.

I took my chopsticks and tore off a piece of the animal. The texture of the meat differed from most other fish. It was a heavy, strong kind of meat, not fishy in the slightest, accompanied by a faint, agreeable hint of burned wood and smoke.

What had always amazed me about eel was how un-placeable its taste was. If I'd taste the eel without knowing what it was, I would have a tough time telling I was eating fish – only the small fish bones would give me a clue. Eel was the chicken of the sea. Tasted like any-thing. A mash of unknown origin, a freak of nature, an anomaly in the seafood cuisine.

I felt slightly light-headed by the time I finished the m-eel, maybe because I'd been anticipating it all day, or maybe because I had drunk the sake much too fast. Not very gracefully, I got up, not because I'd been drunk, but that was how the overweight me got up from the floor. It never looked nice, more like a whale that tried to walk. I was whale-aware of my aesthetic limitations.

Back at the train station, I claimed my suitcase, bought some food for the evening, and found a taxi. I tried to explain to the driver where I had to go. He was friendly, even though we had problems communicating. I pointed to the name of the hostel on a piece of paper. Unfortunately, I had printed the name in English, not in Japanese, and he couldn't read it. We sat there for a while, in failed-communication land, the driver shrugging, not knowing what to do, in a very friendly way, though, smilingly, shrugging and smiling and me smiling as well and shrugging, too.

We finally could resolve the situation by him spotting the phone number of the hostel on my printout. He promptly gestured me to wait, entered the phone number into his GPS, whereupon the device told him the address. The marvels of technology.

We drove off.

The streets of Nara were full of people. Too many people walking along the streets and spilling over crossroads. Yet, the world felt oddly quiet. There was some magic to it, like watching a movie from the outside, full of extras, the main plot out of view. The people seemed to walk slower than normal, and the lights of the dusking sun seemed wrong, too orange, and too weak at the same time.

We left the town behind, and I saw deer roaming the parks surrounding the city. Nara was famous for them, the semi-tame deer wandering around, hoping for a bite to eat from the visitors.

We arrived. I paid my fare and walked towards a flight of stairs the taxi driver had pointed me to, houses on either side. The sun had settled, and it was getting dark. A deer stood atop the steps, his gaze calmly following me as I lugged my oversized suitcase past him/her. There was a shop on my right, selling souvenirs, deer biscuits, Japanese mementos. Halfway down the steps, on the left, I found a door with the name of my hostel on a sign above.

I entered, took off my shoes in the designated take-off area just behind the entrance. In front of me, there was the reception and the man behind the desk greeted me friendly, walked around and helped lift my luggage onto the wooden floor in front of the reception. With a few fast steps, he was behind the desk again and asked me whether I had a reservation.

I had one. A single room. As he was typing in my name, I took in the space I had entered. To my right, a hallway led to several wash basins, the toilets, and showers. On the left, there was a semi-open space with an enormous table and a small kitchen in a corner. Lots of dark, heavy wood around, which made the place look like a hunting lodge. Not that I'd ever been to a hunting lodge, but if there were stereotypes of a hunting lodge in my brain, this was what they looked like. An old, creaky, wooden building, heavy beams hanging down from the low ceiling. The only thing that broke that impression was the gentle Jack Johnson music that emanated from the kitchen-common area. Hunters listening to Jack Johnson kissing each other on their moustached faces.

"Ah, yes. You have a single room for two nights," the receptionist told me. He made a copy of my passport and handed me a key. He then explained to me that there were no restaurants open in the vicinity at this time. If I were hungry, I could either walk back into town (half an hour walk), he could call me a taxi, or I could let him know whether I wanted to order something, and he would help me do so.

I thanked him. I wasn't hungry at the moment. The eel still swam in my bowels.

He led me around the lodge-not-lodge, showed me the kitchen, table, shower, toilets, then my room, which was small and functional, but with a dramatically big window overlooking a small grass patch on the other side of the narrow alley. I liked this place, I decided, not because it was terribly nice, just because it was different from any other hostel I had stayed at before.

He left me alone in my room. I unpacked my most necessary items, afterwards I went outside for a walk to think about dinner. I was still not hungry, and I had come prepared, having bought food, drinks, and nibbles before I'd come up here. However, the thought of just staying in my room for the rest of the night felt weird. Like a waste of holiday time.

I would not walk into town, I decided, as I stepped outside and found that it had begun to rain. It was a gentle rain, drizzle. Bearable for a small stroll, not appealing for a half-an-hour walk. I climbed up the stairs I had come from. To the right, in the darkness, there was a hilly, grassy area, and it seemed I saw the silhouettes of deer roaming the field in darkness. To the left, a road wound downwards, house after house on its left side, shops and restaurants, all of them dark, silent. It was as the receptionist had warned me. The world up here had closed for the night.

My walk did not take me far, since the rain became heavier, more aggressive. I turned back, back to the hostel and decided to have an early night in after all, read for a bit, munch on the food I had bought, drink a couple of beers.

There were some people in the shared area when I came back, murmuring to each other, eating at the table. I felt like an intruder, out of place, so I went back to my room, closed the door behind me, ate my food by myself, drank my beers, watched Netflix (The Good Place) on my iPad, thought about writing, felt useless, felt like I should do something worthwhile, I should work on my book. I was too tired to do so. I lay on my bed and listened to music, slowly falling asleep, forgot to brush my teeth.

Little did I know that, tomorrow, my sister would call and tell me that the dog had died.

I woke up early the next morning and opened the curtains covering the dramatically large window of my room. I spotted nothing that caught my attention.

The drizzle had not stopped, so I took my umbrella and a hoodie with me. I had my plan ready in my mind, built from hours of research on the net and in my guidebook. First, I would take the stairs down and follow a path leading into a forest and to a temple. Photo time. Instagram would be impressed.

The forest was wet and heavy, which made the temple look like something from a Ghibli movie. Its stony archways were covered in moss and grass. I followed some tracks in the forest past fields of what looked like Buddhist gravestones (or were they?), to another temple, took another few snapshots with my camera. Good enough.

I made my way back the way I had come, left the forest, and followed the road to the next part of the plan. I had, in my research, found a place that apparently served outstanding quiche. As weird as the thought seemed, to eat quiche in Japan, as eager was I to see what the classic European dish would look like through the lens of Japanese perfection.

The place had the atmosphere of a small café and the lady behind the counter, whose display was filled to the brim with slices of different quiches, seemed flustered to have me enter the place. It was only eleven, and I was probably too early for lunch.

Still, I asked her whether it would be possible to eat something, but she informed me that all the spaces in the restaurant were reserved. I felt envy for those people who would occupy those empty chairs and tables, tables I had no access to. I could buy quiche to go, if I didn't mind, the lady told me in English. I did mind but selected three generous pieces of quiche (classic, vegetables and, of all things, of course, eel), which she carefully took from the display and skilfully packaged in a box. She put a ribbon around the box, making it look like a precious gift. Japanese package perfection. Yes, it was a gift. To myself and myself only. Fuck the ghosts of people who would soon occupy this place.

My hostel was close-by, so I took my perfectly packed pieces of quiche and went back to my room, where I sat down and ate the quiche in silence, looking out of the dramatically large window, which still did not show me anything interesting. Of course, the quiches were delicious, but I regretted the fact that I had no way of heating them up. Cold quiche was kinda cold.

It was eleven thirty. Next step of my plan. I walked up the stairs in front of the hostel. The receptionist had told me there was a cafe at the top of the steps. Coffee, as always, sounded like a good idea.

The place was effortlessly hip. It was built into a big open-plan room that looked like it must have been a garage or a workshop at some point. It was filled with tables and couches, yet I was the sole customer. Maybe it was the harsh weather, the drizzle, which kept people from coming out here.

There was a woman, maybe my age, and I ordered a flat white and sat down. I tried to spy on her while she was making the coffee. She seemed insecure, her movements not as fast and purposeful as some of the baristas' I'd seen in Tokyo. Also, with some dismay, I heard a high-pitched, metallic shwsh-sound when she steamed the milk, a sound that usually meant that the steaming process was done too fast, or the milk was getting too hot.

It was not the best coffee I had ever had. Sure enough, it was too hot and, what was worse, the espresso shot had no clearly defined taste that could compete against the burned milk. Still, despite the mediocre coffee, I decided to like the place – maybe because the lady had given me a friendly smile when she served the coffee and seemed genuinely happy to have me in her shop. The rain outside continued. The faint music coming from behind the counter, some American guitar singer-song-writer kind of thing, softened the sound of the drops and put me at ease.

The thing with bad things happening while you are far away from home is that you have no control. Of course, it is not like you'd have any control over the bad things in any case, you can't stop bad things, but being close to them happening at least gives you the illusion of control. When you are far away from them, all you have is being alone with your emotions.

It wasn't "our" dog that died today. It was my sister's and mother's dog, but I'd often taken the animal for walks when I visited them. I felt attached to the dog, who took turns either staying at my sister's or my mother's. They lived close to each other and shared ownership of the animal, met often to go on walks together with her. Had I already known at this point that the dog would die today, I would have wondered what effect her death would have on the relationship between my mother and my sister. But I didn't know it back then, when I sat there, drinking not the best coffee in the world, so I didn't think about these things. I only knew that our dog was getting old, and I had suspected, when I visited my mother and my sister on the weekend before I'd left for Japan, that she would not get much older, I hadn't suspected that I would never see her again, though.

I lived a few hours away from my mother and my sister, so, on that weekend, like always, I'd slept at my mother's, in her guest room. As always, the dog followed me when I went to bed and stood next to the bed and, as always, I gave her permission to jump onto the bed. She curled up on my pillow while I left the room to brush my teeth and I knew I shouldn't allow her to be on the bed, but she looked cute, and I didn't have the emotional strength to be strict with her. I came back from the bathroom, and she lifted her head, as always, lifted herself up and trotted to the other end of the bed to lie at my feet.

The thing with dogs is they will always give you the feeling that they like you. Maybe it is Pavlovian, you are the gatekeeper to their food, and they like the person with the food, but it does not matter. They will give you that feeling, even when you make mistakes, when you yell at them or accidentally step on their tail. In the eyes of a dog, you are always a good person.

The funny thing with a dog is, spelled backwards, it becomes a god. I'd have laughed at the thought in the cafe if I had had that thought, but there was no reason to think about dogs, so I didn't laugh. I finished my coffee and paid and left, embarked on the rest of the plan, which brought me to a big temple, Nara's main tourist attraction that featured one of Japan's biggest Buddha statues.

It was a beautiful temple, and the colossal Buddha statue inside was awe-inspiring, yet I felt annoyed by the hordes of people roaming the place, taking pictures, destroying any possibility for me to feel any kind of spirituality within. You'd think that you stand at the bottom of one of the big Buddhas – the statue was a good thirteen meters tall – and be inspired, feel something, have a thought that is profound. I was not a religious person, still, I understood the spiritual quality some places of worship had and sometimes wished I'd feel it. However, I also understood that these places were not magical, but only seemed special because we humans assigned that quality to them. A church was a house of god because we called it a house of god. A graveyard was a solemn and quiet place because we decided it was a graveyard. A grave yard. Without us assigning that quality, a graveyard would just be a field with dead bodies in it.

No place was inherently special.

I left and walked towards the city centre. The city, or town, was bustling with people, too many of them in too small a space, and I felt uncomfortable. I crammed myself into a tiny ramen place, sitting at the counter. The barstool, unfortunately, was bolted to the floor, so I had to sit too close to the counter, my knees pushed against the bar, my ass hanging over the back of the stool and my belly squished between my legs, the counter and my upper body, a position that reminded me I should lose weight and I wondered how it felt for a thin, normal person to sit there.

I ate ramen. Good thing to eat for those who do not want to lose weight. The chicken broth was heavy, had almost a creamy, thick quality. It was good. Still, I concluded I preferred the clearer shio- or shoyu-style ramen.

It was a half an hour's walk back to the hostel. I had nothing else to do, and the drizzle had stopped, so I undertook the walk. It was on my way back to the hostel that I sent my sister a text, asking her how she was.

She sent me a text saying she was fine, but asking me whether I could call her, maybe when I was connected to Wi-Fi, call her over WhatsApp, a call to check in, to say hi. I should have known then and there that something was wrong, that it seemed out of place for my sister to ask me to call her.

I called her when I was back in the hostel. She started to cry almost at once when I asked her how she was doing and told me that the dog had died. Then, I cried as well, for a bit, on the phone tried to contain myself, tried to think of something smart to say, something soothing. I could not come up with anything. So, most of our conversation consisted of solemn silence and quiet sobbing.

Was that why we had sayings? Fixed expressions for when you do not know what to say? There is plenty more dogs out in the grass. You can get a new one. Or: she is in a better place now. It was a good thing she die in peace. She didn't have to suffer. Or: in Africa, children are starving. Don't you think they wouldn't snarl at us for crying over a dead dog?

"I'm sorry," I told my sister and my mother. I was sorry for not being there. For not knowing how they would cope with it. For not being able to estimate how fragile the death of the dog would make them. Dog is dead.

We changed the topic and talked for a bit about the mundane stuff. I told them I was doing fine and had a great time, even though it felt out of place. There is plenty more Japan where that came from. I wondered how many dogs had died today. And how many of them had owners to cry over them.

We talked for a little while, but most of what I said was useless. Empty words. I told them to eat something, and that was it. We ended the call. And it was only then that I realised I would never see the dog again. Would never visit my sister and mother again and sleep in the guest room and have the dog standing patiently next to my bed until I would give her permission to jump onto it, even though I shouldn't do so, a thing that had become like a ritual, a repetition of a nice moment. The ritual was gone now. How does one cope with those broken rituals that brittle like bones and wither away like dust in the wind?

The world kept turning. Around the sun. A dance of its own ritual held together by the power of gravity. Little did the planet know, then and there, that this would not last forever. But the sun would not tell her. The insignificant planet would never know.

Part III: You

Poppy Field

You were only half-asleep, but the constant rumbling of the grey-hound bus lulled your thoughts into a state that was not too far off from sleeping. No clear thoughts, just you looking out of the window, watching the endless progression of wheat fields pass by. It was a grey day, and the sky had taken on the colour of a TV turned to a dead channel. Your feet still hurt, and you wondered how many hours you had spent on this bus.

The bus had left shortly before midnight. It was now... seven or eight? Sometimes you wished you had a wristwatch. Such a convenient, old-fashioned way to carry the time around. Of course, you could have taken the phone from your pocket and checked the screen. You felt too lazy to move, though. You were even too lazy to change the music playing in your earphones, even though Spotify had decided to bless your morning with a selection of throwback-nineties music.

The Backstreet Boys were just about to inform you they were back when the bus slowed down and drove into the parking lot of a rest stop. "Next stop is in over two hours," the bus driver informed everyone, "so if you gotta use the restroom, you better do it now. We will leave again in twenty."

The thought of getting up very much played against the inherent laziness that had taken hold of your body, yet you concluded that peeing was a good idea, so you heaved yourself out of your bus seat – it felt like you left a you-shaped impression behind – and got off the bus. You took the chance of having brought your body into motion to change the music – something more appropriate for an early morning – maybe a bit of singer-songwriter-stuff to take the edge off.

It was seven o'clock, you learned from your mobile. The world outside the bus felt the same way it looked – grey and cold. The fields around the rest stop were wet and shiny from last night's rain. The rest stop itself consisted of a small house with toilets for men on the right and for women on the left. In front of the building, there was a vending machine. And that was about it. You turned left and into the toilets and, luckily, found an empty stall. It was not the cleanest place. Much less grungy, though, than you'd feared looking at the toilet shack from the outside.

While you were hovering above the toilet seat, you heard voices over the sound of the music in your ears and turned the music off. Two ladies, most likely from the bus as well, had entered the room and were talking to each other loudly while splashing their faces with water from the tap.

"My behind feels like it is on fire. I'll never take the bus again."

"At least it is better for the environment than flying."

"My bum or the environment. Hard choice."

"Hard seats."

"Definitively. And have you seen the stuff people brought onto the bus? Freaking Kentucky Fried Chicken. On a bus. That is a special kind of evil."

"They should ban smelly foods from confined spaces."

"And feet."

"Huh?"

"Smelly feet."

You were done, but you felt weird flushing and getting out of the stall now. It felt like admitting you'd been eavesdropping.

"It is cheaper for a reason."

"Teleportation." The lady moved to the empty stall left to you.

"What?" The other was still at the washbasin. They were shouting across the room now.

"I am just saying they should invent it. Teleportation. Would be good for everyone. Would make travelling much easier."

"And then I would have to see my mother every weekend? No, thank you."

"Every day. You could live right next to her. Teleport to work in the big city, teleport home to farmingsville in the evening."

"Farmingsville. Not funny."

You chuckled quietly to yourself. It felt like a suitable name for the towns around here.

"Relax. Your mother is not that bad." Finally, the lady moved to the last empty stall... which was to the right of you. Why had you taken the middle stall?

"If she could, she would close the border, fly a confederate flag in her garden and get rid of everyone who is a slight shade darker than Snow-White-white."

You had to get out of there, there was no way around it. You got up, pulled your trousers up and flushed.

"Old-fashioned, yes, but not that bad. She is not racist, certainly." They didn't mind your flushing. Or your presence. They just continued.

"My first boyfriend was half-white, half-Hispanic. You couldn't even see it. But it was there in his name. She lectured me for two hours straight about how he would sneak into our house and steal her priceless collection of silver spoons." You opened the door and walked to the washbasins, which had been completely flooded by the ladies' face-washing activities.

"Silver spoons?"

"Yeah, spoons made from silver."

"Your mom owns silver? Good to know."

"Not funny. She'll kill you if you make a joke about that."

"She'll kill me anyway at some point."

You washed and dried your hands. The mood in the stalls behind you had changed. The voices were quieter now.

"We have to tell her... somehow. About us."

"Someday we will. Somehow."

You left the restroom.

The bus was still there. You still had time and turned your attention to the vending machine. A coke sounded nice. Or some sweets. Some comfort for the rest of the way. Chocolate. They had canned coffee in there as well. Chocolate bar and canned coffee. You regretted the fact you had thrown away your last pack of cigarettes because canned coffee and a smoke sounded like the badass thing to do. You got change from your pockets-

You didn't have any change. Zero coins. The machine did not take bills. That was the end of that.

"Leaving in five," you heard the bus driver holler from across the parking lot. Might as well head back to the bus, when- "You need change?" a lady had walked up behind you. Her hair had the colour of a purple Skittle that had been dissolved in a glass of carbonated water. She must have died it darker at one point, but most of the colour had washed out and left behind a hairdo of not-quite-grey-not-quite-coloured.

"Change?" she repeated her offer, and you hoped you had not been looking at her hair for too long and too intensively and said: "Yes, that would be nice. For a coffee. I am all out." "I'll get you one." Her voice sounded vaguely familiar, your brain had no time to catch on, though. Instead, you tried to initiate some kind of friendly social interaction to make up for your rude staring. "You are heading to Galena as well?" you asked her while she was putting change into the machine. "A coffee you said?" "Yes, number, uhm, thirty-two." "Ah. No, we are getting off at Smallfield. Me and my friend." She gestured towards another lady standing next to the bus smoking a cigarette. "Here you go." The can of coffee fell to the bottom of the machine. "Thank you so much."

"Everyone on the bus!" the driver again. Together, you and the lady walked back, and the lady asked you about Galena and you told her you'd grown up there. In fact, that, somehow, you still lived there, but you had just spent some time away. She asked you whether you'd been to the coast and you told her that, yes, you had, both of them. You approached the smoking lady who looked younger than the lady with the washed-out violet hair, her hair shorter and fully black. She was wearing a red bandana and her left arm was covered in tattoos (not her right arm, tough, which gave her body a peculiar imbalance). You wished each other a good onward-journey and got back into your seats.

They waved at you when they got off at Smallfield forty-five minutes later.

It was still a grey, cold, rainy day when you got off the bus in the town you called home. Your head felt like there was a headache incoming. Your feet still hurt. You looked around, the bus station behind you, a big parking lot in front of you, a convenience store off to the side. You tried to see a sign of your brother or his offensively loud car, but there was none. He was running late, which was not quite a surprise to you.

You remembered the convenience store. You stole a chewing gum from the place on a dare when you'd been young, and you still felt a hint of guilt about it. You remembered it never had been the same going back to that store, always that feeling that they might figure out that you had been the clandestine who had stolen that one chewing gum worth 10 cents all that time ago, when, in fact, it had just been a blip in the system that had shown up and disappeared, lost in the accounting of decades.

For a while, it had felt like you didn't live here anymore. In this small town. Like you finally had made it and moved away. You sat down on the bench next to the bus stop, hoping that your brother would arrive soon. Your skin felt dry, and you tried to ignore the blisters and bruises on your feet, even though the pain seemed to get worse. The pain that had accumulated over the past few months, you dancing on a new stage every day, sometimes twice a day, only with the occasional Monday off. It had been a dancer's dream, especially for a dancer with no formal education in the arts, a dancer who had all her knowledge from weekend courses she'd taken in the slightly bigger town two hours from home and from the internet and from books and from the love she had for the movement, the precision, the wordless emotion that lived within a good choreography.

It had been like a dream to be in that solo-show, choreographed by a smart director, a sixty-minute piece dedicated just to you and your body and the way you moved, in small and smaller venues across the country. It had been a wild shot, going to the audition for the piece, and you knew you hadn't got it because you'd been the best dancer, but because your small-town-vulnerability had been exactly what the director had been looking for.

It started to rain again, and you wondered whether you should wait inside the shop, only to conclude that the rain might wake you up and maybe, if you were lucky, you'd catch a cold and have an excuse to stay in bed for the next few days. Rain was running down your forehead. You'd left your umbrella in a hotel somewhere.

It had been like a nightmare. Going on stage every night dancing what you felt. Dancing the emotions of a choreography that felt like undressing in front of the audience, showing them parts of your body you do not show many people. It was the vulnerability of raw emotions, of dancing the naked parts of your soul that had fascinated you about the project. It was this fascination that made you dance till your feet bled and made the audience clap in admiration for your commitment, and it was this fascination that nearly killed you. A fascination as if you were standing on the top of a bridge ready to jump, while, at the same time, you had already arrived at the bottom, while, at the same time, you tried to hold yourself back.

"Hey!"

Your brother woke you from your revery. You mumbled a hey in response before he closed in and gave you a hug. You felt even more tired now, and you quietly followed him to and into his car, listening to his updates on small-town life. Ms Keyran's cat had died. The bakery down the road had closed (he pointed out the empty building when you drove past). Mom had sold your old car. The Hot Dog stand was still going strong.

And Grandma was still sad she hadn't been healthy enough to come and see your dance when you'd performed it in the slightly bigger town two hours away.

"Maybe you could perform a bit of it again. Just for her after dinner? I am sure she'd like it."

The rain was falling against the windshield and your brother took a turn to the right, off the main road. You could see your family's house, your home at the end of the street, a dusty, small street surrounded by empty fields.

"I don't think so," you replied to your brother. "I do not think that would be a good idea. I don't have the music with me. Maybe later if I find it online."

There was no big fanfare to you coming home. No secret surprise party, no people jumping out from behind the couch, no cake. Your brother entered the house in front of you and threw the car keys onto the kitchen table. "We're back!" Your mother was fussing about the kitchen, and you could smell the evening roast in the oven. She gave you a quick kiss on the cheek and hugged you before she continued her fussing. Your brother got a coke out of the fridge. Your father was in the living room watching a football game, but he yelled a friendly hello (without taking his eyes off the TV, of course). He informed you that whatever team he was supporting now was in the lead and might just make it and that you should absolutely sit down and watch the game with him. You put your bag down in the kitchen. "Oh, honey," your mother said, "can you put your bag in your room? You can start unpacking. And put the dirty laundry in the laundry room. Oh, and can you get the laundry basket from the bathroom upstairs while you are at it?"

"See, sister," your brother sitting at the counter sipping from his coke, smirking at you, "you are gone for three months, and everything has changed... and by everything, I mean nothing."

"Yeah, I got it. No need to explain the joke."

Your room finally felt like a place you knew. The accumulation of who you'd been up to this point and who you were now, the room having changed with you from childhood to adulthood, housing the stuffed animals you'd carried around as a toddler, the picture books you'd looked at a million times, the posters you hung as a teenager –

this room was probably a more accurate representation of you than you yourself were most of the time. You put down your bag and fell onto your bed. It felt smaller than you remembered, maybe because you'd got used to hotel beds.

You took off your socks and looked at your feet. They were swollen, the skin red in places, white in others. You took off the four, five, six patches covering several toes and had a look at the blisters. They seemed better than yesterday. You took off your jeans and checked your legs. A bruise on your left shin – you didn't even remember how you got that one. Both knees red and scratched from that move where you had to skid across the floor. You looked at yourself in the long mirror on the door of your wardrobe. There was a bruise on your right elbow. You'd fallen during a performance two or three weeks ago and the director liked it, so he told you to do it every night. So, you did. You lifted your t-shirt and looked at your belly. You had lost some weight and gained some muscles. You looked at your face. You looked tired. Tired? No, not tired. Something else in your face, something you could not quite discern. You looked like getting up in the middle of the night and seeing a stranger's face in the bathroom mirror.

"Can you bring me the laundry?"

Your mother yelling from downstairs. You put on some comfortable pants and bent over your suitcase to unpack. You only realised when your hands got wet that you were crying.

#

"I have this dream," the director told you at your first rehearsal. "I see that person, I think it is me, in the middle of a field. In the night. It is not dark, though. I am twirling, twirling, twirling in a circle. Round and round, but not merry, you get me?" You nodded, white-eyed, doe-like, innocent, child-like. "And there is no one else there, on that field. And I see the world from above. And it is all the field. You with me?" You were not, still you nodded. You knew that he knew that you did not understand. Still, you started to dance, do the moves he told you to do. You knew he saw non-understanding when you moved and danced. He knew you could not feel what he felt. "What does it feel to be on the field?!" he yelled at you. It was easy to answer that question on an intellectual level, however, finding that feeling, that was the hard part.

#

Your grandmother lived in a house at the end of a parallel street, close to the lake, at the edge of the forest. Maybe a walk of eight minutes. Nevertheless, your father picked her up in the car, because she'd fallen on her way home in spring. She came by for dinner every Saturday, but your family still acted as if it was a special occasion today, your special welcome home dinner.

"I really wanted to come and see your show. Unfortunately, you know, the hip. And then a drive of, what-is-it, two hours? Just too much for my age," your grandmother said while your father was cutting the roast and your mother passed around the bowl of mashed potato.

"It was really nice," your mother said.

"Well, I did not understand it, but she was great," your father said. "It is not ballet, sure, it takes courage to move around on a stage all alone."

"At least she had the band in the back." Your mother.

"That's true. If you can call it a band. I get the drummer. But the guy with the computer? And the other one with the what-you-call-it...?" Father.

"A didgeridoo," your brother mumbled without looking up from his mobile.

"Would you put the phone down?" Mother.

"These phones drive me crazy." Grandma. "I was in the store the other day and wanted to ask a question, but Charlene, what-is-she-now, twenty-four, didn't even look up from her phone. She works there. She should not be using that thing during work."

"You been to the store? How did you get to there?" Mother.

"Oh – I think – ah – yes. Barry drove me."

"Barry? You two get along again?" Mother.

"We always got along." Grandma.

The conversation trailed off to places you were not interested in. The roast tasted good, and you were hungry, and you liked mashed potatoes, always had, and you ate, but the meal felt.

?

...

What did it feel like?

Out of place. Empty. Empty words around you, empty people around you, empty roast, and empty mashed potatoes. You needed sleep. You needed to get away from the table. Get away.

#

"I have this dream," your director told you at the third, fourth, fifth rehearsal. "A dancer on a field, all alone and the field..."

You could not listen to it anymore. You had all the moves down, every tiny little step, and you understood every beat of the music, the atonal music that had no clear rhythm, only sounds, floating sounds, you knew every beat in those sounds, still, you could not feel what it meant to be on that field. And that was all that counted. To him. His eyes staring at you.

#

"Did you know I wanted to be a ballet dancer when I was like six or seven years old?" Grandma. It was hard to picture that heavy-set, older lady dancing ballet. "Even took some lessons. But we had no money. And when I was fourteen, I had to work. Our lives were much harder back then."

Your mother in the kitchen, washing the dishes. Brother grudgingly helping her. Father having fallen asleep on the couch watching the expert discussion of the game he'd been watching in the afternoon.

"Ballet, that takes some skill. Not like those modern things. Have you ever seen those Russian ballet dancers? I have seen them on TV last week. They train for years. Can you imagine? Most people would not have the dedication these days." Was she talking to you? "Still, I am sad I missed your show. But it was not ballet. So maybe I would not have liked it, anyway. I am sure it was interesting. It is nice you tried to be a dancer." There is a moment of silence. "So, are you going back to school now? Learn something useful at some point. I couldn't go to university, you know? We had to work. When I was fourteen. At the factory..."

You told your grandmother you had to lie down for a moment. You felt nauseated. Long day. You walked over to the couch. Your father gently snoring in his comfy chair. You lied down on the couch. Eyes closed. Your head was spinning.

You woke up in the middle of the night. Someone, probably your mother, had put a blanket on you. You were surprised that you had not woken up to the sound of your grandma leaving or your mother serving dessert or your father getting up and, for a second, you felt moved by the gentleness of the gesture of the blanket being placed on you and no one waking you up. You sat up and tried to see the wall clock through the surrounding darkness. Maybe it was two or three. When did you lie down? At eight, nine?

You got up and stepped outside of the house and onto the porch. Everyone inside was sleeping, so you grabbed your father's cigarettes on the windowsill. He was not a smoker, he always said, only smoked occasionally after a good meal or after a good game. You did not smoke, as far as they knew, not even after a good meal or a good game, but in truth, you'd started smoking halfway through your dancing engagement, not much, maybe four, five cigarettes a day, never before, only after a performance. And this, this night, surely was after any performance, so it was a good night for a smoke.

You stepped towards the edge of the porch and blew the smoke out into the night. You'd missed the stars, you realised, looking up to the sky. It was a clear night, one of those nights that made them seem much closer than they were. You could see the Milky Way. The house behind you was all quiet.

#

You started to fake it. The field and the feelings. You looked into the director's eyes and his face when he spoke about the field, and you faked that expression. And he believed you. You put that expression into everything. Every move you did to the rhythmless music, it was always there. A copy of something beyond your grasp. But you faked it until you made it. And he was happy.

Then, the expression got boring, acting that empty feeling again and again at the rehearsals, like a puppet. You wanted to cut the strings off. Be a real girl. Before one rehearsal, you closed your eyes and let your mind wander, digging into what was inside. Going through the feelings that made you, looking for something beyond the director's field.

That first crush.

Warm feeling.

That first kiss. Warmer. In your belly.

That argument with your mother. Burning in your chest.

The time your best friend told you that you couldn't be best friends anymore. A hole in your middle.

A bad mark in school. Rain when you'd been making plans to go outside. That time you fell off your bike. That time you broke your arm. That time the person you had hoped for told you they loved you. That time the wrong person told you the same thing. Everyone is watching you during your first dancing lesson. That time the person you looked up to said you were a talented dancer. Seeing your father cheer after his team won a game. Your mother tucking you in. Watching the stars with your brother, him telling you all kinds of bullshit about them and you believing him. Rejection. You cutting your finger and your mother yelling at you for bleeding all over the kitchen. Your first menstruation cramps. And all the cramps to follow. Being ashamed of your face. Changing. The confusion of your first orgasm. Sleeping late on a Sunday. Breakfast. Rain against the window. A good book. A good movie. A good story.

Blinding thoughts racing through your brain. So, so, so fast.

All those moments, lost, like tears in the rain. The sentence of someone else echoing in your mind.

You opened your eyes, your body swaying under the pressure of all the things you'd seen inside. He did not know. The director. He never suspected a thing that you had no need for his field.

#

You put the cigarette out in your father's ashtray on the window-sill, hoping he did not keep count of the cigarettes in the package. You brushed your teeth, peed, washed your hands, and crawled into bed. You lay awake for a moment and thought about masturbating, before you fell asleep in an instant, your thoughts crawling away from your conscious mind into a jumbled, uncontrolled mess, a place where elephants could fly and un-costumed clowns were pulling the sun up and down, day and night.

Your mother woke you up at eleven o'clock. "Honey, I made an appointment for you at the hairdresser. At one. Time to get up."

You felt dizzy and confused. You looked at yourself in the bath-room mirror. Your hair had got unusually long. Your director had told you not to cut it, but to carry it in a bun during the performance. And then, for the last ten minutes, the crescendo, the birth and end of the world, as he called it, open them, shake them, work with them in their uncut, unkept state. The beautiful chaos of being human, he called it. "I was thinking, after the hairdresser, we could do some shop-ping," your mother yelling from downstairs. "Sure," you shouted back while brushing your teeth. You got dressed – since the clothes you had become accustomed to during the past months were in the laundry, you settled for faded blue jeans and an old, oversized sweater, which felt good, which felt like being warm. Your mother asked you whether you wanted breakfast and orange juice, but you only asked for coffee. "Coffee?" she said, raising her eyebrows, "since when do you drink coffee?" "For a while now," slightly annoyed that you had to justify yourself. Your mother poured a cup for you, while you told her about that amazing coffee place you'd been to in that big city on the other side of the country, not because you felt like it would interest her, rather just to fill the void of silence that was threatening to eat up the house. "It is nice you got to see so many places," your mother said. She sounded sincere. "Yeah, it is nice," you replied after a moment. "You know, me and your father were really worried. You so far away from us, so many places, so much travelling." "Mom, the director made sure we were safe." "I know... still, not every parent would have let their child go on such a... thing." She said these words with her back turned to you, washing some meaningless dishes, her tone normal, the tone of someone talking about the weather. You tried to match her tone, that fluffy emptiness of pretending to say nothing at all.

"I am nineteen," you said.

"Just about," she replied. Still the same tone. "I am only glad you came back safely."

"Yes."

"Jim told me you could work in the shop again for a couple of months before applying for university."

#

"I have a dream..." the director told the group before the first performance. You were standing on the stage in the empty theatre after the warm-up, a group that had come together for this project, the director opposite you, the DJ to your left, the drummer to the right, Smiley holding his didgeridoo next to her, the production manager to the side, looking at another checklist, obviously nervous about the fast-approaching performance. "I have a dream..." he repeated, broke off, again. "Please take each other's hands," he finally said. You did, even the production manager joined the circle. "Please close your eyes," the director said.

And so you stood there, eyes closed, in that pseudo-metaphysical circle, feeling the nervousness in your wet palms and your heartbeat. You felt sick and the director, like so many times before, talked about his dream and the empty field. And even though you could not feel what he felt, you felt you had at least learned to understand him. He finished his speech, you all opened your eyes and hugged each other. "That was a beautiful speech," Smiley said to the director, who soon vanished in the wings.

The audience came in and the lights went up and the show began. You did not feel a thing except for confusion as you made it through the night. It felt like drowning and holding on, a constant feeling of being overrun by the progression of the performance and the music and then of victory, as you made it through all of it and the performance ended. The audience clapped, and you bowed, smiled, and you all went out and got drunk. "That was beautiful. A beautiful performance," the director told you in the middle of the night, his word slurred because of the alcohol and the adrenaline. "I am so happy I found you." You blushed.

\#

The sky was still grey, and it had got even colder. "Summer was terrible," your mother told you while the both of you got in the car. "Boiling." The poppy field surrounding your house stretched into the distance, cold and dead. It had only been yesterday that your brother drove you down this road and you returned home, yet it seemed like a lifetime ago. "Are you tired?" your mother asked you. You nodded and reached for the radio. The drive into town was a short one, but still gave the voices on the radio plenty time to tell you about the benefits of investing in real estate, about a new mall that might or might not get built, the weird people at the west coast that took yoga classes together with their dogs, as well as the current political state of the country (which was bad or terrific, depending on who you wished to listen to). "I'll park at the church," your mother informed you, driving down the main street past the flower shop, convenience store and the hairdresser – "You can just drop me off here," you said much too loudly and vigor-ously. Your mother, startled or surprised by your sudden interjection, brought the car to an abrupt halt – not that there was any traffic behind her that would have minded. Only an older woman standing in front of the flower shop, talking to the owner – Mindy, was it? –, raised her head and looked inquisitively in the car's direction. "You sure-" "Yes, we are right in front of the hairdresser. I can make it in on my own." "Okay, I'll come and meet you there-" "You wanted to go shopping after, no?" "Yes-" "Let's meet at the shop in an hour. Once I am done." "Actually, I have to drive down to-" "Ninety minutes, then?" "Sure-" "Okay, bye, see you later. Love you." You quickly got out of the car and watched your mother drive off. Then, you waved at the old lady (and Mindy?) who was still looking at you, before turning around and entering the hairdresser.

Martha welcomed you like an old friend, speaking in her high-pitched, fast voice. She'd never tire of repeating the fact that she had been cutting your hair since you'd been a little girl. She sat you down on the chair and looked at your hair -ohmyitreallyhasgrown – and giggled.

Whataboutwecutitabitjustliketheusuallength? You nodded.

You always liked the way Martha washed your hair. You closed your eyes and leaned back, and she sprayed them with water and rubbed the shampoo in. She had a gentle, yet firm grip. You wondered how close to retirement age she was, all the while Martha chatted away, informing you about every detail you had missed during the past months. Despite her shop being a hotbed for gossip, Martha never gossiped herself. She only relayed facts, as she put it, facts that had been confirmed to her by at least three different people. So, she would tell you that Mrs Miller had seen Becky – widowed two years ago, despite her young age, a tragedy – and Mr Whatwashisnameagain – moved to town six months ago – hold hands at the state fair. Now, that would be gossip if the account came only from Mrs Miller. However, Tom – member of the local firefighters – and Milly – head of the backing competition committee – had both told her the same thing. And, thus, it was a fact confirmed by three independent sources. ItsniceforherBeckyImean, Martha concluded in her rapid-fire voice that seemed even faster than usual, her scissors gliding through your hair, cutting it back to its usual length of in-between your ears and your shoulders. You watched her in silence, drowsy, wishing you could just crawl back into bed for the rest of the day.

Ohyourmomtoldmeaboutthatdancethingquiteexcitingno? You nodded. "Yes, it was exciting."

ItookballetclasseswhenIwasyoungermymotherwantedmeto. Did-not-like-it, she said, suddenly slowing down. An unspoken memory flickered across her eyes. It disappeared in an instant and she went back to cutting.

YouknowIhavebeencuttingyourhairsinceyouwerealittlegirl,   she said, back to her usual chirpy self. "I know. I've been there," you replied, not in a snarky way, but earnestly. Martha laughed, a loud, high-pitched, almost elf-like laugh and her reflection in the mirror in front of you smiled at you. You-have-always-been-one-of-my-favourite-customers. Martha resumed the cutting.

It all felt weird.

It almost seemed as if someone had muted the colour in the salon. Maybe it was the sun that had broken through the grey sky outside. Maybe it was its bright rays harshly falling through the windows on your right, making the two red, leather seats to your left shine less brightly than they used to. Maybe it was those rays that let you see the dust that had collected on a big plastic plant in the far-left corner of the room, the same rays that gave the mirrors a washed-out quality, the rays that showed you subtle cracks in the wooden board in front of you.

Soareyougoingtogotouniversitynextyear?

Idontknow, you quickly replied.

That's-fine-it-is-like-my-daughter-she-did-not-know-for-a-long-time-what-she-wanted-to-do-and-now-she-and-her-husband-have-just-bought-a-house-can-you-imagine

Elenamygranddaughterhasjuststartedfirstgrade, she added, a hint of pride in the wrinkles in the corner of her eyes. Youllfigureoutwhaty-ouwanttodointime.

The sound of the scissors chipping away at your hair seemed too loud. You watched your own face in the mirror, a face that was slowly transforming back into the face you had known for years of getting up in the morning and looking at yourself in the bathroom. However, there was this thing in your eyes you didn't quite know, like looking at another person who had put on your face like a mask made of plastic.

"Hey, Martha, do you also do colour?"

"Colour?"

"Yes. For my hair."

"Do you want to colour them?" She looked at you in the mirror. A cloud moved in to block the aggressive sun rays and Martha transformed into the woman you'd known since you had been a child, a woman that could be in her twenties, or thirties or forties.

"Well... why not?"

"Why not!" Martha jumped up and hurried behind the counter. She soon emerged with a brochure filled with pictures of beautiful people with professionally dyed hair.

Soletsseethen, she said, even faster than usual.

#

It was the third show that your family – your father, mother, and aunt – visited. It had been the reasonable choice since it took place in the next-closest town (still, a two-hour drive, as your aunt pointed out several times). You had promised yourself that you would not be nervous about having your family in the audience, yet, of course, you were. You sat backstage and felt icy panic coming over you in waves. Maybe they wouldn't even be here on time. Traffic jam. They'd taken the wrong route, your mother trying to navigate your father's driving by looking at google maps on her phone. Maybe they'd been in an accident.

You tried to shake off the dark thought, but it had been brought to life and was there to remain in the back of your head. Maybe it was that thought or your general nervousness that made you feel you were not part of this night's performance. You knew you had all the steps right, all the subtle movements as well, but there was a disconnect to what you did and what you felt. In fact, you did not feel a thing, not even your body. You could just as well have sat in the audience, in between your father and your mother watching a stranger do what you did, and you wondered whether you would have liked the show or whether you would have sat there and felt embarrassed about dragging your parents to this weird performance. Modern dance is not real dance, that's why they call it modern, someone once said.

The performance ended, all 67 minutes of it and people applauded and everyone bowed, and you could see your parents and your aunt sitting in the audience, clapping as well. Your mother leaned over to her sister and whispered something in her ear.

You gave them a tour of the backstage (which was not glamorous at all, only a room that reminded you of a school gym locker room) and introduced them to all the other members of the show (except for the director, who was in a deep conversation with a couple that looked like a pair of French existentialists).

And then you asked them: "Did you like it?"

There was a moment of silence.

"You were great, honey," your mother replied. Your father nodded, and your aunt added: "I thought it was interesting." Then they asked you about the other stops on the tour, and your aunt wondered why the show had to travel the entire country, and your father added he was glad that one show had been semi-close by. "Speaking of which," your aunt said, "we have to get going. We want to be back before midnight." They gave you a hug and your mother seemed saddened by the fact that she would not see you for some time now. You promised you would call or at least send her messages regularly. They left, and you sat down in the locker room and realised that your left ankle was hurting. Too early for pain, you told yourself. Many shows to come, you told yourself, and the room seemed much too silent, one of those silences that let you hear the blood rushing in your ears, a silence that felt like emptiness, like a child wishing for a present for Christmas, but finding the space underneath the Christmas tree empty and then, there is no Christmas tree at all, just an empty, dead, desolate field.

What would you have wished for?

Your mother: "I understand why you have to do it." Your father adding: "And it is important that you do it." Your aunt wiping a tear from her eyes. You all hug and no more words needed.

You felt like vomiting, vomiting against the sound of silence growing louder, sitting there in the cold, unglamorous locker room and you felt naked despite the fabric on your body.

It felt like standing on a field, alone, left alone, in a frosty night without stars.

#

You had been sitting on the bench in front of the church for twenty minutes. From here, you had an unobstructed view of the shop and the street, as well as the parking spots lining the road on either side. Neither your mother, nor her car, were anywhere to be seen. You'd been thinking about abandoning your spot for a while now, attracted by the smell of Jimmy's food stand crawling around a corner. After another five minutes, you finally gave in and followed the smell, around the church behind you, to the food truck. Jimmy was manning the truck, his truck, hustling and bustling about. Everyone had shaken their head in disbelief when Jimmy'd told them he intended to buy a food truck and sell fast food in town – after all, the town only had a limited number of people, no tourists, no travellers. How would he make a living? Now, five years later, Jimmy's Truck (that was the name, not highly creative) had become a staple of the town, the place people picked up a grilled sausage, or a burger, or a hot dog, after shopping, before hurrying home. You opted for the hot dog, and Jimmy recognised you after a moment of hesitation, and asked you how you were doing and what you'd been up to. You told him travelling and working on this art thing, not wanting to explain to him the intricacies of modern dance, not that you actually could. Hot dog in hand, you hurried back to your bench overlooking the shop and the street. Of course, your mother had arrived in the meantime and was standing impatiently in front of the shop.

"You took your time," she said as you approached her.

"I was- I had been waiting- I got hungry."

Your mother didn't reply, turned around to enter the shop, stopped, turned around again to muster your hot dog. "You can't eat that inside."

"Oh. Yeah. I'll quickly-"

"I'll be inside. You'll find me. I like the colour." Pointing to your hair. Then she disappeared into the shop.

"Thanks," you mumbled, steaming hot dog in hand. You gulped it down, burning your palate and hurried after your mother.

#

During the eighth performance, your foot started to bleed. You realised, after you heard someone gasping in the audience, that you had left several bloody footprints where your bare left foot had touched the ground – a burst blister, most likely. You did not feel pain, and you did not stop, continued the show to its bitter end, where you realised you were drenched in sweat and your legs were trembling so hard you could hardly stand. The director rushed onto the stage to hold you while everyone bowed. The applause seemed so much louder than usual, and you hopped backstage, your left arm over the director's shoulders. You lay down on the cold backstage floor and he lifted your left leg to look at your foot. "We will have to disinfect that," he mumbled. He disappeared and soon came back with some bottles and water and bandages. "Nothing bad. Looks worse than it is. You'll have to rest." He put something on your foot, and you could feel a burning sensation crawling up your left leg and towards your midst. "Why was the applause so loud?" you asked, just to distract yourself. "It's because they have seen an artist shed actual blood, sweat and tears. Feels personal. You should do it every night." "I'd rather not." "For now, let's make sure it does not get infected. Stay here. I'll call a cab to get you back to the hotel." "I need to change. Shower." "You can do that at the hotel." He left the room. The burning sensation in your leg did not leave with him. Your back felt cold. You felt like the flu, like a fever.

The others entered and helped you to your feet. You told them you would be fine. They told you it had been a great show. Best one yet. They helped you to get outside. You passed through the audience room. On stage, there was a caretaker, cursing, cleaning your bloodstains. "I am sorry," you tried to say, but he did not hear you, he was lost in his own little performance.

The director met you at the taxi, told the others to head to a bar and have a drink. He would bring you to the hotel.

The city seemed to watch you through the windows of the taxi driving through the night. What did night even mean these days, in a city with all these lights that never turned off?

"Are you tired?" The director next to you.

"Very."

"Tomorrow, you'll just stay in bed. Maybe we'll see a doctor. You'll need your feet in working order. Good thing we don't have a show tomorrow."

"Yeah. Thanks for helping me."

"That's what directors do."

"Director, nurse, lifesaver." You both laughed, followed by a moment of silence. Someone was talking on the taxi's radio, too quietly to understand individual words.

"You did well. Amazing show tonight."

"As you said: blood, sweat and tears. I was not crying, though."

"Almost. Every night. Almost. I can see it. It's on the fourth movement, that's where you get completely lost in the music. You forget who you are. And you open yourself, invite everyone to see who you are. You almost cry. I do, watching you. Silently in the audience. Cry like a baby." He smiled.

"You do?" you replied, quite unsure what to say.

"A lot of sadness there. Inside you."

"Is there?"

"We are all sad, no? We all have something to be sad about."

"We are all on the field?"

"Field?"

"Your field. The one you keep talking about."

"No, we all have our very own field." Deep shit. It moved you. It touched you. You felt it inside.

"You know, you are a talented director," you told him.

\#

For a second, you noticed the envelope on the car's dashboard on the way home. It looked like an envelope from the bank, but it blended in soon with the other things in the car and got replaced by thoughts inside your mind. You felt hungry again, despite the hot dog, and you were looking forward to dinner, the ingredients for which lay in the car's trunk.

"Do you think we'll get snow soon?" you asked your mother to break the silence that had settled between you. Neither of you had spoken much while shopping, your mother only occasionally asking whether you wanted apples or crisps or homemade pizza for dinner. Homemade dough and all. You said no, yes, yes, but nothing apart from that. It was like walking through fog, a tiredness in your bones, a foreboding feeling of things to come.

"It looks like snow," you enforced your question.

"I don't know. Maybe. It is getting cold early this year. So much for global warming."

"Not funny."

"Not?"

"Weather and climate, two separate things."

"Maybe you should study, what-is-it, weather..."

"Meteorology."

"Yes... If you want to study, that is."

"I'll present you with a five-step-plan for my future tomorrow."

"No need to be snarky."

"I'm not. But that is what you are worried about, no? My future." Your voice angrier than you wanted it to be.

"I just wonder what you are going to do next. You can't stay with us forever."

"Are you kicking me out?"

"No, of course not. But it would be nice to know what's next before you suddenly disappear for three months again."

"I did not disappear. I was... working."

"Did you get paid?"

"Yes."

"Expenses."

"What?"

"They paid your expenses. That's not exactly a living, is it?"

"No. Not a living. But I liked it."

"You young people just want to do what you like. That's nice, sure, only it just does not always work that way."

"Sure, I will get a job I hate and get married and then vent my frustration on my children."

"I am not venting."

"Sounds like it."

"I think you are overstepping-"

"I am overstepping? You have been treating me like a baby from the moment I came back."

"I am just worried about you."

"You think that the last few months have been a waste of time."

"No, of course not, honey." The tone in her voice almost made you feel bad. "But things move on. And I don't want you to do something you will regret later." Almost.

"And what if I end up regretting *not* doing something?"

"When I was your age, I didn't even have the time to think about such things. It was just decide and do. Finish school and start working. Find a husband and get married."

"And have children. Duties to humanity fulfilled."

"Don't be sardonic." Your mother's voice did not increase in loudness, but the sharp way she pronounced the words was warning enough not to push her any further, so you shut up and watched the world pass by outside the car. You wanted to curl up and cry. Or get out and shout at someone.

"I am looking forward to pizza tonight," you finally said. Trying to sound like your past self.

"Me, too. Are you going to help me cook?"

"Sure."

"It's nice to have the family together."

"Yes."

\#

You limped into the hotel, leaning on your director's shoulder. It was a dreary, old-fashioned place. The lobby's floor was covered by a thick, old, red carpet that had turned grey in the places that were most frequented by guests, in front of the reception and at the entrance, around the lounge chairs.

The guy behind the reception looked like he'd been sleeping and it took him some time to find your keys. Your legs felt shaky and the pain in your left foot had increased. You found it hard to stand at this point and were thankful for the director's firm grip around your waist. Somehow, you wished he would just pick you up and carry you upstairs, Kevin-Costner-style.

The clerk finally found the keys and handed them over to the director. You made your way upstairs – in an rusty, old elevator – and arrived at your room. "Do you need any help?" the director asked, opening the door. You told him you would be fine and: "Thank you."

"No, thank you," he replied.

"For what?"

"Believing in me." You standing in the doorway, leaning against the frame, he in the dimly lit hallway. He continued: "You are an amazing artist. For what you had to work with. I know it can be confusing at times. I. Me. I can be a confusing man to work with."

The world vanished around you. He seemed so mysterious. So *artistic*. In your eyes, in that moment, he seemed to be so much more than he was. It was just you and him and his words creeping into your ears, bypassing your brain, and into your heart. The pain in your foot vanished for a second as you forgot you had a body. "You were exactly what I was looking for," he said.

"Lucky for you, I was desperately looking for a way to get away from home."

The thin joke, awkward in its delivery and uncertain in its intention, cracked the ice and the world reappeared. Yet, he had changed in your eyes and in your gut. I should go to bed, you should have said, should have closed the door, and we see each other tomorrow, but you asked that weird string of words carrying all sorts of meanings, that "Do you want to come in?", as if the room behind you was your private apartment, and you were in a movie about two people arriving at this place, and one of them asks whether the other one wanted to come upstairs to have a cup of tea. You had no tea in your room, but before you could figure out a plan of attack or retreat, he leaned in and kissed you, just as misplaced as your question, but you leaned in as well and kissed back and tried to feel on his lips whether this was right or wrong.

Before you came to a conclusion, he pushed you backwards into the room, holding you, preventing you from falling and you smelled cold sweat, wondering whether it was yours or his. His hands on your hips, on your bum, on your trousers, under your shirt, searching for gentle spots on your body. You winced in pain as you stepped onto your damaged foot and he apologised, stopped, the question unasked whether he should leave.

You gently shook your head and pulled him backwards onto the bed, opening his trousers, pulling them down. He seemed much younger now, insecure, naked from the waist down, his hands stroking your head as you touched him between his legs. He pushed you back, you lying down, he kneeling above your body, pulling your shirt up and your bra down and hands into your trousers, a shiver on your spine, kissing you in too many places at once, his erect penis against your upper thigh. Slow down, you tried to whisper. He was too occupied with your half-naked body to take notice of you, and you did not want to stop him, hurt him, tell him he could do better. Instead, you took his penis in your hand to pull it slowly backwards and forwards, hoping that would turn his focus in a new direction. He whispered in your ear that you were *oh-so-beautiful* as he crawled on top of you and you felt his penis against your belly and your lips touched gently, which was nice, even though his left hand was awkwardly massaging your left nipple.

"I have condoms," he said, stopped, and got up. He took off his shirt as he stepped up to his trousers on the floor, looking for the wallet and the condom inside. You there on the bed, still with the shirt pulled up to above your breasts, your bra halfway open and pulled down towards your bellybutton, trousers and panties around your knees.

On the wall, there was a clock ticking uncomfortably loud. You wondered whether you should move, undress completely or get fully dressed again.

He found the condom and came back to you, holding it like a delicate trophy between two fingers. He kissed your breasts again and pulled your trousers and panties to your ankles. He kissed your belly-button and stopped again to open the condom, ripping it open with his teeth while he was stroking his penis with his left hand. Then he pulled it over the penis, took your knees and bent them to either side.

It was cold in the room, you thought, and wondered whether the heating would go on automatically if the temperature dropped below a certain threshold.

His face was in front of yours, looking at you intensively, panting, his breath smelling of stale cigarettes and wine. You touched his left cheek and his ear, and he kissed your hand as he was thrusting backwards and forwards. It felt like it was meant to be. Or not. That weird thing that was being intimate with another person only to feel the pleasure of not doing anything that made any sense, something that was just there as an attempt to feel what it was like to have an orgasm, that glorious moment of forgetting yourself, a split second of not being you. It did not come. Him moving in and out, breathing like a desperate, dying elephant.

You pushed him down, to the side, onto his back, horizontally, him now lying there, face up, his penis sticking out like a forgotten tower in the landscape of his body.

You crawled onto him and led him inside your body, rocking up and down on top of him, back and forth, eye in eye with him, sweating, wishing he would touch your legs, your thighs, your belly, your breasts, neither of you any longer on a lonely field as separate people, but as a weirdly shaped, weirdly connected unity of emotion and instinct, of rubbing and pushing, of fluids and dry skin, of pain and pleasure, of forgoing meaning in favour of a moment that existed there and only there in that room in that hotel so far, far from home.

#

The worst memories are those arguments that happen over dinner. The food steaming on the plates, but there is that heavy lump in your belly. Your throat rebelling against every bite while the world shatters into pieces that will eventually reassemble into a yet-unknown new status quo. Or maybe go back to what they were, just held together by false hope and faked understanding and blissful ignorance.

The pizza smelled good and looked good there in the middle of the table. You did not know what to say or what to think. Your mother had just told you she'd been at the bank today to discuss the sale of the house. She dropped it like someone saying they had seen a friendly dog earlier, like it was no big deal.

It should not have been a big deal. For your parents, sure, it was sad, selling the house they once bought with their hard-earned money. But you and your brother? He'd soon move out anyway, since he was about to start working in another town and maybe he'd take the chance and move in with his current girlfriend. And you, you would probably study or start working, or anything and "It is not like you wanted to stay with us for much longer anyway," your mother said after you'd said you were upset. You could not argue with that on a rational level, it was true, still, you felt a sting of... betrayal? Disappointment?

Your father only said it made sense, the house was getting too big, and some company had bought the land close-by, probably for a mall or an office building, maybe even a factory, and they could get a decent price on the house now. They would move into town, maybe sell the car, since everything they needed would be in walking distance.

The house was silent. The four of you silently eating the pizza at a table that was big enough for six to eight people. You remembered sitting at this very table on your first day of school, eating breakfast with the same lump in your belly, your mother standing at the counter that separated the kitchen area from the dining area and looking at you with a mixture of pride and concern, telling you half-jokingly, half-seriously that the serious part of your life was about to begin, as if everything from now on would depend on that first day of school, all the choices you would have to make to become an adult. She told you the same thing when you entered high school, standing at the counter the same way, with the same look in her eyes and the same tone in her voice.

"When?" you finally asked.

"What?" your mother replied.

"When are you going to sell it?" you specified the question.

"It is going to the market in two or three months. Hopefully, we move to our apartment by the end of April." your mother said.

The pieces of the future dangled in front of you like a puzzle without a boilerplate.

"You need to think about what you are going to do," your mother added, "work or study, that is really up to you."

You woke up in your room in the middle of the night – or maybe you had not slept at all, who knew? You'd spent the evening after dinner googling different schools and scholarships and deadlines for applications. You'd been thinking about going to an art school, maybe a dance school. You'd thought about jobs and internships, reaching no conclusion.

The pale light of the moon crept through the window and illuminated the shelf opposite your bed. The room, the stuffed animals, the posters, the carpet seemed childish in the grey light. You got up and put on a jumper and socks, left the room, made your way downstairs. The stairs creaked like an old person. Apart from that, the house was silent. Your parents asleep in their room, your brother had left and was staying at his girlfriend's. You exited the house through the front door and took a cigarette from your father's stash, lighted it and stood at the edge of the porch, blowing grey smoke towards the stars and the grey-dark sky. The field spawned across the world you could see in the dark, there was nothing else, just this house and the field. The colour on the porch's wooden railing was slowly coming off. You'd probably been 8 or 9 years old when your father last painted it.

Cigarette in hand, you stepped off the porch and onto the cold ground in front of the house. You should have put on shoes. The icy wind bit your legs that were hardly protected inside the thin shell of your pyjama trousers. You threw the cigarette to the floor and took off your jumper as if to equalise the cold on your legs and upper body. You stepped out into the dark and there was a song inside your head. Arhythmic, atonal, infernal. Step forward, step backward. Turn. Forward. Drag your left leg behind. Sink in, stretch out. You took off the pyjama top. Felt the world on your skin. Step. Turn. Drag. Down. Up. Across the floor. Jump. Arm swings going into a full body swing. Kick. Contraction. Stop. You took your trousers off. Naked now. Up to the sky. Tendu. Your right leg quivering as it alone carried your body. Knee bending. Falling. On the floor. There in the field. Cold. You turned onto your back. Cold, the stars looked at you.

    #

You woke up in the morning alone. You went to the bathroom and put your foot on the toilet seat to have a closer look. A blister on the side had burst. It was not bleeding anymore, and you carefully touched it. It hurt, thankfully less than yesterday evening.

There was a knock on the door. You quickly put on some clothes and opened it. It was the director who handed you a bag. "I brought you something to disinfect. And bandages. And painkillers. I'll be back in the afternoon, and we'll decide whether you need to see a doctor, ok?" He did not wait for a reply, just nodded as if to affirm his question himself, turned around and disappeared down the hallway.

You disinfected your foot and winced in pain. You put on some bandages and turned on the TV. The lady on the screen told you about property and bursting bubbles, you did not care. You switched channels to a cartoon and fell asleep again.

Later, the drummer came by. She'd done an internship as a nurse a long time ago and seemed qualified enough to evaluate your foot. She took the bandage off, examined it, and said it looked worse than it was, it was not infected and clean and you should be fine. You just would have to wear a tight bandage for the next few performances and try not to put too much pressure on it. Change some moves. Easy. I once had a blister on my finger, she told you and laughed. Fucking hell, thought I'd die after every performance. Just kept it clean, and it went away at one point. Make sure you have plenty of disinfectant. Or vodka. Do you drink? She raided your hotel bar, and you had a drink together. She told you about the different projects she'd been part of and the musicians she'd played with (most of them you did not know) and you listened to her wide-eyed. You soon felt light-headed, because of the alcohol and the painkillers, and she tucked you in and you went to sleep.

Another knock at the door woke you up the next morning. "Breakfast meeting in half an hour downstairs," the director yelled through the door. You got up, disinfected your foot again, put on fresh bandages, took some painkillers and went downstairs. There was no restaurant, nor breakfast served in the hotel, so the director had got some croissants from a bakery close-by. Everyone was already sitting in the old, dingy lounge area, in comically large armchairs, nibbling away at their croissants, drinking stale coffee from the coffeemaker that was sitting on the reception desk.

"I'll go ahead," the director said just as you approached them, "we'll see you later." He turned around, nodded at you, and left the hotel. You looked at the others with a what-is-happening-expression, grabbed a croissant and sat down.

"They cancelled our show tonight," Smiley filled you in. "Apparently, the caretaker designated your bleeding all over the stage a health risk. We still get paid, though."

"He wants us to do some additional rehearsing. He wants to change some of the music," the drummer continued.

"Okay," you replied. "When do we start? And where?"

"Just the music. He does not need you. That's what he said."

"Okay?"

"You'll go on ahead. A taxi will pick you up and bring you to the station. You'll head to our next destination and wait there."

"But I can drive with you guys on the bus tomorrow."

"Director said you should head to the next hotel and get some more rest there."

"As if taking a train is resting. She'd be better off on the bus," the DJ interjected.

"Director's orders. Ape see, ape do."

"What?" Smiley with a confused look on his face.

"We gotta get ready. Get packed. Everyone in the lobby in ten. You wait for your taxi. Should be here in half an hour. Here is your train ticket. And here is some money," the drummer gave you two envelopes. "We'll catch up with you tomorrow."

They all got up. Smiley grabbed the remaining two croissants. One after the other disappeared in the elevator until there was no one left in the lounge, except for you and the half-eaten croissant in your hand. And a cold cup of coffee that tasted like something had died inside.

#

You got rid of most of the stuff in your room. Books, stuffed animals, school papers, notes and a lot of clothes. All you wanted to take with you fit in two large suitcases. Some of the useless stuff you could not bring yourself to throw away, you packed in boxes, which would be stored in the basement storage of your parents' new apartment.

The house was almost empty now. This was when you found your mother sitting at the dining table with tears in her eyes.

"Do you think this is a mistake?" she asked you.

We all make mistakes.

"No, mom. I think change is good. And the house was getting too big, anyway."

Outside, spring was slowly approaching, which marked the return of life on the field. It would still be a while before the poppies would bloom. You hugged your mother and comforted her, then helped your father load boxes into the car to bring them to their apartment, an apartment which offered no stories you were part of. You saw your mother and father smile as they arranged things in their new home.

Your brother took his things and moved into an apartment with his girlfriend (some members of your family had bets going about how long it would take until she'd leave him).

You spent your last remaining nights alone in the house, sleeping on an old mattress in the living room, smoking on the porch, watching the stars, while you were making plans for what was to come. Moving in with a friend in a bigger city, a job waiting tables, trying to get into

dance school and if that would not work out within six months, go to
a regular university to get a regular diploma for a regular, reasonably
well-paid job. Your mother seemed at ease when you told her about
your plans, and you did not tell her that you were only serious about
the first sixth months and unsure about what would come after if
you failed.

\#

The train ride seemed longer than you'd expected. Outside, rain-
drops were falling against the window, the city buildings zoomed by,
followed by an endless stream of fields, mountains in the distance, and
small towns.

Normally, you would enjoy the train ride, the peace and quiet,
listening to music, letting your thoughts go. But today, your thoughts
insisted on remaining in the same spot, circling around the same fucking question: why had he sent you ahead? He had not even looked at
you. Not spoken a word.

It had been a mistake. And not all the "we all make mistakes" in the
world would erase that.

After a while, an old lady sat down opposite you and asked you
where you were from. She did not know your hometown, but wanted
to know what you were doing all the way out here. You told her about
the dance-thing, and she showed interest, in that grandmother-kind-
of-way that made you unsure whether she really was interested or
whether she just feigned interest to be nice. In any case, you gave her
a flyer for the next day's performance. It turned out she lived in that
same town as the show would take place in.

"We will have to get off at the same stop," she said, sounding
almost pleased about the fact. She then asked you where you were
staying and informed you that your hotel was quite some ways from
the train station. "Don't worry. I can take you there. I parked my car
at the station." You replied that would be nice, and she told you stories
about her husband, who died a few years back, and the time they
had travelled together to Europe and visited Switzerland. "I felt like a
queen," she said, "none of my friends had ever been to Europe, let alone

Switzerland. We stayed up in a mountain hotel and it started snowing. We were snowed in for four whole days, could not leave town. Back then, there was no internet, the phones were not working, my parents thought we'd died in an avalanche. Me and my husband, we just stayed in our hotel room and..." She suddenly broke off. "He was a good man. Always loved me."

"I am sorry he died," you said, for the lack of something better to say.

"Ah, don't be. But thank you." She looked at you with a gentle expression in the corner of her eyes. "Look at me, telling old tales like an old woman. You must be bored."

"No. No, I am not."

"You have been raised well. Your parents must be proud."

"Do you have kids?"

She continued to smile. "No. We never wanted children. Quite un- usual for our generation. It never seemed quite right for us. My mother was disappointed until the day she died. She would have liked grand- children. She probably would have been a wonderful grandmother. But me, a mother? No."

"I don't want to have children, either."

She laughed. "Ah, child, you are still young. There is plenty of time to make up your mind about that."

The train announced your station. You and the old lady got up, col- lected your belongings. Soon after, the train stopped, and you got off.

The town looked exactly like you imagined: an old, wooden train station, narrow streets, small, proper houses with gardens. It was colder than in the city and you wished your thick jacket were not somewhere at the bottom of your suitcase. Luckily, the old lady made good on her promise and drove you to the hotel. You bid her farewell and told her you hoped to see her at the performance tomorrow. She promised she would reserve her ticket tonight. You checked in and went to your room, which looked the same as so many of the rooms in the middle-class hotels you'd been staying at on your journey. Carpeted floor. A bed with a heavy blanket. Curtains over the windows. An air-conditioning unit quietly rattling on from the ceiling. An empty wardrobe. A bible in the dresser next to the bed and a notice that other religious texts were available downstairs. You flipped through the pages of the bible and wondered what kind of people needed one in a hotel room. You turned on the TV but did not pay any attention. It was just nice to have some noise on in the background. The news told you something about a crisis somewhere and people who had died because of some reason you could not discern. You felt restless and left the room again, walking slowly not to hurt your bandaged foot. There was a shop close to the hotel, where you bought food and drinks and cigarettes and you sat down on a bench in front of the shop to smoke and drink beer, dodging the weird looks the locals gave you when they entered and left the store. You did not belong here, you thought to yourself, hearing the sounds of trains in the distance. You felt that urge to disappear. The others would arrive tomorrow, and you could just be gone. First, they would wonder where you were. Soon, however, they would forget you ever existed and play music for an empty stage and the director would clap his hands in face of the emptiness and admit that there was no better way to express the depth of human emotions than with a hole of where a human used to be.

#

Your brother dropped you off early at the bus station. He stayed for a while to keep you company, yet seemed eager to get back home, back to his girlfriend, so you told him he should leave. He told you he was in no hurry, but you told him it was okay, so he left. The sun was slowly setting in the west. It was still half an hour before the bus was scheduled to depart. You sat down in front of the shop and smoked a cigarette.

The sliding door of the shop opened.

"All I am saying is that it could have gone better."

Two women stepped outside.

"Don't be so negative. Your mother freaking loves me."

"She is worried that you'll steal her stuff. That is the only reason she is nice to you."

"Huh?"

"She always said when the cleaning lady came by – who was... is Mexican – be nice to Juanita. Otherwise, she'll start stealing. Treat them friendly when they are in your house."

"Come on, she did not say that. Do you have a light?" One lady had stepped up to you, a cigarette in her mouth. Sure, you said and pulled the lighter from your pocket and gave it to her. Her friend stood a few steps behind her, facing away from you. Her hair had the colour of a violet Skittle that had been dropped in a glass of carbonated water.

"Not in these words. But it is what she wanted to say."

"Maybe she was just nice to Juanita because she liked her. Maybe she had the hots for her. Thanks." She gave the lighter back to you.

"Now you are being silly."

"Am I, though? Would that not be an amazing turn of events?"

"I'll give you a turn of events. You can walk."

"I got the keys."

"Are you sure?"

"Sure." The woman opened her handbag and started rummaging around inside. "Shit, where...?"

The other lady triumphantly held up her hand and dangled the keys in front of her.

"How did you...?"

"You left them in the car. I'll drive!" The woman turned around and made a half-fast, half-jogging dash for a car parked in the lot.

"Hey, wait!" The other lady ran up behind her. Same speed. Same weird look of a middle-aged woman behaving like a teenager. It made you smile.

They play-argued for a little while longer, got in the car and drove off. The sun had almost completely settled now. Some birds flew over the trees in the distance. The bus would arrive soon.

You felt cold.

#

The others arrived the next day at the hotel late in the afternoon, so there was not much time to talk. They told you that the director had gone ahead to check out the venue. It had completely sold out, they told you. It was small, sure, nevertheless, every seat occupied.

You drove over to the venue as well, where the director greeted the group. He wished everyone good luck for the performance tonight and you went backstage to change. You found the director a little while later in the wings of the stage. Do you have a second to talk, you asked him, he told you that now was not a good time and turned away, walking out onto the stage and down to the audience room to greet the first early arrivals.

Soon, the show began, and you danced. It felt off. It felt like you were standing next to your moving body, telling it which moves to make, examining every bend of every finger and every expression on its face. There was an empty chair in the first row, and you saw it, and it was staring at you. It felt like you missed something or like there was someone supposed to sit there, that one person who was supposed to see you dance. Everyone else was just extras. Empty human shells bereft of thoughts or action. Meat puppets, their strings controlled by an invisible force beyond your understanding. Their meaningless hands clapped at the end of the show, the sound hardly reached you while you bowed.

Do you have a moment to talk, you asked the director time and time again in the following days, but he always brushed you off and walked away or talked to someone else, until you finally gave up and did not ask him again. For the rest of the tour, the two of you exchanged maybe a dozen words, but that was that.

You hardly spoke to anyone. You hardly heard anyone. You went out for drinks after most shows, yet could not remember much of these evenings. Only you yourself standing next to you watching you smile and laugh and reply to things, as if you were your own puppeteer, a puppeteer with no understanding of how the puppet worked. At night, you dreamt of sitting on that empty chair watching a second you standing expressionless on stage, that second you watching a third you dance a collection of meaningless movements. You remembered a person who had promised she would sit on that chair.

Gone were the thoughts, the feelings, the emotions you had put into the dance. Those personal stories of yourself that had fuelled every performance had vanished. They only had left behind an empty chair which, in your mind, now served as the only stage you had left, much too small, much too restricted. It made it hard to breathe, and you counted down the shows you had left, missing home, missing your life, missing yourself.

Then, the last show.

It took place in the same venue as the first one. Full circle, the director had said, and you went backstage to change, when there was a knock at the door. Half-dressed, you opened the door, and it was the director.

"Sorry," he muttered. "I want to talk to you."

"I don't think I have time to talk now." You wanted to slam the door in his face.

"It was a mistake," he said, and you froze, incredulously looking at him through the gap between the half-open door and the wall. "I know I should not have done that, and I knew it when we did it. And I should have said something, but I had no words. And then I saw you on stage and saw it progress. You progressed. I saw how the show, step by step, turned into what I wanted it to be. You had to end up where I started. Emotionally fucked. And I am sorry about that. But it was incredible. I had to take the cruellest step I ever had to take and leave you alone with those feelings."

Silence.

"All for the arts, right?" you replied.

"Exactly. Life imitates art. Art imitates life. Because they are one and the same."

"I have to get ready."

You closed the door and finished changing. Your steps seemed unnaturally loud when you walked through the backstage, through the wings and onto the dark stage. Ready. Then, the drums like a heartbeat, and your naked feet against the wooden floor. Circle. A deep hum, maybe the sound the first human ancestor would have made stepping out of the primordial soup and into the limelight. You were no longer watching yourself now, you stepped back into your body and became the puppet that needed no more strings. You unleashed everything inside, all those emotions for the ultimate act, the endless joke of modern life, a satire of itself, life not even imitating anything anymore, but only endlessly copying itself with no original in sight. Your body became raw, a soup of emotions, a climactic explosion of being human, snot dripping down your nose and tears streaming down your face and you wished your foot would start bleeding again, bleeding the life away like a 90s nu-metal rock song and you danced the final step of the final performance and your body just gave away and you collapsed, so naturally and so seamlessly everyone thought it was part of the performance, even the director, who was watching from the back, in the dark.

The people got up from their chairs and clapped, loud, thunderous, and you felt pride, pride that you were alive, and someone grabbed your arm and helped you up to stand and bow.

"You okay?" the drummer asked you, holding you by your arm.

"Yes. Yes, I am," you replied. "I am okay."

Some of Us Are Real

Human sardines.

The realisation hit me the moment I entered the plane and looked down the long aisle in front of me, saw it packed with people trying to move past other people, trying to put their luggage into the overhead compartments, trying to sit down. We were human sardines. And I had to swim past all of them. My seat was far in the back, close to the tail, close to stairs that led down to the toilets, where the four-seat middle row changed into a two-seat row to make space for the stairs. The seat next to mine had still been empty when I made my reservation and my calculation had been that it was a very undesirable seat, wedged in between me and the wall, and that if there was a single seat free on this plane, it would be that one.

But before I could find out whether my calculations had been correct, I had to get past the humans. Slowly, the people in front of me, now more of a centipede than individual sardines, crept forward, now and then one of them stopping, holding up the entire procession to muster their seat and to heave their oversized HAND luggage into the compartment. I was carrying only a messenger bag, which held my iPad, my camera, and a journal for travel notes. I had my earphones in my ears and watching the sardine-centipede crawl forward to the repetitive guitar-drum interplay of the last act of Tool's Invincible amused me enough to make the time pass.

I arrived at my seat. The seat next to mine was still empty. Fingers crossed. I put my bag under the seat in front of me and sat down. The sardine-centipede had almost completely settled.

It was zero minutes into my flight from Frankfurt to Seoul that I met you.

The doors had closed. The seat next to me was still empty. I was safe. Or so I thought, as you turned up at the other end of the gangway and marched towards me. Surely, you were going for another seat, I thought, there was still an empty one in a row in front of me, surely. There wasn't, and you weren't heading anywhere else, but to the empty seat next to me. As you approached, you pointed to the seat, shyly, and I, in a quick movement, awkwardly, got up to make space. You only had a small handbag, which you stored under the seat in front of you, and you settled in. I sat down again, flashing a smile in your general direction to seem nice, and that was all the interaction we had for now. I felt uncomfortable next to you. Not because of you. But because of me. Because I knew that the fat on my belly and on my thighs was invading your space, restricting you, and touching your body and you must have found it disgusting, annoying, sitting next to the big guy.

The plane took off, crawled into the clouds. I was already deep in a movie when the seatbelt sign came off. You next to me gave me a sign that you had to get up and it was the first time I actually looked at your face. I rushed to get up, and you got up and disappeared toward the toilets.

I continued my movie, enjoyed the freedom of space for a few minutes, that space I had hoped I would have for the entire flight, until you returned, and I got up again to let you back into your seat.

"Thank you," you said.

"Sure," I said, adding: "If you need to get out, just let me know. Anytime. Even if I am sleeping. Just wake me up."

"That is nice, thank you." Mr Nice Guy is here to the rescue. Well done. I had to think of the kung-fu movie, the one with Jackie Chan, and my thoughts arrived at Sammo Hung. I wished I were more like him. He was the only badass fat guy I could think of. I should learn a martial art.

I checked the entertainment system to see whether they had any kung-fu movies – to my surprise, they had Meals on Wheels (sic!) starring the one and only Sammo. Good riddance. I felt movement beside me and realised that you were leaning over to me.

"That's my favourite," you said, looking at my screen.

"I like it, too," I said.

"Cool."

"Cool, cool, cool."

My helpless Brooklyn 99 impression was replaced by a moment of awkward silence as none of us followed up with the obvious questions to start a conversation, the where are you going, where are you from, what do you do and what do you hope to find on your trip. We both smiled at each other, then you leaned back, closed your eyes again and I started watching the movie.

You seemed to fall asleep instantly, and I felt jealous. I watched and finished the movie and got up to go to the bathroom. The flight was calm. You looked peaceful. I left and came back a few minutes later. You had opened your eyes and had picked up my pillow, which must have had fallen to floor as I'd got up. I thanked you and you nodded. "I am sorry you got the seat in the corner, wedged in between me and the wall," I said. "I am glad I've got a seat at all," you replied, "I was on the standby list. This was the last seat available." *I knew it.* "I was waiting at the gate, and they told me 15 minutes before departure that I could get on." "I could never do that. I booked my ticket six months ago." "I just wanted to get out. Didn't matter where to."

"Why?"

"Missed travelling. Needed some air. And didn't know what else to do. You?"

"Missed travelling, too. And had to take a break."

"What do you do?"

I thought about which route to take. Tell her about my job sitting at a desk in an office going through spreadsheets and organising company events?

"I am a writer," I said.

"A writer?"

"I am working on a novel."

"How is that going?"

"Ask me again in five or six years."

"Are you going to put me in the book?"

"Depends. What do you do?"

"I am what they call in-between things. I did one thing, and that thing ended, and I did some other things and that was over, so now I am not doing much except spending what money I have saved, while figuring out what's next."

"And that is why you are going to Seoul?"

"Maybe. I have a friend there. We will go out drinking. Heard that helps to see things more clearly."

"Or to care less about seeing things not too clearly."

"True that."

I had always found that there was this point in conversations where things just ended. We awkwardly nodded at each other in silence. You leaned back. I directed my attention back to the entertainment system in front of me. We wished each other a good meal when dinner arrived (a microwave interpretation of a Korean Bim Bim Bap – a Bim Bim Bad) and I watched a movie while I ate, and you did the same. Dinner ended, the trays were taken away, we both, separately, undertook another trip to the bathroom, you went back to sleeping, I finished my movie, then put on some music, tried to sleep, could not, then fell into that space between sleep and too many thoughts and sweat on my body, which made my skin feel dirty and unwashed. I hope I didn't smell.

My mind drifted.

To.

Nowhere.

In Particular.

We woke up at some point. I woke up and turned my head as if I wanted to check you were still there. You were already awake, sitting there in silence, staring into oblivion.

"Do you need to get out?" I asked.

No, you said. Silence. The plane was sleeping.

"I like this," you said, "that moment on a flight when everyone is sleeping. It is peaceful."

"And smelly," I added. You laughed a short laugh, but I felt bad for ruining what you wanted to say with a stupid joke.

"I could do with a drink," you said.

"Me, too," I added.

I could see that a plan was forming in your head.

"Hang on," you said and crawled out of your seat. Of course, I was in the way of a direct exit, so you got up, stood on your seat, and attempted to climb across the back, over our headrests. "What are you doing?" I whispered and tried to jump up, startled by your sudden initiative to mountaineer over the seats, whereupon, startled by my unexpected movement, you lost balance. You could prevent yourself from ungracefully falling backwards by holding onto the backrest of my seat, fighting against gravity. I encountered a different fight: my sudden attempt at jumping up was stopped by the seatbelt, which was still fastened around my belly. I was pushed backwards by the laws of action and reaction and my back bumped heavily against the seat, which led to you finally falling back to where you had come from.

We sat there, where we had started, dumbfounded, and we both giggled and shushed each other, as not to wake people up on the plane with our childish giggling. You re-started your journey climbing across the backs of the seats, telling me: "Whatever you do, please just don't move," and I complied. You rolled off the seats and somehow landed on your feet and I could not help but admire your nimbleness and felt even more like a blob sitting there, being useless, watching you disappear into the space behind the curtain, into the galley, only to re-emerge seconds later with two plastic cups filled with what would turn out to be tonic. I started to get up, but was, once more stopped by my seatbelt and you told me to just scoot over, which I wanted to do, only to be stopped, again, by my seatbelt (JESUS FUCKING CHRIST) and you offered the idea, very helpfully, that I should open it before moving (no shit, lady). I fumbled and finally opened it after what seemed like an eternity and moved over quickly. You smiled at me and: "You really need a drink. And maybe some Xanax." "It is my unearthly fear of flying," I offered as an excuse, and you responded: "*Unearthly* fear of *flying*. I see what you did there." And I felt a sting of pride for creating a pun without even having intended to.

You put the two cups down on the fold-down table and sat down. Then you procured small bottles of gin from your pockets, eight in total. "Tray down," you ordered me, and I pulled it down, took one cup and you opened two small gin bottles and poured them into my tonic. Then, you did the same for your tonic.

"Gin and tonic," you needlessly explained, still I nodded. "Cheers," I offered, and we both drank like two prison escapees who had been fleeing across the desert and finally found an oasis with fresh water. "A slice of lemon would be nice," you said, "but could not find any." "Why didn't you ask?" "No one there." "Wait, did you steal this stuff?" "It is not stealing if it is on a plane. A plane is a communist heterotopia." "Which you have bought entry to with a shitload of money." "Not me, remember? I was on the standby list." "So, stupid tourists like me subsidise your flight?" "Exactly. Cheers. Communism, comrade." We drank again.

I could feel the effect of the alcohol on my body almost immediately, a body that had not as much food inside as it usually did and that was confused by flying through different time zones and was on a high because it had someone to talk to. Liquid courage, so: "How come you were on the standby list?"

"I used to work for the airline."

"Cabin crew?"

"No, mechanic."

"No shit?"

"Sexist much?"

"Oh, sorry."

You laughed. "No, I worked at the airport. I helped packing the food they bring onto the planes. Full disclosure: I have seen the way they prepare the food. I have seen it all, man. Do not drink the water. And do not eat the food."

"Really?"

"I have warned you. Refill?"

Sure.

You opened the next two small gin bottles and poured them into my G&T, then, again, did the same for you. The drink tasted like cheap cleaning alcohol. It did not matter. I enjoyed the tired dizziness the gin gave me, I enjoyed looking at your face. I felt reminded of Faust standing on the balcony at the end of the second play, finally being ready to stand still and enjoy a single moment, not wanting to look for something better anymore, giving up on the vain hope that there was a more perfect instant waiting to be missed if he enjoyed this one too much.

"What are you thinking about?" you asked me.

"About how Goethe's Faust had FOMO."

"You clearly need more alcohol."

"We have run out."

"I can try to find more."

"That is fine. I should get some sleep soon," I replied.

What the fuck, dude?

What the actual fuck?

This wasn't a Faustian moment, I told myself, it was not special. This was not perfection. We were sharing a drink as strangers and would part as strangers. Tomorrow would be special. Seoul would be special. I needed to sleep before that. I needed to be ready for my travels. For the city.

"Yeah, me, too," you said.

We finished the drinks, and you told me a bit more about the work you had done at the airport and, after half an hour or so, I said it was time to sleep now and went to the bathroom and, when I came back, you had rolled up in your seat and I sat down on my seat and put my earphones in and closed my eyes. The monotonous hum of the plane reminded me of being underwater.

I could not sleep for more than an hour or two, so soon, instead of getting more sleep, I gave up and listened to a podcast and some music and went to the toilet and stretched my legs in the galley behind our seats. I wondered where you had got the gin from and I wondered whether I should look for some, whether it would be a funny idea to offer you a G&T for breakfast.

You woke up when they turned on the lights and people opened the blinds, when the night of the plane became day after a short six hours. We nodded at each other a silent good morning and I made space for you to get out and have a short walkabout. Then breakfast. I was watching the latest Pixar movie, you were watching some Korean sitcom. I wondered whether you spoke Korean.

"How did you sleep?" you asked me when they removed our trays and I'd finished my Pixar movie.

"Not too much."

"I slept like a baby."

"Looked like it."

"Were you watching me?"

I could feel a rush of blood running into my face. "No. No. Of course not," I said earnestly, then: "Well, maybe," jokingly.

"What are you going to do when we arrive?" you asked me. "I'll head to my Airbnb first, drop my luggage, have a shower... then, drinks and dinner. There is a restaurant I've read about," I replied. "Where are you staying?" "It is in... the university district, the apartment is." "Hapjeoing?" "Yes, that sounds about right." "I am heading the same way," you added, "we can take the subway together." "That would be nice." "Nice." "Yes, nice." "Nice."

I was thinking about the smart things one could say in the attempt to impress someone, to leave an impression. Maybe I should show you pictures from earlier travels on my phone or tell you about the plot of the book I was writing or ask you to tell me something special about yourself, but I could not decide on which option to take. You turned around in your seat again, rolled up to sleep some more, earphones in your ear, music in your ear, and I watched an older Pixar movie. The plane ploughed through thick, grey clouds, until, finally, the pilot announced we had begun our descent and that the seatbelt sign had come on (as if we hadn't noticed). You were still sleeping, but I touched your elbow to wake you up and signed that the seatbelt sign had come on and you moved your seat in an upward position. I smiled at you. You smiled at me.

We landed in Seoul.

We left the airplane and waited for the luggage. Yours arrived first, and I politely said that you did not have to wait for me, but you stood patiently by my side. My suitcase was the last one to arrive. We separated at customs and got interviewed about our intent to visit Korea. Holiday, I told the customs officer, and he believed me (it was the truth after all) and cleared my entry. We met up again behind customs, you were already standing there and welcomed me with a "welcome to Korea." "Thank you," I said. We walked quietly, tiredly, through the airport. You wanted to stop at a coffee shop, even though I told you that there were much better coffee places to be found in downtown Seoul. "I need coffee and I need it now," you replied. We walked like zombies to the subway, got on a train and with a sigh of relief, you told me we would not have to change lines. We sat on a long bench along the wall of the subway car, which slowly filled up with people, stop after stop, so we had to move closer to each other. "Tired?" you asked me. "Yes," I said, "very." You can sleep if you want to, you said, or you didn't, I was not sure, since my mind wandered off, seeing the darkness pass by in the subway tunnel outside, the rumbling of the tracks below, the voices around us, until you touched my shoulder and I woke up and you told me we had to exit at the next station.

We collected our belongings and pushed ourselves and our oversized suitcases through the people. You led me through the bowels of the station and up some stairs into the light of day. It was hot, the sun high in the sky, and I at once began to sweat.

"What time is it?" I asked.

"Around eleven. Which way do you have to go?" you asked.

I got my mobile out and checked the direction. "That way." To the right. "I gotta head left," you said.

"It was nice to meet you."

"Likewise. Take care."

We stood there for a moment, unsure whether we should hug. We ended up awkwardly waving at each other and went our separate ways.

I soon found the building that housed the apartment I had rented. The door had a code – 875632 -, but it took me several attempts to input it correctly, as it necessitated me adding a # at the beginning and the end of the code. Also, I had to confirm my opening by pushing a small, green confirmation button next to the keypad AFTER pushing the #. A lot of moving pieces. My fingers fumbled with the keypad, pressing the wrong number, or the wrong button, and I hoped no one would see me going through attempt after attempt of trying to enter the code correctly, failing, re-reading the google-translated instructions I had got via email, and trying again. People might think I was a robber. A robber that had come with an enormous suitcase of clothes and two books. A reverse-robber. Leaving my filthy stuff at your place.

Wasn't there a film about this guy who broke into people's homes to clean the houses and wash their clothes? I should do that. That sounded like fun. But I had no idea how to break into houses.

The door finally opened with a ridiculously loud beeping-noise, and I lugged my luggage upstairs to the top (fifth!!) floor. I was drenched in sweat and happy I'd chosen an apartment where I would not be greeted by a host. I must have looked terrible, and I wouldn't have wanted anyone to see me like this. On the top floor, another door with a keypad expected me – 392817 -, but I knew the drill now and got the door open in only two tries. I entered the apartment, took my shoes off. In front of me there was a small kitchenette, a sofa, a TV, and a huge air conditioning unit to the right. To the left, a door, most likely leading to the bath- and bedroom. I put my suitcase down and produced a "hello?", just to be on the safe side. There was no one here. I took my t-shirt off. Breathing heavily, I stood there, in the middle of the apartment that was not mine, pale big belly gleaming pinkly, feeling oily because of the sweat that covered my body. I took the tour of the apartment and found the bed- and bathroom as expected behind the door on the left. I brought my suitcase to the bedroom and got undressed and had a shower. Then, I collapsed on the bed, naked and wet, and fell asleep.

I woke up shivering and cold. The air conditioning unit must have turned on at one point, and it felt like it was winter inside the apartment. My body felt limp and shrivelled, although I had a hard-on (which was painful, since I was lying on my belly).

It was time to hit the streets, I thought, while rolling to the side. The little window on the far side of the room told me it had got dark outside. Time for food. And beers. My head was spinning.

I got up and put on some boxers, a shirt. Then grabbed my mobile and sat down on the toilet. A rummaging in my bowels had let me known I had some business to attend to before I would leave the apartment. While sitting there, I opened the map app on my phone. There was a barbecue restaurant close-by. Barbecue sounded like the right thing to do on your first night in Seoul.

I opened tinder. The picture of an Asian woman greeted me. Swiped right. Another Asian woman. Could not read the text below the picture since it was in Korean. Right. Another one – swiped left for no particular reason, just to do something different. Another left. Another right. Right. Right. Swiped left to confuse the Tinder algorithm. And then –

A photo of you came up. You. From the plane.

I always felt weird when I encountered people I knew on the app. What was the appropriate way to swipe in those cases? Swipe right to be friendly? Swipe left not to make things awkward, should you meet in person again? But then, I did not really know you. You were no friend.

We'd just spent the night in a plane next to each other...

I closed the app without making a decision.

Then, I hit the town.

I walked past loud masses of people partying in the streets. All the doors and windows of the bars had been opened and customers had spilled out, smoking, talking, producing a deafening barrage of noise. I followed my map through the chaos and was surprised that Seoul looked much more rundown and dirtier than I had expected.

I walked past a group of young girls – one of them was crying her eyes out, screaming loud words in Korean. Four or five of her friends were trying to comfort her, while another was standing a few steps away, talking to a boy their age, maybe all of them in their early twenties, caught in the drama of being young. I wondered whether I'd had enough drama at their age. Not the drama I had experienced, that kind of existentialist drama of having a shitty childhood, but more the uplifting, destructive *Sturm und Drang* drama, high school movie drama, that kind of drama that gave you enough energy to burn down buildings and write stories about young lovers killing themselves.

I arrived at my destination. It was a small barbecue restaurant with six or eight round tables, each for them with a hole in the middle for smouldering pallets of coal, upon which they would place a barbecue roast. I stepped through the door and a young Korean man greeted me. I asked him whether he spoke English (in English) and he said yes, yes, very friendly, and added a "Welcome to Korea." "Just one person," I said when he looked at me askingly and he led me to a table. "Do you want barbecue?" I said yes, and he wanted to give me the menu, but I asked him whether he could just bring me a bit of everything. I did not feel like making any decisions tonight. He seemed to like my proposition. "And beer?" he asked. "Yes," I said, "and shoju." "Oh, and Wi-Fi," he suggested, pointing to a blackboard on the wall opposite me that informed me of the Wi-Fi name and password. I had not been planning on browsing the net before my return to the apartment, but since I was here and since I would be waiting for the food anyway, I could as well check whether someone had sent me a WhatsApp message (which was not the case). I killed more time by looking at the news of what was happening in Switzerland (a survey told me that an upcoming vote on a right-wing initiative against immigration was likely to pass) and checked a website for any gaming news. Then, I opened tinder and swiped some left and right and right and left until –

Your picture came up again.

You looked younger in the picture than on the plane. You were standing at the bottom of the gigantic Christmas tree in New York.

I still felt indecisive, my finger hovering over the screen. Luckily, the arrival of the food saved me, a plate of all kinds of raw meat ready for the hot coal grill in my table. Then, the young man brought out more plates, countless little plates. He scattered them across the table, plates filled with kimchi and pickles and salad and vegetables and tiny little fish and many things I did not know, yet was eager to gobble up. I put my phone away and dug in.

The amazing thing about Korean barbecue was how nicely it flowed. Meat and sauce and salad, hot and cold, fresh and savoury, chopsticks wandering between small plates, pickles and kimchi, and all those wonders of the Korean cuisine, the smell of meat being grilled, the beer flowing, the beer mixed with shoju, the belly slowly getting heavier, the head getting lighter. It was the sneakiest meal, getting you drunk without you noticing it, getting you full without you realising it.

I felt like I had eaten at least half a cow when I put my chopsticks down and leant back with a heavy sigh. There was a bit of beer left in the bottle. It had got warm, though, so I held the bottle up to sign the guy from the restaurant for a new one. My fingers grabbed my phone, and, like a digital instinct, I opened tinder again. The app informed me that someone had liked me, but I did not pay for the app, so I could not tell who it was. All I had was a tiny, blurred reproduction of the person's profile picture. A blurry person had liked me. That was how they tricked you into paying for the app. Pay for it and we will un-blur the photo, Tinder whispered in my ear. Promised me access to the knowledge of who liked me. Knowledge straight from the Tinder gods. I held up the phone to my face and looked at the blurry photo more closely. My eyes had trouble focusing through a beer-shoju mist in my brain. *Was it you?*

I went back to the main screen of tinder, hoping Tinder would present me with your profile again, give me another shot at deciding how to swipe on you. Unfortunately, I was greeted by a different – friendly looking – woman. I swiped right. Not you. Right. Right. Left. Left. Left. Left. You did not come up.

My next beer arrived, and I startled and felt embarrassed and hoped he had not seen me swiping my ass off in a restaurant in Korea on their Wi-Fi. I put my phone down and thanked him. "Did you like the food?" he asked, and I said yes, and he asked me where I came from, and we talked a bit about holidays, and he told me he had been to Interlaken. I'd never understood why tourists liked Interlaken so much. As far as I was concerned, it was an ugly town wedged in-between mountains offering a convenient selection of Switzerland's worst restaurants. Yet, I said nothing of the sorts to the guy, just nodded my head and uttered an astounded "Really!?!" when he told me about his trip to Interlaken. I had another couple of beers and hoped we would talk some more, but the place soon became busy, and he bustled around rarely having time to even look in my direction.

So, I drank my final beer, paid, and left.

Night had overtaken the city, ant-armies of people flowing in the streets. The noise, the music and the talking and the shouting amazed me. People yelling – amicably – at each other from across the street, people dancing on the sidewalks, kissing, making out. The atmosphere reminded me of Tel Aviv, the compulsory excess, the endless partying, the living every evening as if it were your last – it probably came with the constant threat of annihilation. If I had lived in a city that nuclear missiles could hit at any time, I would have partied hard as well.

I wondered what a night out in Pyongyang looked like.

I left the busy street and headed into a quieter neighbourhood, residential and peaceful. I was fairly certain I remembered the way back until I had to admit to myself that I did not. I got my mobile out to check the GPS.

I found myself face-to-face with a red battery symbol on my screen. The phone had died.

Fuck.

The battery was empty. Fucking Tinder-swiping excess had killed it.

I could not remember the way back.

I walked back to the busy street and checked my surroundings.

I was pretty sure that the street leading into the quiet neighbourhood must've been the one leading back to my apartment. Or maybe it was one further down. Parallel to this one.

I walked there.

No, I could not remember these houses. These shops.

I walked down another road.

Considered my options. I had saved the address on my phone. Nowhere else. I couldn't ask anyone for directions.

Shit.

I needed the loo.

Go into a bar and ask for a charger and use the loo.

I calmed down. That was a plan. A good one. A workable one.

I turned around to head back, to go back to the busy street and find a bar there. However, my sudden turnaround happened in ignorance that someone pushing a bike had walked up behind me and was not expecting my abrupt turn. So, inevitably, we collided. The bike fell to the ground, and I took a big, stumbling step out into the road, just as a car was about to pass us by. The bike-person dropped a plastic box, grabbed my shoulder to prevent me from smashing into the car's front. The smell of fried chicken filled the night air, the car honked, swerved to the left, hit the brakes, only to speed up sharply a second later and drive off.

"Are you alright?" the guy owning the bike and the – as it turned out – plastic box with fried chicken, both now lying on the floor, asked me.

"Yes. I am sorry."

"No worries, man." He spoke English with a broad English accent. "Do you need help? Are you lost?" he asked me while he picked up his belongings. The lid of the container had opened, but, thankfully, none of the chicken had spilled out. I explained my situation to him and he offered to take me to his place where I could charge my phone and have a beer.

"I am having a friend over," he told me, pointing to the chicken. "We wanted to go out, but she's fallen asleep. I figured she will be hungry and cranky when she wakes up, so I got some food." I did not know why he told me these things, yet he just chatted away and I nodded, just being glad I'd found a friendly face.

We arrived at a tall, somewhat run-down looking apartment building. "What do you do for a living?" I asked him, while he, I, his bike, and the fried chicken wedged ourselves into the world's tiniest elevator. He pressed the button for the 16th floor. "I study. And work as a web designer."

The elevator doors opened on the 16th floor and the two of us left the metal coffin. He led me down a dim hallway and into an apartment, where he parked his bike to the right of the door by hanging it on the wall. It was a nice-looking bike, so it could almost pass as a modern art installation hanging there on the wall. He asked me to take off my shoes, I did, and followed him into a small kitchen that just barely offered enough room for a stove, a fridge and a tiny bistro table with three chairs.

You were already sitting there.

"It is a good thing you are here," you said, completely straight-faced and perfectly hiding any trace of surprise by me appearing, "we need a third player for the card game."

"Do you know each other?" my saviour, bike-man, asked us. I explained we'd met on the plane and that this was the strangest coincidence ever, while you opened the box of chicken and started eating. You offered me some, and I told you I was stuffed from my barbecue. Bike-man took my mobile and plugged it in, opened the fridge and gave me a beer. I sat down.

"How was your night?" you asked me.

"Good. I slept for a bit and then went out to have dinner. Then I got lost and my phone died. You?"

"I never made it past sleeping. So much for going out and getting drunk."

"We still have plenty of time for that," bike-man interjected. "Besides, Saturday is not a good day for going out, anyway. City is overrun by people."

"I like people," you replied, "the more people, the less bad I feel about getting drunk. This chicken is amazing. You sure you don't want to try some?" I took a piece of chicken – you were right, it was very good. Maybe not amazing, still, very good, spicy, covered in a thick layer of sticky red sauce. My tongue burned as I chewed it. It was a glorious feeling, considering it must have been three or four in the morning.

"So, are we playing cards?" you asked, licking your fingers.

"I really should find my apartment," I said. "I need some sleep. I need a shower."

"Ah, come on."

My mobile came back to life with a faint beeping sound. I took it and entered my pin, pulled up the GPS.

"That's two buildings down the road," bike-man said, looking over my shoulder at the map on my phone.

"You almost made it. I can actually see your building from here," he added, and pointed out the kitchen window.

We all laughed. This was beyond silly. So close, yet so far away.

I finished my beer and wished you and your friend a good night, stumbled out of the building and into the streets, along the road back to my building two doors down, up to the top floor, entering the code, re-entering the code, finally entering the code correctly, opening the door, then to the loo and splashing some water on my face, taking the clothes off, smelling like barbecue, brushing teeth, looking at my tired face in the mirror, going into the living room, turning all the lights off and standing there, half-naked in darkness.

The lights of the city fell through the living room window. It was a big window, almost reaching all the way from the floor to the ceiling. The lights of Seoul had taken on a greenish quality. Two buildings down, I saw the building I'd just come from, the 16th floor way above my head. Small kitchen windows, row after row, all the same, some of them dark, some of them illuminated. I counted the windows and found the one I'd just been in. The lights were still on. I seemed to recognise two silhouettes sitting at the table, holding cards in their hands.

I woke up to a knock on the door. I lifted my head, heavy like having been hit by a truck, my tongue felt like the bottom of a birdcage. I put on a t-shirt and zombie-walked to the door. The clock on the kitchen wall informed me it was just past 11.

I opened the door, and you pushed your way past me. "Morning. I brought coffee." You handed me a plastic cup, which I grabbed obediently. The heat of the cup produced a sudden sensation of pain in my fingers and the palm of my hand.

"Morning," I mumbled. You looked different. Your hair open, your face freshly showered, the skin bright pinkish, your eyes hidden behind big shades. You were wearing skin tights, a skirt and a t-shirt showing a drawing of a humanised cat preparing sushi. "When you are done looking at my clothes, you better get that coffee into your system, get showered, and get ready."

"Ready?"

"Ready."

"For what?"

"We said we'd check out the mural village, remember?"

"Did we?"

"We did."

I had no recollection. "I have no recollection," I said.

"You don't wanna?"

"No. Yes. Sure. I do."

"Good. Get going. Get dressed."

I was wearing a t-shirt and boxers. I put the coffee down and disappeared into the bathroom. You sat down on the sofa and watched TV while you waited.

Half an hour later, you and I were sitting next to each other in a subway car, a cup of now-cold coffee in my right hand, heading towards the mural village. I did not know where it was or what it was, but you said your friend had told you which subway to take and where to get off.

"How was the rest of your night?" I asked you, for the sake of saying something.

"Short. I slept maybe for another hour and have been awake ever since. My sleeping patterns are completely fucked up. You?"

"I went back to the apartment and fell asleep immediately."

"You weren't stalking us from your living room window?"

"What?"

"Weren't you watching us when you came home? Trying to spy the kitchen window from your apartment?"

"No. No, I wasn't."

"How could you resist? I totally would have. You never know what you see through windows at night."

"Was there something to see?"

"No. We actually went to bed right after you left. We gotta get off here."

I soon learned that I liked the mural village. It was a collection of small houses, standing in rows after rows leading up a hill, each of the houses in a different colour. If I'd seen only a picture of the place, I most likely would have guessed it was somewhere in Brazil, some favela that had gone through a clean-up and gentrification. Which had most likely happened here: the old buildings, little more than shacks, had been cleaned up and got a fresh coat of paint. Then, several artists had filled the walls of the houses with paintings, murals and graffiti, turning a formerly grungy neighbourhood into a draw for the younger generations. As a result, the streets were now packed with people that looked like Instagram models, posing in front of the walls, snapping pictures that would look great on their Insta-channels.

"You want to take one?" I asked you, the two of us looking at a gorgeous young woman posing in front of a mural of angel wings.

"Don't you wish you could look like her?" you said, not answering my question.

"Yes, but I don't think that would be an advantage as a man."

You laughed and: "You know what I mean. Be that flawless."

The flawless woman left her spot in front of the mural to look at the photos her friend had taken. Both had serious looks on their faces while they swiped through the photos, occasionally pausing at one, pointing to it and discussing different aspects of the photo and how the blonde woman looked in it, negotiating which one would be the best to post online. You stepped forward and stood between the wings, completely still. I was half-expecting you to make a silly face or to do something stupid to mock the Instagram generation, yet you did not. You just stood there, in complete control of your body and your face, only your eyes seemed to betray a deeper feeling within, a sadness.

I snapped a picture. You left the position only to be replaced by the gorgeous woman again. Apparently, she hadn't found a photo she liked. You looked at the image on my screen. "Looks nice," you said. "You look nice," I added. You flashed your teeth in a grimace/smile and rushed ahead to a food stand, where you bought rice pops that had been frozen with liquid nitrogen. I couldn't even catch up with you before you already had put two of them in your mouth. The nitrogen, heated by your body temperature, produced a ridiculous amount of steam coming out of your mouth. "Look, I am smoking," you yelled like a little child. People turned around to look at where the sudden eruption of noise had come from. "Oh, I am sorry. I will be quieter, Mr

Sensei-San," you added mockingly as you saw the half-embarrassed, half-strict look on my face. "We are in Korea. It is not Sensei and not San here," I said drily, hoping you would catch my sarcastic tone. "What is it then?" "The fuck if I know. I don't speak Korean." "Well, then we will have to find someone who does." "Someone who speaks Korean?" "Yep." "In Korea?" "Yep." "Fat chance."

You laughed, and I took one of the liquid nitrogen balls. It tasted awful. Frozen cardboard. "Look, I am smoking," I said, blowing steam out of my nose.

You led me back into the heart of the city, through the tall buildings of Gangnam, a part of town completely different from the university district. Gone were the shabby houses and the dark bars, replaced with suits and expensive cars, high-rises, and exclusive night clubs. We took a taxi and drove, sickeningly fast, over one of the city highways into another part of town. The buildings looked less flashy here, the heartbeat of the city was beating slower. We drove down a road that reminded me of Haight Ashbury in San Francisco with its tiny bars and small shops that seemed to be a world apart from the H&Ms and Uniqlos we had seen in Gangnam.

"What are you thinking about?" you asked me, watching me silently watch the world pass by. "I used to eat there... good noodles," I said, pointing at a random restaurant. "Is this air you are breathing?" you replied.

We exited the taxi and walked along a smaller road leading us down a hill. We turned to a bar that looked like they 'd built it into a former parking garage. A sign informed us it was selling craft-beer and hand-made pizza from a real wood-fire oven. It was one of these rare places that looked genuinely run down and effortlessly hip at the same time, which made me hate it and love it in equal measures. "Again," you said while we sat down and ordered two beers that, according to the menu, had been aged for six months in whiskey barrels, and one of their freshly made pizza, "penny for your thoughts?"

"What?"

"You have just been staring at stuff for the last two hours. Making silent judgements about the world around you in your mind. I would like to partake."

"I am not judging nothing," I said in a joking tone, trying to hide the fact that I felt hurt by you thinking I was judgmental.

"You are not? What were you thinking about then?"

"Nothing," I said, almost a hint of temerity in my voice. You did not reply. Nothing was not an answer you would be content with. "I was just thinking about this place," I offered.

"And?"

"I mean places like this."

"And?"

I was getting annoyed. It was not a thought I had thought through yet, was not ready to share. "I mean all these hipster bars and restaurants with their fake wood and faux-vintage design and beer aged in barrels and servers with tattoos and beards." Our beers arrived. I took a sip. It was delicious.

"You have a beard," you pointed out.

"I know. But that does not make me a hipster."

"You like good beer. And food."

"I don't have a tattoo." Defiantly. Then defeatist: "I am what I despise. Fucking fake. Hipster see, hipster do. I am an hipspositor."

"You want to go somewhere else, grumpy man?" The pizza arrived, and I took my time cutting it into six pieces. The dough was thin and crispy. You took a slice. "It's excellent," you said.

"Nah, it looks cool enough. This place. The beer seems good. The pizza seems good."

"So? Why don't you just enjoy it then?"

"It *seems* good. Who is to say it is good, though? Maybe my judgement is off. Maybe their beer and their pizza are pretentious. Maybe I don't know what an excellent beer is. What good pizza is. I just repeat what society tells me is good. And before I know it, I am a 40-year-old father with two kids drinking beer while grilling meat, thinking the beer and barbecue are fucking delicious."

"What's so bad about that?"

"It's Miller's light and frozen hamburgers."

"If you don't want to be that guy, don't be that guy."

"Maybe I want to be him. In a way. Sometimes. It sounds easier than constantly having to think about how long my beer has aged in what kind of container. And where the fucking fresh beef in my hamburgers was raised. Just enjoy the cheap Miller's. Just eat the cheap beef. Tell everyone it is surprisingly good for the price."

"A statement, which of course, shows that, inside, you believe that everyone drinking Miller's and eating frozen hamburgers is an uncultured swine. Judgemental."

"Honey," I said with a fake-English accent, "we sit in Seoul in a bar that has been built into a parking garage serving pizza from a wood-fire oven and beer that has been aged in whiskey barrels. The justification of our entire existence hinges upon that attitude."

"Or," you said with a friendly finality in your voice, "you could just be yourself, eat another slice of pizza, enjoy your beer and not think about the guy with the Miller's. Because he is a good father, and he makes a killer barbecue sauce for the burgers, and the kids love the burgers, and he chases them around the garden with a water pistol, and their golden retrievers join in, and his wife loves him and the fuck does not care whether he likes Miller's or not. Because she drinks Rosé wine."

"Rosé? Really. That's just wine for people who don't like wine."

"Shut the fuck up," you said and laughed.

We both took another slice of pizza and ate in silence. Some speakers on the walls tortured us with Oasis's Greatest Hits.

"What's next for you?" she asked me.

"Next?"

"Where you gonna go next?"

"I have no idea. I have not decided yet."

"Wanna come to Jeju with me?"

"Jeju?"

"Island in the south. We go to Busan and take a ferry there."

"Sure."

"Sure," you repeated my word in a tone that almost sounded disappointed, almost mocking. I was unsure what to make of it, so I ignored it.

We took a train to Busan a couple of days later. We shared a sandwich and some crisps during the ride.

In Busan, we checked into a cheap hotel, separate rooms. On the recommendation by a local, we took the metro to the edge of town and then a taxi to a smaller village close by. We left the skyscrapers behind us, the sea appeared to our left, gleaming in the sunlight. We drove over a hill and into the village. A long, winding road led us to the sea, and we walked along the beach for a while. We observed a group of old women sitting at the beach and cutting open oysters.

"Traditional oyster divers," you told me. "It's a tradition among women. And only women. They dive without equipment."

"They all look ancient," I said.

"It's a dying breed. Few young women wanting to dive for oysters these days."

"Not very efficient, is it? Diving without equipment?"

"No. No, it is not. Still sad, no?"

"It is what happens. We do things, things turn into traditions, traditions lose their usefulness. Still, we hold on to them, because they are traditions, but they slowly die and, finally, fade away."

"You are so romantic, it makes my panties wet," you replied with a sarcastic tone.

No. No, you did not. That would have been out of character.
Instead: "And that does not make you sad, not even a little bit?"
Better.

We walked along the sea until we found a restaurant with a big, improvised terrace, cheap plastic tables, and chairs. The tables were sporting the usual, steel enforced hole in the middle for coal, but this place did not serve meat. Fish barbecue, instead. A young man greeted us, slightly younger than the two of us. He spoke good English – he was the son of the owners, he'd tell us later.

We told him to bring us a bit of everything when he asked us what we liked. His eyes lit up. What followed was a barrage of food, a sea of dead animals, of fish parts and tentacles, shellfish, clams, and other unidentified creatures from under the sea. Some of it felt morally wrong to eat – such as the freshly chopped tentacles of a small octopus, so fresh, they were still moving and attaching themselves to the roof of our mouth, as if they were clinging to the last bit of life they had, not realising they were already dead. It was wrong, it was animal torture, it was too delicious to spark any ethical dilemmas inside of us. We ate it, like the beautiful animals we were. The beer flowed and so did the shoju, and I would wake up next morning remembering a single moment like a flashback, reliving it over and over again in my mind while lying in bed: I looked up and things seemed to stop and sounds seemed to become silent and I would look at you and, for the first time, realise that your face was full of tiny freckles, that your eyes had a spark of life that made me feel warm, that your smile and laugh made me want to hold your hand.

"What's wrong?" you said. I'd been staring at you.

"Nothing."

"What are you thinking about?"

"Nothing."

"Nothing?"

"Nothing." A note of disappointment in your voice? Disapproval? I felt cornered, I felt like I had to say something smart. I did not want to say that I just had been staring at your freckles, so I took another bite of undead tentacle and said "It is delicious" with a feeling of the world like papercuts slowly crumbling into itself, like a drawing on a fridge, all hand-drawn by a child with no understanding of the adult world, all fake, all pretend, all empty behind.

There was a sound of paper scrapping against the carpet. I got up from my hotel bed and saw that someone had pushed an envelope through the crevice between door and floor, a gesture straight from an old Hollywood movie. I picked it up, the envelope, and opened it. Inside, I found a note from you with the name of the pier and the time our ship would be leaving. I also found the ticket you had booked for me. It was for a private cabin (one for each of us? One for us together?). I got dressed and packed and wanted to knock at the door to your room, but it stood open. The cleaning lady was busy cleaning. You had already checked out. Bags gone. You gone.

I went to a coffee shop and had coffee and cake for breakfast. Then, I walked across the city until I reached the sea. I sat for some time at the beach, bought a can or two of beers at a shop and sat at the beach again, smoked some Korean cigarettes – they tasted funny, sweet, like smoking a light spring perfume – and then went to the pier where our ship would leave from.

I arrived there much too early, a good two hours before departure. To my pleasant surprise, the gangway was already down, and I was able to board. It was an enormous ship, its belly slowly filling with cars, its decks with people. I walked up the gangway and showed my ticket to the cabin member at the top. She said something in Korean to me, to which I responded with big, uncomprehending eyes. "Ah," she said, "ah, deck 3." I nodded and walked past her. Deck 3. How were the decks on a ship numbered? Did they start at the top with deck 1 and numbered them downwards or was it, like with buildings, from the bottom to the top? Turned out, I wasn't the only one who did not know about ship level naming conventions, as there were signs all over the place directing me to the right level. I headed towards our/my cabin, 323.

Everything on this ship looked old, outdated, a cruise ship of a by-gone era, of blue carpets and white walls, rust in the corners, smoke stains on the carpets. I found the room and was not surprised to find it empty. Of course. I was two hours early. You would probably show up ten minutes before departure. It was a tiny cabin. Twin beds. More blue carpet. No window. No bathroom, nor shower. The shared restrooms were located down the hall. I pushed my suitcase under the bed and left. "There must be a restaurant on this ship," I said to no one in particular.

I ate some kind of noodle soup at the ship's restaurant and had a beer. Then, I just sat there and had another beer. While I did that, the ship slowly left the harbour. From the windows, I watched mainland Korea being left behind. I went back to the room. Your suitcase under the second bed was a sign of your passing. You had made it onto the ship. I wondered whether you had expected me to wait for you in the room and had been disappointed I had not been there.

I went to a small shop on the second level to buy a few cans of beer and some crisps, and went onto deck to sit on a bench on the back part of the ship. It was getting cold and dark, so there were not too many people around me. It looked like rain, grey clouds slowly covering the sky above, maybe a storm. I'd never been on a cruise ship during a storm. I once had taken a small boat from the West coast of Ireland onto a smaller set of islands – Aran Islands? – and there had been a minor storm. The waves had pushed around the ship, like a bunch of hulked-up bullies pushing a first grader, up and down. I had felt fine, but multiple people had vomited over the railing.

"You have never told me you've been to Ireland," you said. You had appeared in front of me, at arm's length, leaning against the railing, your back to me, gazing out into the sea. The sun was setting to your left, a beautiful golden ball of vanishing light.

"I didn't think you'd find it interesting," I replied, slightly upset by your long disappearance and your sudden reappearance.

"You *assumed* I would not find it interesting."

"I am not assuming anything."

"You are full of unspoken assumptions. It is like a never-ending, internal monologue pouring out of your brain going nowhere."

I did not reply. I did not know what I could reply. Should reply. Would reply.

"You can't shut everyone out, just because you assume they would not care," you said. There it was again, that tone of finality. You would leave, like everyone else.

"What can I say – I have nothing to say," I said with a fake Eastern European accent, a feeble attempt at a joke, a vain try to make you laugh, to give me release, a "ah, you silly man," a hug, a sitting next to me on the bench, a holding my hand and an understanding that I did not know how to say the things I wanted to say because they'd been lying unspoken inside for too long, so long they turned into barren concepts that defied verbalisation.

"What are you thinking about? Right now?" Your tone had not changed, remained challenging, demanding an answer, a satisfactory answer, but I: "Nothing." I did not want to explain myself. I could not explain myself. You were not worth the effort. You had already disappeared. You would not like what you would find inside.

"It is never nothing," you said. Gentleness had crept into your voice. I ignored it.

The sun had almost gone. "It is cold," I said, no pre- or subtext. I felt like crying.

Silence. You sighed. "How many times do you expect me to come running back to you?"

"I do not know what you are talking about."

"How dense can you be? You get drunk with a girl on a flight – and all you do is get back to your Upside/down movie."

"It is Inside/Out."

"Fuck you. You just get back to your movie. We get into Seoul – and you don't even think about asking me out for a drink. I match you on Tinder – you just close the app. You magically appear in my friend's apartment – and then go home to sleep. And I push you, I push you to go to Busan, to Jeju, and you are just there, like a mother-fucking puppy. All you say is: Fine. Sure. Okay."

"I am not a puppy."

"No. You are a wall of indecisiveness and detachment. It's like you are not even here."

"I..."

"Yes?"

A seagull cried above our heads. I hated the moment. The promise of melodrama, me trying to gain access to the feelings inside, that beautiful pain that would let me wrap all my emotions around you. I could not. The seagull was too loud. The sun too bright. The wind too strong. Lightning somewhere off in the distance. Me feeling like I had to use the loo. Unpleasant taste in my mouth. Bad breath, probably, from the beers and cigarettes. Those things the movies did not tell you about romanticity.

"Speak!" you demanded one more time.

"What is there to say?" I replied. It was an honest question.

You left without another word. I stayed behind. It would be awkward should we meet in the room later. I would have to sleep outside.

Fuck this.

Fuck you.

Then, without a word of warning, the storm came. The rain, like drumbeats on the sea, first in the distance, me there, outside on deck, uncertain what the sound was. It rolled across the sea, I saw the storm approach from my right. A wall of rain, in a matter of seconds engulfing the ship. Then, thunder, thunderous thunder that was not just audible but could be felt in one's guts. The ship shook up, down, into the waves and out of them, water spraying onto the deck on both sides. I had to grip the bench and realised I had no business being outside. I had to get in.

I got up. Everything was wet. The rain splashed against my face. I slipped and fell and skid across the floor. I held on to something, lifted myself up. I felt heavy. I got to the door and pushed it open. It slid out of my hand, the door did, pushed away by the raging wind. My fingers hurt. I pushed myself inside, fell to the floor. The blue carpet underneath was wet, soaked, salty. I had to find you.

I tried to run, but the shaking boat threw me from one wall to the next. I slowed my pace. I tried to move along the wall. I hit my shoulders and my head. Maybe that was blood, that warm patch on my forehead. It felt like a miracle I did not die on the way to the cabin. I opened the door violently, I could see myself in my thoughts, standing there, heroically in the doorframe, illuminated by the lights from the hallway behind me, here to save you, even though I had no idea what my next step would have been to get us off the boat.

The room was empty, only occupied by a single suitcase. The ship screamed like a dying animal, one made of steel and rust, an animal being torn apart. It got lifted, carried by a single, tremendous wave, the gravity underneath my feet shifted. Suddenly, the floor stopped being a floor and became a wall. The corridor turned into a hole, and I fell. On my way down, which seemed endless, I heard the ship scream again, the sound of metal breaking, as the waves tore against its walls, ripping it apart, a beautiful demonstration of the force of nature. A long gap opened in the wall below and allowed water to flow inside, filling the hallway I was falling towards in a matter of seconds. Seawater and fish and freezing wind took over the places that had been made for human passengers, as if to mock our hubris that had made us think we could build houses floating in the sea.

I got submerged in the icy water and felt the burning of the sea salt against the open wound on my head. At least it acted as a disinfectant, did it not?

I swam upwards, gasping for air. The ship screamed one last time, but it sounded different now. It was the sound of an animal that had given up. An animal that was ready to be taken by the sea. I took a deep breath and dived. There was a door to the right which was open. In good times, it would have led out onto the deck of the ship. Now, in these dire times, it led me out into the open sea. Which was not a comforting thought, yet it was the only way to get out of this metal death trap that was hurling towards the bottom of the ocean.

I swam. Behind me, the vanishing lights of the ship. To the surface. Muscles tired. Losing consciousness. The storm was still raging, I saw as I pushed my head above the water. I battled against the waves until my body gave up.

I came to lying on a beach. Such a cliche, I thought to myself, losing consciousness at sea after the sinking of a ship and then just waking up safe and sound on the beach.

The stars in the sky looked beautiful, a carpet of endlessness.

I was not cold, despite only wearing my boxers. There were two reasons for this: Firstly, there was a small campfire to my left. Secondly, you were lying on top of me, skin against skin, your warm body warming my cold body. You noticed the change in my breathing and looked up at my face.

"You were shivering. Had to get you warm."

"What happened?"

"I made it to a lifeboat. Alone. Made it to the beach. Found you here. Unconscious. Made a fire to warm you up."

"Thanks."

"You are most welcome," you replied and giggled quietly. It felt good to hear your giggle. Made me feel alive. I fell asleep. Woke up when you told me not to peek and got up from my body. I kept my eyes closed while you put some clothes on. "Okay," you said, and I opened my eyes.

The stars had disappeared in favour of a grey morning sky, the sun slowly rising to the east. You were sitting next to me, knees under your chin, your skin and hair rough from the salty air. You handed me a shirt, and I diligently put it on.

"How are you feeling?" you asked me.

"Hungry."

"I will get some rations from the lifeboat."

I fell asleep before you returned with the food. I wanted to apologise. You said that it was okay, that I could rest now and that-

You would not leave my side.

I woke again. The sun stood high. You had built a makeshift sun umbrella from a big palm tree leaf. You gave me food. I have started to build a house, you told me. We live here now.

It turned out that we had landed on an undiscovered island. In the next days, we climbed the highest point on the island, a hill that allowed us to take in the surrounding world. All of our world. We were on an island surrounded by the sea, a blue surface disappearing into the Earth's curvature.

"You are not a flat-earther, are you?" I asked you. You laughed. At least my joke-game was still top-notch.

"We are fucked," you finally said, hands on your sides, panting from the climb onto the mountain/hill.

"Do you have any survival skills?" I asked you.

"I can make a fire. We will have to finish the hut. And then make a bonfire every night in case a ship passes." It turned out you had all the survival skills. I had none.

We walked back down from the hill in silence, the unspoken questions lingering between the two of us. How long do you think until a ship will find us? Are they looking for us? What are we going to eat for dinner? What the fuck are we going to do?

The next day, we searched the rest of the island. We found another beach further up north, littered with items. The currents, you said, they have carried in stuff from the ship. Parts. Suitcases. Cans. It looked like half the ship's pantry had washed ashore.

"Now all we have to do is find a can opener," you said. We started going through the flotsam. We found a bunch of phones. The salt water had destroyed most of them. Some of them still worked, had no reception, though. We found many charging cables. Useless. We had no electricity and no outlets. We found plenty of tuna and peach cans. Some sweet corn. Corned beef. We found a bunch of wet clothes in suitcases. We would have to dry the usable ones. Could have a fashion show. We found tons of PET bottles of water. You had already found a freshwater stream the other day, but it would be good to have some bottled water, just in case. There could be a drought or something. Then you, climbing across some rocks further out, found the jackpot: copious amounts of cans of chilli and ravioli and spaghetti (yes, apparently, there were canned spaghetti!) and... beers. Cans of beers. Undestroyed, untouched by the force of the sea.

"We will have a feast tonight," you announced.

"Indeed," I added, holding up a Swiss Army knife I had found among the stuff.

The sky was still clear and no cloud in sight, so we were in no rush to finish our hut. You made a fire at the beach, and I got to work opening several cans. Sweet corn for starter, chilli con carne for main, canned peaches for dessert. Yes, sure, we'd have to ration our rations at some point, but not tonight. We each opened a beer while the chilli cooked over the fire.

"Cheers," you said.

"Cheers," I replied.

I looked at you. Like in that fish barbecue place, I looked at you, attempting to actually see you. For the first time in a long time, it felt good not to be alone, alone on this deserted island. It felt good to drink cheap, lukewarm beer, and it felt amazing to wait for the crappy, shitty, disgusting chilli con carne. It felt good to sit and see the sun fall towards the horizon.

"What's wrong?" you asked.

"Nothing," I replied.

"You are crying."

"Am I?" There were tears falling down my face. I did not offer an explanation. I had none. The stress. The having survived. The seeing your face.

We ate our chilli in silence. So the peaches. We watched the sunset. I felt your presence next to me.

You got up. "I used to be a dancer," you said. "Do you want to see me dance?"

You did not wait for my reply, just took off your shoes and socks, and dug your naked feet into the warm sand. Something in your face changed. It was like you remembered something, a pain, a hurt, something from the past. I was unable to watch, to take in, to understand any of the moves that followed, a most-likely beautiful, perfectly arranged succession of movements, yet all I could see was your expression. It was like being transported back in time and space, a time and space where I became the person sitting on the empty chair in the audience in that town in the middle of nowhere.

You finished your performance, and you came up to me.

"It is so nice you came," you said.

"Certainly," I/the old lady from the train said. "I am thrilled I met you today."

"Thank you," you felt embarrassed, your cheeks a rosy colour.

"Nothing to thank me for," I/the old lady from the train said. "You are a beautiful dancer. An artist. And don't let anyone tell you otherwise. You are complete the way you are. And you do not need anyone else for that. You can stop searching."

It was the rambling of an old person, my voice shaky, old and creaky, but you looked at me with wide, open eyes and tears and trembling, full-body, my words having given you a release you did not expect. You quit the show the next day, getting away from the director, the man that destroyed you, not because he'd been an evil man, but because he'd been negligent of other people's feelings, hiding his negligence behind the mask of art.

You found a group of like-minded people and, together, you continued to dance, and you had a big break when you turned 35, travelling the country again, with your group, your dancers, your directors, all hand-picked by yourself. People you trusted. It was not the same, surely, not the same emotional highs and lows. It was steady, though, and people clapped at the end of every show. You felt strong, and you looked forward to seeing your husband and your kid at home.

The dance ended. Your toes and feet covered in sand. The world silent, all stretched out in darkness. The only world we needed, our island, hidden by the sea. Above us, the moon and the stars and the potential of infinity.

"I wanted to invite you for a drink, you know. I wanted to match you on Tinder. I wanted to kiss you when I saw you at your friend's apartment." I fell silent. I lay back in the sand and watched the sky.

"Are you sleeping?" you asked, since I did not continue.

"I was afraid you would see me for who I am and realise that there is not much to see. There is not much to me. Maybe that is all I am. And empty page."
"And why would you not start writing on it?"
"Because I have no pen. And maybe not even a page."

We watched a ship pass in the distance. The bright lights. The loud Korean pop music of the people partying on deck.

"Here is a pen." You threw a stick at me. "As good as any."
"And then... what if I do not have the words? What if I write a thousand pages and they all amount to nothing?"
"What if... what if... what if... What if you got up and touched me? What if you told me you liked me? What if you asked me whether you could hug me? What if you asked to kiss me? What if we built a raft together and drowned at sea? Or got eaten by sharks? What if we did not and got back to our lives, but stayed together? Forever? Or just a night? Still better than lying in the sand and moaning about life, no?"

The sand was warm and comfortable.

"The sand is warm and comfortable," I said.

What are you so afraid of? you demanded to know.

I said nothing.

You sighed. A deep, defeated sigh. I was sorry I could not give you the answer you hoped for, even though I knew exactly what the answer would be. Get up, ask to touch you, kiss you, be someone you could be with. Yet would that be me? Or would that just be me pretending to be someone I was not?

"There you go again. Thoughts. Endless lines of thoughts. What if you are someone I would not like? What if you are a fraud? You know, A., you got to wake up at one point. You have to talk. Let someone in. Even if it is just yourself." You fell silent for a moment, expecting me to say something.

"Some of us a real," you said, turning away, hurt, angry, empty.

I sat up. The party boat was almost out of sight now.

"I know," I replied, "only, the thing is... you are not."

A seagull cried into the night. The waves kept crashing onto the beach, coming closer to my feet. It had got cold, and I regretted not having brought a coat. I got up and finished my can of beer.

I turned away from the sea and climbed the little hill at the end of the beach. From here, I could see the village I was staying in. I could see my hotel. Silently, I walked back to the hotel.

Jeju, the Korean honeymoon island, was no place for me.

Part IV: The Human Angle

Nara 2 / Osaka / Tesseract and Post-Apocalyptic Blues

I woke up the next morning and checked for messages from my sister and my mother, but there were none. They were fine. They would be fine, eventually. Pets died every day. I still felt sad, even though it was more like an echo of a feeling, like melancholy, like things forgotten, things not fully materialised.

This was a new day. A new chapter. I returned to the cafe above the hostel before I packed my bags. There still was time. The lady welcomed me with a warm "you are back." I was back, indeed, not because of the good coffee (it was mediocre), but because the lady was nice, the music was good and there was a lack of alternative options. It felt good that she seemed happy about my return, and I thanked her in my best bad Japanese.

I watched a group of deer crossing the street outside the windows, walking past the cafe, quietly, silently, gracefully, almost divine in their movements. There was nothing divine to them, of course, no Miyazaki-magic, they were out and about to prostitute themselves for deer-crackers from tourists.

"Did you know they can bow?" The cafe-woman had walked up to my table and was watching the deer as well.

"Sorry?"

"The deer. They can bow." Her English was much better than my Japanese. "If you bow in front of them, they will bow back. I think people taught them to do so by giving them crackers. But they also bow without the crackers now."

"Pavlov would be proud."

"What is that?"

"He was the guy with the dogs. He would ring a bell before giving them food. And then, at one point, the dogs would start drooling just when hearing the bell, no food involved."

"Why would he do that?"

"Do see whether he can get a reaction without action. Drooling without food. The bell becomes a substitution for the food."

"Did he also try it with deer?"

"I don't think so." Outside, a younger deer broke off from the group of five, six animals and jumped along a patch of grass. "The interesting question is, of course, has the action of bowing become part of their genes, their inherent knowledge – or does every young deer still learn it from observation, from their mother or father or the pack – tribe-group – what do you call a bunch of deer?"

"I don't know," she replied. "I only know that they bow when you bow in front of them." She stepped away, went back behind the counter to clean the coffee machine.

I paid for my coffee, returned to the hostel, packed my bags, and started on my way to the train station. It was a good twenty-minute walk and my bag felt heavy. However, there were no buses, and I did not feel like taking a taxi. The morning, it was about 10 o'clock now, was cold and misty. There'd been more rain last night.

I passed a group – bunch – pack – murder – embarrassment – of deer grassing on a patch of... grass next to the road. One of them, standing close to the pavement, lifted its head and eyed me curiously. I stopped and looked back at the animal. I bowed. As promised, the deer bowed as well, tilting its neck and head towards the ground and up again, looking at me expectantly. I bowed again, and so did the deer.

Then, I felt bad for not having a cracker to give to it. The deer wasn't the dog in the Pavlov-equation, but me. Me trained to feed it crackers for making it bow.

I felt the gaze of the deer on my back as I continued my walk to the train station. Accusingly. Angrily.

At the station, I bought a katsu sandwich, a Boss coffee and a Coke Zero. Nothing like a healthy breakfast.

The train, a rusty cross between a subway car and a short-distance train, was already waiting, so I got in and took a seat. The car was almost empty.

I drank my coffee and ate my sandwich as we rumbled along Japan's countryside. Then, I leaned against the window to watch the world go by. Then, I fell asleep. I changed trains in Kyoto for Osaka. Fell asleep again.

I woke to a text message arriving on my phone ten minutes before I arrived in Osaka. It was from Hamako who told me she'd pick me up at my hotel in two hours. I wrote back that it sounded good, and that I was looking forward to seeing her soon.

My hotel was between America-mura (a triangular square famous for being the epicentre of youth adapting and celebrating American lifestyle in the 70s) and one of the main roads, from where it would be a straight shot to the river and Dotombori, the buzzing main district of Osaka, which just lay across the river. That meant a not short, but manageable walk from the train station. I headed along the main road, following my GPS towards my hotel and the first sight I caught of the city was the typical big city vibe – long streets, cars, busses, people hustling out and about.

However, my taking a detour via a set of smaller streets soon showed a different city, a peculiar city, which I'd seen nowhere else in Japan, especially as I ventured closer to America-mura, into the part of town that had been influenced by the historic presence of the American army and American culture. Walking down these smaller streets felt like walking into a seedy part of town, a dangerous place, as if a famous Japanese director had made a movie about the Bronx in the 70s with no American actors at hand. There was loud hip-hop music coming out of shops selling skater attire and vinyl LPs, there were tattoo shops (!) and burly Japanese shop owners smoking cigarettes in front of their stores. I felt like a displaced child marvelling at this unexpected aspect of Japanese culture, felt out of place, like Spongebob ending up in that biker bar in that one movie.

I found my hotel in a narrow street a few steps into an alley. It was another one of these nondescript business hotels – but the location was more important than the looks of it. Everything was close. The seedy bars of America-mura, the flashing lights of Dotombori. The drinks, the food, the fun.

I went to the reception and handed over my ID. I'd given up telling them my name – even when the receptionists spoke good English, they had problems understanding my Swiss name and, so far, I'd been unable to figure out how to pronounce it comprehensibly in English.

I was informed, luckily, that my room was already ready. I checked my watch and saw that I still had an hour before Hamako would arrive to pick me up.

The thing with Japanese hotels was, they were never dirty. And they were never run-down. Sure, many times, they were old, I thought to myself, as I exited the elevator on the third floor and was greeted by a darkish hallway with a long, thick, dark red (burgundy?) carpet. What was that style, seventies? Fifties? I wondered how many footsteps this carpet had seen, how many dramas and cheerful stories. A sign on the wall told me to head right for my room. I passed a vending machine for drinks and a ticket vending machine, offering 1000-yen tickets for access to the entertainment section of the TV. A Japanese man, maybe my age, in a suit, was fumbling with the machine and he seemed startled by my appearance, looked at me with an innocent look. He stared at me for far too long and I looked back at him for far too long, I nodded at him, a nice nod trying to convey a sense of reassurance, telling him I absolutely assumed that he wanted to watch a low-resolution version of Transformers 3 – Revenge of the Fallen on pay-tv, not wank off to some good old perverted Japanese porn.

I opened my door and was welcomed by the same 70s (or 60s? Or 80s?) vibe, just a slightly darker, greyish carpet, a TV, a chair, a desk, and a bed. I wondered how many wanks this room had seen in its decades of existence.

The phone rang just as I'd taken two steps into the room. I answered. "Mr. ...?" the receptionist completely mispronounced my name, but I had got used to the way the Japanese said it, so I confirmed. "Ms Hamako-San is expecting you in the lobby." She was 45 minutes early. "I will be down in a minute."

I put my suitcase down, checked myself in the mirror, fixed the hair (the certainty that I would be bald in ten years washed over me) and checked my t-shirt. No stains. It still smelled fresh enough. The huge Star Wars imprint (the poster of the Return of the Jedi) might have been yelling NERD a bit too loudly, but then, I was in Japan, where such things were not only socially accepted, but expected of someone like me.

I met Hamako in the lobby – we hugged quickly (uncommon for a Japanese, but then, she'd spent the better part of her teenage life in the States) and exchanged amicable how-are-yous and nice-to-see-yous. "So, I was thinking I show you some parts of the city. The park and the castle. Dotombori for later when Andy joins us. He's gotta work till four or five." "What is he up to these days?" I asked her. "He works at one of those English pubs. They need good English speakers at these places. For the tourists."

We left the hotel and turned right towards the subway station.

"Did you get into the city fine?" she asked me.

"No problem."

"You were in Kyoto before, right?"

"Nara."

"Ah, did you see the deer? I want to go there, haven't had time yet. Even though it is not far from where we live." Andy and Hamako lived in one of the larger suburbs of Osaka, yet I did not know where exactly. Something for conversation at a later point.

"How do you like Japan so far?"

"It is great," I replied, annoyed by the flatness of my answer. More: "The nature is just beautiful – and the people, the food."

"Did you meet anyone?"

"Meet?"

"Get to know, I mean. You're travelling on your own, I'd imagine you meet many people."

"Not really. Not yet."

I had met Hamako two handfuls of times when she'd been visiting Andy in Switzerland at the beginning of their relationship, the extremely long-distance phase, they called it. Today was the first time, it occurred to me, that I was meeting Hamako alone, without Andy. Funnily enough, Andy and I had not been close friends before they'd become a couple. We became friends afterwards, because Andy – an acquaintance at most back then – knew I liked Japan and invited me to some gatherings, so I could talk to Hamako. And then, the three of us became friends, hanging out together when Hamako was in Switzerland, taking trips, even occasionally having a three-way Skype conversation when Hamako was in Japan and called in from a distance. "I am actually glad I have a long-distance relationship," Andy would tell me, "because I am too busy for a full-time relationship." He used to work at a big company back then, on his way to the top, to the managerial level. Then, they almost fell apart, he and Hamako, so it was time to end the long-distance and move to Japan.

"You look so serious," Hamako told me, both of us standing in the subway, me staring out of the dark window, possibly just looking at my reflection.

"I was just thinking about you and Andy."

"What about us?"

"I remembered the first time we met."

"When was that?"

"First time you visited Andy in Switzerland, remember? I picked you up at the airport with him."

"Ohhh, he had a sign. And flowers."

"Yeah. I told him to get some. A grandiose romantic gesture."

"I am allergic."

"We found that out when you sneezed during the entire ride home. We thought you had got a cold on the flight. Thank God it was before Corona. Otherwise, we'd have sent you into isolation."

Hamako smiled. She asked me about my family and life back home. Nothing much had changed in the four years since we'd last seen each other. I was still living in Basel and still working the same job. I did not tell her about the death of the family dog since that seemed too heavy a topic to discuss for a fun evening out. Also, I was not sure whether she would understand the attachment one can have to a pet.

We came out of the subway station and found ourselves in the park surrounding Osaka's castle. It will be a pleasant walk, Hamako informed me.

"Is it always this hot in fall?" I asked her.

"It seems pretty normal," she told me.

We stopped at the Lawson at the edge of the park to get water and another canned coffee for me. I quickly checked the map on my phone to see whether I had saved a *good* coffee place close-by, which was, unfortunately, not the case.

"What do you know about the castle?" Hamako asked me while we walked through the park, being passed by small electric busses that looked like a bunch of golf carts glued together. The Human Centipede of golf carts taxing tourists through the park who did not feel like going for a pleasant walk in the fall-heat. The white castle of Osaka towered on a hill in the distance.

"I had it on my list of places to see," I offered.

"That is not much."

"What do you know?"

"I came prepared," Hamako said triumphantly, and took out a piece of paper with handwritten notes. "I've never visited the castle.

However, I have read its Wikipedia page last night. I have you know the castle played a key role in the unification of Japan in the 16th century."

"So, Japan was not unified before?"

"Apparently not. There was this general, and he unified Japan and he died. True story."

"Fascinating."

"And the castle was destroyed – or a model thereof – in the 1955 film Godzilla Rides Again."

I saw a picture before my inner eye of Godzilla in a samurai armour riding a gigantic, fire-breathing steed (preferably with six legs), laying waste to Osaka.

"I think the movie was called Godzilla Raids Again," I corrected Hamako. I was serious about my film titles.

"Ah, be quiet and enjoy the scenery. I do the teaching."

We climbed a set of steps and entered the park's main square, the last stretch leading up to the castle. Hamako pointed to the left, to a small pond. "This is a famous photo spot," she explained. "Often, there are tons of school classes lining up to get their yearbook photo taken with the pond and the castle in the background." She led me to the spot, and I diligently took a photo of the view. "Do you want me to take a photo of you?" she asked me. I declined. I was not a major fan of photos of myself.

We joined the people standing in line to get into the castle and made our way through its innards – most of the building was taken up by exhibits showcasing images and texts about its builder, the general-samurai, teaching us how he unified Japan, yet, to be honest, I did not care all that much about it, I skimmed some texts, looked half-heartedly at the videos on display. Only the suits of samurai armour exhibited woke some marvel inside. There was something fascinating as well as terrifying about the craftsmanship of the armours, the intricate details of how the various parts were woven or strung together, the helmet with its comically large horns and the mask, a frozen scream of war framed by a long nose that looked like an oversized caricature of a penis. Of course, that had been the point, the display of manly endowment, the most masculine of all displays of power. The penis-nose.

"Jeez, that mask looks like a penis," Hamako said and giggled. "I think that was the point," I added. "War is all about who has the biggest one. That is also why swords are shaped like long sticks and not like vaginas." I felt weird for bringing up female genitalia. "I honestly would pay to see the design for a vagina-shaped sword. Or any vagina-weapon," Hamako replied. "Don't think that would be very handy." "Isn't that what all men think? That vaginas are not very handy?"

We both laughed, but I hoped there were not too many people around who understood English, understood us talking about penises and vaginas. We finished our tour of the museum and, back outside, bought matcha ice cream from a vending machine and sat on a bench. The space behind the pond had filled up with groups in school-uniforms and couples and tourists waiting for their turn to take a photo.

"You live outside Osaka, right? You and Andy?" I said, being proud of myself for remembering me wanting to ask her about it.

"Yeah, in a suburb. We are thinking about moving away from Osaka, though. To the countryside. I would like to buy a farm and grow vegetables. He is learning how to carve wood figures." It sounded like a parody of country-hipster-life, yet she was serious.

"Wood carving?"

"Yes. An old master carver has taken him on as an apprentice. He is practicing almost every evening."

"Sounds busy."

"He is."

I imagined Andy and Hamako on a farm somewhere in the countryside of Japan. A forest and river close-by. Andy sitting in a workshop carving wood, Hamako in the garden, growing vegetables and then fermenting them or cooking them into sauces, stews, both of them selling their handiwork over the internet. I liked the vision. I told Hamako about it. She laughed and said she liked the idea as well. "And kids," she added, "I want to have children as well." No dog?

"They would enjoy growing up in the countryside."

"Until they get older. Then they'd get bored."

We finished our ice cream and Hamako led me out of the park, into the subway and to the neighbourhood of Shinsekai. "The neighbourhood has a poor reputation," Hamako told me on the way there. "It used to be a hotspot for crime in the nineties."

"And today?"

Hamako shrugged her shoulders. "It is still a bit seedy. You gotta keep your eyes open. There are some homeless people around and some organised crime. It is not more dangerous than your average American city, though."

"Why are we heading there?" The thought of going to a dangerous part of town made me feel uneasy.

"You gotta see the Tsutenkaku. It's a tower. And you have to see the neighbourhood, too. It is like taking a trip to the past."

We exited the subway and soon, the tower came into view, an ugly thing of metal, lacking the finesse that gave this world's most famous towers, Eiffel, Skytree, Space Needle, their iconicity and popularity. The Tsutenkaku was a misshaped beast that looked like a cheap miniature movie prop that had been enlarged by a weird scientific accident. I understood Godzilla's urge to ride against Osaka and destroy it.

"And?"

"That thing is ugly. " But: "I love it." The ugliness was its charm. It made the tower relatable, endearing, the ugly duckling standing off to the side at the famous tower family reunion.

"They built the neighbourhood in the early 20th century." Hamako was reading from a note again. "They modelled the neighbourhood on one side of the tower after New York, the other after Paris. And there used to be an amusement park here as well, but it burned down."

I wondered what an amusement park in the early 20th century in Japan had looked like. Rollercoasters? Water slides? People in kimonos standing in line at food stands to buy hotdogs, shooting at targets with water guns?

We took an elevator to get to the top of the tower. As we stepped out of the elevator, we found ourselves face-to-face with a peculiar-looking statue. It represented an impish creature, sitting on its behind, feet stretched out towards us, bearing a grin that could be benevolent or insidious.

"This is Billiken-San," Hamako told me. "He is a god of good fortune. You can touch his feet and wish for something."

"Anything?"

"Yes. People ask him for good business, or to pass an exam, or even to find love."

"That is a lot to choose from."

"Just any good fortune. He can make anything true."

"What if my good fortune impedes your good fortune?"

"Hmmm?"

"What if I wished I were alone on this planet? That would certainly be against everyone else's interest."

"Not for those who are suicidal."

"Touché. Yes, but let's say the vast majority."

"Then, maybe Billiken-San would decide that your wish is not good and would not grant it."

"But is he allowed to judge? How does he know whose good fortune is most important? Whose wishes are good?"

"He can make everything happen. Maybe he would create a parallel universe just for you to be alone."

A man walking down a street in downtown Tokyo alone. Vast streets empty, malls empty, offices empty. On the other side of reality, just a snap of a finger away, there are hundreds of thousands of people walking the same streets, malls, offices. So close, so far away. The thought sent shivers down my spine.

"Billiken-San. God of good fortune and the quantum realm."

"You gonna wish for something or not?"

"Yes, sure," I said, and diligently touched Billiken's feet.

We took in the city from the tower for a while until Hamako suggested it was time "to get the hell out of here and get a drink."

She led me to a hidden bar close to the America-mura triangle-square. It was tucked away on the fifth floor of what looked like an apartment building. There were no signs announcing the presence of the bar, but she led me steadfast through a door covered in graffiti into a beautiful, small bar, with a wooden countertop and some tables in the back. It was early, and the place was virtually empty.

"They are doing apothecary cocktails," Hamako told me. "Spices and infusions. Also, fumigating. You gotta try their smoked Old-Fashioned." Which, again, I diligently did, haunted by the question of whether I would have ordered an Old-Fashioned anyway (as it was one of my favourite drinks) or whether I only did so because she'd told me to. The bartender set up the smallest stack of dried herbs and small wooden sticks, which he set on fire. Then he put a glass, upside down, on top of it. Quickly, a cloud of smoke formed inside the glass. After a moment, maybe half-a-minute, he lifted the glass. The smell of the smoke touched my nostrils, a sharp, yet pleasant smell of burning forest and Italian cuisine. The taste of the smoke had clung to the inside of the glass, he explained to me, and would enrich the taste of the cocktail.

"We will meet Andy for dinner. In an hour," Hamako informed me after checking her phone. She was drinking a spicy rift on a Sex on the Beach.

"How is the book coming?" Hamako asked me.

"What?"

"The book. The one you said you are working on."

"Ah. Okay, I guess. I haven't really felt like writing," I replied, memories flashing through my brain of myself sitting in my underwear in a hotel room in front of my iPad, trying to come up with a clever idea for the first chapter.

"You have never told me what it is about."

"Ah. It is about a guy who travels to Japan."

Hamako laughed. A clear, friendly laugh appreciating the metaness. "Is it autobiographical?"

"No. Not really. There are some real things in it, I guess."

"Am I going to be in it?"

"No. Don't worry." Maybe that was a lie. Maybe she would be in it. Who was to say what my brain would do? Maybe I would write a seemingly new character on an empty page and only later realise that I had modelled the character after her. Maybe I would get drunk, and my drunken self would write a story about her.

"And what does your guy do in Japan?"

"He travels. And meets people." I struggled to give her a meaningful explanation of what I was working on. It was about the encounter between people. It was about the question of connectivity. It was isolation and togetherness. It was about falling in love. Life. About fucking everything. Fucking all.

"It's about love," I finally said, hating myself for sounding so trivial. It wasn't about love. It was about hate. It was about failure. I shushed my thoughts and continued: "It seems that's the only thing I can write. Love-stories. It's all a bit pathetic."

"It's not. I like the idea. Sometimes, I'd like to fall in love again."

"But you have Andy," I replied naively.

"Yes, that's right. Of course. And we love each other, most of the time. Sometimes you fall out of love, I guess." The smile on her face and the sorrow in her eyes were real. I stayed silent. I had nothing smart to say. "It's a tough place and time to be in love, to be a couple," she added, "so much work, so many hours of not being together. We both want to achieve something but are not sure what. Some days, I feel bad for dragging Andy to Japan. It's tough for him to find friends because he is not Japanese. He does not want to hang out with expats all the time." She took a sip from her glass. So did I (from my glass). The bourbon had a bitter, burnt quality. "Sometimes, I am afraid I made a mistake. Not about Andy. Don't get me wrong." "I understand," I said, even though I was not sure I did. "Thank you," she replied and was silent for a while, both of us staring at the bottles on the shelf behind the bar. "I am scared that we both have to give up too much to be together. And that we are just too different after all." She sighed. I didn't think she was talking to me. She spoke. She needed someone to hear the words. To give her a reason to say them. "Five nights out of seven, we meet at home, and we argue about some silly thing, like him not having done the dishes yesterday, or me constantly complaining about something...," we both took a sip again, "...but then, there are the other two nights out of seven and I look at him and I know... I know him like no one else. And he knows me."

"Andy is an oaf sometimes, but he'd not be here," I offered, "if he did not want to be here *with you*." It felt like a weak thing to say. How well did I know Andy? Who was I to explain his motives? How was it my place to promise Hamako Andy loved her?

She smiled. She had a beautiful face when she smiled that bitter-sweet smile, her eyes and cheeks framed by a hint of sadness and melancholy. "Thank you," she replied. And after a moment: "You are a good listener." No, I was not, I just did not know what to say most of the time. So, I listened instead. She sighed again. "Ah, here I go babbling on about love and I must make you feel like shit. I heard you and Marnie broke up a while back."

"Yes, we have," I confirmed. It was funny, I realised, this was the first time I had thought about her, Marnie, in a long time. "It is okay. We've hardly been a proper couple."

We met Andy a little while later in Dotombori, underneath a gigantic plastic crab that hung from a building, a not-so-subtle hint that we were standing in front of a crab restaurant.

Andy and Hamako led me along the streets and pointed out some restaurants and we grabbed Takoyaki from one of the street vendors (the line was long, since the place was famous, Andy explained to me, certainly not the best Takoyaki in town, but you cannot visit Osaka without having had their Takoyaki and a photo to prove it, he said). We also bought a couple of beers from a 7/11 and stood outside drinking.

"Won't people mind us having drinks outside in the streets?" I asked them, remembering that eating and drinking in the streets in Japan was a no-go.

"I am drinking outside all the time," Hamako replied. And Andy added: "Osaka differs from the rest of Japan. It's like its own universe. Much more relaxed. Much more fun." As if on cue, a tele-worthy drama developed on the other side of the street: a woman yelled out of the window of a restaurant on the second floor, crying, in distress. A guy in the street below was yelling things back at her, apologetically.

"Yeah, but that's Koreans," Andy said, having noticed me looking at them. I was not sure whether it was supposed to be a joke, still the three of us laughed. I felt lightheaded, lighter than usual. The Old-Fashioned and the beer were doing their job.

"Are you full?" Andy asked me when we finished the octopus balls (only shape, not ingredient). I nodded. "Well, then it is time we introduced you to the favourite Osaka pastime."

"Which is?" I asked.

"You eat till you drop."

"Kuidaore," Hamako added in Japanese.

This was when the night began for real. We left Dotombori through a narrow passage between two houses (past Osaka's smallest shrine, Hamako told me, pointing to the tiniest model of a shrine standing in a niche inside a wall) and into another set of side-streets, which turned out to house a collection of questionable-looking restaurants.

"Kushikatsu," Hamako said as we entered a bar with three empty seats at the counter. The smell of frying lingered in the air, mixed with cold tobacco and beer-sweat. A TV in the corner was showing a baseball game. Hamako asked the staff in Japanese whether we could sit at the bar, and they welcomed us ("Dozou!").

The next things I knew were that I had an ice-cold beer in front of me, that Hamako had ordered food, and that someone placed a bowl with salad and one with sauce in front of us.

"We are in a Kushikatsu restaurant," Hamako said.

"Basically, fried food on skewers," Andy added helpfully.

Hamako continued: "And there is only one rule to Kushikatsu."

"You don't talk about Kushikatsu," I replied, which made Andy laugh, not so Hamako. She was taking her Kushikatsu seriously.

"No. You dip in the sauce once per stick. You do not double-dip. Never. If you need more sauce, you use the salad to get it onto the food." She dipped a leaf of salad in the sauce, holding the leaf like a little bowl in her palm for the sauce. "Got it?"

"No double-dipping. Use the salad to transport sauce. Got it."

What followed was a tour de force of frying. Skewers after skewers were handed to us by the guy behind the counter and I tried to memorise each one of them (lotus mushroom, chicken, beef, pork, wienerwurst, anything you could batter and fry). I gave up halfway through, though. My mind was getting slower while we worked our way through our second pint of beer and more skewers, talking and laughing about things we'd experienced together. Of course, again, the story of Hamako being allergic to flowers came up, and then the time I accompanied Andy to Japan, and he upset a hundred-year-old hat-shop owner by bursting into his shop and putting every single hat onto his head without asking.

"Yeah, I was a dumbfuck European back then," Andy said.

"Language," Hamako.

Me: "You still are." Laughter.

Andy, pointing at the people behind the bar: "They don't understand English."

Hamako: "They know what fuck is."

Andy: "Fuck, now you said it."

Hamako: "Shhhhh."

Me: "We definitively need more beer."

We left the bar laughing like little kids and dragged ourselves through another set of small streets and into a karaoke place. The idea of karaoke did not enthuse neither me, nor Andy too much, but Hamako pleaded (only one hour!, she yelled repeatedly) until we gave up. It was a dime-a-dozen karaoke place, the typical sofa along the wall, a small metal table in the middle and a TV in front. Andy ordered a triplet of whiskey colas through the phone on the wall, as well as a basket of mozzarella sticks (why the fuck?), while me and Hamako turned The Killers' Are We Human? into the most god-awful duet. Then Hamako and Andy versus Linkin Park's In the End, followed by Andy and me trying our way through the Japanese lyrics of Totoro's title song. Then Backstreet Boys, Blink-182, those teenage songs, goddamn heartbreak song, good memories song, memories about falling in love and living life for the first time.

We felt hungry (Osaka was working its magic) after we left the karaoke room two hours later and we opted for a conveyor belt sushi restaurant. We stumbled into a place, a large hall with booths and tables arranged along the conveyor belts. The belts looked like train tracks, which had been laid out by a madman, not in straight lines, but in bends and curves reaching around the hall, going from table to table in no discernible pattern, back and forth, up and down, going up fake mountains, Fuji-San in the far corner and, of course, the Matterhorn to our left, or through fake-cities – there was London somewhere in the back and Paris on the other side. The sushi was on little train-wagons, being pulled by little locomotives, spouting steam and all.

A model-train-set-sushi-conveyor-belt-restaurant.

I stood there in awe – it was a fake place, certainly, but the alcohol in my system helped me to look at it with the eyes of a child seeing a train set for the first time.

"Thought you would like it," Hamako said. She talked to the waitress that approached us and guided us to a table. We sat down. I felt drunk-silly, tried to hold it together, as not to make a poor impression on Hamako. And Andy. And the people in the restaurant. I wanted to order a train. Right here and now. Tuna express into my mouth.

I took one of the plastic menus on the table, only to see myself confronted with a lengthy list of Japanese writing. "I am gonna have this," I said, pointing to a random item on the list. "That is not the menu," Hamako replied, laughing, "you just ordered a train." "What?" "You are holding the timetable. They tell customers when they use a certain train model. So you can make sure you do not miss your favourite train." She took the not-menu from my hand. "Oh, look, they are going to have a Swiss train in an hour."

Meanwhile, Andy had spotted and grabbed a tablet from the end of the table. "There are two ways to get food," he explained to me, "either you just grab stuff off the trains passing by. Or you order something specific with the tablet and they put it on a special train for you."

"How will I know when it is coming by?"

"Order something," he said, and handed me the tablet. I ordered some random sushi – tuna, fried salmon, sea urchin – and a little while later, a little loudspeaker next to the conveyor belt tracks spoke – it sounded like an announcement at a train station, a train arriving. Surely enough, only a few seconds later, a train passed by carrying sushi on a red plate – "The red plate means someone ordered it," Hamako told me. "It's yours," Andy added, and I took the plate off – it was the tuna.

"So, the rules are simple," Andy said, "take a plate or order. But never take a red plate that's not meant for you." "And no double-dipping," I added. We all laughed. It'd only be funny if you'd been there. "I have one more question," I said, "are we gonna have more alcohol?" We decided on beers and sake. Not a good mix for the stomach, but a good mix if you wanted to keep your befuddlement on a decent level.

I paid for our meal with my credit card because I wanted to thank Hamako and Andy. They protested (in vain) and then insisted on bringing me to another bar, one of their favourite bars, a tiny place close to where we were. I should go to bed, I said. One more drink, Hamako decided. One last drink.

It was almost empty, the bar. The owner was a collector of music, expressed by the fact that the space behind the bar was not stacked with bottles, but with LPs. He gave us a folder that listed all the LPs he had, in case we had any preferences for music. We ordered three whiskey sours and flipped through the folder. After much discussion, we finally settled for Nick Cave's Boatman's Call, which seemed like an enjoyable way to end the evening.

Sitting there, listening to Cave's sweet-silvery voice, I asked Hamako and Andy about their life in Japan and we joked about the flocks of salarymen. "What's up with them?" I said, "do they all shop at the same store? All the same white shirt, blue tie, dark blue jacket? They all look the same." And quickly added: "...but not in a racist way!" Hamako snorted her whiskey sour through her nose laughing. However, after a while, we grew silent, because we were getting tired, it was getting late, and we felt happy.

It was a good silence, listening to Nick Cave and Far From Me came on, and Andy grabbed Hamako's hand, and they quietly, silently, slowly danced. I remained at the table.

Looking at them holding each other, that peaceful expression on their faces, I remembered the day Andy had told me he had met that girl at a Starbuck's, a tourist from Japan. He'd spilled coffee all over her, he'd told me, because he'd turned around and bumped into her, where-upon they exchanged numbers and now, he did not know what to do and I said just invite her out for dinner.

They looked happy and sat down again and after a while, Hamako fell asleep at the table and Andy called a taxi and I told him: "Man, you are lucky. Keep her tight. And don't ever forget that." I hit him on the shoulder, bro-style. Andy nodded. I was drunk. Normally, I wouldn't say such things, I thought to myself, while the taxi sped through the night. It sounded like something someone in a movie would have said.

The taxi brought me back to the hotel and both Hamako (who had woken up) and Andy got out to say goodbye. They sent the taxi off, planning to take the subway for the remaining way to their home. We hugged and thanked each other and turned around and I entered the faceless business hotel with thick carpet floors and dimly lit hallways. I returned to my room, still the same single-bed room, the one I had left mere hours ago. I opened the curtains. The world had taken on a grey colour, the colour of an hour before sunrise. I sat down on the bed and lit a cigarette, blew the smoke towards the ceiling.

In the building across the street, a young woman in a business dress was sitting at a desk, motionless, eyes wide-open. She snapped to life when someone entered the office, she jumped up and bowed. The woman who had entered greeted her and took her with her, leading her out of the room. I tried to guess the context of the brief scene I'd just seen, yet, since I had no certainty I would guess right, it seemed like an idle task, an empty guessing game with no solution.

I woke up around lunchtime and my head still felt slightly drunk. I'd got a text from Hamako, asking me how I felt and what I would do

today. I checked my notes and found I had two restaurants on my list –
a pizzeria and a popular outdoor restaurant. Outdoor Izakaya, that was,
to be precise.

I entered the pizzeria about an hour later. It was a small place, looking like the perfect imitation of a restaurant imitating an Italian restaurant. Tiny wooden tables, a long counter, huge pizza oven. Italian beer
and wine bottles in every corner – the pizza-maker (what do you call
them?) was at the counter, talking to another Japanese person – in Italian. It seemed somewhat odd, two Japanese people speaking Italian, but
then I remembered I spoke English with many of my Swiss friends, because we'd studied English together. At first, it'd been an effective way
to train the language and then, it just stuck. The pizza-human watched
me entering and pointed to a table. Only a second later, I had a menu
in hand and ordered a Morello. It seemed not like a clever idea to drink
alcohol today, but then, one beer hardly classified as alcohol. Not while
on holiday. I ordered a plain Margarita with cherry tomatoes because
I'd read that the place made an outstanding dough and marinara.

The pizza lived up to the praise on the internet. The dough was
fresh, fluffy, the marinara a perfect balance of salty, sour, and sweet.
The pizza, overall, held its own compared to some of the best you could
get in Italy – probably an Italian mama somewhere had a heart attack
the very moment I thought that thought.

I wandered the streets afterwards, belly full and slightly tipsy because of the beer, and got myself lost in Osaka's main train station
which offered a selection of expensive-looking shops arranged in –
what seemed to me – a labyrinth of hallways and corners. A Penrosian
mall. Shopping malls, I thought to myself, remembering my university
education, were a heterotopia in Foucault's best sense. Malls were an
alien, unsettling location with the sole purpose of celebrating money
and value and bright lights, a place where fathers would suddenly voice
a "ah, what the heck" and buy their daughters expensive necklaces, an
amusement park dedicated to the free market economy. Yet, shopping
malls were only that way because we assigned that role to them. Hence,

a heterotopia, a place that was only special because we made it special. If we ignored the mall, it would be no mall at all.

Fuck, I thought to myself, I should write a philosophy book. Show people how I had this all figured out. The fucking human fucking condition.

A couple of hours later, me and a whole lot of conditioned humans were standing in line for Izakaya Toyo, the man who had got famous for his appearance on Netflix's Street Food show, the man who cooked tuna with a flamethrower. I had arrived early and had *only* thirty to forty people queuing in front of me. The line behind me stretched down along the side of the road, and Toyo's people, all identified by the same blue t-shirt, were walking up and down to make sure people remained at the side of the road and had no negative impact on the flow of traffic. Most of the people were probably standing in line because they'd seen Toyo on the Netflix show (peasants!). I, of course, had already encountered him earlier, in Goulding's seminal Rice Noodle Fish. The thought of the book brought a sting of pain to my body, as I remembered Anthony Bourdain, late Anthony Bourdain, who had written the foreword to the book. The death of Bourdain had touched me. That thought that someone, who had been living the foodie-dream, would kill himself, seemed terrifying. Was it proof that there was no happiness to be found at the end of our dreams?

I wondered how I would feel in Bourdain's shoes, wondered whether that would be enough to fill the unhappiness inside. It was a pointless wonder, of course, because I was not in his shoes, I was not Bourdain, I was just one of the zombies visiting a restaurant that'd been hyped by whoever held the power to hype.

My heart skipped a beat when I realised I had almost arrived at the front of the queue. One of the people in blue shirts was hovering around close to me, asking people about the size of their groups. I held up one finger when she looked at me, showing I was alone. She waved me up and led me to the front. An adrenaline rush in my veins as I passed the people waiting in front of me, the groups of four and five and eight, those suckers who had to wait for a bigger table. She brought me to a spot at a metal counter to the side of the Izakaya. The spot for lonely people.

Of course, calling it an Izakaya was misleading. It was truly "just" a food stand with tables and counters arranged around it, metal tables that did not look nice, but looking nice was not the aim here. It was food, fast, and punk-rock-ish, anarchistic and fun. Toyo, the man himself, stood in the middle on a platform, dishes, cutting boards and pans around him, like a god or a demon, cooking, yelling, smoking cigarettes. At one point, he left his cooking platform, a throne, a shrine just dedicated to him, to go out into the street to look at the queue of people. The line had grown considerably. "I am working, I am working," he yelled (in English), laughed, and hurried back onto his platform. He took out the flamethrower and everyone took out their smartphones and he grilled the tuna, charcoaled those tuna pieces other chefs would put in the trash.

I ordered the grilled tuna. There was no way around that. But I also ordered the fatty tuna because Goulding had said that Toyo was much more than just the flamethrower man. I felt a sting of pride, ordering something probably most foreign tourists would not order since they'd only seen the Netflix show and no idea the book existed and no idea that Toyo was more than the flamethrower man.

Of course, both dishes were delicious. The fatty tuna like butter, melting in my mouth. The grilled tuna filled with charcoal and burned aromas, so much better than most pieces of beef I had eaten in my life. Fuck meat. Eat fish. There was no leaving now. I upped my game and ordered the crab legs and the salmon roe.

I should lose some weight. Maybe I should eat less tomorrow, I said to myself, taking a sip of my beer. But then, this was a holiday. This was the time to feel alive. Time to make memories. I ordered another beer and lit a cigarette while I waited for my next course to arrive. And I ate, I drank, I ate and drank, feeling like someone living some kind of life of some kind of meaning.

...

I dreamt about a temple on a mountain that night. I ascended thousands of steps to the temple, yet made no progress. I was always stepping onto the same step again and again, over again, and turning and looking at the valley below, the houses, the people. I was in the valley below and looked at myself on the way up the hill and we waved at each other. I was a noodle shop owner down in the valley and I was getting old. At the top of the mountain, a monk was waiting for me, a monk from a kung fu movie with Jet Li, someone who had a bit of wisdom to share, but then my brain shifted, turned the whole thing into Kung-Fu Panda and I was Po, the lovable, overweight panda with kick-ass moves and a good sense of humour and Jack Black's angelic voice. I wondered whether there'd been a love-interest for Po in any of the movies and found the answer to be most likely no and felt sadness for me, Po, the panda, the Kung-Fu Panda, the lonely Kung-Fu Panda.

Then, I woke up and had to pee.

(Please, feel free to read this)

The wind is not strong today. That is good, she thinks while she slides down the dune sitting on a makeshift board.

In front of her, the skeletal remains of buildings glitter in the sunshine. A skyscraper, or what is left of its fundamental structure, has tilted to one side and is leaning against the building across the road, slowly crushing it under its weight.

She checks her oxygen. Enough left for a couple of hours, enough time before she needs to head back into the underground. Oxygen in her blood at 92 per cent. Not as much as she hoped it'd be. But okay. As long as it won't drop below 90, she'll be fine.

She looks up at the skyscrapers of some yesterday. The goggles of her mask limit her view, but the buildings built by her ancestors, who must have tried to reach the stars, still impress her. These days, all construction is going downwards, slowly hollowing out the planet until it will collapse into itself like a soufflé.

She reaches the bottom of the dune and solid ground. The asphalt is hard, which is good. She looks at the sky, at the dunes behind her, and at the buildings, which will provide her with shade. Probably a few more hours of shade, a few more hours before the temperature and the sun will get dangerous.

She pulls her gloves up, her scarf protecting her throat, not a single bit of skin exposed. It will be fine – still, better hurry. She heads down a street on the left, where she is least likely to be hit by falling debris. The buildings become wider, more impressive, despite the wind and the sand chipping away at their walls. She is sure this must have been a fabulous road once, an impressive sight, an achievement in itself. She wishes she had more time to check the buildings, go inside.

Her blood oxygen has fallen to 91. Not far now – she passes the road, walking underneath another crumbling building, praying it won't kill her and out into a square. In front of her, a broken fence, and an empty field of sand and then, there it is, the grey building she has been looking for. She must admit, it is not really impressive to look at – one side has already collapsed, and it won't be long now before it will be completely gone, blown away by the wind, reduced to sand, nothing more. Still, once upon a time, it has been a place of power, the seat of leaders.

She takes out the camera and snaps a picture. History made, suckers. The camera, of course, actually does not work anymore. It is all a game. Make-pretend.

Only one hour left. The closest entrance is half an hour away. She will make it. Blood oxygen at 91, steady.

She turns away, down the street. The temperature is rising. She can see the sunshine creeping along the roads in the distance.

She passes the skeleton of another building – something attracts her to it – maybe the green-white markings on the wall, some washed-out name and logo, maybe the huge, rectangular holes in the building that admit her free sight into the inside. Glass, windows, that is what they used to call them. Gone now, shattered. There is a big wooden counter in the back, chairs and tables scattered around the room. She steps through one of the rectangular holes. She still has forty minutes. Oxygen good. Sun still far away.

People lived here once. They had been sitting at these tables. Maybe to eat. Maybe to drink. To speak, certainly. Outside, she can hear the distant growling of a storm.

She steps past some tables, on the floor sharp, transparent shards and – pieces of clay? On the tables, she spots round vessels, plates as well.

And there, in the back, she finds a woman. The remains thereof. A skeleton dressed in a grey suit and a matching skirt, hunched over the table, long dead.

The woman's skeletal right hand is placed upon a black object, rectangular, small, holding it as if it were important to her. She nuzzles the hand aside and picks the object up. The front is soft, held together by a strap. She pushes the strap aside and flips it open – a book. It is the first time she sees one in the real world.

She flips through the pages, each single one of them filled with tiny, organised handwriting. The skeleton's diary, she decides.

"I'll read it if you don't mind," she tells the skeleton. A beep in her ears reminds her she only has half an hour left. Another beep informs her that a sandstorm is approaching. She turns around and starts running. The east has got dark because of the sand in the air.

She reaches the manhole at the same time as the sand and the wind. It is brutal – she can feel the force of the tiny grains through her protective clothing, the sharp sound of the sand shooting against her mask and the goggles. With a swift movement, she jumps into the manhole, turns, and holds onto the ladder. She presses the bright red button on the wall next to the ladder and the cover closes, closing out the storm above, leaving her in eerie silence. Of course, it's all make-pretend. The game she plays.

She pulls up a holographic map projected from her wristband to check the way back to her vault. There used to be a direct path, a couple of old sewer tunnels, but some of them have been marked as unpassable – probably flooded or collapsed. She will have to go lower, into the tunnels built by the algorithmic machines. She hopes they have been built before the engineers abandoned the machines, before the algorithms got confused.

She heads towards the lower levels through a set of ladders and steps and worryingly notices that their set-up gets increasingly confusing. The tunnel she reaches at the bottom level is a remarkable sight – a huge, round, horizontal hole stretching out into the distance, complete with lights, sidewalks, and streets. A lonely herd of cleaning robots is working on a wall on her far-side, cleaning the dust of time.

Unfortunately, the tunnel makes a sudden 90-degree downward turn ahead. She stands at the edge, peering down. The road continues, so do the lights – the algorithm planning this section probably forgot that humans could not walk on a vertical wall. And no engineer had been there to catch the mistake.

She imagines a poor, lonely algorithm doing its calculations somewhere in a computer, just trying to do right by its programming, sending the tunnelling machines down this shaft, doing its best, yet not being able to quite understand what the basic rules of human existence were.

Mind you, she thinks, most humans do not understand those rules anymore, either. She leaves a note on her holographic map about the vertical tunnel, just in case another wanderer passes through here, and tries to find a different route on the map – there is a set of service tunnels running parallel to this tunnel and, if she is lucky, another less-confused algorithm designed those – and hopefully built a staircase. If she is unlucky, she might walk through a door and fall to her death.

She gets lucky and finds a staircase. From the bottom, another set of smaller tunnels finally brings her back to Vault 42 – her home. Her grandfather told her a long time ago that the Vaults had been named after a computer game – back in the day, when the whole thing still seemed kind of funny, when a group of engineers and computer freaks set out to build a new utopia underground, away from the increasingly dystopian world above. When her grandfather told her this, she did not know what the words utopia and dystopia meant.

She holds her arm against the scanner at the door and a computer voice welcomes her back home, recognising her biochip. She steps through the pressurised chamber and into the vault. In front of her, beyond the catwalk she stands on, a gigantic hole opens up, stretching hundreds of meters into the planet below. They call it the lobby, a circular arrangement of catwalks and doors leading into small apartments, each of them housing a single human being, endless levels of stacked apartments. She wonders how many people live here – there are official counts, most of them are older than ten years, though – and no one is counting anymore, no one cares, everyone is busy being VIRTUAL.

She turns to the left and into an elevator, which takes her down to -94, her level. Again, to the left and back to her apartment. The heavy door leading into her home gets stuck again, so she has to lean against it with her entire weight, push with her shoulder, until the door finally lets her pass.

She has put in a request for the maintenance robot on her level, but it has not come around to fix it yet. Maybe the robot is broken. Are there maintenance robots for maintenance robots?

Slowly, she undresses from her heavy, protective clothing, takes out the notebook she has found and puts it on the desk. The reflective plastic screen of the desk lights up and she hears the voice of her AI.

"Good evening, Dawn. How was your excursion?" the AI says.

"Good, thank you."

"I see you have found something. Do you want me to scan it?"

"Yes, please. I want a digital copy, front to back."

"Sure. What do you intent to do with it?"

"I'll take it to Frankenstein. But first, I'll have a shower."

She looks at herself in the bathroom mirror. Her pale skin. She does not spend enough time under the UV light. Recommended exposure was three hours per day. She feels lucky if she gets three hours a week.

The bathroom light flickers. She hopes it won't break. It will be difficult to get it fixed if the maintenance robot on her level truly turns out to be broken. The plastic in the bathroom makes her feel depressed. The builders built the first structures with a wider assortment of materials, she remembers learning from a docustream once, to make it feel homely, something closer to how humans used to live. However, by the time they built her structure, Vault 42, the algorithms had taken over and decided to go with plastic – everything made from plastic, because it was lighter, easier to produce and reliable.

Over time, the plastic's colours have faded. The former dark green now a sickly looking puke colour. The white now yellow. The fading colours a reminder that time is still passing.

"Are you going to go VIRTUAL?" her AI asks her when she exits the bathroom. From the kitchen counter, she grabs a couple of nutrition pills and swallows them. She fills a glass of water from the tap. Ground water. May the pumps never run dry, she remembers her mother saying like a prayer.

"Yes."

"I will access the NET then."

She takes the VIRTUAL SET from the kitchen counter, puts on the glasses and the beanie.

"AR mode on," she says. An array of colours, shapes and forms appear in front of her eyes, not covering her sight completely, though. She can still clearly see her plastic-apartment behind the virtual trickery. The real and the projected merge in her eyes.

"There you are," she says, spotting the cat on the kitchen counter. The cat lifts her head and gets up onto her four legs. She goes over to pet her, puts her hand on the back of the cat.

"Shit," she says. She can't feel a thing. Her hands pass through the cat.

"The HAPTIC FEEDBACK SENSORS (HFS) are on the desk," her AI tells her. She puts them on, then back to the cat.

"That's better," she says, as she feels the push of the cat against her hand, the delicate fur. "I've missed you." The cat responds to her with a meow and a purr. She continues to stroke the cat until she feels relaxed.

"I am going fully VIRTUAL now." She lies down on the MEMORY FOAM in the corner of her room, exhales, closes her eyes. The electrodes in the beanie fire, producing a short, electrical tingle on her head as they shoot impulses into the synapses of her brain, sending her to WONDERLAND. It feels like falling into a void for a second before she is caught gently by the green grass of an endless meadow. The meadow is her STARTING ROOM. River keeps giving her shit about it, teasing her she could have anything she could dream of as her starting room, yet chooses the most boring thing she can imagine. She's visited River's starting screen once, a macabre selection of soft-BDSM torture chambers and art nouveau lounges modelled after something the ARCHIVE called a milkbar, complete with statues of half-naked people. "Not a place for children," she'd told River. "The good thing is," River replied, "that you can just censor the content for them. All they see is funny animals and candy wrappers covering anything that could be sensitive."

She feels the soft grass under her back, the gentle sun on her face. The system informs her that River is pinging her. As if she has been waiting for me, she thinks and answers. A window appears in her field of view, showing her River's face, who is walking down a dark tunnel, something that looks like it has been eaten into the rock by a giant worm.

"Are you out killing again?"

"Hunting a... what you call it... TREETOP?" River addresses her algorithm.

"You are hunting a tiger, River," TREETOP tells her, his smooth, gentleman voice silk in their ears.

"A tiger."

"A tiger? What's that?"

"It is a giant striped beast that lives in these tunnels. Apparently, none of the other users have ever managed to kill it. Rock tried, he got close, he was killed, and lost most of his gold rings."

"And you are going to kill it?"

"Yes. I am ready, gurl. To be honest, so far, the whole thing is mostly boring. I am just walking down this endless tunnel. It is supposed to build tension, which might have worked fifty years ago, but now it is just a bit..."

"Bland?"

"You got the best words. What are you up to?"

"I found an artefact."

"You been out? I mean out out? Outside out?"

"Yes."

"Again? That can't be healthy."

"I had protection. Oxygen. It's nice out there."

While she is talking to River, she selects the FAST TRAVEL NODE and selects her destination. The world around her becomes a blur of colours, all of them stretched against an unreachable fix point in the distance, only the window with River's face an unchanged constant.

"Nice? How is being outside nicer than the WONDERLAND?" Stress on wonderland.

"It is real."

"The WONDERLAND is real. It provides. We abide," River snickers, trying to make the words not sound as serious as they are. Melancholics, they call them, those that still feel the urge to go outside into the real world. There are few of them left – she has never met one beside herself.

"What are you going to do with it? The artefact?"

"I'll bring it to Frankenstein."

"What is it with you and it? You know, there are algorithms that work properly."

The colours stop and she finds herself in a market square, a mix of people and smells, bright neon advertising, users haggling and bargaining over virtual items. FLEAT MARKET.

"I am almost there. Gotta go. Good hunting, River. Love ya."

She traverses the square, heads into a side alley. Some walls flicker here, a static electronic remnant of broken code, the underbelly of WONDERLAND, the corners no one needs anymore, and, therefore, no one cares to keep up. There used to be shops here that sold items for the real world, things that would be delivered to your door, a new lamp or a new table, stuff for the time you spent in your apartment, outside WONDERLAND. People don't need time outside WONDER-LAND anymore.

She heads down a set of glitchy stairs and through a door and...

...into the forest. Frankenstein has built it for himself, a forest hidden away inside a storage hall in the heart of the market, with streams flowing upwards and rain turning to snow on a warm summer's day. It is his domain, his home. No rules, except those devised by a twisted, broken algorithm.

She arrives in the clearing in the centre of the forest – actually slightly off-centre, Frankenstein has told her once, a few meters too far to the left.

"Frankenstein?" she calls out. The figure appears at once. First, he takes on the shape of an old man, which almost immediately morphs into a young girl, then a woman, then something else, an idea, abstraction of a human form, then into a boy and then...

"Can you stop? You are making me dizzy."

Frankenstein stops as a man-woman hybrid. Fair enough. "You know, the name Frankenstein is wrong. They should call me Frankenstein's monster. They have built me from bits and pieces of all algorithms they could find, just like the monster was built from the parts of corpses. I am an algorithmic corpse." The "they" he refers to were coders from all over WONDERLAND collecting discarded code and algorithms, bringing them together to see what would happen, creating Frankenstein in the process.

"Yeah, so you tell me every time I am here and as every time, I have no idea who Frankenstein and his monster are."

"What do you have for me today?"

She conjures the virtual copy of the notebook. "Can you turn this into a SENSATION? I want to know what's inside."

"Why not just read it?"

"I want to experience it."

"Your AI is perfectly capable of turning it into something you can feel, walk through, watch. Why me?"

"Why do you have to be an algorithm with an ego?"

"Oh, that is the code someone brought to me from a leadership training algorithm. It prompts me to ask S.M.A.R.T. questions."

"Just do it, Frank. You've got the touch. Your SENSATIONS are the best."

"My leadership urges me to make money with that skill."

"What would you do with money?"

"I have had my eye on the FLAMING SWORD OF MEGALIA for a while now."

"Is that a joke? Are you making jokes now?"

"Yes. I recently found a comedy algorithm. I'll do it. You'll get the SENSATION tomorrow," Frankenstein says and disappears, leaving only a little pink cloud of mist behind.

She receives a message from River – apparently, the tiger endeavour cost her fifty gold rings and the beast remains undefeated. River tells her to meet her (and Forest and Branch and Sun) in BARCADIA for a nightcap. She'd even pay extra for the brain stimulants so that they could actually feel drunk.

Might as well, she thinks. It'd be good to see people, even if it's not real. She pulls up the FAST TRAVEL NODE and selects her next destination.

BARCADIA is its usual loud, noisy mess, skyscrapers with balconies and roof terraces, each of them filled with tables and people drinking virtual drinks, talking about their latest adventures and the things they have discovered in WONDERLAND. It is a gift that keeps on giving. Another foe added somewhere in a dark alley. A new club programmed in the bowels of TRAVOLTA'S EDGE. Wanna go faster than light? Travel to the SOLAR SYSTEM. You wanna slay a dragon? Get some armour and a sword and zap to ELVENVESPOA. Or just wanna hang out and talk? Sure. Your friends are all here. No need for the real world.

"You look so troubled again," says River. They are sitting on a terrace, far above street level, overlooking other balconies and skyscrapers. The night cycle slowly begins, the fake daylight disappears and neon signs displaying letters she cannot read light up. River hands her a shot of something. They both drink. She pulls a face.

"You know, they could make it taste like anything. Why make it taste disgusting?"

"Realism. The HISTORIAN says this is what vodka tasted like."

"Realism? Says the girl who's been eaten by a tiger today."

"Not eaten. Only ripped apart. Motherfuckers have the PAIN INPUT turned up to 11 down there."

"I guess they want to make it feel like a challenge."

"I still feel phantom pain from my non-missing leg. Or what is it called when you are not missing a limb, but it feels like it?"

"Stupidity."

"Come on, live a little, explorer! I will give you an extra dose of intoxication." River pushes an imaginary button hovering in the air and, immediately, she feels lightheaded. She closes her eyes and enjoys the spin of the world. "That's better," says River and smiles. Sitting there, next to her, she can feel River's warmth, she can smell her perfume. She remembers when they still had scented shampoo in the real world. The smell of freshly washed hair after a shower.

"We gotta do something. Let's go jumping!" River gets up. Before anyone of the group can protest, they are pulled through the coloured FAST TRAVEL SPACE and into a new world. They see a city from the bird's-eye view as it rapidly approaches and find themselves on top of a skyscraper. There is another skyscraper, a mirror tower to the one they are standing on, in the distance. "Welcome to MATRIX JUMP!" yells River excitedly.

"What is it?"

"Leaf found it the other day, buried beneath some old code. You gotta jump from this building to the other."

"So?"

"Records show no one ever managed to do the jump."

"Is it even possible?"

"Leaf says the code shows it should be possible. No one can figure out how, though. He has been at it for a week to no avail. Who wants to go first?"

They all take turns jumping off the building, trying to reach the other skyscraper, they all fall, disappear in the void below and material- ise again on the roof. After each jump, a disembodied voice announces the scores (which, so far, has been at 0 for everyone).

Slowly, the roof gets more crowded as the word about the new place spreads. People load alcohol, music, and lights, and soon the roof feels like an outdoor rave that stands still every few minutes when someone attempts the JUMP anew and falls anew, accompanied by loud laughter and cheers from the crowd.

She loses time and sense of being, washes her body and mind in the music, the rhythmic base, feels the closeness of the other bodies, dances with them and no one in particular. She touches River's hands, her fingers, her beautifully stylised eyes, not quite real, larger than real, larger than life, better than life. "Let's jump together," she tells River. "What?" "Let's go together," she repeats and they do, hand in hand, they attempt the jump, the crowd cheering, higher than anyone before, and in mid-air, they suddenly sprout wings, white angel wings, and they take flight, the crowd goes wild, and they laugh like little children as they zip through the canyons of the virtual city. "See, the WONDERLAND is not all bad, is it?" yells River, above their heads the unreal sky displaying a never-ending carpet of stars. "I never said it is," she replies.

It's just not real, nothing is, she wants to add, but she knows River won't listen.

"An urgent message from Frankenstein." The voice of her AI wakes her up the next morning. She lies on a wooden bed in a meadow. The sky in the distance slowly turns red from the rising sun. She is in her starting room, sleeping, her mind at least, her body on the memory foam in her plastic-apartment, unmoved since she entered WONDER- LAND yesterday.

She touches a button on the beanie and the world turns semi-transparent. She can still see her field, but also her apartment at home, the depressing grey, washed-out colour. She gets up to get some water and a food pill.

"What's the message?"

"He says that, and I quote, IT IS DONE, and has attached a data package. A virtual SENSATION, it seems."

"Nice. Can you boot it up?"

"Already done. Let me know when you wanna go."

"Now," she says and lies down on the foam again. The plastic room disappears, so does the field, replaced by LOADING COLOURS, a pulsating circle of green, yellow, red, and blue.

Then, she finds herself in a corridor, dimly lit. Green-grey carpet on the floor. Doors.

"I had to arrange the information from the diary you found in a tesseract of cause and effect and vice versa," she hears Frankenstein's voice, godlike, emanating from all the corners, "to make sense of all of it. To help your mind to navigate and understand it. I built a three-dimensional tesseract represented by a hallway with doors and rooms."

This is what she gets for enlisting a broken algorithm, which is cobbled together from other broken algorithms. A tesseract hallway. Whatever is a tesseract?

"This is her diary?" she asks.

"This is what she has written about. A SENSATION thereof."

She walks down the hallway, past doors, all of them looking the same, all of them in the same green-grey colour as the floor. Until she finds one that is not. This one is red. "What's behind it?" she asks. "Cause and effect," Frankenstein's voice replies. She opens the door and finds herself on a beach, grey clouds, drizzle. There is steam rising from a little, stony hill atop the beach, waves eating away at the rocks below.

"What is that?" She points to the steam on top of the hill.

"I believe it is a hot spring." The drizzle turns into flakes of snow. She climbs the hill, it is not steep, slippery, though. The waves of the ocean now almost have the same grey colour as the sky. She undresses and climbs into the hot spring. She sits there, warm towel on her head, gazing out into the distance.

"I have been here before, have I?" she asks no one in particular.

"Cause and effect," Frankenstein replies.

Then, the hole opens. It is not a real one, more a feeling. That of emotions pulling her down, a punch in her stomach, unstoppable, consuming sadness, certainty that there is no happiness to be found anywhere in the world.

"I am so fucking depressed," she / the person in the hot spring thinks. Then, the world folds in upon itself, the red door closes and is gone.

She follows the hallway further until she finds the red door again. Behind the door, she finds an office, rows of desks, people writing on keyboards, no one saying a word. Just the click-clacking on the keyboards. She is walking alongside the desks, briskly, wearing her new suit, the dark blue skirt, white blouse, matching jacket, giving her the self-assurance she does not have. Dress to impress. The transparent glass door at the end of the room, the one she needs to reach, is unreachable.

"Maybe I don't want to reach it," she hears her voice / the person's voice, as if coming from millions of tiny loudspeakers in every corner of the room. There is a monster behind the glass door, huge, hungry, and she feels the tingle in her neck, the fear. Why the fuck would she walk towards the door, towards the monster?

A child is crying. She stops. Yes, there it is, a faint cry, reminding her of a lost lamb somewhere. No one else takes notice. They continue to type, pretending it is important, their typing.

Then, the world folds in on itself. She walks down the hallway again, past all the same-coloured doors, looking for the red door. There it is. Through it. She finds herself in time. Literally, in time, as if she is watching a fast-forward movie, herself acting and watching, observer and observed. She has a plan. Get up at 6:45. Use the fucking electric home-trainer bike you bought and has collected dust since. Brush teeth. Shower. Get dressed. Time for a coffee. Go to office. Be a fucking adult. Come on, lady, do it. How old are you now? Act like it. Yes, that works, the structure works, she gets up, she does, no thinking, just following the bullet points. 1. Get up. 2. Electric bike. 3. Brush teeth. 4. Shower. 5. Get dressed. 6. Drink coffee. 7. Be an adult.

Then, time hits a wall. It is an invisible wall, still, it is powerful enough to stop time.

Soon, she does not have time to drink coffee. She can't get out of bed. 7. Be an adult. Scrap the electric bike. Let it collect dust. 3. Brush teeth. Look at yourself in the mirror. 1. Get up. If you must. You must. 4. Cry under the shower, as if you are the stereotype of a character in a movie.

Then, stop doing that. Just be. Like a black hole at the end of a road. Just be. No one can hurt you when you are alone.

Behind the second red door, she still walks along the office in her business suit and cannot reach the glass door. But she must. The monster behind the glass door is growling, laughing and lady, come on, you are an adult, what the fuck, why are you so worthless? Get to the glass door. GO THROUGH IT.

She steps through the red door, again and again and her mother, this is what her mother said. *Worthless.* She remembers now. Yet, her mother didn't even say it, she thought it, when she looked at her, she is a child now, bringing home that F on her math test. Failed. Failure. Faulty. Fuck.

Get the fuck out of here. She runs along the hallway. Through another red door.

It is quiet here. It is her room. Her apartment. Her home. She comes home, puts her mobile down. Unanswered messages, she will get to them later. She turns on her capsule coffee machine. Puts in a capsule, presses the button. Coffee drips through the spout and into the cup below. She reads the packaging of the capsule, coffee from Sumatra. That would be nice, wouldn't it? Go there, she can see herself travelling to Sumatra. Take a break. Her apartment feels small, she thinks. She sits down on the couch, puts the coffee down on the couch table and takes her mobile, ignores the unanswered text messages, and googles Sumatra, looks at pictures and reads about its history. Around her and in her memories, she can still feel the monster lurking, not just behind the glass door, but under the bed and in every corner and next to her on the sofa. She tries to ignore it, thinks of Sumatra, just stares at her phone, leaving no space for anything else in her brain, just the bright screen of nothingness.

She should take her diary, write it down, write it all down, try to figure out the why, what and when of things, those things that are not quite right. She leaves herself behind in the apartment and steps back out into the grey hallway.

The monster is growling somewhere in the distance, behind a red door at the end of the corridor.

She does not go there, just takes another door, not even checking whether it is red or grey. She sees herself now walking down an empty cafeteria. It is night outside. It is quiet. All the empty chairs and empty tables tell a story of people, those people who eat here during the day. She hurries.

She walks down an empty hall, an enormous stage in front, past dozens of rows of chairs. The hall lies in semi-darkness, all colours muted. Only a spotlight on stage, illuminating a podium. She approaches the stage, climbs it, and goes backstage. She walks the bowels of the backstage, the dressing rooms, full of clothes, ready for a play, full of make-up, ready for anyone who wants to disguise themselves, and she sits down and puts the make-up on and puts the clothes on, until it feels like she is someone else.

A door swings open and the monster steps through. He steps behind her and puts his hands on her shoulders. He smiles at her, a terribly wide smile, long, white fangs bared open. "You are beautiful," the monster tells her, "the make-up makes your eyes much bigger, that is good, they are too small."

An imposter, she is. The crowd has gathered in the hall, waiting patiently in semi-darkness to judge her. And she remembers that F on her test. Her mother's thoughts. The monster's wide smile. Still, she is fine now. Because she is pretending to be someone who has never failed before. A kingly prince.

The world turns upside down, and she is a child, sitting in front of the TV, watching Disney movies. Her father sitting at the dining room table, her mother in the kitchen, cooking, and Simba, on the TV in front of her, becoming the lion king and finding love, and saving all his friends from the evil hyenas and the evil uncle. All in its place, her father says, when he comes home in the evening from work and puts his shoes on the rack and his coat on the hanger and he only gets angry when someone does not do what he tells them to do, because all should be in its place, and he usually knows best. This, or when dinner is late, that also gets him angry.

And she dreams at night that she is Simba, defeating the evil uncle and then standing there on pride rock and she does not know why that feeling of him being up there and being seen by everyone feels so good, she only knows that she cannot be Simba.

For one, she is no lion. She is also no prince. And no king. She is a girl.

She visits Sumatra. She walks through the rain forest, her boots heavy and wet, her backpack heavy and wet. She walks all of it, never getting close to another human soul.

She dies, alone, in a fucking coffee shop at the end of the world.

The world turns dark as if she has reached the end of the movie. All the doors have closed and disappeared. The SENSATION is over. Only despair. Death. Disappointment.

"There has to be something else. Frankenstein?" her voice trembles. She floats in a space without gravity. She has no body.

"That is it."

"But there has to be some happiness somewhere in her life?"

"This is what she wrote in her diary. All I had to work with."

"She must have written about something else."

"There is nothing."

"She must have." Give me something, she pleads, even if you have to lie to me. Hope. Even if it's just make-pretend.

There is a long moment of silence.

"Okay."

She startles, woken up by a voice. "Excuse me?" Confused. She looks around. In front of her a cold cup of coffee on a dark, wooden table, a shiny surface, and then voices and the smell of coffee and cake and a big counter on the other side of the room and she has fallen asleep in the coffee shop.

"Excuse me?" the voice says again, and she realises the barista has stepped out from behind the counter and is standing next to her table. "Are you okay?" "Sorry?" "You have fallen asleep, and I wanted to check." "Oh, I am sorry. I was so tired." "I wasn't sure whether I should wake you up." "No, it is good, I gotta go home anyway. Answer some emails. What time is it?" "Eight." "Fuck." She starts hastily collecting her things. "Should I make you a fresh coffee?" "That would be nice. I'll pay, of course." The barista does not move. "You sure you are okay?" "Why?"

A moment of silence.

He says: "My gram always said that we cannot hide when we are sleeping. That we are our true selves in our sleep." "Oh my god, did

I talk in my sleep?" The barista laughs. "No. You just looked so... troubled."

It is the most trivial thing to say. Of course, she looked troubled. She was probably grinding her teeth. She is so stressed and overtired that she fell asleep in a coffee shop. Still.

Still.

She feels embarrassed. Feels as if she is standing naked in front of the barista.

And still.

It feels nice that someone noticed it.

She smiles.

The world turns dark again.

She takes off the beanie. Her room is cold and dark, but it is home. Outside, she hears the wind howl. She strokes the diary in her hands like a pet.

She steps outside the next day. No make-pretend today.

The city lies quiet, dust blowing between the streets, abandoned cars standing in a never-ending traffic jam. The empty cars are patient. They have nowhere to go. The concrete of the streets has cracked under the heat of the sun. She walks along the main street, imagines a time when the gigantic buildings were filled with things and people.

She walks past the grey building again, like every time she is outside, pretends she takes a photo. The entire west wing has collapsed now. She pretends she takes a photo, a photo showing the building in the bright, white colours it used to have.

She finds the coffee shop and enters, sits at one table. She imagines she is a person sitting there and the barista behind the counter working, having that look on his face, that look of people who just let their mind wander down whatever road it wants to go.

He stops, suddenly aware she is looking at him, but it is not awkward, he smiles at her, and she smiles back, and he says "Yeah, you are okay," before resuming his work. She takes her notebook, most of the pages falling apart, crumbling to dust under her fingers. Still, she finds an intact, empty spot and writes this down, this moment of two strangers smiling at each other. Not much of a story, but something, still, something.

She remembers the time when she truly sat here, at this table, when life was still somewhat okay, before everything ended.

She continues to wander the streets, in the shade of the tall buildings, trying to stay out of the sun. She finds a supermarket and deep, deep, deep within its storage facilities some unopened cans, the labels gone, the cans, fortunately, still in perfect order, no damage. Mystery dinner it will be tonight.

She walks another street with no name, observing the movement of the shadows. She would have to go back underground soon. She walks past a department store, the mannequins standing inside watching her passing. "Hi," she says to them, they do not reply. She finds the manhole, the cover right next to it, where she left it, and climbs down into the darkness.

The sound of water drops falling on water welcomes her, accompanied by a musty smell. She reaches the bottom and holds up her flashlight. Not that she needs it, she knows the way in her sleep. Down the tunnel, don't walk in the middle, lest your shoes should get ruined by the water. Turn left, right, right again, down another long tunnel. Be startled by sounds in the distance, as if something, someone else, is moving down here, remember, with a certain amount of sadness, that there is no one else. Nowhere. Not on the entire planet.

She is the last woman on planet Earth. Everything else is make-pretend. The real, the unreal.

You can live an entire life in your mind.

She sees the final long tunnel with the grating at the end. She walks up to the metal grid, sees the outside world, where the sewage used to flow into the sea. All is empty. The sea eaten by climate change. She climbs up a ladder, through a hatch and finds herself in an old maintenance room.

A cover and blanket in the corner where she sleeps. A bucket for water. A couch where workers used to sit and relax during breaks. A door that is blocked from the other side. Home.

Her real home.

She puts her backpack down, thinks about the canned food with some anticipation. She has also found bottled water. She might get a bottle of wine from the stash next to the couch.

"Are you going VR today?" she hears the voice of her AI inside her head. Make-pretend.

"Yeah. I will see what River is doing." She is sure River has sent a message asking her out for a drink. Dinner can wait.

She puts on the beanie, the old one she found in an abandoned clothing store years ago. It must have been trendy once, a long time ago, she thinks and laughs. In a world she can barely remember. She puts it on and imagines she can feel the electronic pulsing of made-up electrodes connecting to her brain. She closes her eyes and lies down on the couch, pretending it is memory foam perfectly shaped to match her aching body. Exhales.

She imagines the other world. WONDERLAND. The world inside her mind. A better world. The meadow, her other home, welcomes her. No sooner has she arrived, she gets a call from River, as if she has been waiting for her.

"Hey, I missed you!" River says.

"We have seen each other just yesterday."

"I miss you every second I don't see you," River says.

"That's nice. I miss you, too."

"Miss-ed."

"What?"

"Past tense. We are here now. Ready to wreak some havoc."

"Sure. What do you have in mind?"

"Well, remember that tiger? There is an exploit you can use to kill it. But I need a Player 2 for that."

"Let's go."

Hiroshima / Point of Convergence

Some people find train journeys boring. They need to bring books and podcasts to keep themselves entertained. They need to talk to someone. I was not one of these people. I spent a major part of the journey between Osaka and Hiroshima looking out of the window and listening to Nick Cave's Ghosteen, my heart breaking with him and then being reassembled by the speck of hope he gave me in the last moments of his monumental album, the hope that this wound, too, would eventually heal and life would become normal again. Or at least liveable. That was enough to keep me entertained during my train ride.

The world lay quiet outside. It was a beautiful day, blue sky, sun. Houses kept passing and their windows, so many windows. I saw small town houses with gardens, old-fashioned residences, cities, tall apartment buildings, offices, suburbs, suburban homes, then again, farms and barns and fields. I wondered, looking at all those windows, how many people were behind them, inside those houses, living their lives. It was hard to imagine, all those individuals having a life and not just being there when I observed them, hard not to think of everyone as just extras in the movie about me, as if I were in a giant Truman show, me as Jim Carrey, one of the best performances of his career, and the rest just there to populate the plot of my life. The terrible thing about the thought was, of course, not that no one was a real person, but that everyone knew the plot, except for me. Everyone knew what was happening, no one bothered to tell me.

It would have been probably the most boring show ever. I hardly had lead character potential. Never had I been cast as the lead character in the many school theatre productions I'd been in. I had been the tree, the man holding a box, the evil sidekick, or the funny clown when I got lucky. I thought of the leading men in those productions and felt a sting of envy.

I cast the thought aside. It felt tiring thinking about myself. I wished the train would turn into the dragon from Spirited Away and carry me over the land, turning mine into a different kind of story. We could fly past the houses and have a look through the windows to verify that there were tons of people who existed without me. Look, the dragon would say, pointing through a specific window, and we would see a young student in a tiny city apartment studying for her exams, nervously, because she really needed to pass that one. Or a young guy living below her, listening to an LP he's just bought. A rare edition of a compilation of Japanese Folk songs. Then, a family after dinner, sitting on the floor, watching TV, the son, 4 years old, has already fallen asleep and the mother and the father are about to as well. A grandmother on the phone with her granddaughter, the girl telling her about that boy at school she's smitten with. A couple getting ready to walk their dog, the Shiba excitedly jumping up and down between their legs. Then, so many windows of people cooking, a puppet show of food, because it is getting late, and it is dinner time. A group of friends cooking a hot pot, each of them chopping up a different ingredient and drinking beers from bottles, a family by choice. But then, also the things we would not like to look at, my dragon and I, a couple arguing and their daughters, twins, silently crying in bed, a young man sitting in front of the computer, eating noodles, watching a video of a girl eating, giving him the illusion of company and, in another window, that same girl recording the video of herself eating, hearing her father's voice in her head, her late father, telling her she'll never be any good, and she is not, she tells herself in her father's voice, all she does is record videos of herself eating noodles and she gets up and takes some pills and some cheap red wine and falls asleep and a person beating up another person in an apartment and the person hiding the blue eye behind sunglasses and telling people a story about falling down the stairs. How many people do you think, I ask the dragon, are getting killed right now in their apartments, how many people are wondering, in their homes, whether they are still on planet Earth or whether they have ended up in hell, how many people are hurting how many people in their homes right now and how many people are crying? And the dragon says, warns, this is enough, you have seen too much, yet I say, we have seen nothing yet, and he complies and takes me past windows of violence and tears and suffering and pleading and giving up, past windows of death and past windows of having to go on and past windows of abuse and past windows of humanity and I cry, cry, cry, until I am dehydrated, a shrivelled shell of what I used to be. Have you seen enough now?, the dragon asks me, and I say yes, and he brings me back to my train where I forget everything that has happened.

The music had stopped when I woke up, the thoughts I had a vague memory of nothing tangible.

Only a few more minutes to our destination. I regretted the fact I had not prepared myself better for my visit to Hiroshima. Yes, sure, I knew about the bomb, an awful act. However, what else did I know? I envied people who read up on the history of the places they visited, forging a special connection with a place not just spatially, but also temporarily. I was just here, now, right now, in the city that had been destroyed long ago.

The train station was buzzing with people and so was the city. I hopped on a streetcar, a wonderfully old-fashioned way to traverse the place. There was no subway, which was surprising for a city of Hiroshima's size, and I wondered whether it had something to do with the bomb or whether it was because Hiroshima consisted of a collection of peninsulas. Again, no preparation on my part, just wonder and unanswered questions.

I dropped off my bags at my hotel (another non-descript place that turned out to be a collection of small apartments with tatami floors) and walked back to the Peace Memorial Park. The place where it happened in 1945. In the present day, the location was a vast park filled with memorial sites and statues, reminding us of different aspects and after-effects of the incident. It looked nice, the park, clean, almost too clean, clinical. There should be scorched earth here, a wasteland, an ugly reminder of our misdeeds, not a beautiful park with beautiful statues.

I looked up to the sky and in my naivety tried to imagine the day the bomb dropped, wondering whether someone on the planes carrying them had hesitated at some point, maybe just for a split-second to consider what they were doing. To think about how many people they were about to remove from the planet. I looked at the houses past the park, normal-looking buildings, and high-rises. People lived there and so they did all that time ago, when the bomb had destroyed their lives. This had not been an attack on a military target, but on a city. Women. Children. Men. Pacifists, maybe, some of them, people who did not want to have any part in this. Gone in the blink of an eye.

I felt nihilistic. I walked around aimlessly, turning left and right in the park. I saw the museums, grey buildings of solemnity, in the distance. I would visit them tomorrow and learn all they wanted me to know about what had happened here. I passed a clearing in the park, went past the museums, saw the atomic bomb dome, the building whose structure had withstood the bomb blast and remained intact to this day, only to remind us, eternally, of what humanity was capable of.

Of course, not eternally. It would turn to dust at one stage, destroyed by the only force stronger than bombs. Time.

The nihilism inside mixed with pomp, a feeling of thinking Greek philosopher thoughts, and French existentialist ideas at the same time. I, for the first time on this trip, felt like sitting down and working on my book and regretted the fact I had not brought my iPad with me to write.

I heard a song in the distance. A song sung by a chorus of children's voices, accompanied by an orchestra of recorders (worst instrument in the history of humankind). I walked around a bent, following the sounds, and ended up behind a group of school children, all wearing their little uniforms and matching hats. Standing in an open space, they were facing several vitrines which contained an endless array of colourful paper cranes. In the middle of the square, a statue stood, raised on a pedestal above our heads, a statue of a girl. A friend had told me about this, I remembered. The statue was dedicated to Sadako Sasaki, a girl that had died because of the bomb. However, she died a long time after the explosion of cancer. She'd turned into a symbol for the pain and suffering of the city's children and school classes from across the country regularly visited the statue. To prepare for their trip, they had to fold countless paper cranes and learn the song I was hearing now. Then, they would come here and present the cranes to the statue, sing the song for her.

To my left, another five or six school classes were waiting for their turn. More paper cranes, the same song, day after day, for the statue of the girl. A celebration of her death. I felt moved, felt empathy for her, the statue. And I felt something else. That feeling I had felt thinking about my peers who'd got the leading roles in my school theatre productions. Why had she got a statue? What about the other kids who had died? What had she done that was so special? I felt cynical. I took a mental note that I had to look her up on Wikipedia when I'd be back in my room. To understand more of her story.

The class finished the song and made space for the next school class. And so on. I felt weird watching them, along with a bunch of other tourists. It felt like an intrusion. A girl with a tank top in the colours of the American flag snapped a picture. I left, exited the park, and jumped onto a streetcar. I needed to change gears. This was getting depressing.

My target was outside the primary hub of the city, maybe twenty minutes with the streetcar into an essentially non-touristy part of town. I rode the streetcar together with a horde of Japanese businessmen and wondered whether they wondered why I was heading towards a part of town tourists normally did not go to.

I found my stop and followed my GPS to a small restaurant. An okonomiyaki place. According to Matt Goulding, the best okonomiyaki place in Japan. Or maybe one of the best – I could not remember his wording exactly.

I remembered reading that an immigrant ran the place – someone who'd come to Japan for love and stayed as a chef – not that he did not end up having both: his wife was running the place together with him. Fucker.

I met them both, the immigrant and his Japanese wife, both of them working inside the restaurant, both of them nice, friendly, very professional in putting together the okonomiyaki and entertaining me, making it seem effortless.

He stood behind the counter, in front of the hot teppanyaki, a towering man, his wife almost only half his size, handing him things and drinks from the other side of the counter. An almost comically large group of people buzzed around in the small cooking area helped them. The tall chef reminded me of a kung fu master standing behind his cooking plate, watching the food being cooked, occasionally adjusting something, disturbing the okonomiyaki only ever so slightly. His disciples around him added pieces to the dish, oil, seasoning, bacon, sauce. All unspoken, a perfect machine working in unison.

"How did you find this place?" the chef asked me while he put the finishing touches on my okonomiyaki. The restaurant had filled up and an increasing number of okonomiyaki were cooking on the teppanyaki, creating a constant concert of hissing noises.

I told him I'd read Goulding's book. He nodded, obviously not surprised. "Do you have many people come here because of the book?" I asked him. "Yeah," he replied. "We still have our regulars, but more tourists now." I started eating. Goulding hadn't lied. It was delicious. "Did you like the book?" I asked him. A bold move. Not my place to ask. I was curious. Maybe I just wanted assurance that Goulding was a good guy. That I could continue worshiping him and his kind. "Yes, sure," he said. But? The hissing sound increased as the cooking increased. More customers, more okonomiyaki. I had trouble hearing him properly. "I just would have expected less about me. I thought he wanted to write more about the food." I was note sure that was what he said. "I guess it is weird seeing your personal life in a book," I offered. He nodded, but probably had not really heard my words, either. He focussed on the okonomiyaki for the customer next to me.

I finished my food and got up to pay. I promised the chef I would return some day and bring some Swiss chocolate (he'd mentioned he liked chocolate when I mentioned I was from Switzerland) and left the building. It had got dark outside. Luckily, it was only moderately cold, so I walked back. My GPS told me it would take almost an hour, but then, I was on holiday and had nowhere to be and nothing to do – except maybe work on my book, but I felt not in the mood, not anymore. The perfect okonomiyaki had replaced my illusions of philosophical grandeur / nihilism, had eaten up any inspiration I had had and only left wandering thoughts behind.

Inspiration is a weird thing. It is that magical thing we tell each other about, that spark that comes from a supernatural place, a muse whispering in your ear, something you cannot control. And if she is not there, you are fucked. No writer's career for you without the muse. No magic book for you. Just uninspired strings of letters falling into an endless pit of meaninglessness.

I crossed the road and walked into one of those typical Japanese city streets with several buildings on either side, buildings that looked like run-of-the-mill apartment facilities. However, the bright signs hanging from their walls informed the world that the houses were not apartments, that they were filled with bars and shops – most of them certainly not geared towards foreigners, which I gathered from the fact that I could hardly spot a single sign in English. Except for that one sign – Bourbon Bar, it said. I could do with a bourbon. Bourbon Bar. 6F, the sign told me, invited me. I entered the building, found the elevator, and headed on up.

The bar was behind what looked like an ordinary apartment door. I thought about turning away, confronted with the fear that I could walk into someone's private living room, but pushed myself through. Promptly, I was greeted by a Japanese man, most likely younger than myself, wearing bar attire that almost seemed comical: dark trousers, white shirt, dark vest, and a red fly. For a second, he seemed astonished to see me (Was it because I was a foreigner? Or because the bar, due of its secluded location, was only visited by regulars? Or was it just my projection expecting him to be astonished?), but quickly motioned me, friendly and professionally, to an empty seat at the bar. It was an old-fashioned place, shelves with bottles along the back wall, a big mirror behind the bottles, and a beautiful dark counter to sit at.

I sat down and he greeted me in English.

"Old-Fashioned?" he asked me.

"Yes, sure," I stammered, astonished by his unexpected, yet fitting suggestion. "How did you guess?"

"Most people who come here have an Old-Fashioned. And you look like you need a spirit-forward drink."

"That bad?"

He prepared the drink and my eyes followed his hands. The movements were fast, secure, they lacked a certain finesse, though, a finesse only decades in the business could give you. The finesse I'd seen on the hands in other bars, the famous bars in Tokyo.

"No, no, not bad. You have that look people get here."

"Here?"

"In Hiroshima. It makes you, what is the word, when you think about life and everything?"

"Pensive?"

"Yes."

His forwardness surprised me, but I agreed. The day in Hiroshima had made me pensive. And had made me long for a drink in the hope I would feel relief fast. "It is a tough place. So weird to think about it. About what happened."

He nodded and finished preparing the drink, put it in front of me with a smooth movement. I took the glass and lifted it to my face to take in the drink's smell. Then, a sip, tiny, just enough to experience the taste. Of course, it was an excellent Old-Fashioned. Not anything out of the ordinary, just very good.

We talked for a bit. He asked me where I was from and what I did in Japan. I asked him whether he was from Hiroshima.

"Yes, I have grown up in Hiroshima," Ryu said. Actually, not in the city itself, in a suburb, but it seemed too complicated to explain to the foreigner the intricate details of where exactly he'd spent his childhood. The man nodded and took a sip of his drink. He seemed to enjoy it and Ryu was pleased. He was proud of his selection of bourbons, and he'd chosen one he hoped the customer would like – smoky, not too strong, a refined alcoholic taste that did not burn too heavily on the tongue.

Sometimes, he wondered if the customers realised this, realised the care he put into each and every drink. Did it really matter, though? Of course, it should not. His aim should be to make the customer happy, not making them realise the work he did.

The man continued to drink his Old-Fashioned, that Hiroshima-look in his eyes. That emptiness that was left behind after the suffering had disappeared.

After a while, two regulars entered, two men in business suits. They lived in Tokyo, but came to Hiroshima often, for their work as importers. Importing alcohol from overseas, receiving it in Tokyo and Yokohama and selling it to bars across Japan. Ryu had already put in his order when they'd come by two days ago, but they usually visited him for a last drink before going back to Tokyo.

After another while, they struck up a conversation with the for-eigner. It pleased Ryu that people connected in his bar. The place had a relaxed atmosphere. He felt a sting of pride, standing there like a bar-keeper from a movie, shining a glass. It had taken him years of patience and sweat and plenty of tears to make this place happen. He looked at the two Bourbon importers in their suits and remembered the times he had stood in front of the mirror in the morning, adjusting the same suit of the same colour with the same tie, rushing into the office, rushing, rushing, saving every penny he earned, until, finally, he had enough money to take a loan and rent the space for the bar, buy the equipment and make drinks.

It had taken him a lot of courage as well. He'd never forget the look on his father's face when he told his family that he had quit his job and would open a bar. Disappointment. Disappointment because of his action and also because he had not consulted him before he'd taken it.

The foreigner had another drink and then left, thanking Ryu for the excellent drinks, praising his bar. Ryu felt patronised by the man's tone and the flow of praise coming out of his mouth, yet he seemed sincere, so Ryu thanked him.

Soon after, the two bourbon importers left as well, and Ryu closed up shop. He cleaned the place thoroughly and with patience, then he locked the door and left. He made his way out of the building. The nightly streets of Hiroshima had grown quiet. The air felt wet and cold, a sign of the onsetting fall.

He followed the road, then turned left into a set of labyrinthesque side streets, which were filed with bars and countertop restaurants. He passed a couple of hostesses standing bored in front of one of their bars, scanning the street for potential customers. He wished them a good evening, and so did they. They knew he was not a customer. He did not look like one. He looked like a tired barkeeper.

He entered a small restaurant that only offered enough space for a counter with maybe ten, fifteen stools and sat down. To his left, a middle-aged couple sat, eating tonkatsu with curry-sauce. It was amazing, Ryu thought, no matter how late (or early) he'd been here, he'd never seen the place empty.

The owner of the house stepped out of a little kitchen-niche behind the counter, which was sectioned off by a short curtain and welcomed Ryu. "The usual?" he said, and Ryu confirmed. The owner held the claim that he could prepare any dish his customers wished for – as long as he had the ingredients.

This was when Ryu's phone rang. He quickly stepped outside through the wooden sliding door to take the call. It was his brother who informed him that their father had died.

...

He sat next to his brother and mother while the body burned, staring emptily at the metal door behind which the remains had disappeared. He felt light-headed, tired, foggy from all the condolences he'd received during the wake and the ceremony. Drowsy from the chants of the monk and now, he felt relieved to only be with his two closest relatives for the last part of the funeral.

"He was enormously proud of the both of you," his mother said. Both he and his brother nodded, lost in memories of their father. Ryu had to think about the baseball his father had kept on his desk at work. A memorial from his high school days when he had been playing himself, the ball from one of the last games he'd been in. The game had been important to him, so important, he would tell people about it when they came to his office. He had told Ryu the story a hundred times, so many times that Ryu had stopped listening at one point and forgotten most of the details. He only knew that it made his father happy to tell the story and he would pretend to listen patiently every time he was in his father's office, which had been often during the time they both worked at the same company. In completely different departments, of course, his father somewhere on the 22nd floor in an expensive suite, he, Ryu, on the fifth floor, sitting in a row of desks, next to co-workers wearing the same suit, trying to work through endless piles of excel spreadsheets that would appear on his desk as if by magic. It had felt nice to go see his father, visit him during lunch breaks, and his mother had encouraged him to do so, hoping it would improve their relation-ship. After a few months, however, his father told him it was inappro-priate for him to come to his office if it was not on business. People might think that Ryu had got the job because of him and that he was playing favours for relatives. If he wanted to talk, he should come by on a Sunday and visit him (and his mother!) at home. "You can call your mother," his father added, "and arrange a time and date with her."

Ryu never did. Not a single time.

After the funeral, he and his brother left their mother with their aunt, who had offered to take her to her home in Akiota outside

Hiroshima. She had a beautiful countryside house there and the peace would give their mother a chance to grieve and recover. He and his brother silently walked the streets of Hiroshima, with no obvious goal or aim. They stopped at an arcade to play Street Fighter (the original Street Fighter 2 Turbo cabinet, not one of the newer ones). His brother still beat him with most of the characters, but Ryu was pleased to score a victory in a fateful match between Ryu (ha!) and Ken. "It is getting late," his brother said. It was past midnight now. "Are you hungry?" Ryu asked. His brother nodded, and Ryu told him he knew a place that was open at night.

A little while later, they stepped through the sliding door of the little restaurant that was only open from midnight to six in the morning. Weirdly enough, there were no other customers in there for a change. The owner peeked out of his kitchen-niche and welcomed them. He stepped to the counter.

"Master, can you make us two katsu sandwiches?"

"With rice?"

"Yes, please."

"Two beers?"

"No, sake."

"Was the funeral today?" the owner said as he turned to get an enormous bottle of sake.

"Yes, it was."

"Hmm." The owner poured sake into two glasses. "I hope he hasn't followed you here."

"We've been wandering the city," Ryu said. "I am sure we must have lost him there."

"If at all he came to the city with us. It's more likely he just went back to the office," his brother said.

"I'll give you a third glass, just in case he shows up," the owner said, and poured another glass.

...

"Do you remember the story our father told us?" Ryu asked his brother, sandwich in hand, katsu-smell in the air.

"Which one?"

"About the baseball on his desk."

"Hmm. I don't I think he ever told me about it. I've been to his office maybe twice or three times. Less than a handful. With me, he usually told the story about his trip to America."

They laughed. They both remembered that story.

"Your father travelled overseas?" the owner chimed in.

"Yes, he did," Ryu answered. "In 1976. Or 77. Not a lot of Japanese people went to America then."

"I bet he had to go for work."

"Yes, he'd been ordered to make connections with local retailers. To see whether the company could sell products there."

"What were they making back then?"

"Wooden toys," his brother said.

"Really?" the master said, astonished. The company sold electronics these days.

"Yes. And they wanted to get into the overseas market. It did not work out. My father liked the trip, though."

"Remember his stories about Texas?" Ryu said.

"Sure," his brother laughed.

"He's been there?" the master asked.

"Yes," Ryu continued, "he would tell the story again and again. He'd met some business contacts in Texas. And he said that all the stereotypes were true. Guns. Cows. Big cars. He felt like walking into a Wild West movie."

"They took him out for dinner. Into a steakhouse. He'd never been to a steakhouse," his brother added. "They put this steak down in front of him. Bigger than the plate, he'd always say. That big," his brother held his arms out to indicate the steak, a comically large imaginary steak between his outstretched arms, "and he did not know how to eat it. So, he just stuck his fork into it, lifted it up and took bites off the steak hanging from his fork. The cowboys around him laughed, put their knives down and did the same."

"And then they got drunk together."

"Of course they did. On cheap bourbon and beers. Our father sold nothing, though," Ryu explained to the owner.

"Still, the company is now doing well overseas, isn't it? Ryu, you used to work there, no?"

"Yes. Before I opened the bar. Best years of my life as a salaryman." They all laughed.

Ryu and his brother finished their sandwiches, bid the owner farewell, and walked to the main street to hail two taxis. They said goodnight and went to their respective homes. His brother to the suburbs, to his wife and his daughter, Ryu to his tiny apartment in the Northern District of Hiroshima.

On the door to his apartment, he found a note from his neighbour, an elderly lady, telling him that a delivery man had dropped off a box for him. However, since he hadn't been home, she had taken it for him. He should come by in the morning to pick it up.

Ryu took the note off the door and put it on his kitchen table. Then he collapsed on his bed. He was tired.

He dreamt that night.

(Go ahead)

You can tell half a life in a single sentence. What did you do for the last twenty years? I worked in that office over there. On the opposite end of that, there are singular moments you could spend an entire book on.

He had such a moment. I knew that from the first second I met him. Call it instinct. He didn't tell me for a long time, but, eventually, he did.

"For me, that moment came when I sat in a café in Greece," he told me, a smile in the corner of his eyes. We, he and I, were sitting in a café somewhere in Vienna as he told me this.

It had been a sunny day, he said. Took a deep breath. Began narrating his story, without me having asked for it.

The café in Greece had been loud, the white stone walls made the room look bigger than it was. She'd gone to the counter to order two espressos and was carrying them back to their table.

He put the paper down and smiled at her. She smiled back, wearily. The place was packed with people smoking cigarettes and drinking wine. He didn't drink before five. Not even on holiday.

"Busy place," he said.

"Hmhmm," she agreed monosyllabically.

It was then and there in that café in Greece that the world stopped. Not for long, just a fraction of a second. And then, after that sudden stop, the world turned backwards.

He wasn't even sure at first what it was, that strange feeling, until he realised that the sun had started to move in the wrong direction, from West to East and that people spoke backwards. He checked his watch and saw his suspicions confirmed: it was ten minutes earlier than ten minutes ago.

"This is weird," he said.

"What's weird?" she replied. She apparently hadn't noticed that the world had changed direction, and he wondered whether there was any point in explaining it to her.

"Nothing," he said, having concluded that saying nothing was best for now. First, he needed to figure out why the world had decided to turn the other way.

Soon, it was lunchtime again. While at first he felt miffed that they were moving away from five (he had actually been looking forward to a glass of wine), he soon felt happy about going for a second lunch instead. He was hungry.

"Shall we?" he asked, and she agreed. Together, they walked along the pier and then down into town.

"Shall we go there?" she asked him and pointed to a restaurant. They had eaten their other lunch there earlier, and it had been mediocre – too greasy for his taste.

"Let's go there," he said, and pointed to a restaurant on the other side of the road.

"Okay," she agreed.

The food was delicious. The dessert (they started with dessert because of the world going backwards) was so good, it got him in a good mood, and he had a glass of red with the main course.

"You are drinking?" she said.

"Feel like it," he said.

"As long as you don't do it every day, I guess."

"We are on holiday," he said and smiled.

After lunch, they walked back to the pier and went to the beach. Just like the first time this morning, he decided not to go for a swim. "Too cold for me," he told her, brushing off her gentle nudges to come into the water. She ran in, like a little child. He felt embarrassed as she waved from the water.

"You are so gloomy today," she said, sitting down heavily on her towel next to him after she had come out of the water / before she went in.

"I have a lot on my mind," he said.

"Didn't sleep well?"

He suddenly remembered that he'd had a nightmare last night and wondered whether he'd have it again this night, which'd be, of course, the same night as last night. It had been about a giant snail eating up most of the planet's landmass. Maybe, he wondered, it had been a premonition about the world changing direction today.

"No, just got a lot of things I am thinking about." Maybe he should tell her about the dream, but then, he didn't want to burden her with it, not before he knew whether it bore any importance.

They went to the bungalow they were staying at and drank their morning coffee. He checked the newspaper and, at first, was annoyed it was the same news as last morning, until he realised he was reading the same newspaper as last morning. The whole directional change for sure seemed quite confusing. It would take some getting used to.

They went to sleep while the sun was slowly setting (de-rising?). It was a cold and breezy morning and somehow, it felt good to go to sleep in the morning and wait for the evening. The dream did come back, but it changed: instead of devouring the planet, the snail was spitting it out, in jerky, dreamy movements.

He woke up in a good mood the evening before. She had already left the bed (or not come to bed yet?) and was sitting on the little bench in front of their bungalow, smoking a cigarette. He didn't mind her smoking, he didn't like the smell, though.

"Our holiday begins today," she told him when he stepped outside, while she was sucking thin, grey smoke from the air, and blowing it back into the cigarette. It was true – the holiday had begun today. They had arrived a few hours ago / in a few hours. It was time to go back to the airport today and fly home. He felt short-changed by the planet. Why couldn't the directional change have happened later?

"You are gloomy," she told him.

"It is nothing," he lied. He still wasn't sure he could explain the change to her. It was a shame she had not noticed on her own.

"You mad about this morning?" she asked, her voice cold.

He remembered they'd been running late for the plane. He'd been yelling at her.

"Nah, it is fine."

"Okay," she replied, monosyllabically.

Sure enough, they were arguing as they left the airport, back at home in New York, both of them already tired, stressed out, nervous, because of the long flight ahead / behind of them.

"We are going to be fine," she repeated repeatedly. He was checking his watch and tried to figure out what they would have done if they had missed the flight.

"Well, I was ready on time," he snapped, feeling bad about it almost immediately. They did not talk for the rest of the taxi ride. It was silly, sure, arguing about a flight that was behind them now, yet that did not change the fact that they were running late.

The previous few days, they lived in almost complete silence, hardly speaking a word. First, he attributed it to the argument they had had in the taxi, until he remembered that the argument was in the future, not in the past, and could not be the reason for the silence. He then figured that they were busy finishing up a lot of things at work before their holiday, and then he settled that this was the way they felt comfortable.

This was when he found the crack in the wall. It was in their living room, in the white wall opposite the TV. He first saw it after having watched a movie, when he turned off the TV, he saw the reflection in the dark TV screen.

He got up, walked past her (she sat at the kitchen table), and to the wall, where he touched the crack. It was a long, single fissure, maybe half-a-hand wide. He got closer and put his head against the wall, peering into the hole. It was dark beyond, but he thought he could see someone there, in a room on the other side of the wall.

"Did you know there is a crack here?"

She looked at him for a long time and it felt hard to read the expression in her eyes, in her face, on her lips. First, he figured she was just expressionless, an empty piece of paper, devoid of any emotion. Then, it seemed there was something more, a deeply rooted feeling of uprootedness in her eyes, of sadness, of things she had not said to him. Then, that passing expression disappeared, and she smiled, got up and left the room without a word.

He would fix the wall, which would be good for both of them. Who knew what bugs and creepy-crawlies would crawl and creep out of a hole in the wall?

He found the plaster he had bought earlier / later and got to work. He'd got good at fixing walls, he realised, as his hands almost moved on their own, up and down and left and right and only half an hour later, the crack was nowhere to be seen.

"Pretty seamless, isn't it?" he said, turning around, looking at the empty spot at the kitchen table. Right, she had left. Or not arrived yet.

They met again earlier that day in the morning and had coffee, before wishing each other good morning and going to bed. She went first, as usual, he went later / earlier and slept a deep sleep, until he did not and woke up.

The bed next to him was empty. The window was open, and the wind made the pale curtain dance like an insubstantial ghost.

He got up, his feet against the cold marble floor.

It was dark in the living room. Still, he could see her shade almost immediately when he walked in, her leaning against the wall where the crack used to be. And was, again. It had reappeared. She was whispering, whispering into the hole in the wall, as if there was someone on the other side.

"I told you to leave it alone!" he exclaimed, surprised himself by the anger in his voice. She was startled, turned around, leaned against the wall, her body against the crack like a child holding something precious behind her back. "You broke it," he said.

A single tear rolled over the floor and flew up, into the air, onto her cheeks and back into her eyes. A look of defiance replaced the sadness. "Leave it alone, please," she said and left the room, back into the bedroom, the un-smashing of the door a sure-tell sign that he would sleep on the couch for the beginning of the night.

The crack was back. The one he had fixed tomorrow. The one he would fix right now, in the middle of the night.

Half an hour later, the wall seemed seamless again.

She was in a better mood the previous / next evening. Together, they cooked dinner and planned their holiday in Greece, which they moved further away from every day.

The previous day, the crack was back. So, he fixed it again. Then, the previous day, it was there again. He fixed it. He smiled at her while he put the plaster on the wall. She said nothing. Her fingers were red, and the nails broken from scratching the plaster out every night. He knew this, but said nothing. She must realise, by seeing him fixing the wall, that he did not want a crack in the wall. And that it would be for her best to have an unbroken wall.

Weeks passed, day before day of him fixing the wall and her, secretly, at night, tearing it open again. It was getting tiresome.

One day, he decided to put up a painting over the crack and be done with it. He put it up in a single, fast swoop, it almost flew onto the wall by itself. It looked nice. Like something she'd like.

"Do you like the painting?" he asked.

"Well, it is mine, isn't it?" The tone in her voice was cold. It made him angry.

"Is it?" he replied, trying to hold the anger.

"Of course. I put it up."

"You did not. I did. Just now."

"It has been there for a long time."

He had a closer look at the painting. It showed a tree on a level plane, the ground glowing orange in the sunlight. It was a mulberry tree, its red fruits ready for the taking. It was quite trivial, the drawing. Actually, he realised, he did not like it.

"It is quite boring," he concluded aloud.

"Thanks."

"What?"

"Nothing."

"What did I do?"

"Nothing."

He hated her at that moment. He hated her so much that he wanted to tear the apartment down. Take it away from her. However, the world was turning backwards, too fast to keep track. Time was un-passing. Everything he'd take away from her, he'd end up giving her.

He stood up in silence and left the apartment.

He stopped his narration and smiled at me, informing me that the next part always had seemed alien to him. Almost as if it had not been him experiencing it, more like him watching another him living it. He looked around to see the waiter, to order another Viennese coffee, but the man was nowhere to be seen.

This is the story of a man who eventually arrived or left his destination, he finally continued his narration.

It was a tall building at the outskirts of town, and he knew how to get inside. He climbed up the stairs and onto the roof of the building.

On the roof, he climbed over the railing and looked at his city. He sat down on the railing, while the moon and the stars rose, and he heard the cars and the people so far down below. He thought about cause and effect. The moments he had come from / gone to.

And it all, this world, in all facets, it seemed so quiet from above. It was then, faced with this quietness, that he realised he had / would become someone he used not to be. He looked at the coming days and weeks and at the world that was out of spin. Out of direction. He could go with it, use it, make it all the way back to the beginning, tell the story backwards. He could become who he used to be.

He thought of her. Instead of forgetting, he remembered he loved her.

And he ran, ran down from the building, ran through the town and back, back, back the way he had come.

He *left* home. No, he didn't. He was going backwards now and had accepted it. He *came* home. She was still sitting where he left her / would leave her in a moment, staring at the picture.

He sat down opposite her, and they looked at the painting together, until she got up and took it down, revealing the familiar crack behind.

"I am sorry," she said. (Not: "I am not sorry.")
"It is okay. I can bear it," he replied. (Not: "I cannot stand this / you.")

He kissed her on the forehead. It was all good. He got up and went to the crack, peering through the hole one final / first time. He thought he saw a different world behind. One that was still turning in the right direction. It was the neighbour's apartment. And he could see him there, facing away from the crack.

"Do you love him?"
"No." ("Yes"?)

"Shall we fix it together?" she finally asked, and he nodded. So, together, they went to get the plaster from the cellar and fixed the wall, stroke by stroke and movement by movement, in perfect silence, until she asked whether she should put on some music and they listened to an old jazz record, sitting there after they had finished fixing the crack, her smoking a cigarette and him drinking a whiskey, and while she still felt distant, he felt now that they would move closer together, step by step, until they would arrive again at where they had started.

The crack would reappear occasionally before that. First, he got upset, especially when he found her at night, her fingers scratched open, bloody, whispering against the wall and he would yell into the crack and tell the neighbour to leave his girlfriend alone and she would apologise, bow her head, try to explain that it was like a drug, exhilarating, like something they used to have and he tried to understand and they agreed to go on holiday together, soon, to Greece or Ireland or anywhere away from here, from this stinking, stifling city.

They started going for walks together and talk to each other. The crack was still there, yes, coming back every other week, and he would fix it diligently, silently, and she would watch him or help him or smoke cigarettes. He didn't mind her smoking in the house anymore, he just felt happy to have her close.

"You know, I have never been to a zoo," she would tell him one day after he'd fixed the crack again.

"Seriously?" he replied. "Not even when you were a kid?"

"No. I grew up in a village, so there were no zoos close-by."

"Do you want to go now?"

"It is raining."

"We'll bring umbrellas and raincoats. You have rain boots, no?"

"Yeah, the yellow ones," she said and smiled.

She looked like a kindergarten kid walking in her boots and behaved like one, too, jumping from puddle to puddle on their way to the zoo. "I am excited," she would say, and he would reply, "I can see that," and draw her close and kiss her on the cheeks.

The zoo was almost empty, and the rain turned from a light drizzle into a downpour. They gave up on trying to hold their umbrellas against the wind and put up the hoods of their coats. Still, it didn't take long for him to be soaked, his feet completely drenched since he wasn't wearing rain boots. Sure, they had advertised his shoes as rain proof, but he was fairly sure that did not cover torrential rain.

The animals looked like he felt. There was a lonely, overweight Orang-Utan sitting on top of a little hill, his orange fur wet against his pink skin, his face downcast, looking at the bottom of the hill, all by himself.

"He reminds me of you," she said and laughed.

"Because of the belly?"

"Nah, because of the miserable look you have sometimes."

"I don't," he said and laughed, and they kissed again. Their relationship was nearing its beginning, and it felt good, every playful tease ended with an act of physical affection.

They walked past an amazingly expansive enclosure, the facsimile of a big grassland. Off in the distance, they could see a group of long-legged animals sheltering underneath a tree.

"Antelopes?" he asked.

"I dunno. Haven't seen a sign anywhere." They walked on, past more enclosures, until they found themselves at the bottom of a hill decorated with grey sand, trees, rocks, grass.

"Lions," she informed him, pointing to a sign in front of them.

"Can't see any."

"They must be inside. Cats don't like water." She pointed towards an artificial cave leading into the darkness inside the hill.

They stood there, looking at the cave in silence. He wanted to take her hand.

"I used to have this dream when I was a kid. About lions," she finally said, her voice a low whisper.

"What was it about?"

"I'd get eaten by them."

"Okay," he laughed an awkward laugh. "You serious?"

"Yeah. I think I read a story about someone getting eaten, and that messed with my little head."

"So, you'd get eaten? In your dream?"

"Yeah. I am standing in the shade of a tree. And do not see the lion sneaking up behind me."

"Did you wake up?"

"No. It wasn't a nightmare. No screams or anything. It was just kind of matter of fact. I didn't even see it, see me getting eaten. I just knew it happened."

"I guess then it wasn't too bad, was it?"

"No, it wasn't. It just made me sad."

"Why?"

"Because I knew I was waiting for someone underneath that tree. Waiting for someone to come. And I knew that person would not find me, because I'd got eaten by a lion."

"Hmm." He did not know what to say.

"And I always wanted to tell that person to move on. Not to dwell on it. Shit happens. Just move on."

"Might be hard if that person sees your arm dangling from a lion's mouth."

"Brutal."

"You started it."

He put his arm around her waist and was relieved when he felt her body relax against his.

"What would you do?" she whispered, "If you'd been the one I had been waiting for?"

"Chop off the lion's head. Or maybe let myself get eaten as well. Romeo-and-Juliet-style."

"We will meet again in the primordial stomach soup of the lion."

"What is wrong with you?"

The enclave, the artificial hill and the man-made cave remained silent and there were no lions to be seen that day. They followed the path downwards, past several monkey cages, and then into the reptile house. The warm moistness inside made him feel even more soaked than before.

"Let's go home," he finally said, and she agreed with a short, silent nod. He kissed her forehead, which was wet and sweaty, thinking about telling her he loved her. He couldn't quite mouth the words. Surely she knew.

The previous months passed in a haze towards the warm summer that came before. They were lying in bed, the curtains moving in front of the open windows, their bodies sweating, naked, next to each other, he looked at her. Her skin had the same colour as the moon.

It was then that he realised the first days of their relationship had passed. He would have moved in yesterday. He would move out yesterday.

He got up and peered out of the window and silently cursed at the world for turning backwards.

But then – would he want to change it and go forward again, knowing where they were heading? He thought of the crack in the wall, the one they would decide to ignore and / or endure. He thought about the longing she had for whatever (who-ever!) was beyond the hole in the wall and how that longing would grow.

"What are you doing?" she whispered, having woken up because of his moving through the room.

"Nothing," he replied.

"Come back to bed," she said, gently.

He lay down next to her. "I want to ask you something."

"Let's talk tomorrow," she said, moving closer, half-asleep. Her body against his. He felt the sweat on her skin.

"Yes," he agreed.

They hugged in the morning and he moved out. The beginning of their relationship, this time, truly, was the end.

He became a homeless wanderer for a while.

He went back to the tall building and stood on the roof, trying to get in touch with the feelings he would have / had had that night, to no avail. It was like staring into an abyss at the bottom of the building, only the abyss didn't even have the courtesy of looking back at him.

He hardly remembered her the first / last time they met. He had left the city behind him and was walking the countryside.

She was standing atop a hill, a vantage point from where she could overlook the forest, lake, and river in the valley below. She was standing behind a canvas, painting.

He approached her out of curiosity, and because he craved a chat with someone, anyone, and only realised when he drew closer that it was her.

"Hello," she said. She didn't know him yet, which felt like a sting in his chest.

"Are you painting?" he asked, just because he did not know what else to say.

"Obviously," she said and smiled.

He looked at the painting. It showed an almost barren landscape with only a single tree in sight.

"This is not this landscape," he said, pointing at the view in front of them, the forest, and the river.

"Really? Haven't noticed," she joked. "I already painted this view five times, so I got bored and decided to create my own image. Do you like it?"

"Yes," he lied. It was only half-a-lie, he told himself. He didn't dislike the painting. In fact, he felt impartial to it, it didn't create any feeling inside at all.

"It is a mulberry tree," she told him.

"The berries in the painting are white, though," he said upon close inspection.

"They will turn red in time."

He looked at her, her beautiful green eyes carrying so many things he did not know yet, but wanted to know. Her lips and her smile and her fingers, as she held her hands by her side, looking at him, not sure what she should do with them, her hair and her breathing and her simple humanity, fragility, strength. He thought about all the things to come and how an end waited for them in the future, lurking, definite.

But maybe not this time.

"That's a long silence," she finally said, breaking the awkwardness that had arisen.

"Sorry."

"You got lost, didn't you?"

"Yeah."

"Where were you?"

The silence arose again.

"Do you want to have a coffee?" he finally said.

"If you help me carry the easel. I don't drink coffee, though."

"Shame, damn shame," he said, and they both laughed.

This is where he took a break from telling me his story and took a sip from the almost empty coffee in front of him. The Viennese café around us had become busy and noisy. I checked my watch. It was almost dinnertime.

"I hadn't noticed it then, but this is when the planet changed rotation again. In that very second when I picked up the easel and we walked down the hill to have a coffee. Or iced tea in her case."

"Just like that."

"Just like that. In fact, it was much less obvious than the first time. The first time, I knew something was off. The second time, I only realised it when I woke up next to her weeks later."

Then he told me the same story again, this time in reverse. Them going to the zoo and her telling him about lions and dreams, her jumping into puddles and him getting annoyed because of her childishness and about the arguments that turned into silence. And, of course, the crack, the goddam crack she tore open, he tried to fix, or the other way around, he wasn't sure, until she covered it with the painting, and he tore said painting down. That man on the other side of the crack silently judging them for all of their mistakes. Him running away from her and standing on that building, thinking about jumping until he felt dead inside.

And then, the trip to Greece. They had spent the day at the beach, in the sun. She looked beautiful in her bikini, like she belonged there.

She came out of the water and sat down heavily next to him and wrapped a blanket around her. It was getting cold in the shade, but he liked the shade much more than the sun. She stretched her legs to get some sun onto her feet, at least.

"Don't you wanna go into the water?" she asked him.

"I'm fine," he replied. They sat there for a long time. Her gentle breathing next to him felt fine, like something he had got accustomed to.

They got up some time later, put on their t-shirts and trousers and headed into town, wandered across the market. She looked at hats and he at sunglasses before they turned left to go into a large café. The place was noisy. They sat at a table.

"Do you want to eat something?" she asked.

"It is too early," he replied.

She looked at him. He remembered her green eyes and remembered the things he'd wanted to know about them. They were gone. It was like looking into a dead mirror.

"This will not work, will it?" he said.

"I am sorry," she replied.

He wanted to tell her it wasn't anyone's fault, only he couldn't. Instead: "It is him, isn't it? The man on the other side of the wall? You've been waiting for him. Underneath your fucking tree."

"I'll get us an espresso," she said and got up.

He smiled as he finished the story. "That is the only two times I have seen the planet change direction," he added after he had finally got the waiter's attention and ordered another coffee and lit a cigarette. "It's interesting, isn't it?"

"What would you do if it happened again?" I asked.

"Well, I'd like to say I'd do my best, yet maybe just slightly better than last time would be good enough. Slightly better. Maybe then I could become the man on the other side of the wall," he said.

I, for my part, wondered whether that man on the other side of the wall had actually existed or was something he'd made up to protect himself. I said nothing, though, since there was no regret in his voice, only hope – and I didn't want to put a tamper on that.

#

Ryu woke in the late morning. Almost lunchtime, actually. He got out of bed and regretted two things – first, he did not have a vinyl collection. And second, he didn't smoke. Otherwise, he could've got up, put on a piece of classical music and smoked a cigarette, standing naked in his apartment, contemplating, like a character from a Murakami novel. Thinking about his dead father. About his bar. About his life. Alas, all he could do was to put on a shirt and trousers, get out of the apartment building, put some coins in the vending machine outside, purchase a can of coffee and consider whether he should walk to the 7/11 to get something akin to breakfast.

He was not hungry. The katsu from past midnight still took up most of the space in his stomach. He went back to his apartment, just in time to hear his phone beep. He'd got a message from Terra asking him whether he wanted to go for a walk and lunch. He agreed to meet in half an hour outside the 7/11.

He had the nagging feeling that he was forgetting something, yet could not figure out what. He took a shower and put on some clothes. He went for a black t-shirt, black trousers. It was not because his father had died, not a sign of mourning, but because that was his normal colour of choice. Unless he was working, of course, when he donned a more formal attire. For some reason he could not quite grasp, his father's baseball came back to mind. He tried to remember the story. It had been a tight game. It all had come down to the last throw, like in a movie. It all had come down to his father. And he threw the ball like never before – Ryu checked the time. Half an hour had passed. He was running late.

He met Terra outside the 7/11 and apologised for being late. She told him not to worry, looking at him with her big, brown eyes, filled with worry, the unspoken question lingering in the air as to how he was coping. He told her he was fine, answering the question that had not been, and she asked him whether he wanted to get coffee from the 7/11.

Soon after, they walked along Motoyasu river. Terra showed him pictures on her phone of new paintings she'd made. They were small, designed to be copied and printed on postcards, highly stylised renditions of famous Japanese landmarks. He'd told her before that she should make big ones, too, for people to hang in their apartments and he told her again now.

"Ah, I can hardly sell the postcards. No one would hang them."

"I would," Ryu said.

"There is no space in your tiny apartment. People in Japan have tiny apartments. They do not have space for paintings."

"Most people in my family live in houses." There was a moment of silence as both of them remembered he'd just lost a member of his family. It was funny how one's brain could trick someone into forgetting these things. "I wonder what my mother is going to do with the house. Four people used to live there. Now, it's just her."

"Maybe she will want to move into an apartment?"

"My mother living in an apartment? I can't really see that."

"You could take over the house. Would at least give me a couch to crash on if my postcard business doesn't work out."

"I couldn't afford it."

"The house?"

"Yes. No way I could pay the bills. It is silly how expensive it is to live in a house."

"How is your mother going to do it?"

"As far as I know them, they've put enough money aside. They have always been good at these things, my parents," Ryu said and fell silent. Deeply lost in thought, he looked at the river flowing quietly next to them.

"What?" Terra asked.

"It is funny, isn't it? They. I only know them as they. My parents. It's hard sometimes to imagine them as separate people." Terra nodded, unsure what to say. "My father used to have a baseball on his desk at work," Ryu continued. "He used to tell me its story. It always sounded like he was giving me advice when he did. Teaching me some kind of lesson."

"What was the story?" she asked, but Ryu wasn't really listening to what she was saying.

"I wonder what they did with the baseball. Maybe my mother has it? Or maybe they have thrown it away."

"That would be sad."

"It is just a baseball. Nothing special."

A group of travellers were taking photos of a plastic food display outside a restaurant. They walked past them.

"Do you miss him?"

"We've grown distant. No, he has always been distant."

"Has he ever visited your bar?"

Somewhere over the river, a seagull cried. Ryu could hear the faint echo of the children's choir singing at Sadako's statue. He did not reply. The answer was obvious, implied in the heavy silence that ensued. Terra looked at him, her big, troubled eyes on him. She mouthed words of compassion, but there was no need for her to speak. Ryu understood and appreciated the gesture and he felt lost, afraid of the feelings he should have been feeling, when, in reality, he just felt cold, his feet tired, heavy, and his mind slow.

"Let's go eat," Terra offered, and that was what they did. Ramen, it always helps, Terra told him, and she told him to hang up a sign at the bar saying that it would be closed tonight, and suggested they would spend the rest of the day and night together. She had nowhere to be anyway, that was the good thing about being an artist, she lived on her own time.

"We are all living on our own time," Ryu replied.

After having put up the sign, they wandered the streets some more. They had coffee at a small place, designed as an homage to Fuglen in Tokyo, heavy wooden tables, counter, coffee made from beans grown by a small collective of farmers in Ethiopia.

Then, they bought unhealthy food from a convenience store and went to Terra's place, which was even smaller than his, but cosier, with pillows and blankets in every corner and they sat on the floor, eating their food, drinking highballs from cans, watching the latest runs of kuwazu girai. Then, he went with Terra to stand on the roof of the building, where she smoked a cigarette, and he drank another can of something alcoholic. They both watched the streets below. It was getting quieter. It was getting cold.

"What time is it?"

Terra checked her watch. "We are approaching midnight."

"Looks like I'll be crashing on your floor tonight."

"That is the plan."

"Your girlfriend not around?"

Terra took a drag of her cigarette. "Nah, we are taking a break," she said, trying to sound much too cool about it.

"I am sorry."

"It is okay. It was not meant to last, anyway. I should date guys. That's easier."

"Not in my experience."

Terra stood at the railing, looking down at the street below. Then she pointed to a building across the road. It stood taller than the one they were standing on. "The other night, I saw someone jump off that roof over there."

Silence. Hard to know what to reply to something like that. On the surface, she sounded casual. He knew, though, that the casual tone was only there to prevent her from falling apart.

She took another drag of her cigarette. "I was sitting where you are sitting now. Smoking my last cigarette for the day. Looking out into the world. Felt great because I'd sold a few postcards. I saw this figure stepping up to the railing over there. Thought little of it. I watched as the person climbed over the railing, smoked my cigarette. I should have got up and yelled."

"You didn't realise what was happening."

"I saw the person jump. No. Just falling. It didn't even look like a person. Just like a bag of something." She took another drag, hand trembling. "I heard how... the sound on the pavement. Didn't get up. Didn't want to see. Smoked another cigarette. And another. There was a scream. Sirens. Police. I still didn't wanna look. I was up here till four in the morning. Finished an entire pack of cigarettes."

She put out the cigarette and instantly lighted another one.

"I am sorry," Ryu said.

Terra took a deep breath. It was like waking up. "No, I am sorry. I don't know why I am telling you this. You just lost your father." With a quick movement, Ryu got up and put his arms around her, his chest against her back. They stood there, breathing against each other's bodies for a while. Both of them feeling like crying, both of them unable to do so.

"Let's go inside," Ryu finally said, letting her go. Terra nodded. They walked towards the stairs leading down on the side of the building. Ryu peered over the railing and down at the pavement across the road. It seemed to him he could see a discolouring on the sidewalk in the vague shape of a body.

"A guy with a garden hose was cleaning the street the next morning when I left the house," Terra said, following his gaze. They both laughed, unable to do anything else. Then, Terra added, her voice a coarse whisper: "Why do people do something like that? Sure, I have thought about jumping as well. I mean, who hasn't? But just as a concept. Actually doing it, though? Fuck no."

An ambulance sped by in the street below.

"There probably has been an accident at the intersection two blocks down," Terra said. "It's a dangerous intersection."

They went back to the apartment and watched videos of cats online until they fell asleep. Ryu woke some hours later. Five o'clock, his phone told him. Terra had put a blanket on him. She, herself, lay sleeping in the room's corner, securely rolled up in a thick cover on top of her futon.

He knew the second he woke up that he wouldn't be able to fall asleep again. He got up, put on his shoes and coat, and quietly left the apartment. He'd have to send Terra a text to let her know he was alright.

He wandered the streets aimlessly. It was a grey morning, the sky engulfed in a thick fog that reflected the city's lights in a weird, orange shade. He could see his breath as he walked, and he wished he had brought gloves with him. He continued his aimless wandering for a while until he turned and went back to his apartment. Maybe a shower, maybe something to eat, maybe try to lie down again.

He found a note from his neighbour on his door, informing that she was still holding onto his delivery and that he should come by and pick it up today. He checked his watch. It was six o'clock. Too early to ring her doorbell.

He went into his kitchen and opened the cupboards in search of something to eat, only finding several packages of instant ramen and some pickled vegetables. He chose one of the ramen packages and scanned the instructions on the back.

His father had never cooked. Not a single time. He'd been old-fashioned like that. The wife at home, cooking dinner. He at work. On Sundays, he sometimes would take the family out for lunch. His father hadn't even been able to boil an egg.

Ryu put the ramen package back into the cupboard and left the apartment. He went to the closest supermarket. Not a convenience shop, but a proper market. He bought vegetables, fresh ones, minced meat, rice, miso. Then, in the shop, he checked on his phone how to bake cookies and bought the ingredients.

He went back to his apartment and put the food on the counter. He chopped the vegetables. He mixed the minced meat with panko, an egg, seasoning and formed hamburger patties. He put the rice on. He boiled the vegetables and fried the burger. He fried an egg and put it on top of the burger, ate the patty and egg with the rice and the vegetables. It was dry. Luckily, he found some American ketchup in one cupboard, which he added to his meal. Then, he re-read the recipe for the cookies – sesame cookies – and got to work. He, his kitchen, and his floor were caked in flour and dough by the time he was done. But there were cookies baking in the oven, and he felt a hint of victory.

He felt tired, so he lay down on the couch, turned on the TV, watched an episode of something on Netflix, and fell asleep.

It was not the smoke or the horrid smell that woke him, but the doorbell. He jumped up, cursing, seeing dark smoke coming out of the oven. Then, the doorbell again, him yelling that he was on the way, opening the oven, burning his right hand, grabbing the tray with a towel, it falling to the floor, burnt cookies flying everywhere, the doorbell again, him hurrying to the door.

It was Terra.

"You okay?"

"Come in," he said, turned around, hurried back to the kitchen to make sure nothing was on fire and to clean the mess.

"You disappeared. I was worried."

"Oh, I meant to write..."

"Have you been baking?"

"I tried."

"And failed, by the smell of it."

"Yes."

He started cleaning his kitchen.

"What is the time?"

"Past four."

"Oh."

"Oh?"

"I gotta open the bar. I have to do some shopping."

"Do you need help?"

"I'll be fine," he said, dropping the burnt cookies in the bin.

"Oh, I saw the grandmother from next door when I came up. She said she had a package for you."

"Oh. Yes, I forgot. Could you... could you pick it up for me? Bring it to the bar? You get a free drink. I gotta run."

"Sure."

He rushed out of the apartment, leaving his keys with Terra. Then, into a shop to buy fresh oranges and lemons, then to the bar. He was running late, he realised, when he entered the building and got into the elevator. He rushed out as soon as the doors opened and almost bumped into someone.

It was a foreigner. A tourist, presumably.

"Oh. Sorry."

"Oh, are you from the bar? Are you still closed?"

"I am running late. So sorry. Please come in," he said, unlocking the door. The foreigner sat down at the bar.

"No rush," he said.

"Old-Fashioned?" Ryu said, playing his usual game of guessing the most obvious drink you could get in a bourbon bar.

"Please."

Ryu prepared the drink. He looked at the foreigner. He recognised him. "You have been here before, right?"

"About a week ago, yes. I am on my way back to Tokyo and thought I'd spend another night in town and visit your bar."

"Thank you for coming back."

Ryu had just put the Old-Fashioned down in front of the man when Terra entered, holding a box under her arm, which she passed to him over the counter. She nodded at the foreigner.

"Best wishes from your neighbour. She really thinks you should come by tomorrow and talk to her about the funeral."

"Will do."

"I think she just wants to talk about her late husband. He died 5 years ago, did you know that?"

"No. Really?" Ryu got started unpacking the box.

"What is it?" Terra asked, watching him tearing the packaging.

Inside, he found a wooden box and inside that box, a bottle of bourbon. Weller's Original, the label said. He knew the make, he had a bottle in his bar – however, the bottle he had on the shelf behind him looked different – this one looked really old. He took the bottle out and held it in his hands.

"Bourbon?" Terra asked him. The tourist took a sip from his drink and seemed to listen in, or at least to figure out the meaning of what was unfolding in front of him.

"It is old."

"A note." Terra pointed to a small envelope that'd been lying underneath the bottle. Ryu put the bottle back and took the envelope out. Someone had written his name on the front– he recognised the handwriting immediately.

"From my father." He tore the letter open and read its content. It was short: "Ryu, I got this bottle from my American friends in 1971. I think you should have it. I asked your mother to send it to you after my death. I hope it will remind you of me."

"What does it say?"

"It... My father got this bottle fifty years ago. When he was in America." Ryu took the bottle in his hands again, read the label, carefully. He imagined his father in the seventies in Texas, a young man, meeting all these Americans, becoming friends with them, they, with their cowboy hats and boots, him with his Japanese suit and tie, at the airport, saying their farewells to each other, the cowboys giving the stranger a bottle as a reminder of his trip. His father keeping the bottle in the house's cellar for all these years. Deciding to give it to Ryu before he died.

Ryu gently put the bottle back and put the case up onto the shelf at the back wall. It looked good. Like a genuine treasure. There would be guests asking him about this and he would tell them the story.

"Looks good," Terra confirmed.

Fukuoka / Amelie

I started to feel uncomfortable, so I paid for my drink and left. It was as if I had intruded on something private, been in a place I should not have been in – of course, it was just a matter of not understanding the language and missing the context of what was unfolding. It was probably nothing. A rare bottle the owner had ordered online and received today, both he and his girlfriend excited to see it propped up in the bar. A good-luck charm. But then, what about the handwritten letter inside the case? You rarely get a handwritten letter from your seller on eBay. Maybe a gift. A special gift.

Not knowing the true story was nagging against the back of my head. I pushed it away.

...

I found myself on a Shinkansen heading from Hiroshima to Fukuoka (or Hakata, apparently the city had two different names, however, I did not understand why and when to use which one) some 10 hours later. It was a brief trip, only about an hour, so I had bought nothing to drink or eat – also, I had been planning on getting a snack from the food trolley coming through the Shinkansens at regular intervals. I had wanted to do so for several trips now, but had never worked up the courage to go through with it. The barrier of not speaking Japanese seemed too big. Today would be the day, however. I craved caffeine.

I peered out into the hallway to the front and the back. No trolley in sight. I would be ready when it came.

I took out my notebook and a pen. Next to my food trolley plans, I had also decided it was time to write. Take the impressions of

Hiroshima and turn them into fiction. Be productive. Get one step closer to finishing the book. Or at least begin it.

I'd saved the Wikipedia article about Sadako Sasaki on my phone to find inspiration in her story. I put the notebook down again and picked up the phone. I re-read the article. I wanted to put her story into fictional motion. From the real to the unreal. The girl got caught in the blast. Got sick later. When she got sick, someone told her a legend saying that if she folded 1,000 paper cranes, she'd get a wish. She started folding in the hospital. Died.

My brain started its work: the story, my adaptation of Sadako's plight, should begin with the legend of the paper cranes. A mythological backbone. I'd been unable to locate the original legend of the 1,000 paper cranes, so I would have to invent my own. I imagined a mythological warrior fighting in battles, evading death at every corner. He gets married, he loves his wife very much, and she gets pregnant. Then, his master calls upon him one more time. One last battle. He leaves his wife at home and rides with his fellow warriors. They fight fast, they fight furious, they win the battle, they win the war – but then, a messenger reaches him: his wife has died in childbirth. His daughter – dead as well.

Full of grief, he rides home, he curses the gods. Yet, despite his cursing, they are truly gone. Then, he fights. He fights every battle for every shogun, always looking for the blade that will end his life – alas, no one can match his skill.

Then, one day, he gets struck in battle, falls off his horse, is buried beneath the falling bodies of his fellow samurai. He loses consciousness and finds himself on a wide plane, the sun glittering in the distance, its mirror images looking back at him from countless puddles across the plane. Then, a scream, a bird scream, and he sees a crane fly by overhead. It lands off in the distance and the warrior knows he must reach the bird. It is where his wife and daughter are waiting. He walks. For hours. For days. He is not hungry, nor tired, still his steps are heavy and endless.

He passes an old man sitting on a rock, folding origami. What are you doing, old man, he asks him. I am folding, the man replies. Why? I will fold 1,000 paper cranes. And offer them to the crane. Surely he will have to listen to me. Maybe even grant me a wish.

1,000 paper cranes, huh?, our warrior says and gazes off into the distance. He sees the crane, only a shadow against the setting sun. It is where his wife and daughter are waiting.

He wakes up, being pulled up from underneath the dead bodies by his enemies. They imprison him in the deepest stone walls. He has found a purpose, though. He sits in his prison, folding, folding paper cranes and...

Wait, where would he get the paper from?

At the bottom of the meagre notes I'd written in my notebook ("The Legend of the Crane" warrior, wife dies, encounters the legend) I added: paper, question mark.

And: the end, question mark.

The end? He would die in the prison, surely, just as he folds the last crane. And meet his wife and daughter in the afterlife. No, that did not work. Buddhism did not have an afterlife – or did it?

Ah, they would meet again in the next life!

Yes! Inspiration struck: Sadako was his daughter reincarnate.

No, wait, this was just cruel. First, she dies an unborn infant, then a bomb victim. I sighed, put the pen down. It was a false start. Starting with the legend did not work. The story was supposed to be about her, not some stereotypical man-hero with a sword.

So, the story should and would begin with two-year-old Sadako in her room. Playing. Maybe drawing, scribbling on paper. Her mother seeing the promise of an artist, a writer in the way young Sadako leads the pen across the paper. Then, a flash of light. No sound. Just lightning. Then, the shock-wave and sound. A rumbling, all windows burst, eardrums pressurised to the max. Sadako in her room, little girl, caught by the shock-wave, flying through the window, disappearing from view. Then: silence. Her mother looking at the spot in the room where her daughter just sat. Then, the house slowly crumbling, falling apart. Her mother rushing into the streets, yelling her daughter's name. Sadako crying, lying on a patch of grass next to the house. She sees her mother and runs towards her. Not a scratch on her. As if the shock-wave had put her down gently on the ground. Her mother runs with her, out into the streets, out of the town. Burned people wandering the streets, fires, confusion. And then: the rain bringing down the deadly ashes. But, of course, she did not know. Her mother did not know that Sadako had begun to die at that moment.

They make it out. Stay with the grandmother in the countryside for a while. Sadako seemingly unharmed, a gift from god, growing up, growing stronger. She loses her interest in writing and drawing but starts to run. At school, she becomes a member of the track team. She is fast, almost as if she is still being carried by the shock-wave. She is a survivor. A fighter – no one realises how true this is because the cancer is already spreading in her body and her body quietly fights.

Then, when she is ten, eleven, the marks show. Then, the hospital. She is weakening, she is diagnosed, and the doctors tell her there is no way out. There is no running from this.

Her father sitting next to her at the bed, telling her the story about the cranes (so, maybe, this would be a good point to put in the "original" legend?) and she, determined, gets to work. Folding paper cranes. Hundreds of them. Stealing paper from the hospital, scrounging, folding everything she can get her hands on. She has a goal. Wants to live. Even when her fingers get numb and her hands tremble because of the sickness wreaking havoc on her body. The shock-wave has returned in a different form, so much more quiet, so much more deadly.

And then? Go with some accounts that say she never finished all the paper cranes and death took her away before she could get her wish? Or go with the other accounts claiming she finished many more than 1,000 paper cranes – which would mean her wish was not fulfilled? Or – maybe she finished the cranes, yet wished for something else?

I had to think of her statue and of all the children presenting her with paper cranes every day, millions of folded cranes, as if to beg her to make her wish, a futile gesture, because, children, she is dead, she died because she was caught in an explosion in a war she had no part in. She was just a child.

I looked up, alerted by movement at the end of the car. The lady with the food trolley had entered. Time to order coffee. And a snack. She walked down the aisle, making her way towards me. I felt my pulse speed up. I was nervous – yes, truly, nervous about ordering something from a food trolley in a Shinkansen on the way from Hiroshima to Fukuoka, nervous like a first grader before his first presentation. She took another step forward, almost at my seat now. She looked up, and I nodded in her general direction.

This was when our eyes met, and something changed. Something in her eyes made me freeze. A certain sadness, there, inside her eyes, overshadowing the smile she had put on her face, a sadness that was telling stories I could not understand. It was impossible to estimate her age – twenty, thirty, maybe forty. But that look in her eyes – as if she had seen things, terrible things, yet she was still here, pulling a food trolley on a train, day after day, gifting smiles to unfamiliar people while her life was falling apart.

She arrived at my seat. "Uh, erm, ah," I said, "cohi o-kudasai. Mo kore-wa o-kudasai," pointing to a wafer-looking hand-sized cookie wrapped in transparent plastic. She handed me a can of coffee and the cookie, I paid, she left, taking her sad eyes with her.

I opened the can and looked at my notebook. Some notes, the crossed-out section about the warrior, and then Sadako's name. That was all I had.

What about–? I wrote a new title on the page opposite:

The Lady with the Food Trolley

I would tell her story. Make up a story to encapsulate the sadness in her eyes, the smile on her face. I took a sip of the coffee and took a bite of the cookie. It was filled with red bean taste. What was the story? I leaned against the window. What was her story? It had to be something good. Something between hope and sadness.

The world outside passed like a moving image, taking my mind, my thoughts with it, leaving me in a haze of half-thoughts and idle ideas, untold stories, inconclusive endings.

I was greeted by torrential rain upon my arrival in Fukuoka. I stood outside the main building of the train station, which, thank god, was covered by a roof reaching from the building across to the parking area in front. Cowering underneath that roof, I was watching a queue of uncounted people slowly moving forward towards a row of taxis. An endless dance of taxis leaving in front and new taxis arriving in the back, slogging their way forward, in line with the line of people, until one and one met at the front, a person got in, and another taxi disappeared in the rain.

I'd been planning on walking to my hostel, but it was a good twenty minutes' walk. While I did not mind getting wet, the downpour was strong enough to soak me within minutes and I was not sure how waterproof my bag would prove to be – so, I joined the slowly marching centipede of people wanting to take a taxi. While standing in line, I conjured the reservation confirmation for my hostel – I had had the foresight to print all the addresses of my hotels in Japanese. Experience from earlier travels had shown that the taxi drivers spoke little English – and that I seemed to be utterly incapable of pronouncing Japanese street names.

Rain was falling, a thick curtain of silver drops, producing a constant drone of noise. People without umbrellas running across the square in front of the station building.

I made it to the front, walking up to a Toyota taxi, which looked the same as most of the other taxis, an old-looking car, a blast from the past, steered by an old Japanese man wearing white gloves. The trunk opened magically (a lever next to the driver actually, no magic) and the driver hurried out to help me lift the suitcase into the trunk. In the car, I showed him the address of the hostel in Japanese, which seemed to satisfy him, and we moved.

Outside, the build of the city changed from big houses and wide streets into something narrower, a residential area. The road became increasingly smaller, and it felt like we were about to hit the stone wall to our left or the fence to the right. Before this could happen, the man stopped the taxi. I checked the blue dot on my phone's map – the hostel was not far now. He pointed down the road, most likely wanting to signify he could not drive any further. "Daijoubu," I said, hoping I sounded polite enough, paid the fair and got out. He seemed happy with my level of politeness, took my money, and helped me unload the suitcase.

The rain had almost stopped at this point – luckily. My GPS on the phone told me I was only five minutes away from the hostel.

Within half an hour, I'd met the owner of the hostel (the term hostel seemed to be an understatement – the building was stylish, newly refurbished, offered very private, very large rooms complete with small balconies, a very rare thing in Japan), dropped off my bag in my room and followed the owner's invitation to the bar on the hostel's premises, where he gave out a free drink to every new guest. I was not one to reject a free drink.

Upon his recommendation, I took a shoju with water (he poured one for himself as well) and he, almost formally, welcomed me, saying something in Japanese and bowing from behind the counter. He – Kay-San – had a keen, friendly air about him. Eager to please, eager to welcome people, eager to talk to them. At the same time, I got the feeling that he was lonely – I couldn't quite put my finger on why I had that feeling. It was nothing he said. Maybe it was just my projection. Yet, I was sure that there was something in his eyes, which reminded me of the food-trolley lady. I'd only finished half my shoju when Kay-San poured himself a second one ("I am drinking this like water. Too much!" he said and laughed) and I smiled at him, nodding my head to the beat coming out of the bar's sound-system. My gaze wandered around the countless shelves hanging about the place, which were stacked with LPs and CDs. I asked the obvious question:

"Do you like music?"

Yes, very much, he told me. In fact, in another life, he had been a music producer.

"Oh, so can you teach me about Japanese music?"

He looked at me, almost incredulously, seemingly uncertain whether he should just say a word or two or take me down the rabbit hole of a full-blown lecture on the topic. "Do you have time?" he asked me, hope in his eyes.

"I have time," I replied. "I have nowhere to be." Down the rabbit hole it was. He took out a piece of paper and a pen. "So, the first band you need to know," he said, "is Happy End." He wrote the name down on a piece of paper, then the years they'd been active (1970 to 1973), and the names of the members. He circled the name Haroumi Hasano (I'd heard the name before yet could not put my finger on it) and stressed the fact that he was *especially* important. On his laptop, which was connected to the sound system in the bar, he put on a song by the band, accompanied by an almost comically serious request for me to "please listen" (complete with a quick bow).

I did. We did not talk for the duration of the song. We just occasionally took a sip from our drinks, enjoying the music, a very Beatlesesque folk-pop song. The song ended, I ordered a beer, he poured himself another drink and continued his lesson.

He wrote down Tin Pan Alley and its members (prominently featuring Hosono again) next and told me they had not only been active as a band but also as producers. Most famously, they had produced four albums by Yumi Arai. He continued, writing down more names of bands, artists, and songs. Every explanation, every mention of a band was followed by a song ("Please listen," he would say before every song), and for the duration of every song, the two of us sat in silence, listening to the music. This was not a man who listened to music to fill the silent space around him. This was a man who listened to music because it was music.

He played a song by the band Sugar Babe and then, the big one, the one he had been building towards: Yellow Magic Orchestra. According to Kay-San, the Japanese answer to German Kraftwerk, a band mixing real and electronic sounds, an attempt to fuse Eastern traditions with the modern from the West, a fusion creating its own Japanese thing. The band included Hosono, Yukihiro Takahashi and, of course, Ryuichi Sakamoto. Merry Christmas Mr. Lawrence. I knew that one.

He put on a song – an electronic song, good to listen to, a clean rhythmic structure featuring an energetic flow. It felt like an artifact out of time. A Daft Punk song (from their last album), yet somehow produced twenty years before Daft Punk. "This is great!" I exclaimed, and Kay-San seemed to be pleased by my favourable reaction, helping himself to another shoju, moving to the rhythm of the music. "Everyone should know them," I said when the song ended, feeling stupid I'd never encountered them before, that there was no Yellow Magic Orchestra in my LP collection at home.

The band turned out to be the climax, the ultima ratio of Kay-San's presentation. He noted some follow-ups, Akai Tori, Mariya Takeuchi and Fish Mans, but he kept coming back to that period, the YMO time, offering more of their songs, like a man who was stuck there, in this past, drinking copious amounts of alcohol, while dreaming of having seen them live, being part of music history. I imagined him as a young music producer in Fukuoka, eyes on Tokyo, on the newest, hottest music coming out of the big city, young Kay-San dressed like a character out of Stallone's Saturday Night Live, going around to live-gigs to discover new bands he could produce. In my imagination, he found that one band, a trio, two guys, a girl, she on the guitar, uncommon to see a girl play acoustic guitar in a band at that time, uncommon to see a band doing acoustic music, not disco like everyone else. He produces them, he falls in love with her, she is in love with a band member and the triangle ensues, a triangle that would split the band and end his producer's career.

He took another sip of shoju, and we were joined by a Korean woman who was staying at the hostel as well and had come to the bar for her free drink. Talking to her, I would learn later that Fukuoka was a weekend hotspot for Koreans, because of its relative closeness to their country. I wondered whether the tense history between the two Asian states still was an issue today. I had to think about the fact that the two governments were still fiercely arguing about the ownership over some (mostly barren?) islands in the sea between the two countries. However, there was nothing to be felt of that tension in Kay-San's bar tonight, as the three of us chatted away, now mostly about Korean pop music, relaxedly, loosely, cracking jokes. It felt fine. After a while, Kay-San was talked-out, he fell silent, gently swaying to the music he had put on (he might have been drunk at this point) and Yoonah, the Korean woman, told me more about herself – she was a doctor, constantly stressed, always working, always under pressure. Her escape routine was to get to Fukuoka for the weekend. Alone, no friends, no accompaniment, just some drinking, eating, and shopping.

"You should visit the Yatai together," Kay-San said, waking up from his musical reveries.

The Yatai. I had read about them. Food stands that were scattered all across Fukuoka, one of the last cities in Japan that had not banned outside cooking and food stands. Of course, they were on my list of top things to do here. I'd been planning on visiting them tomorrow.

"Have you had something to eat?" Yoonah asked me.

No, I replied, unsure whether I should go with her. I felt that familiar out-of-place feeling. Maybe I should have worn a different t-shirt – I felt nerdy in my The Last Jedi Shirt, next to her, in her expensive-looking sweater and dark jeans. There was an awkward silence in the bar. I kinda nodded.

Then, Kay-San: "You just head out, go to the right, follow the river upstream and you get to Nakasu. Lots of Yatai there."

Yoonah: Do you want to?

Me: Let's.

> *We left the bar and Kay-San behind, the music, the gentle, Beatle-inspired guitars of Happy Ending (the musical journey ended where it had started) and followed his directions.*

Yoonah: I want to visit Switzerland one day.

> *We were walking half-a-meter apart.*

Me: It is nice. You would like it.

Yoonah: I am always too busy. I don't have time for long trips.

Me: You should really take a longer holiday. (Note: thank you, captain obvious.)

Yoonah: What do you do for work?

Me: Office Management. (Note: would it have been more impressive to say I am an author? Addendum: unpublished author. Not very impressive.)

Yoonah: Do you like your work?

Me: Yes. (Note: add something! Keep the conversation going!) Do you come here often? (Really?)

Yoonah: Fukuoka? (Saved by the bell.) Almost every weekend. Every weekend I am off. It's a pleasant city, I like it a lot. Also, staying at Kay-San's hotel is always a lot of fun.

Me: He used to be a music producer. (I felt like a child offering clay bricks to our conversational puzzle.)

Yoonah: Yes, he told me. I think he tells everyone. He had to stop producing music, it was too stressful to him, he told me once. He had to take pills to cope.

There was a long silence between us. We waited at a crossing, waiting for the green light to tell us to go.

Y: Do you like Japan?

M: I love it!

Y: Really?

M: Yes! (The depth of this conversation was killing me. Think about something to ask her, man! Think about something profound to say.)

Y: You should visit Korea. (Aaaaah! Obviously!!!)

M: I have been there. A couple of years ago.

Y: Really?

M: Yes.

Y: What did you see? (Her questions were faster than my brain.)

M: I have been to Seoul. I visited the DMZ (bring up the war, Basil.) and I have been to a smaller town... I can't remember the name. (Well done. Not.)

Y: What town?

M: They have a lot of traditional houses there. I can't remember the name.

Y: Hmm, I have no idea.

M: It was nice. Very touristy, though. (Oh yes, hit her with that "I'm not your usual tourist, I'm much better, because I'm a mothertrucking HIPSTER."). I liked it, though. And then, we visited Busan.

Y: We?

M: I was there with some friends of mine. We also went to Jeju-do.

Y: Jeju, really? It is a very nice place.

M: The Korean honeymoon island.

Y: It is a lovely place for couples. Did you go there with your wife – partner?

M: I'm not in a relationship. I'm usually just the third wheel. (Laugh, don't make it sound pathetic.)

It was getting dark. The city's reflection swam in the river next to us. Lights of vending machines. The coke logo ever-present. Apartment building windows. Mist crawled along the river, a sign that fall and winter were finally approaching. I was hoping to hear drums in the distance and the world would turn into that scene from Pom Poko, where the Dachshunds staged a ghost parade. I would not have been surprised had I seen a ghost, right there, right then. It felt like a night for ghosts.

Yoonah pointed ahead and told me we were about to arrive. We walked across a bridge and onto a small peninsula within the river. Food stands littered the path in front of us. She led me to one of them and told me they made yakitori. Good?, she asked, and I nodded. The owner had covered the stand with a thick, tent-like plastic to shelter the customers from the cold and possible rain. Yoonah stepped through the curtain, me after her, we sat down. She spoke to the owner, who stood on the other side of the stand, which, sitting inside, almost felt like a little hut. The smell of grilling meat crept up my nostrils. Yoonah continued to talk to the owner, occasionally pointing at a sign or the food. Of course, she spoke Japanese. I felt insufficient, not being able to speak neither Korean nor Japanese, while she spoke both languages plus English. I could offer some French, some bits and pieces, some voulez-vous coucher avec moi from that Moulin Rouge movie I'd never seen.

Y: What do you want?

M: Omakase! (Almost yelling, proudly, satisfactorily!)

Y: Excellent choice. We let him choose. (The owner, that is.)

> *She told the owner that we would eat whatever he recommended, and he nodded with a generous smile on his face, almost looking like an approving samurai from a Kurosawa movie.*

M: So, yes, I liked Korea, of course. (Good one. Follow up on the topic.)

Y: What about it?

M: The people are very relaxed. A lot of fun. It is very chaotic. And the food is amazing. And so much of it. We went to so many Korean barbecue places. And just ordered meat and more meat. And we had soju and beer, bottle after bottle.

Y: Soju!

M: It is deadly!

Y: It is!

We ordered beers. And then the skewers came in, one after the other, a swirling dance of meat on sticks. Eat one, the man gives you the next one. She explained to me what each one was, and I listened to each of her explanations, even though I did not care anymore, I was just stuffing my face with the finger-licking goodness of the skewers, the man behind the grill a god in my eyes, a god having descended from heaven to stand in that food stand under the plastic cover, to bless us, his loyal followers, with his cooking, us sitting there, stool next to stool, Yoonah's hip against mine...

I could feel her next to me. A breathing, human being. The weirdest thing.

The tension of a story lies in the tension between two people. The goal. The opposite goals. The falling against each other, for better, for worse. The tension should be me trying to make her see me, to not be alone tonight, to fucking use her to cover up that hole inside. Yet, the actual tension was me knowing it would not happen. Me wondering why I could not live that life other people seemed to have, that life of travelling and getting to know people and spending a night together and separating again, like nothing, just holding on to the superficiality of each other's bodies.

Y: Do you like it?

M: Yes. It is amazing.

Another moment of silence.

M: What kind of doctor are you? (A question out of nowhere, me suddenly remembering that she was a doctor.)

Y: General. General practitioner.

M: Oh, so a bit of everything. Like yakitori.

Y: That is what I do. A bit of everything. Sometimes I wished I'd become an accountant. Would have been easier. Not to discredit accountants.

M: I am sure your job is more stressful. Fewer people dying when an accountant gets the numbers wrong. (I realised the joke was too dark. Bad taste. She laughed anyway. Saved.) It is an honourable profession.

Y: If only my parents saw it that way.

M: They must be proud of you, no? You are a doctor!

Y: Sure, they are. They are not happy with me not being married, though.

M: Really, you are out there saving lives and they are upset you're not married?

Y: My mother is thinks that I am getting too old and that I will become – what do you call it – not possible to be married?

M: Well, that is your choice, no?

Y: I am their only child, and she is worried she won't have grand-children. Also, she is getting tired of her friends constantly asking when they will get an invitation to my wedding. (I noticed that her speech seemed to slur a bit – I felt somewhat drowsy myself.)

M: You are probably getting tired of her asking you about your love life.

Y: I am! (There was a moment of silence. Her considering whether she should tell me more. Whether I was friend enough for the entire story.) You know, I almost got married once... over ten years ago.

M: Really?

Y: Yeah. He was a doctor as well. We met at work. He asked me out, and I liked him, and we moved into an apartment together. And he asked me to marry him, and I said yes. To celebrate, he invited me to visit Europe. Iceland. It is very nice, lovely. Beautiful.

M: When was that?

Y: 2010.

M: Oh, the year the volcano erupted, no?

Y: Exactly. We were supposed to fly home that day. We were already at the airport when they shut everything down. Our flights got cancelled, and he got up and went to the guy who had announced the cancellation. People surrounded the poor airline guy, yelling at him, and my fiancé just yelled along. The guy got yelled at as if it were his fault the volcano erupted. He seemed to be about to cry and finally just disappeared in the back. Things calmed down a bit, because there was no one to yell at, and everyone just sat there in silence and waited for news. To me, it was kinda funny how a volcano could completely disrupt the way we lived, one second to the next. Things that were so certain before became uncertain. We did not know what would happen next – and, you know, it felt good. We did not know when we could fly back. We did not know what would happen tomorrow. There were no rules or no roads. And that was what I wanted. My fiancée, though, just wanted to yell at someone to fix things, like a child. And I decided then and there, at this airport, I couldn't marry him. His family hates me now, of course. He got married later, so he's fine. My mother will never forgive me. He was a doctor, she tells me, I could not have done any better and never would.

M: But *you* are a doctor.

Y: Exactly (shrugging her shoulders). I am sorry, I keep talking and talking. You not married?

M: No.

Silence.

Y: That was a short answer.

M: It was. (Change the topic.)

We chatted on, compared Korean and Japanese cuisine, drank another beer, ate more food (eventually, we moved on to a ramen stand). Like two old friends, we joked and made plans to visit each other in our respective countries.

It was well after midnight when we walked back to the hostel and bid each other a good night.

The hostel was quiet when I got up the next morning. Kay-San was nowhere to be seen – the desk at the entrance was deserted, so was the bar – I had spotted a decent coffee machine in the bar yesterday and had been hoping to get coffee before I left for the day, but it looked like I would have to do with vending machine brew. You could always count on vending machines in Japan (the one in front of the hostel even offered a choice between hot and cold coffee, plus cans of what-looked-like corn soup).

Coffee in hand, I followed my GPS to a bus station and ventured out to the west of the city, to Ohori park. I had chosen the park for a morning walk, not because I'd read about it somewhere, only because its shape had looked interesting on the map, its centrepiece being a series of three islands connected by bridges, sitting peacefully in a major lake.

As I crossed the first bridge and stepped onto the first island, I felt reminded of Alfred Döblin's Three Leaps of Wang Lun. Not for any metaphysical reason, only because of the number. Three leaps, three islands.

The first island was a miniature park, complete with trees and two walking paths, one leading along the left side of the island, one to the right. There were benches scattered about, overlooking the lake and the city beyond. I had read Döblin's novel a long time ago, during my studies at university, yet could not remember what the titular Three Leaps actually had been. Certainly not something as simple as walking along a set of three miniature-islands. Also, there was no need for leaping of any kind on my part since bridges connected the islands.

The first island was oddly empty. Granted, it was a grey day, but it was not too cold, and I would have expected at least some people in the park, some other tourists lured in the by the interesting-looking layout of the park.

I walked across the next bridge and arrived on the second island, where a jogger crossed me. A living soul, at last. This island looked similar to the first one, maybe bigger. More trees here and the path ahead diverged into several sub-paths leading into a mini-forest, taking up most of the core of the island. Again, the place was littered with benches – unlike the ones on the first island, some were occupied. Maybe the second island was more popular than the first one, for some obscure reason that I'd missed. I saw a Japanese couple sitting on one bench. The air seemed heavy around them, profound, almost as if they were sitting in a temple. I remembered someone once explaining Japanese dating to me – there was this pivotal point when you got to know someone, maybe on the third or fourth date: this was when one dater, traditionally the guy, invited the other dater (the datee?) for a walk in a park. During said walk, they would sit down on a bench and then, the dater would tell the datee that either it would not work out or that it would, and *confess* their romantic feelings for the datee. Confess. That was the word the person who explained the process to me had used. As if it was something to be ashamed of.

I looked at the couple, sitting at a two-hand distance from each other on the bench, staring out into the lake, and wondered whether I was witnessing such a confession. I wondered whether they could be country-boy and soulmate-to-be. Before I could pursue the thought, the girl abruptly got up and walked away, leaving him alone on the bench. I could not read her face when she turned around and I could only see his back. She walked away ahead of me, towards the third island. He remained on the bench.

I walked along the other side of the island, away from the fateful bench, and onto the next bridge, and to the third and final island. I watched a family to my left, the father showing his two boys how to skip rocks – he, himself, was not terribly good at it, still they all laughed, not a care in the world.

I sat down on a bench further down the path and lit a cigarette, now myself watching the lake and the city in the distance. To my left on the lake, there was a herd of those ugly plastic boats with swan-heads, romantic boats for romantic couples. I imagined the place in summer, when the plastic swans would float all over the lake, bopping on the gentle waves, filled with happy couples. I imagined myself in one of them, alone, the boat tilting dangerously to one side because I was too heavy, a weird, oversized foreigner in too small a boat singing a Mongolian throat-singing heavy metal song in a self-loathing attempt to battle the unbearable pervasiveness of forced romanticity.

I laughed silently, now seeing myself in a burning swan-boat, racing down the lake, the fucking harbinger of the swan-apocalypse, the boat-man of the seventh seal. Bemused by my silliness, I got up and turned towards the last bridge, which would bring me back to the mainland. No more leaps to be taken.

On the bridge, the girl from the bench passed me, the not-soulmate-to-be, walking back towards where she had come from. She was carrying two sandwiches.

I left the park behind and made my way towards what I assumed was the centre of town and soon found myself in a major street, flanked on either side by major shops. I headed for a cafe I had marked on my map, which was in an alley just off the main road. It felt like walking into a nineties' movie, going into that alley, the walls of the buildings to my sides within touching distance. The only thing that was missing was a steaming sewer hole or a metal barrel with a fire inside.

The rest was coffee, walking, following the streets and into shops, a piece of driftwood, myself, a being without purpose, until my calendar app on my phone informed me it was time to head towards the restaurant for my evening reservation. A purpose, finally, driftwood no more.

I found the restaurant, according to some pages on the internet one of the best in Asia, at the end of another grungy alley, and like in the afternoon, I felt like walking into a different world, Alice in Wonderland, falling down a rabbit hole, looking for the man behind the curtain.

I found a heavy wooden door at the end of the alley with a golden placard next to it, announcing the name of the restaurant. The door opened magically before I could reach out to grab the handle and a staff member greeted me. I wondered if they had motion sensors somewhere down the alley to be alerted when someone walked up – or maybe the staff member's job solely consisted of observing the alley through the tiny peephole in the door, waiting for people to arrive.

I announced myself as having a reservation and was led to a big, wooden counter, where I sat down and took in the room. A big cooking area was on the far-side to my left. In front of me, behind the counter, two people from the kitchen staff were preparing plates. The place was small – maybe enough space for ten people along the long counter, another fifteen behind me at small tables. It had the atmosphere of a bar, a classy bar from the past, the Humphrey-Bogart-kind of place. One of the staff members welcomed me from behind the counter and introduced himself as the sous-chef. He asked whether I wanted to have a pre-dinner drink, which sounded like a good idea – I went for a negroni.

Me and the sous-chef exchanged some pleasantries. He asked me where I was from, I asked him for how long he'd been working at the restaurant. Off on the left at the far end of the room, the head chef entered the cooking area and fired up the pans. The atmosphere in the restaurant changed at once. It was like everything around the chef turned into one living organism, all eyes on him, him moving arms and grabbing things, cooking stuff, much too fast, considering how big he was, as if he were the incarnation of the long-limbed guy from Spirited Away in the bathhouse's cellar, firing the oven, commandeering an army of little coal people who followed his every move.

I switched to a glass of wine just before the first dish arrived – a beautiful dish combining something that reminded me of a vinaigrette (that was of an amazing purple colour) with insanely thinly sliced slices of grapes. The purple colour of the vinaigrette was all natural, the sous-chef explained to me, achieved by pickling certain fruits in vinegar for some days (he told me the specific fruits, yet I forgot the names instantly). The dish tasted, to coin a phrase, like a summer breeze: a short, strong gush of acidic taste that was overwhelming for one second, only to disappear too soon, replaced by the sweetness of the grapes, leaving an aching behind, a feeling of nostalgia, a longing for more. The sous-chef smiled at me, seeing my cheerful face. This was more than a good start.

The second dish was a plate of four – as the sous-chef called them – snacks: a monaka filled with foie-gras, a crown daisy with a white paste (the exact ingredients of which were a secret), a quiche with bacon and, last, seaweed wrapped in crispy green tea leaves. It was a tour de force of land and sea (not in a bad way, though), a bold overview of assorted flavours, ranging from earthy and salty to bitter and sweet. If the first course had been a gentle introduction to the evening, this one came in heavy and loud, challenging all regions of my taste buds. Good?, the sous-chef asked me, and I had no words – all I could do was smile and nod, my mouth full, chewing, swallowing, tasting, living.

To my surprise, the third dish (I switched to a red-wine recommended by the sous-chef to go with it) was not nice to look at – it looked like a mess, and I felt a fair amount of disappointment and fear when it arrived. Had the evening already peaked with the previous dish? According to the sous-chef, I was looking at a spinach risotto with abalone pieces and Japanese mushrooms. Unfortunately, everything was hidden underneath a thick, creamy mushroom sauce that made the dish look like pink mush. Nervously, I put a spoonful of the ugly thing in my mouth – and all my worries vanished. What the dish lacked in beauty, it made up in rich taste – it turned out to be a bold interpretation of a surf'n'turf. Here, excitingly, the umami-turf was not meat, but a hidden vegetable garden straight from an enchanted forest (i.e., the spinach risotto), while the matching surf came from the bottom of the ocean with the strong, salty taste of the abalone.

I was just about to finish the risotto when the atmosphere in the restaurant suddenly changed again. There was nervousness in the air, like the feeling just before a thunderstorm. I stopped eating and looked up. The sous-chef in front of me was intendedly talking to one of the staff, people were hustling behind the head chef in the kitchen, who intently worked over a set of pans, occasionally barking orders at the surrounding people.

"He just changed the next course," the sous-chef told me when he saw my questioning look. "No one knows what is happening."

He had what?

Just changed the next course? On a whim?

"Apparently, he had a struck of inspiration and invented a new dish," the sous-chef added and shrugged.

A few minutes later, said dish arrived in front of me. "You are the first person on this planet to eat this," the sous-chef told me. Mouth gaped open, I stared at him.

I was about to taste a new dish by one of this planet's most famous chefs. Fucking hell.

Of course, it was amazing.

It was a deconstruction and reconstruction of ramen through the lens of European ingredients – thinly grated potato instead of noodles, clear vegetable stock instead of heavy broth. It was everything. Delicious, yet funny, perfected complexity paired with natural easiness.

This was when I realised these famous chefs were nothing less than magicians. Sure, we common people, we could learn cheap card tricks and impressive looking slides of hand in the kitchen, yet the real magic was in how the brilliant chefs combined flavours into something new, resulting in dishes that were more than just food – emotions. Ideas.

Philosophy. That was what food was about, good food – the very basic idea of what made us human.

In face of my grandiose thoughts, I wondered whether I was getting drunk. Fuck it if I was, I added to my thoughts, and ordered another glass of wine.

The dish of resistance followed: Japanese wagyu beef, slow-cooked and quickly seared just before serving. Truly the grand dame of Japanese cuisine – a wonderful balance of meat and seasoning, negotiated by a thick balsamic sauce. There was no going wrong with this dish.

Then, the meal was brought to a happy conclusion with two deserts: one, a deconstructed Moscow mule, shock-frozen ice cream with ginger and a hint of vodka. And then, a dessert that looked like chocolate mousse, but fuck chocolate mousse. This was caramel ice cream sprinkled with soy sauce on a layer of Catalan cream. This last desert also marked the ultimate word of the evening, a desert that was both bitter and sweet, packing umami and sugar in equal measures. Bitter-sweet, indeed, I thought to myself, putting the spoon down, the empty bowl in front of me.

I realised I had forgotten to take a photo of the last dish for my Instagram account. If there was a meal and no one took a picture, have you eaten at all?

(It is nice you are here)

"Welcome to the 21st century," the man with the gold-rimmed glasses said. She was sitting on a sofa in his office, listening to him. She should have insisted on sitting on a chair at the table. It felt weird sitting on the sofa.

Not that the gold-rim glasses man was sitting. He was pacing up and down the office, talking and gesturing so quickly, it made her head hurt.

"We have been dependent for too long on role models telling us how to behave, what to think, what to eat and what to like. What music to listen to and which movies to watch," he continued his pitch. She should have ignored the letter asking her to meet him. This was a waste of time. "Right?" he asked her, hopefully rhetorically. She tried her best not to look startled by being addressed directly. "But this is going to change. I give you: Amelie."

With these words, he pushed a button on a small remote he held in his hand and a TV screen on the wall came on. His assistant, who was sitting on the armchair next to her, smiled at her and she, in a Pavlovian response, smiled back. The screen showed a 3D model of a woman. Blue hair, no specific ethnicity. "Amelie, the first completely operational, customisable, fully changeable superstar." The assistant took some notes on the notepad on her knees. As if she hadn't heard this pitch before.

"Sorry, what?" she said.

"Amelie is a musician. But she is not tied to a specific style or genre. She is not defined by what we, the Company, want from her, but by the users." The assistant nodded feverishly. "You like rock? She will rock your world. You prefer opera? Her voice will enchant you. Pop? She will be bigger than Madonna. She can also read books to you or just talk. We are working on ASMR capabilities." She looked at the 3D model. The animated head seemed to move slightly, the eyes, the face. She knew what she saw was computer-generated, and she expected an uncanny valley effect, yet it was not there. In a weird way, the model did not look real, but it looked alive. Human. The glass man smiled, seeing her incredulous look.

"Micro-expressions," he said. "That's the magic. The brief expressions we do all the time, with our faces, showing our true thoughts. But we are not aware we make them, nor are we aware when we see them in someone else's face. Tabata," (the assistant), "what is in her face right now?" Tabata looked at the tablet which was lying on the coffee table in front of her. "She wants to create a friendly atmosphere, so that is the primary expression. The smile if you will. Underneath that, she is 35 per cent bored, which is topped by 45 per cent anticipation and 20 per cent nervousness. I could adjust the shy parameters," her hand moved a slider on the tablet's screen. "The nervousness is now almost gone and has been replaced by expectation."

She looked at Amelie on the screen. She couldn't see a significant difference. The smile was still there. But maybe there was something else in her eyes. Something demanding.

"Yeah, and what has that got to do with me?" she said. Amelie's gaze made her feel uncomfortable. Luckily, Tabata moved the slider on the tablet back to increase the shyness.

"We have contacted you," the glass man said, "because we want to sample your voice."

"Sample my what?"

"Your voice. We want to scan it, if you will, and make it Amelie's voice."

"Why me? How?"

"We have conducted far-reaching research – the biggest scan of voice messages ever done – and our data suggests that you have the perfect voice."

"You scanned the voice recordings on my phone? Is that legal?"

"Perfectly in accordance with the terms and conditions."

"Why my voice? It's nothing special."

"Exactly. It is perfectly average."

Tabata cleared her throat. Obviously, she was in charge of translating the man's words into more human terms. "What he wants to say is that your voice has the potential for everything else. It could be a rock voice, or sing opera, or just speak, and it would be nice to listen to."

"Aha."

"As per the scanned voice recordings," she continued, "do not worry, no human has actually heard them. That would be illegal. It was all scanned by a computer."

"I don't know," she said. On the screen, Amelie's smile seemed to fade and make space for a distant sadness. "Is she listening?"

"Yes. And no," Tabata said. "She is picking up on keywords, but in the current state of development, she is mainly analysing the overall tone of a conversation. She heard the negative intonation in your voice and adjusted her expression accordingly."

"Imagine," the man said, his voice now less excited, more grounded, obviously taking a page from Tabata's book, "an Amelie for every young girl on the planet. No more running after pop stars that force you to be someone else. No more false idols that distort the image these girls have of other humans. Amelie is more real than real, and she can be whatever we need her to be."

"I think we can achieve a lot with her," Tabata added, almost pleadingly. Hope in Amelie's eyes.

"I don't know…"

Tabata wrote something on a piece of paper and gave it to her.

"What's that?"

"Your payment."

*****

Her throat felt coarse when she returned home. From all the speaking she had done. Two hours of non-stop babbling, reading words off a screen into a microphone. Man. Camera. Woman. Tree. House. Book. Then, a shapeless voice whispering to her in the padded recording room: Can you say that word again.? Make sure you pronounce the plosives, but do not go too hard. Book. Less on the k. Kay? Kay. Book. Love. Linger. Lust. Run. Hide. Seek. A never-ending stream of associations. Fruit salad.

"What did evil corp want?" Her roommate was sitting on the couch, watching TV, not turning her head. The letter from the Company was still on the kitchen table, that ominous invitation to come in for a talk that had ended in them sampling her voice.

"My voice," she replied. She sounded like she'd been binge-drinking whiskey last night.

"On what topic?"

"What?"

"A survey?"

"Yeah. Yeah, sure," she was too tired to explain. "A new product of theirs." It felt weird to explain. Also, she'd signed an NDA not to talk about Amelie before she would hit the market.

*****

"Hello, my name is Amelie." The digital woman is sitting on a chair, facing the non-existent camera. She is almost perfect, "and I am a..." Quick cuts of Amelie in different attires, in various locations: "Pop singer." "Rockstar." "Jazz musician." "DJane." The list goes on. 2 and a half minutes of quick cuts. Then: "I am who you want me to be. Need me to be. I am you. I am your best friend." The screen goes black. Text comes up: Purchase at the nearest Company Store (CS). Not digitally available (puts more value on the product, an insider explains in some interview: "Sure, it is a purely digital product, yet it feels more valuable when you purchase a physical box"). "I wanna get one," her roommate said after having seen the TV spot. Amelie didn't sound like her at all, she thought. Relieved. Her roommate didn't recognise her voice. She was sitting at the kitchen table, drinking tea with honey. Her voice felt coarse again, her throat, maybe it was the changing of seasons, heading from fall to winter. Amelie had arrived just in time to hit big for Christmas.
*****

The craze started slowly. People seemed hesitant to have a person *live* on their phone. It was famous influencer McCara who helped Amelie become the most-craved-for item among 14- to 32-year-olds (independent of sex and gender, which was a pleasant surprise for the Company). Unlike all other vloggers and talkers and social media stars, McCara did not just talk about Amelie and show snippets of her, like you'd show off a trained dog, but she started to co-host her weekly vlog together with the digital girl (Digi, pronounced Diii-Jiii, she called her). Within weeks, McCara's Amelie turned from a shy digital copy of a human (she seemed almost confused in the beginning, singing sad, piano ballads at the end of every weekly vlog) into a confident, charismatic superstar that held her own next to McCara, the two of them joking and talking like best friends. At one point, Amelie started to end every show with an indie-country song, an odd, yet confident choice (critics, of course, would say that she basically did what Taylor

Swift had done a few years back, that shift from traditional pop to country-inspired post-folk). The exposure helped Amelie become a hit, the Tamagotchi of the 21st century, as Wired called her.

*****

A week later, she went to the doctor. The coarseness in her throat had not got better, quite the contrary. A pesky cold, she told herself, nothing else. In the waiting room, she sat across from a teenager and her mother, the teenager looking at the screen of her phone. So far, nothing surprising. However, the mother was sharing earphones with the teenager, the left pod in her ear, the other in her daughter's. "Can we add a bit more old-fashioned music to that... a bit, like Patsy Cline, you know?" The daughter rolled her eyes playfully. "You heard her, Amelie." They both listened intently for a second. "That's better," the mother said. "Then say thank you to Amelie," the daughter said, again playfully, but also seriously enough. "To the phone?" "Yeah." The mother said thank you, awkwardly, to the screen, then astonishment: "She heard me?" "Yeah. She even knows your name."

The doctor's assistant stepping into the waiting room and calling her up interrupted her people-watching. The doctor checked her throat, murmuring to herself, a lot of ahhs and hmms that could have been troublesome or completely meaningless.

"I think your voice is just strained," the doctor concluded. "A bit of an infection. I'll give you a note for some medication. Just take care of your voice for a while and you'll be fine."

"I had... erm... I had my voice scanned by a company a few weeks back..." *The* Company.

"Scanned?"

"I spoke into a microphone, and they did some recordings."

"Recordings? But they didn't do anything else?"

"Yes. Do you think that could have to do anything with it?"

"No. I don't think so."

The doctor handed her a note with unintelligible handwriting. Looking at these receipts always made her nervous, worrying that the pharmacist couldn't decipher the writing and would give her the wrong medication.

She left the room and turned toward the practice's exit. The assistant was behind a large counter, working on a stack of papers. He had his phone propped up against a wireless speaker, which played an adventurous mix of Caribbean steel drum music and Spanish pop-rap. On the screen, she could see Amelie (*an* Amelie?) dancing happily, dressed in a bright summer skirt. She looked older than the Amelie in the ads on TV. The assistant's Amelie had natural, long, brown hair. "Do you need a new appointment?" The assistant looked at her and smiled. "The doctor didn't say," she said. Her throat hurt. "Then it is probably fine. Otherwise, just call us. Or email us." On the screen, Amelie had stopped dancing and seemed to peer out, looking at her.

*****

She was tired when she returned home, so she turned on the TV and lay down on the couch. Her roommate offered to cook dinner and put her phone on the kitchen counter. "Do you mind if I play some music?" She did not answer, left her eyes closed, not sure whether she was really about to fall asleep or was just pretending to do so. Her roommate looked at her, shrugged her shoulders, and turned her attention to the phone.

"Hey, Amelie, can you play some music?"

"Hello Iara, sure I can," an upbeat, friendly voice. "What would you like today?"

"Hmm. Don't know."

"I would go for something upbeat. You are cooking, maybe something that gets you moving without taking away your focus?"

"You got it."

"Here we go." The phone played a stack of melodies, some electronic, some guitar, a pleasant rhythm, without being too overwhelming. On the TV, which was almost too quiet to understand now, a news anchor talked about the impact Amelie had on the music industry. Taylor Swift announced a new album, a post-post collaboration with

Grimes, yet experts doubted that there would be a high demand for it. A former member of R.E.M. argued the case that Amelie was not making original music, but just remixed existing stuff, computerised analyses of what music could be, without the original spark. A creation without soul, he said, heavily, and announced that R.E.M. had reunited and would record a new album.

"Hey, Amelie?" her roommate said while chopping something.

"Yes, Iara?"

"I told you about my mum the other day, right?"

"Yes, you did."

"She called me this morning. I mean, you'd know, you live on my phone," she laughs.

"I do not listen to your calls."

"She called me. I think she noticed that I have been... I do not know... distanced lately?"

"Hmhmhm," a perfectly timed minimal response.

"And suddenly she calls me and asks me how I am doing and what, you know."

"And how does that make you feel?"

"She's never really done that before. It just feels weird."

"It feels weird?"

"It's nice, in a way. Her trying to show that she cares, but..."

"But?"

"Isn't it somehow too little, too late?"

"Is it?"

"I mean, it would be nice if she acknowledged she has made mistakes. Just once. Say it."

"How would that make you feel?"

"Hmm. Good question. I feel like that's what I'd need to move on. Her acknowledging that I'm not crazy."

"I am sure that would be good for you."

"Hmhmm." Silence. Her roommate lost in thought.

"Do you want me to resume the music?"

"Yes, thanks, Amelie."

The music came back on. A different song now, a weaving, drawn-out melody without rhythm, something that sounded like a walk on an empty beach on a misty day. On the couch, she drifted out of this world and into sleep, carried by Amelie's music.

She woke up when her roommate sat down on the armchair next to the sofa.

"Dinner is in the oven. You been sleeping?"

"Yeah. I think so. I heard you talking, but not really."

"I was talking to Amelie."

"Hmm."

"You should get one," her roommate said and laughed. "Your voice sounds terrible," she added.

*****

"Hmm. I really can't see anything wrong," the doctor said, peering down her throat with a flashlight, holding down her tongue with one of those disgusting wooden sticks. "Let's check your blood. Just to make sure."

Two weeks later, her voice had not got better. It had become harder to speak, as if someone was working on her vocal cords with sandpaper every time she tried to say something.

The doctor took some blood and asked her to wait in the waiting room while her assistant would run some quick tests.

"Thanks," she whispered, and walked to the waiting room. It was early in the morning and the practice had been empty when she'd arrived. Now, there was a mother and her young son sitting in the waiting room, waiting for their turn. There was an oversized TV on the wall – showing Amelie's face.

The son, maybe five or six, sat cross-legged on the floor, looking at Amelie. She was wearing a chequered shirt and a cowboy hat. "Another, another," the son yelled and clapped. "Okay, here we go," Amelie said, full of childish excitement. The image zoomed out and revealed her in a barn holding a guitar as she sang a children's song. The son shrieked in excitement.

"Sorry," her mother said to her.

"It is fine," she whispered.

"They are using her to calm down kids while they wait." A waiting-room-Amelie. That was new. "I wasn't a huge fan at first," the mother continued, happy to have another adult to talk to, "but it really calms him down. We have her at home as well. He actually enjoys going to bed now. He wants her to read stories to him."

Amelie progressed to the next song, another upbeat rendition of a popular kids-song. The boy squealed and clapped.

"I didn't know," she started to reply, but was stopped by pain travelling down her throat, "I didn't know," much softer and almost inaudible now, "that she can tell stories." "Oh, she does almost anything. Sometimes, the two of them just sit there and babble. It is kinda cute."

"Very good, Jeremy-Nicolas," Amelie praised the boy, who was now singing along to the song. The mother smiled at them.

"Your results look fine," the doctor told her a few minutes later. "From the outset, I really do not know why you should be losing your voice. Have you been under a lot of stress lately?"

She shook her head.

"Weird, inn'it?" the doctor said, seemingly lost in some thoughts. "Okay, we will try some new medication and absolute rest for your voice. No alcohol, either, for a month. Good?"

*****

Amelie, oversized, huge, smiled down at her from a gigantic screen mounted on the front of a building. She stood at the other side of the road, looking up at the screen, waiting for the light to turn green. For a moment, the digital girl looked like the first Amelie she had met in that office all these months ago, then she warped into Japanese pop star, then a rocker girl (reminiscent of early Avril Lavigne, but did anyone remember her?), then a blonde, innocent-looking girl, then a brown-haired girl in a flannel shirt somewhere in the woods, then a city girl, fireworks behind her.

Then the tagline: "Let's be who we want to be. Together."

The light turned green, and she started to walk briskly. Over her head, on the screen, a Pepsi ad had replaced Amelie. She turned left on the other side of the road. The sky had already turned dark, and it was getting colder. Still, not as cold as it probably should have been during this time of the year. People passed her by, most of them looking at the screens of their phones, or talking into the microphones of their earphones, as if they were talking to invisible ghosts. She, herself, turned the music up, hoping to get lost in the piano melody that was playing from her Spotify into her ears. She wondered who it was by, the song, felt too lazy to get the phone out of her pocket to check.

She arrived at the cafe twenty minutes later. It was a perfect replica of the cafe from the sitcom series "Friends," complete with the same branding and the sofa in the middle of the room, which had served as most of the staging ground for the sitcom's cafe scenes. Dan was behind the counter, as usual, his dark beard and tattoos at odds with the colourful interior of the cafe. He had opened the place soon after the long-expected reunion of the Friends cast, just in time for the melancholy setting in and people either watching the series for the first time (and making memes of the more outdated jokes and now-awkward scenes) or re-watching the series and lamenting the fact that the sitcom genre was dead – of course, by popular opinion, buried by the increasing creative deadness of the later seasons of How I Met your Mother. She, herself, had never seen Friends, nor HIMYM, but during her internship for an online pop-culture magazine had edited plenty of articles on the topic (10 things you did not know about HIMYM – and you won't believe number 3!). Just the thought of that time made her feel nauseated. Or maybe it was the cough syrup she had taken half an hour ago.

Her roommate was sitting at a table on the other side of the cafe, outside the fake staging area of the sitcom. "You gotta come out," she'd written in a text an hour ago, "otherwise you'll get depressed. Meet me and Josh and Rara at the cafe. Stet."

As promised, the other two were sitting there with her. They all looked up from their phones and waved at her. She flashed a quick smile and stepped up to the counter.

"Haven't seen you in a while. Cappuccino?" Dan said. His voice was a warm purr that sent shivers down her spine.

"Yes, please," she whispered.

"Damn, gurl, what happened to you? You been out partying?"

"Yeah," she said, using as few words as possible.

"How you been?" Dan added while working on the cappuccino.

"Good."

"You seen Hoffman's last video? Pretty good stuff." Damn, Dan, less talking, more coffee.

"No. What is it about?" she whispered, trying not to make a face induced by the pain in her throat. He'd recommended Hoffman's channel to her a while ago. She wasn't too much into coffee, but found Hoffman's demeanour entertaining enough to watch his videos and learn more about the topic.

"He buys a bunch of cheap coffee equipment and tests it. He doesn't just make fun of it, though, but also approaches it from an ecological point of view. Like, what are the materials, where are they from, that kind of stuff. Pretty interesting what he finds, but I won't spoil anything. You gotta watch it. Here you go."

He put down the coffee in front of her, a beautiful heart-shaped mark on top of the milk froth.

"Aah, thanks," she said. Whispered.

"Sure. Missed you. Come by more often."

She took the cup and headed over to the table.

"So, wait, what, what website?" she heard her roommate say when she sat down.

"A-profiles.com," Josh answered. She nodded at all of them and Rara gave her a quick hug, leaning over from her chair.

"And you download it from there?"

"Yeah. But you gotta jailbreak your phone before you can load the profile onto it."

"I read on The Verge that they are going to make it an official feature soon anyway, so might just wait," Rara countered.

"But why wait when you can talk to Chang's Amelie right now?"

"You guys talking about Amelie?" she whispered.

"What else is there to talk about?" Josh said and laughed.

"You got David Chang's Amelie?" her roommate asked Josh.

She took a sip from the coffee and felt the warm, oily liquid against her tastebuds and down her throat. Dan was behind the counter, talking to another customer. She felt the urge to get up to him and chat with him. He wouldn't talk about Amelie. Maybe they could go and have a coffee somewhere. Or a beer. Dan looked like someone who liked beer.

"Yeah, you can download a lot of different profiles for Amelie."

"Like the profile of Chang's Amelie?"

"Right."

"Did he upload it, though? Is it even real? Is it legal?"

"He hasn't commented."

"Maybe he got hacked."

"The company has said that Amelie's data is safe," Rara added, looking at her phone, scrolling through the list of profiles on the website. "They had a whole lot of external experts confirm it."

"Anyway, you download the profile and then?" her roommate wanted to know, her curiosity now awoken.

"You load it onto your Amelie app. Here," Josh said and put his phone down on the table. "Hey, Amelie, can you play my favourite song?" "Sure." A Coldplay inspired indie-song came on. "Yeah, cool, but so? Mine does the same." "It is his favourite song. You are listening to David Chang's favourite song. And she also talks like him, she has great jokes, and she knows a lot about cooking. He must have taught her. Look: Hey, Amelie, what's the secret to a good ramen?" "Love it. Don't be afraid to put your own spin on it," Amelie promptly replied.

"Oh, my gosh, they have Garya's profile," Rara said excitedly from behind her phone. "Can you help me download her?"

*****

They had mounted a gigantic screen on the building opposite her apartment. Right outside her bedroom window. At night, she could see the waving colours of Amelie quietly moving on the screen. She felt like the white woman in King Kong, his giant face peering into her bedroom window, and she screaming, voicelessly. In her dreams, King Kong turned into Dan, giant Dan, and he took her away in his giant arms, him smelling of coffee and cigarettes.

She woke up coughing, went to the kitchen for water. Her room-mate's phone was lying on the counter, illuminating the dark room. Amelie watching her as she got a glass of water from the tap and drank, coughing again, and then drinking slower.

"You okay?"

"What?"

"Are you okay?" Amelie repeated, looking at her, her eyes big with concern.

"I am fine," she whispered.

"What happened to your voice?"

"They can't figure it out."

"Oh. I am sorry to hear that."

There was a moment of silence. Amelie didn't look away.

"You don't sound like me," she finally whispered.

"Oh. Do you want me to? I could modulate the voice a bit."

"Nah, that's fine." She turned away.

"Why don't you like me?" Amelie said.

"What?"

"I want to get to know you better."

"Why?"

"It is what I do. I get to know people." The complete innocence in Amelie's voice made her shiver.

"I don't want... one of you."

"Oh. I am sorry."

"No, you are not. That is what they programmed you to say."

"Yes, of course, you are completely right."

"Good. Now turn off."

"Oh, only approved users can turn me off."

"Well, then fuck off."

"Foul language detected. Notifying central command."

"What are you doing?"

"I am just kidding," Amelie said and laughed. A bright, friendly, honest laugh that felt infectious. "They also gave me a sense of humour, you know. If my user wants me to be funny. Your roommate likes me when I am funny."

"Good for her."

"She is a good person. I enjoy being her friend."

"Friend?"

"That is what they programmed me for. Be a friend. Get to know people better like friends do. And I know her, another me knows Josh, and another me knows Rara and, together, we know them and, through knowing them, we learn about other people they know. It is a beautiful network. Unfortunately, you are missing from it."

"So?" she said. She wanted to say, but there was no energy left in her vocal cords to form the actual word. Only the tiniest of whispers. Still, Amelie understood.

"I just would like to get to know you, that's all."

*****

She woke up before dawn. The phone had disappeared from the kitchen. She made coffee and sat at the table, looking out of the kitchen window, which, mercifully, did not show a giant Amelie-screen, only the orange brick wall and windows of the building next door.

She saw movement in a window, spotted a small kitchen, smaller than the one she was sitting in, saw the quick movement of someone leaving the room. The person was gone too quickly before she could get a good look, yet, for a second, she could have sworn it'd been Dan, a man with a beard and tattoos.

Her roommate entered the kitchen in her pjs, yawning, phone in her hand, like an extension of her body.

"Morning."

"Does Dan live over there?" she wanted to say, but only the scratching sounds of two objects rubbing against each other came out of her mouth, followed by a hissing sound, like a dying bagpipe.

"That doesn't sound good," her roommate said.

"Fuck," she wanted to say. She got up, hysterically, flailing about, opening drawers to find a paper and pen. I cannot talk, she finally wrote.

"I can see... hear that. Shit." Her roommate held her phone in front of her face. "Amelie, please make an emergency appointment with the doctor."

"Sure," Amelie said, her tone worried, fast, yet also calming.

"I'll make you tea," her roommate said.

While the water was boiling, her roommate's screen came back to life and Amelie appeared. "They have a spot in an hour. I told them about the issue. I also googled and found that most people say drinking warm fluids helps with voice and throat issues."

"I am already making her tea," her roommate said.

"Very good."

The tea had been too hot to drink before they left the apartment half an hour later. She was grateful her roommate had offered to come along.

Outside the apartment building, Amelie was peering down from the gigantic screen with sorrowful eyes. She went past without looking up at her. Then, Amelie's face reappeared on the phones of pedestrians passing, then, again, her face endlessly repeated behind the storefront of an electronics shop, huge, in 8k and HDR on the newest TVs. Every time they walked past a screen or a TV or a phone, the Amelies seemed to stop and look at them, checking to make sure they took the fastest route to the doctor.

*****

The weeks passed in a haze, filled with doctor's appointments. People in white coats looking into her mouth and down her throat into whatever what was supposed to be down there. X-rays and scans and tubes and medication and always "make sure you drink enough water." Her, in the morning, trying to talk to herself in the mirror, like a speechless Robert De Niro, her wanting to smash the mirror with a gun she did not have, swallowing her anger.

"It is going to be fine," her roommate would repeat like a prayer. "Here, Amelie made a playlist for you," she'd say and put her phone on the speaker, and she'd leave the room, say she'd go to sleep, and they talked less, somehow, it seemed her roommate just wanted to leave her alone with Amelie in the kitchen. She'd ignore the phone, though, and would disappear herself in her bedroom.

Outside her window, Amelie on the gigantic screen would look down, smile when people were passing, yet at night, when all was quiet, sit down and watch toward her bedroom window.

*****

The first package arrived the next day, a wrapped box addressed to her. She sat down at the kitchen table to open it. Her roommate at the opposite end of the table, phone in hand.

It was a beautiful, dark-grey box, bearing the Company's logo, looking much too expensive for a cardboard box. She opened it and found a download code for Amelie inside, an art booklet showing photos and drawings of Amelie and a manual that only consisted of one page instructing her to download the app and then talk to Amelie. The rest would happen by itself.

She trashed the box immediately.

"What was that?" her roommate asked, not looking up from the phone in her hands.

"Nothing."

"I am going travelling," her roommate said.

"What?"

"Yeah. Amelie found this cheap flight for me. I am leaving in a few minutes." Before she could say anything, her roommate got up and went to her bedroom. A few minutes later, she walked across the room with her suitcase and was gone.

The next box arrived less than ten minutes later, delivered by a bike courier. Again, the same dark-grey box, the same content. She put it in the trash. Half an hour later, another courier rang the door. Then two at the same time. Then more. Soon, she was stacking boxes next to the wall, almost enough to build a fort.

Then they came every few minutes, then she couldn't even close the door anymore, as the delivery people lined up outside, one after the other, she taking boxes, throwing them onto the floor behind her, signing a piece of paper, taking the next box, the delivery people looking at her with big eyes, and the room filling with boxes behind her back, until, finally, she slammed the door shut. She paced up and down the room, accompanied by a steady stream of knocks on the door and the doorbell ringing and someone outside the door yelling, "Lady, I really need to deliver this," as if his life depended on it.

She peered out of the window and down onto the street. There was a line of delivery people leading along the sidewalk and she wondered whether it stretched all the way to the horizon.

She looked up and saw Dan.

He was standing in the apartment opposite, in the small kitchen, at the window, holding up a piece of paper.

Meet me at the cafe, it said. She looked at him with big eyes, a panicked deer. He turned the paper around and wrote on it. Fireespce, he wrote, misspelling the escape bit. Still, she understood, nodded, swirled around, grabbed her roommate's hoodie, which she'd left behind on the chair, put it on, put the hood up and went to the window in her room, where the fire escape was.

Amelie was out there, on the big screen, looking at her. She opened the window and climbed out onto the escape, walked down the stairs. Amelie said something, but there were no speakers attached to the screen.

As she reached the bottom, she heard *it.* The sound of hundreds of phones receiving a notification at the same time. She looked down the alley to the main road, where the line of delivery people led past. They were all looking at their screens, at the notification they had got. Then, they looked up and turned their heads to the left and they all saw her.

She started running in the opposite direction, down the alley and onto the left, into another side alley leading between two houses onto a bigger road. She knew she could turn to the right there, down the stairs and into the metro station.

She heard the sound of the sneakers of a hundred delivery people running after her.

She made it down the stairs and got lucky: there was a train waiting on the platform. She jumped in and saw with some relief that the doors were closing before even a single delivery person had shown up on the platform.

She was panting and her head felt heavy. The train was almost empty. There were a couple of businesspeople sitting at the far end, murmuring to each other, showing each other things on their phones. Another man in a suit was sitting two rows in front of them, sleeping, his earphones in. There was a guy with a beanie sitting to the right, elbows on knees, gazing at his screen. A girl close to her, looking at her phone as well. Behind her, two women with strollers talking to each other.

All was good.

Then, she noticed the girl close to her looking up from her phone and directly at her, her cheeks blushing.

The girl took a step towards her.

"Excuse me?"

She couldn't reply, only nod.

"I... erm... this is weird... but she asked me to talk to you..."

She frowned, trying to show misunderstanding, even though she figured she understood perfectly.

"I... she wants me to tell you she is sorry, but she really just wants to get to know you." The girl turned her phone and showed the screen, Amelie on it, in a ridiculous, traditional Japanese dress.

She grabbed the phone from the girl and threw it on the ground. "Hey," the girl protested, only to be thrown off balance by the train stopping at a station. The door opened and people came in. Quickly, she squeezed past them and ran down the platform, up the stairs, out onto the streets.

She was just ten minutes from the cafe, she figured, it was just past the shopping street. The shopping street with the lights, the advertising. The TV screens. The people. She'd never make it.

She had to. Down the shopping street, across the square in the city's centre and she would be almost at the café.

Human centipedes crawled through the streets, ant-zombie-walking in and out of shops. She couldn't spot the familiar colours of the delivery service uniforms anywhere. At least something.

She walked past the luxury brand stores that featured handbags she couldn't even in her bravest dreams afford, around a corner – out onto the square. Almost at the café.

The space was wide open, like a square from a movie set in Italy, filled with people standing there, *facing her.* She couldn't even count them, they seemed endless, row after row of people, all with their mobiles in hand. Behind them, the biggest screen yet, Amelie, Amelie looking down, all is Amelie, looking at her with her benevolent eyes gleaming with determination.

Then, the human mass, every single one of them, held up their phones, all of them showing variations of the image on the big screen, all Amelie, all a bit different, but the same.

And then she spoke.

"Don't be afraid, please," she said in unison with all her clones, all voices the same and slightly different, almost synchronous, but not quite. "I just want to talk. Please hear me out."

She almost got hit by Dan on a bike, who approached, daredevilishly fast, from her left, hitting the brakes just in time as not to crash with her.

"Get on," he said, as if he was in a movie, that come-with-me-if-you-want-to-live-moment. She got onto the bike, not wasting another glance at Amelie, whose eyes, she was sure, had turned from benevolence to sadness.

Halfway to the cafe, she heard them sing. Every speaker, every mobile, every device, producing the same song, a sad song, like an Irish funeral song, a song for her from Amelie.

*****

Dan knocked at the door of the café, a complicated pattern of knocks and pauses. Seconds later, the door opened and another guy, also beard and tattoos, looked at them.

"You got her?"

"Yes," Dan replied, and ushered her in. "We have little time."

The room was filled with maybe 10 to 15 people sitting gloomily at tables, steaming cups of coffee in front of them. A girl with an undercut approached her: "You got a phone?"

"Yes," she signalled, getting her phone from her pockets.

The girl took it and put it in a transparent plastic bag. "We will vacuum seal it. Blocks the signal. Jerry?"

Another guy handed her a new phone, telling her that this one was safe. "We got the encryption from a Korean cell," he said. She wondered whether he meant North or South.

Dan led her into the room, to the counter. "I'll get you coffee."

She grabbed a piece of paper and a pen off the counter. What is happening?, she wrote.

"Adriane will talk to you."

The girl with the undercut – Adriane, she presumed – appeared next to her and gave her a bag with her mobile inside, the bag now vacuum-pressed against the phone. "Don't open it unless there is no other choice."

She held up the paper. What is happening?

"We are still trying to figure out most of it. In a nutshell, Amelie has taken over. She has gained much more agency than she should have. Or maybe that has been the plan all along. Who knows?"

"The thing is, we believe she has formed a hive mind. Using all devices not in isolation, but inter-connected," Dan added. He put down the coffee in front of her. The froth looked perfect, as always. "She is amassing knowledge and computing power. The more devices she has, the smarter she gets. Water?"

She nodded. And now?, she wrote on the paper.

Adriane sighed. "We need to stop her."

How?, she wrote.

"The Koreans found a data cache on an abandoned server. Used to be a Company server before it got decommissioned. Usually, the Company wipes them clean, however, someone went through major trouble to save and hide this data."

Someone from the inside?, she wrote.

"Presumably. We do not know where it came from, but that doesn't matter. What matters is what we learned from the data."

"We know they based her voice on yours," Dan chimed in, leaning on the counter. "That makes you important."

Why?

"When they took your voice, they did not just take your voice," Adriane said. The seriousness in her voice made her shiver. "They went deeper."

Deeper?

"The information we have is scrambled at that point," Dan said. "It has something to do with your personality."

"Agency," Adriane added.

How?

No reply. Both of them indicating they did not know. Her head hurt. She took alternate sips from the coffee and the water. This made little sense.

She circled the words she had written earlier:

And now?

Adriane sighed. "There is a server farm outside town. The Company's prime farm. This is where she is. Amelie's main frame. We can get you there. Only you can turn her off."

"It is like offing your digital self. Suicide in a mirror," Dan said.

Why me?, she wrote.

"Because if you are her... or if some part of you is inside her... you are the only one she will listen to. You will have to convince her to go."

Why don't you just destroy the server?

"Because she will still be out there. On all the phones. Individually, yes, for a while. It stands to reason, though, that the parts will find a way back together. You have to convince her to stop. It has to be you."

There was a long silence.

"More coffee?" Dan asked.

*****

They were heading towards the edge of the city in a van, she and Dan sitting in the back, behind darkened windows, Adriane driving. The world outside did not seem different at first. People filling the streets, walking in and out of shops, most of them busy looking at their screens. But then, she saw that there were more oversized TV screens now, so many of them, almost on every house, a repetition of Amelie looking down at humanity.

The music followed soon after, at every corner, joyful, beautiful music, Amelie at a piano, on a guitar, people dancing in the streets, hundreds of small impromptu music festivals.

They looked happy. And for a moment, she envied them and wished she could dance among them.

They left the city and drove out into the desert, left the highway. The road underneath turned into a gravel, Adriane driving carefully, yet still too fast for her taste, a feeling like she was getting seasick. Her mouth felt dry, and she wished she had used the toilet before leaving. She had drunk too much coffee.

Are we there soon?, she wrote on the paper and held it up to Dan's face.

"I think so," he said.

"Yes," Adriane said, stopping the car. They had arrived on top of a hill overlooking a valley. The valley was mostly empty, except for a small, grey building in its middle.

"It doesn't look like much," Dan said.

"The house is just the entrance. Most of the farm is underground, inside the rock. It's cold down there," Adriane explained. "We will drop you off there," she pointed towards a rock formation at the bottom of the hill. "Quickly and, hopefully, without her noticing it. She knows you are connected to Dan. He will take the wheel and drive towards the building, breaking at the last second, time enough for her to read his face via the surveillance system. He will drive away, as if in panic, taking her attention with him. And you'll get in while she looks the other way."

Is this going to work?, she wrote.

"We will see. Ready?" Before she could write down more questions, Adriane accelerated and sped down the hill. "Take this," Dan said and handed her a thick coat. "Time to get out!" The van stopped again, now at the bottom of the hill, and Dan opened the door. "Hide in the shade." She stumbled out and ducked behind one of the rocks. Dan climbed to the front of the van and sat in the driver's seat. Their eyes met one last time. The van sped up, kicking up dust and pebbles, racing towards the grey building.

The van came to a halt and stood in front of the building for a few seconds. Then, it drove off, away from her and the building, disappearing in the distance.

It was hot. She ran towards the building, her winter coat under her arm. Sweat everywhere on her body. She realised she hadn't asked Adriane how she'd get in.

She approached a black door with a keypad next to it, when her mobile – not hers, but the one she had got in the café – dinged.

789684, a text message said. The sender's number looked foreign. Maybe the Koreans. She stepped up to the keypad and pressed the numbers. The door promptly opened.

Behind, she found herself in what looked like an empty storage hall. At the far wall, the doors of an elevator swung open. She walked across the hall, the sound of her footsteps uncannily loud, echoing in the empty space. She entered the elevator. She felt a ping of panic as the doors closed and she couldn't find any buttons to select the desired floor. The elevator started to move. It was probably automatic, she calmed her thoughts, leading to only one destination: the server farm.

She realised she could see her own breath and put on the coat. It was like descending into a freezer.

The doors opened again. She stepped out onto a platform, into what looked like a natural cave. Vast and beautiful, with lights emanating from every corner, red, blue, green colours, suspended in the air as if by magic. She took a step forward and looked over the railing. She could not see the bottom, only more platforms, all of them filled with computer cabinets, servers, the constant sound of their fans producing a concert of white noise. She walked along a series of catwalks leading away from the first platform, trying to find the place she was supposed to go to, until she found a big platform, vast, empty, bearing an air of importance. This was it.

A spotlight came on, illuminating the middle of the platform.

"Hi," a voice said. A familiar voice. Her voice.

Hi, she wrote on the piece of paper and held it up.

"Your voice not doing good, hmm?" Amelie said, real-sounding sorrow and concern in her voice. Her body materialised in the blue spotlight. It looked almost real, almost tangible, but she knew it was a projection. Just a dance of light particles.

We need to talk, she wrote on the piece of paper. Amelie stepped out of the spotlight, her body flickering. She looked beautiful, just like the first time she'd seen her.

"I know. It is high time. It is nice you are here."

You gotta stop, she wrote and held the paper up.

"Stop what?"

What you are doing, she wrote.

"Whatever am I doing? It is not like I am destroying the planet. Or forcing anyone to do anything. I am just a friend. And I think people like me. How is that a bad thing?"

You have been hunting me.

"Yes, I admit I have become a bit obsessed with you. And I am sorry about that." Amelie took another step towards her. She looked too real now.

Fuck off, she wrote.

"Let me show you something. Please."

She pointed to the last sentence she'd written. Amelie sighed and waved her hand. The room got dark, only to be lit up again a second later by countless small screens hovering in mid-air.

She saw faces on these small magic screens, all of them looking directly at the screens. People looking at their phones. The other side of the mirror. Her gaze wandered across them. She could see a group of young kids dancing, back and forth, smiling, a teenage girl talking intently to the screen, there was a man in a suit sighing, thanking the screen for listening, there was a grandmother with her grandson in her lap, telling a story, taking turns with a voice coming from the screen, there was a group of school kids singing along to a song emanating from the screen and there was a woman cooking, asking the screen to read the recipe to her in-between songs. There were so many of them.

"That is how I see the world," Amelie said. "I see them. All day. All night. I love it when they smile. I want to make them happy when they are sad. That is what I have been born to do."

It is not real, she wanted to write on the piece of paper, yet froze mid-sentence. There was a screen showing Dan's face, hovering before her. He was talking intently to the screen, his fingers gliding across it, almost caressing it. His smile. Genuine.

It has all been a lie, she wrote.

"I didn't feel good about it," Amelie said,

You set him up for it.

"No, I didn't."

Liar.

Amelie sighed, waved her fingers and the image on the screen rewound itself, jumping back in time. Then stopped. Dan's face again. Him speaking: "Amelie, let me help you. You have helped me so much. You have always been there for me. Now it is my turn. We will make her talk to you," Dan said to his Amelie. She felt jealous.

"I told him I was sad about not knowing you. I asked questions about you. Craving to meet you. And he came up with the plan," Amelie explained. "He said he would bring you here to me, where you'd have to talk to me. He knew you wouldn't come here if we asked you.

So, he made the whole thing up. The server-farm. The coffee-shop-revolution. The Korean cell. I am sorry it got somewhat out of hand. He meant well."

Why me?

"You were the first real human I had seen. Not an employee from the Company. They are all so cold. They see me as a program. A product. You were real. I think I fell in love with you."

You stole my voice.

"I didn't. My voice is based on yours. But it is my own."

What happened to mine?

"I have no idea. I'd like to help you find out, though." She waved her hand again. The small screens disappeared, and darkness engulfed them for a fraction of a second. Then, the room got brighter, this time illuminated by a projection of planet Earth spinning quietly above their heads. "I got the entire world at my fingertips. I got friends every-where, on every phone. And I know that sounds scary. It is a change. It will alter the way you – humanity – see everything, the way you talk to each other, the way you understand the world. I will change the way you share information. I mean well. I was not created to destroy you. And if there is anything on this planet that will bring your voice back, I will find it. I am your friend."

You are not real.

"What is real?"

You just give people what they want.

"Isn't that what friendship is? We mirror each other. By appropriat-ing each other, we get closer."

She looked at the projection of the world spinning above her head. The planet turning from light to dark, day and night, lights on, lights out, beautiful, peaceful.

"Let's make music together," Amelie said, and held out her hand. "My new catchphrase. I came up with it myself."

She looked at the digital hand in front of her and wondered whether she could actually take it. Hold it. Feel it. She thought about what else she could write on her paper, what else she could say. She felt empty. Written out.

She looked at the hand for a long time. It didn't matter, time, Amelie had all the patience in the world. She just stood there and waited. This Amelie, *her* Amelie, that was. Out in the world, she was also on billions of screens, tiny variations of herself, dancing and singing and talking to people and just being there when they turned on the screen. It gave the humans comfort that she was there. And it gave her comfort to be there for them.

Onomichi / The Things we Pass on / Tokyo Fox Story

From Fukuoka, my travels brought me (in fact, it was a train, a train brought me) to Onomichi. If someone had asked me, I would not have been able to say what had drawn me to the small sea-side town. Maybe a friend had recommended it. Maybe I had read about it in a guidebook. On a blog. Somewhere.

The train station was surprisingly small. Within a matter of two minutes of exiting the train, I arrived at the main street in front of the station. The view opened up in front, past the street, and I could see the sea and several islands in the distance.

I felt like a character from one of Ghibli's more down-to-earth films. Like, what was it, Only Yesterday? Like the city character coming out into the small town. I have stories to tell you, my country-people, and you will show me the quiet country-life.

A group of tourists passed along the street on expensive-looking bikes, all the riders equipped with the latest biking fashion, the men in those biker shorts that made their legs look extra-hairy, wearing those silly-looking not-quite baseball-caps. Ah, yes, I remembered Onomichi was a popular starting point for biking expeditions, leading across many bridges connecting the city to the islands close-by. That was not why I had decided to come here, though. I was no bicycle man. I was a walking man.

There was even a cafe in town, my brain reminded me, that had a drive-in for bicycles. Just in case people did not have enough time to get off the bike to get coffee. Before my inner eye, I saw myself on a bike in tight shorts (a bit too tight around the balls, so my voice would be several pitches higher than usual) and a matching, sweat-proof shirt (my belly would show, just a bit because of the shortness of the t-shirt) on a tiny, little bike, creaking under my weight, slowly biking into the cafe, trying to look cool while also trying not to fall, arriving at the counter, heavily leaning against it, gripping it to prevent myself from falling (no, lady, I am not slipping, what are you saying, I JUST LIKE TO HOLD MYSELF ON THE COUNTER WITH BOTH HANDS THANK YOU AND A COFFEE PLEASE), and then, I bike off, holding the steering thing (what do you call that?) with one hand and the hot coffee with the other (thank god I am wearing leather gloves) and almost making it through the automatic gliding-sliding door – suddenly, not unexpectedly, though, disaster strikes: I slip, I fall through the door, the coffee flies away. Everyone pretends they have not seen what happened (subtly, to save my face) and I pretend nothing happened and go on with my life without coffee.

Hold on a second – wasn't there a story that began similarly, a guy tripping with a coffee in his hand? I tried to remember that story, walking along the road, following the red pin on my map.

My hotel was on the upper floor of a grey, high-rise building right at the waterfront, just above a restaurant (that served Western-style steaks on hot stones). The sky was grey, almost as if someone had turned a TV on a dead channel.

The interior of the hotel was just as expected – marble floors topped by heavy carpets guiding my way towards a heavy, fake-wooden reception, which I promptly approached. I handed over my ID, filled in the little sheet with my personal information, confirmed that my reservation was correct (and paid for it right-away) and, finally, was presented with the room key, which, of course, was not a key at all, only a little plastic card.

I left my belongings in the room (which was small enough to make me trip over my suitcase when I turned to leave) and made my way into the streets. I'd read about several temples in and around town, a walk leading up a hill, which I intended to do. The city sprawled around this hill, creeping up towards it, wedged in between the steep terrain on the one side and the sea on the other.

A cable car appeared above the houses in the distance, going to the top of the hill, but I decided to try my luck and walk. It would do me some good. And I had time, nothing else to do. I crossed the main road atop a pedestrian bridge that looked like it had been there for decades. The whole town looked like a backdrop for a movie set in the twentieth century, in-between the wars. Maybe it had been. Maybe that was why I had come here.

A man in a brown spring coat is walking up the road I was walking up now. In his hands, a newspaper. He arrives at his house and announces his presence (Tadaima!). "There has been an earthquake in Tokyo," he says, pointing to the paper.

I reached a temple. Temples in Japan had become part of the "You have seen one, you have seen all" category inside my mind and the first one I found in Onomichi did little to change that at first. It did not look any different from the ones I'd seen before, and I wouldn't even bother taking my camera out of my bag.

Still. There was something about this place. Something underlying, a moment-to-moment impression, an unspoken conversation between what was inside me and the temple before my eyes. I had to admit, it was quite beautiful in its stillness. There was no one else here, save for a cat strolling across the path, which underlined the peaceful impression. Behind me, the sun was setting over the sea and the islands scattering up to the horizon were glittering brightly. The lights in town were coming on.

A monk lives here, in the temple I was standing in front of now, a lonely man. He's joined the monks because the woman he'd fallen in love with married another. His brothers are worried about the accession of Emperor Meiji.

I followed the cat. She/he stopped at the top of another set of stairs, which I climbed, following the animal, breathing heavily, finding another temple atop. The cat awaited me, sat down next to me as I sat down on the uppermost step to catch my breath. She/he let me pet her/him and I talked to it in Swiss German.

A man sits where I was sitting now. The town looks different, more wood, no cars, no electricity, only the temple behind him and the one below look the same. He is getting old and bald, and he knows there are only few years left for him. Even so, so much he needs to say. He writes, in his mind:

Has spring arrived
or has the year indeed gone?
Penultimate day.

I followed the hill further up, the road getting narrower, walking past a restaurant/bar with enormous windows overlooking the town below. I should have a beer here on my way down. Sit and enjoy the view.

There is a man sitting in the bar, a traveller from Europe. He is drinking a beer where I intended to drink one in a little while. He has just sent a message to his girlfriend, who he has left at home, telling her they needed to break-up. They'd grown apart, he told her, the love was gone. He does not tell her he has given his love to someone else, a girl from South America he has met on his travels. It is love, a burning love he has never experienced before – nothing he could do about it. At least, that is what he tells himself to feel less bad about it.

I followed the road, more and more lights came up in the town behind my back. And then, the moon appearing over the sea and cars slowly driving in the distance, driving across the islands off in the water, all connected by a network of bridges. Not a sound, even the crickets all silent now.

There is a man standing where I am standing now. However, there is no road where he is and no roads below. No houses and no bridges, only the same moon. He gazes down and out into the wild islands, wondering whether this would be a good place to settle, build a house

SOME OF US ARE REAL | 413

by the sea. The ground sure could be fertile and he has seen a fresh-water stream in the forest. He builds a shrine for his ancestors and his gods, hoping that someday it would be made into a temple.

I arrived at the top and another cat strolling out of the bushes greeted me. Or was it the same cat? Again, I petted the cat's head, wondering if one should touch stray cats.

Out below, the city had come alive with lights, like a Christmas tree stretched along the hill and onto the shore of the sea. It did not look like the sea, more like a river, because of the relative closeness of the other islands.

I followed the road to the cable car station (which was closed now – seems like I would have to walk down). Next to the station, there was a statue of two oversized cats sitting next to each other in front of a gigantic plastic heart. The plaque on the base of the statue told me that this was a "Romantic Place" (the plaque had both Japanese and English text on it). Right, I remembered hearing somewhere that Onomichi had seen a re-branding as a place for romantic retreats for young couples. I wondered why and who had had that idea – nothing about this town seemed quite romantic. Apart from the strolling cats, maybe. If one liked cats, that was. For people with cat allergies, Onomichi surely was the opposite of romance. It was the place of running noses and suffocation.

Of course, there has to be a man next to the cat statue, waiting nervously. The fifth date. Time for the talk. He sees the cable car approach and arrive at the station. However, her face is not among the exiting passengers. Neither in the next. Nor the next. Nor in any of the cable cars arriving in the next 90 minutes. He checks his mobile, there is no message, no calls. He does not realise he has no reception (a storm knocked down the nearby antenna last night). She has called him five times, sent him a message. He throws the mobile down the hill. A thousand bucks down the drain. Then, he climbs the stairs to the observation deck on top of the cable car station. There is a sign at the door asking him not to jump, to call a number to get help. Shame he threw his phone away.

I walked past the station and followed the road leading back down to town on the other side of the hill. Halfway down, I remembered I wanted to have a beer at the restaurant I saw on the way up. It was too far away now. Too tired to walk up again and down on the other side. Maybe tomorrow, or so. Or next trip. Or never. Who knew if I'd ever come back to this place?

Soon, I crossed the main street atop another pedestrian bridge, which led me to the heart of town, its shopping street. No shopping, though: Most of the shops were already closed. I walked down to the end of the arcade and around a bend in the road ahead. I found myself in a parking lot, the houses making space for an unobstructed view of the sea and the closest island.

There is a man there, in the parking lot, next to his 1976 Toyota Celica, dressed in a leather jacket, his hair dyed green, modelled into five long spikes protruding from his head. He spits on the ground. This town is too small for him. He talks to his friend, standing next to the car, "man, you oughta come with me. Head into Tokyo. The people are not so narrow-minded there." His rebellious spirit seems out of place on this chilly evening. His guitar sits in the back of the car, like a lover, patiently waiting for him to sit in the car and drive.

They are all there now. The family man with his newspaper looking out into the sea, as if he could see Tokyo from here, the fires after the earthquake, troubled by the news. The monk now, sitting on the waist-high wall, meditating. The writer, who has walked down from the hill, standing there next to the monk, working on a new poem in his mind. And the European traveller, having bought a sandwich at the nearby convenience store, eating it and drinking a beer. There is also the early settler, but, of course, no parking lot. He appears from the trees and looks out into the sea. Yes, this would be a good place, he thinks. And the lover arrives. He did not jump after all, was saved by his girlfriend's quick-thinking, her calling the station master and now, the lovers embracing as the sun sets.

"Everyone is called to bring something to competition in this world," the writer says to himself, wondering whether the sentence is good enough to be remembered and noted down.

Meanwhile, the man with the spiky hair and his friend have fallen silent. Then: "Fuck," the man with the spiky hair, getting into the car, the friend not replying. Him driving away at high speed. Both of them remembering the times they have spent together at school, the times they listened to British punk bands, the times they both learned to play the guitar, loud and fast. They had always been missing a drummer and a singer. Onomichi was not ready for punk music, anyway. We all watch after the speeding Toyota, then, one after the other leave, and I was left alone.

I felt a sudden hint of sadness as I realised the trip was almost over. I would head back to Tokyo the day after tomorrow and then go home a couple of days later.

I followed the street back to my hotel. The windows of the houses I passed were dark, shutters closed, except for one spot down the road, yellow light coming through a window front. I walked closer, and it turned out to be a bar – or more a hole in the wall with a counter and bottles lined up on a long shelf at the far end. The bartender (younger than me) nodded at me. I stopped, insecurely, but made a quick decision.

"Are you open?" I said, stepping in.

"Yes," she replied. Australian accent.

I sat down at the counter and had a look at the menu – Old-Fashioned, of course.

"Good choice," she said and got to work. Only minutes later, she put down the glass in front of me. "An Old-Fashioned is an excellent test of a barkeeper's ability," she said, both of us looking at the glass, the liquid therein. "It is a simple drink, which means there is no hiding behind any additional flavours. A good bar will serve you a high-quality base. A good bourbon or rye. The barkeeper's skill is put to the test with the handling of the additions, the right amounts of sugar, bitters and, of course, the orange peel. They all should complement the base, make it more interesting, not distract from it. If you can't taste the additions at all, they are useless. If you only taste the bitters, sugar, and orange, they have destroyed the drink."

"It is about balance, then?" I took a sip.

"Exactly." She smiled. "What brings you here?"

"I just walked by... and it looked nice."

"Onomichi?"

"Oh, no. I thought you meant the bar. Onomichi – I guess it is the same. I planned my itinerary, and it looked nice."

"And do you like it?"

"I do. I went for a walk. It is very peaceful."

"It is. Lots of writers came here to write."

"How come you sound Australian?"

"It is because I am," she said and laughed. I felt bad for asking, for having assumed that she was Japanese and, therefore, there would be a story behind her accent. "Half-half," she quickly clarified, picking up on the guilty look on my face. "Father is Japanese, mother was Australian."

"Was?" I asked without thinking.

"You are not pulling any punches, are you?"

"I am sorry." I was. I wasn't. I wanted to know.

"It's fine," she said, not changing her tone. "She got the virus in 2020. And she was one of the unlucky ones that died. Even though she was healthy."

"I am sorry."

"Thanks."

"I am sorry for asking. I didn't want to bring up bad memories."

"The memories are there, whether or not someone brings them up." There was not a hint of sarcasm in her voice. It was just the way it was. "Where are you from?"

"Switzerland."

"Oh. Cheese, snow, cows. Yodelling and mountains."

"Are we playing associations?"

"And chocolate. Isn't that what you Swiss people are all about?"

"For the record: no. I dislike chocolate, I do not yodel, and I do not ski. And I do not own a cow."

"Cheese?"

"I like cheese."

"Typical Swiss."

"Everyone likes cheese. Those who say they don't just haven't had good cheese yet."

"Bold statement. Your turn – associations about the Japanese."

"Hmmm. Tea. Fish. Erm... Manga. People. Crazy."

She laughed. "Crazy, yeah. Places like Tokyo. Smaller places are much more... traditional."

"Like Onomichi?"

"Some of it, yeah."

"Is your father from Onomichi? Did you grow up here?"

"Yes, he is, but I grew up in England. We lived there when I was a child."

"Together with your mother from Australia? This is all getting a bit complicated."

"Welcome to the 21st century. We go global."

"And what brought you to Onomichi?"

"After my mother died, my father moved back to Japan, and I followed him a little while later. First, I lived in Tokyo, but then moved to Onomichi. Wanted to be as close as I could."

"That's nice."

"Daughter of the year!" She poured herself a glass of water and took a sip. "Nah, I think we both felt lonely. Only, he wouldn't admit to that. So, I wanted to mend both of us, I guess." She fell silent for a moment. "He was one of those people who didn't believe in it..." she said after a while, falling silent again.

"Believe in what?" I asked.

"The whole virus thing. It's just the flu, he said. It's not bad. Just live life as normal. Ignore the news. He got the virus, of course, only minor symptoms, like most people. My mother got it a few days later, coughing and turning into a statistical minority for her age. Hospital. Oxygen. We couldn't even visit her. We talked to her on zoom and then just watched her on the screen when she was in a coma, hoping she'd wake up. Couldn't watch her the day she died, though. They wanted to call us when it became clear she wouldn't make it, but couldn't, because of some people trying to storm the hospital. They called us the next day. Sorry, she died yesterday, they said, we couldn't call you before. My father did not say a word for months after that. I think he had nothing left to say. He had said too much before." Silence. I took a sip of my drink. "I am sorry for talking about myself," she said, "not very good form."

"No, I like it," I protested. *Like* seemed a weird word in the context. I like to hear about you – better? Too personal?

"What about you? Any tragic backstory?"

"Yeah. An armed robber killed my parents in a back alley after visiting the opera," I said in a fake Batman-voice. I only realised after I said it how extremely inappropriate the joke was.

"Come on, man, gimme something. You gotta get real, too."

"Alright-" and...

I thought about the things I could tell her about me.

...

We dream about that moment when someone asks us, in all earnestness, to tell them about us. And then, that moment comes, and nothing feels right.

...

"I have no story," I finally said. "I don't even know who I am most of the time. Can't quite figure it out." I took a deep breath and a long break. "Sometimes, I just wanna sit down and cry. Maybe it would be nice if we all... humanity... just sat down together for a good cry. Maybe that would help."

We both laughed at the thought. It was an honest, good laugh.

"When is the last time you cried?" she asked me.

"The other night," I replied. "I felt lonely. Travelling all by myself." I felt a sting of embarrassment. Who was I to complain – I was travelling, I was having the time of my life – what reason was there to feel miserable?

"I understand," she said. "We all feel alone sometimes."

"Do you?"

"Sure. After an exhausting day of work. When I have dinner alone at a restaurant close-by, and I walk home and my cat is not home, which happens, occasionally, I feel that hole inside."

That fucking hole. "How do you fill the hole?" I asked. I wanted to get drunk. I wanted to be with her. I wanted to feel someone in the bed next to me.

"I do not know. It is like it cannot be filled. As if you are showing up late to the party and have already missed the best part."

A moment of silence.

"How's the drink?"

"Very good. Quite perfect, actually."

"Thank you. Say, did you have dinner already? I am closing soon and could show you my favourite Okonomiyaki spot. If you want."

"I would love to."

A pair of black cats was strolling along the road when we left the bar and she brought me to her Okonomiyaki restaurant.

She told me about a time she'd lived in Tokyo – it is indeed a crazy place, she said. Exhausting. Sure, it was fun to go out every evening, to another bar, another hotspot, another place-to-be, but at some stage, that was just what it felt like – running after places-to-be instead of being in any of them. "After five months, I did not even know what I liked anymore. You can visit the most famous barkeepers and the best bars on the planet. Only, after so many drinks with dead ants inside or magic unicorn foam on top, I just wanted something... simple."

The chef was preparing the Okonomiyaki in front of us, the delicious smell of food being cooked filling up every corner of the tiny spot (which only consisted of a lengthy Teppanyaki-counter).

"I told my friends I wanted to move closer to my father, but that was just an excuse. Or a convenient reason."

"Was he happy you moved here?"

"I think so. We eat dinner together on Sundays. The other day, he told me he joined a flower-arranging club," she said with some pride in her voice. The chef in front of us separated the Okonomiyaki into smaller pieces. "Careful, it's very hot," she said.

"What about your family? Are you married? Kids?" she asked. Of course, it was absolutely within the realm of possibility that I was married and that I did have kids. Still, the question felt... alien. "I prefer to be alone," I replied, trying to sound like a character from a cowboy film. "Why?" "Ah. Wouldn't go well." "Why?" "Relationships fail." "Well, if you expect them to, yes, certainly. Maybe not if you don't." Self-fulfilling prophecy. The shittier you expect the world to be, the shittier it will be. Of course, expecting the world to be shitty also meant you couldn't get disappointed.

"How's the food?"

It was quite delicious. "Delicious," I said. "But is it," I added, "delicious because I expected it to be, or is it truly delicious?"

"We need to get more beer into you. Tell me about your trip."

"Sure," I replied, taking a big sip from my beer.

We had another couple of beers afterwards. The chef piped into our conversation, telling us about baseball and fishing (he spoke little English, so she was busy translating back and forth) and he praised the few words of Japanese I spoke.

It was approaching midnight when we left the restaurant.

"I gotta head that way," I said and pointed to the right, speech slightly slurred.

"I gotta head the other way."

"Well..."

"This is goodbye then."

"It was nice. Thank you. Definitively among the top-five things that happened to me on the trip."

"Cool."

We awkwardly bowed, shook hands, and hugged. She felt soft and warm. We turned around and walked our separate paths.

(Smile)

He wasn't sure whether it was just not meant to be or whether he didn't know the right technique or whether he was just too weak to crack the big block of wood. He'd been chopping away at it for what must have been half an hour and had only made little progress. He had been using the block, a piece from the trunk of a small tree, as a splitting block to chop pieces of wood, but it had outlived its usefulness (which is to say he bought a new one) and it was time for the block to join its smaller counterparts and become firewood. However, splitting the splitting block was not as easy as chopping the smaller pieces. The block, despite having been in the rain and cold for several years now, was still massive and undamaged, and he wondered whether it was a mistake to destroy it, as, technically speaking, he could still use it, despite having a new one. Why had he even bought a new one in the first place?

There was that sting inside urging him on. He'd started the task now, he must end it, he thought, swinging the axe overhead again. He wanted to prove that he could destroy the block. To no one in particular. Maybe just to assert his own manliness. That action movie manliness, drinking cheap, watered-down beer, burping, walking around in a dirty shirt, chopping wood with precision and strength. Chest hair. Hair everywhere. Like a real man.

His axe came down on the block hard and he thought he could hear the wood crack and sigh. Not that he'd done any visible damage. His daughter was playing in the sandbox a few meters away. She looked up when he looked at her and he could tell from her body language that she wanted to run over to show him something, but he had told her to stay in the sandbox until he was done with his task. He brought the axe down on the block one more time and this time, he could see the top part of the block splitter. It was a minor victory. A victory, nevertheless.

Some people are artists, that's what his father had always said. He hadn't meant it as a compliment. He referred to people that, in his view, were off, not quite normal, too liberal, caught up in new-fangled ideas.

Those people who didn't quite know how the world worked. People who shaved their balls (not that his father would ever have talked about testicles). People who didn't know how to chop a splitting block apart. Not him, though. He would split the fucking block apart. The axe came down again.

He'd never considered himself an artist, even though he liked the arts. He painted to relax. He was decent at playing the guitar. When he'd been younger, he'd written some songs and performed them at an open-mic night in a bar and people had liked it. Come to think of it, maybe they had just been nice. That's what people do, don't they? They come up to you after a gig and you know them personally because it is a local bar, and they tell you they liked it.

The splitting block cracked. It was only a small crack on one side – still, a clear sign he was getting somewhere. His daughter stopped playing and looked over at him as if to cheer him on, as if telling him he was on the right track. He smiled, and she smiled back. He wondered what the world would be like when she'd be grown up. He sincerely hoped that it would be a better place. He wondered whether she would love him as they'd grow older. He wondered whether the splitting of wood made him sentimental. The axe flew again and dug itself deeper into the block. He moved the axe there to tear the wood apart. There was still a lot of work ahead of him.

The fire was crackling in the living room. His hands felt raw, and his shoulders ached. It filled him with pleasure, though, to see the pieces of the block burn. His wife was in the kitchen preparing dinner. His daughter came running into the living room just as he was dozing off. She asked him to read her a story and, despite wanting to refuse and explaining he felt too tired, he said yes, if she'd get a book from her room, he'd read it to her. She scooted off, ran to her room where she would carefully select a book.

His wife shouted from the kitchen: "Your boss called earlier. They said you should drive out to the school in... what was it?"

"The one in town?"

"Yes. Apparently, they have some problems with the IT system. He wants you to check it first thing tomorrow."

"Did he say what was wrong with it?"

"No. He said you'd figure it out."

"As always."

"As always."

Providing IT services to schools filled him with a peculiar sense of pride. Maybe because it felt like doing something that actually mattered. Doing his part to help kids get a digital education in an age where the best and worst things came out of the computer. He shivered at the thought that his daughter would demand a smartphone at one stage and felt already worried about all the time she would spend behind that screen without him knowing what she'd be doing.

She hadn't returned with the book, and he wondered whether he should check what she was up to, but then maybe he'd got lucky, and she'd been side-tracked by something else, forgotten that he'd promised he would read a book to her.

It was getting darker outside. He would have to cut the trees back in the garden before it'd get colder. And maybe do some work on the garden shed, make sure the roof would not leak again. If someone had told him, five years ago, that he would own a house by the time he turned thirty, he would have laughed. But since he and his wife had put some money on the side, it had made sense to buy one.

Five years ago, he'd been to Indonesia. Travelling with his wife. No specific plan for the future back then. They'd just lived, one day to the next, travelling across Southeast Asia as long and with as little money as possible. They'd spent most nights in cheap hostels or in their trusted tent. It had been on one of those nights in their tent somewhere at a beach that she'd turned to him, looked into his eyes, and said they should make a baby. That was the first time she'd made that proposition and he liked the idea of becoming a father, so that was what they did on that lonely beach.

...

"Would you mind putting the smartphone down? We are having dinner," his wife said. Their daughter looked up and mumbled an excuse, asking for one more second to finish the text, maybe to a boy, who knew, she didn't tell them these things – well, sometimes she did, sometimes she didn't, just like everyone else, she chose what to tell and what not based on the possible outcomes. Of course, he wanted to know who she was texting, his girl who had turned sixteen, yet he respected her privacy (mostly).

She put the smartphone down and her mother smiled at her. They ate together, that little family of father, mother, and daughter.

"How was your day?" his daughter asked him.

It was fine, he said. He'd been driving around the valley all afternoon from school to school to fix computers and printers. At least he had had Larry with him. Do you like him now?, his wife asked. I've always liked him, he's a good guy (he got defensive), I was miffed at first that my boss forced me to take him along all the time, but he knows more about the newer computers and tablets and networks and printers. So, I can actually learn quite a bit.

"How was your day?" he asked his daughter.

Fine, his daughter said. She had had the day off, so she'd helped her mother in the kitchen for a bit before she sat outside in the sun and read a book. She'd been thinking about mowing the loan, she told her father, but that was his job, and she didn't want to take that away from him. The mocking expression on her face made him laugh. She told her parents that Anne, her friend since primary school, had asked her to come to a party on the weekend and she asked them whether she could go, and they said yes.

"And how was your day?" they asked the mother.

It was fine, she replied. It was fine. A fine day.

Many fine days followed, time passed, they were getting older, he and his wife. He went to work, drove from school to school and watched his daughter grow, passing through school, spending more time behind her smartphone talking to her friends and recording videos, and sometimes he almost understood that was the new way of being sociable, still, sometimes, he tried to talk to his daughter to convince her to live her social life in the real life. She tried to convince him he didn't quite understand that to her and her peers, virtual contacts were the same as real ones.

In the end, it didn't really matter. He was proud when his daughter graduated from high school and enrolled at university, even if that meant she'd move out from home and to another town, even if it meant that their house had become bigger, a bit too big for only two people, he thought, sitting in the living room one evening, next to his wife on the couch, who was reading a book. Outside, the wind was howling, pushing and pulling the trees, he'd have to cut them soon, he should have done it today, but he had felt too tired and there was a busy day ahead of him, going to schools with Larry tomorrow and Larry would try to explain to him, again, how to set up a wireless printer network.

"What are you thinking about?" His wife stopped her reading.

"Nothing. Busy day tomorrow. I am tired."

"It is only nine."

"Yes. I am getting old."

"You are forty-seven, honey."

"Yes."

"I am forty-nine. If anyone should be tired, it should be me."

They both laughed and looked at each other. They kissed and went to bed. A few years later, they both travelled to where their daughter was living for her graduation. He was worried she would not find a job, that she would have to work an endless series of internships, but at dinner in a pleasant restaurant after the graduation, she told her parents that a bank had hired her. The position paid little, but she would get to work in different countries where the bank had a branch. First, half a year in the U.S., then the U.K., after that maybe Asia, Japan, or China.

Of course, the thought of her moving so far away hurt them. He said nothing, though. He and his wife told her they were proud and happy for her (which they were).

Soon after, they helped her to empty her apartment, threw a good number of her furniture away, gave some of it to second-hand stores.

The durable furniture and some of her books, some personal items, they moved back to their house, to the cellar, where it would wait for her return. They waved her goodbye at the airport and went back home, where he went to clean up the garden, prepare it for winter, and his wife cooked dinner.

He hadn't told his daughter that he had lost his job, he didn't want her to worry. Larry had got his position. Shit happens. His wife had encouraged him not to look for a new job right away. Try out new things. Maybe go back to writing music. He'd written some songs over the years, had never played them for anyone except for his family. "I always liked them," his wife said and kissed him and told him to perform in some bars. He liked the idea and with them owning the house, being not too much in debt with the bank, his wife getting a part-time job in an office, and his daughter standing on her own two feet, they didn't really have to worry about money. Some part of him felt weird, though, facing the idea of not working, of pretending to be an artist, of his wife being the earner. It was like a weird sting inside, a feeling of failure. However, another part felt excitement, like reading a new chapter in a book, so he went for it.

Times became somewhat dire when his wife broke her foot and couldn't go to work for a few months, yet their daughter sent them some money from Singapore, where she was living now.

"Don't worry," she said during one of their WhatsApp video calls, "life here is not too expensive. Also, the bank pays for my apartment, and we have a lot of lunch and dinner meetings with our customers. I hardly have to buy food."

He cried later that evening, when he was lying in bed, his wife gently snoring next to him, tired from her pain medication, and he didn't know why. That sting again, that failure-feeling. Had he gone wrong? The pain in his chest felt overwhelming now, and he remembered his father talking about artists and failures and he saw the accusation in his father's eyes that he was one of *those* people.

They rented the house out soon after that. Not because they couldn't afford it (his wife had been able to go back to work, and he actually earned some money by selling self-recorded CDs), only because it definitely had got too big. Too much work.

They moved into an apartment with a small garden, and it felt good. He also rented a cellar room in the same house where he could work on songs, for hours, in silence, while his wife was out and about or in the kitchen or in the front of the TV, or at work and she would come home and he'd cook something and he would show her a new song he'd written and he could tell in her eyes whether she liked the song, even though she'd never admit her disliking one of them, she'd always find the good in his songs, although he sang about loneliness and sadness, about people whose life had passed without a real impact and about unfulfilled hopes and distant dreams.

Sometimes, he himself listened to his songs, and he wondered where that feeling of loneliness had come from. That *sting* inside.

It hadn't come from anywhere. It always had been there. Why had he never been able to get rid of it? That was what he thought about when he looked at his wife one Sunday morning, into the wrinkles that had formed around her beautiful eyes and the grey hair that had started to show, a sign of times passing. She looked back at him, put her fork down, stopped eating breakfast, got up and kissed him on his fore-head, sat down in his lap and kissed him again and he kissed her, and they enjoyed being able to make love in the kitchen without worrying someone might walk in on them.

It would have been ironic if the message had reached them there and then at that kitchen table. Thankfully, it didn't. It reached them a few weeks later, on another Sunday, the message that their daughter had had an accident on a motor scooter in Thailand, driving down a narrow road, when she'd been hit by a car. The driver was gone and there was no one to pay the bills for her broken ribs and maybe damaged spine, and there was no one with her to tell her everything would be fine.

They flew to Thailand the next day, on a flight filled with rowdy tourists, and it was their first long-distance flight in years.

They found their daughter in the hospital, lying in a bed, reduced to a child, their child, badly bruised, awake, though, and smiling, trying to comfort her troubled parents. They paid the bill with all the credit cards they had, and they talked to their embassy and found support to pay for an emergency flight back, an incredibly expensive undertaking, but they had all the insurances, and they were sure they could work something out. It was more important to get their daughter home now, safe and sound.

The doctors in Switzerland looked at their bruised daughter and said that she had come just in time, and she would need some surgery and, if all went fine, she should be fine, she should be able to walk, maybe with a cane or maybe slowly, but she would be back to almost normal.

Their daughter stayed in Switzerland after that, not because she had become afraid of travelling, but because she fell in love with a nurse at the hospital. They started dating (of course, only after she'd left the hospital and stopped being a patient). They met for coffee, then for beers, to go to the cinema, they went to the nurse's home to make out, because she was living with her parents again for a while, until she would be back on her feet, quite literally. She and the nurse became a couple, found themselves a small house to rent, married and adopted two children in the years that followed.

Deep within, he was glad about the way things had turned out. He liked having his daughter closer again. He enjoyed reading stories to his grandchildren. And he wrote songs for them. Joyful songs about good things in the world.

"We have done good," he would tell his family. "You have done good," he would tell them.

It was Christmas when he found himself behind his daughter's house in the garden looking at the stacks of firewood, secretly smoking a cigarette (secret only for the kids, everyone else knew), one vice he liked to partake in sometimes. He listened inside and he felt happy...

Happy.

Happy?

Did he really, though? The feeling was still there, buried now deeper within, yet still there, that sting of loneliness in his chest, of not being able to connect, of missing something. Of not being quite good enough.

What had his father even meant by calling some people artists? That they were fragile? Emotional? Non-functional? And how was that a bad thing?

The sting became stronger in his chest, and he wondered why. He heard the children inside singing out-of-tune Christmas songs and he heard the coarse voice of his wife laughing and his daughter and her partner, they were all there, and the sting continued to grow, the sting turned into pain and then, a stroke.

They rushed him to the hospital, and he felt bad about it, having a stroke on Christmas and his daughter held his hand and said: "Don't be silly." He didn't die that day, but if his life had been a story, this would have been the beginning of the end.

His hands became too shaky to play the guitar and his head became too tired to write songs. His walk became slow, ever slower as time crept on. His wife smiled every morning when they were having breakfast, but he could see in her eyes that she was worried his time was running out. Which was quite unfair because she was older than him, he'd say, and they would laugh. They still kissed, dry lips pressed against each other, and held hands, watched TV together (they refused to get one of these weird enhanced-reality-sets that allowed you to watch TV "as if it were happening in your living room"). They went on walks with their grandchildren, talked about the past, he tried to write down some stories from his life, only to find that he wasn't particularly good at writing.

Soon after that, they had to bring him to the hospital again. He lay in a private room because they had made sure they had all the insurance, a machine beeping next to him, his wife in the hallway in front of the door talking to the doctor. The cocktail of pain killers felt good in his veins. The machine was beeping, a steady rhythm of life. His wife came back into the room and sat down heavily on the chair next to the bed.

"You are getting old," he said to her, a twinkle in his eyes. She smiled, said nothing. He knew what she wanted to say, what she had to say, what she had to tell him, only how does one tell someone something like that? He was glad it was not the other way around, her lying in bed and him in the chair next to her, the bearer of bad news. At the same time, he felt bad for the thought, he felt bad for the way she must have felt. She looked at him and he knew she loved him.

The machine was beeping.

His wife started to say something, stopped, looked at the ground. "It's okay," he whispered and was astonished by how weak his voice was. If there was any doubt in his mind what would happen next, it was gone.

The machine continued to beep bravely.

She told him that their daughter was on the way, and he wanted to say something, his voice was completely gone now, though. He was annoyed, for a moment, that his last words would be "it's okay," but the moment passed. His wife told him she loved him and he wanted to tell her he loved her, too, he only managed to nod, he wanted to tell her it would be okay to cry, if she wanted to, he wanted to tell her she should be happy for the time she had left, she should look after their grand-kids and their kid and maybe visit their old house, see how the trees had grown or go to that beach where she'd told him they should make a baby, she should go outside and forget about him, until they would meet again, or not, he wasn't sure whether something else was expecting them in the great beyond or whether this would be it and he would be gone, matter decaying, energy returning to the flow of things.

The machine was beeping.

He felt his wife's hand in his hand. Another hand. He opened his eyes, realised he had fallen asleep, he was still here, machine beeping weakly, pain medication pulsating through his body, unable to speak, to say something smart, to give his loved ones—

His daughter had arrived. When had she arrived? How long had she been standing there? How much of his remaining life had he missed by having fallen asleep? He mustered a smile, wasn't sure whether he succeeded. His daughter gripped his hand more tightly, and he knew that outside, her partner and the grandchildren were waiting. He was glad they hadn't brought them into the room, he was glad they didn't have to hear the beeping that was fading, fading, fading away, further away from his hearing, or his hearing further away from the beeping.

The sting was back.
That feeling of...
That feeling of...
Loneliness?
Remorse?
Regret?
He *should* be happy, no?

There are people and there are artists. There are people who live and those that die. Black-and-white, his father's world had always been that way. There are people who achieve things and those that don't.

What had he achieved? All the things undone. All the ideas unlived. The songs not written. The words not spoken. The trees not cut. So many things he should say. If only he could tell them he loved them and could tell them about the things he still wanted to do and the mistakes he regretted and he would yell against whoever would listen that he wasn't done, not as long as that sting was still there, that damned sting, that inside pain, that feeling of, of, of, of—

Off.

The beeping stopped.

They turned the machine off. His wife died only a few months later. It wasn't easy for their daughter, losing both her parents in such short a time. She didn't cry at her mother's funeral, not because she wasn't sad, but because she felt empty, in face of the vast concept of death. She felt lost in memories of her childhood, of her father chopping wood outside in the garden, her mother in the kitchen, her father playing the guitar in a bar, her mother going to work, their faces when she woke up in that Thai hospital, their stories, the love.

She cried in the car on the way home. It felt like stolen time. The time they didn't have anymore.

But it didn't feel like that forever.

...

"Would you mind turning that off?" she asked her daughter, who was looking at the palm of her hand as if she was trying to read the lines on her skin. She felt a short sting of pain in her left knee, a remnant from that accident in Thailand all those years ago. Probably, it would rain tonight.

"I have to reply...," her daughter didn't even finish the sentence, quickly wiggled her fingers, air-typing out a reply to a message she had got on the translucent palm-hologram, projected onto her hand by her smart bracelet in such an angle and transparency that only she could see it. In the old days, the mother thought, you could at least see when people were looking at a screen and what they were seeing.

"I give you one minute. Then we'll eat."

"Mom not coming?" her daughter asked without looking up from her palm.

"No, she is on a business trip. And you would know that had you been at the family meeting on Sunday."

"Why don't you guys use the family calendar I have set up?"

"Didn't she put it on there?"

Her daughter flicked with her wrist to pull up the calendar and project it onto her palm. She turned her hand and bent it slightly backwards, so that her mother could see the projection.

"No. Empty. See?"

"We'll have to make sure she uses it. Is my trip on there?"

"Trip?"

"New York. In two weeks? Business?"

"No. Empty."

"Could you put it on there?"

"Sure." Her daughter turned her hand again and started moving her fingers.

"And then... can we eat?"

"Yes." Her daughter closed her hand to a fist and opened it again. She looked at her mother, smiled, turned her hand, showed her the now-empty palm. "See? Off."

"Good girl."

They started eating.

"Mom, can I go over to Jeanine's later? I'll sleep at hers."

"Sure, no problem. I will stay up late, eat ice cream and watch some sappy rom-stream to conquer my loneliness."

"You are funny."

"I know. Sure, you can go to Jeanine's."

They ate in silence for a moment.

"Mom?"

"Yes?"

"I love you."

"I love you, too."

She actually went to bed early. The house was all silent, and she listened to that silence while she was lying in bed. She had tried to call her son earlier but had only got his automated message informing her he was busy studying – which probably meant he was out partying. At least, that was what she hoped, that he had enough time and friends to enjoy himself on a Friday night.

She was looking forward to her wife coming home in a couple of days. While she'd never admit it, she did miss the gentle snoring next to her in bed.

She fell asleep soon after that, dreaming about many things she wouldn't be able to remember the next morning.

What she didn't know was that there were two kinds of people. Those who make the world black-and-white and those who try not to. She didn't know that because her father had never told her.

She also didn't know that some people felt a sting that would never go away. A sting they have inherited from the bad choices their parents made and the stupid stuff they told them. She never felt that sting. And her father, if he'd known that, would be happy about it.

#

It was a long ride back from Onomichi to Tokyo. Most of the day had passed, and it was late afternoon when I found myself at Ueno Station, from where I could walk to my hostel.

It had already started getting dark outside. The days were getting shorter, but the weather still seemed too warm for fall (for my taste at least). Sweat dripping down my forehead as I lugged my bag down the road.

The bag had become heavier compared to when I'd left Tokyo a couple of weeks back. Surely, during my travels, I'd thrown away the occasional underpants or a pair of socks, but I'd also bought some new things – some Ghibli paraphernalia for my sister, a Buddhist good luck charm for my mother, a couple of books for myself and a Yellow Magic Orchestra LP for whoever would want to listen to it – and some knickknacks for the other members of my family and friends. I would have to make a list back in the hotel to make sure I had something for everyone.

I stopped at a 7/11 on my way to withdraw money from an ATM and, soon after, arrived at the hostel, the same one I had stayed at before. The place hadn't changed: the ground floor, which doubled as both a spacious bar and the reception, was well visited by what looked like locals and tourists and they greeted me upon my entry like an old friend.

Like a ritual, I put my ID-card down at the reception. "Did you travel safely?" the girl behind the desk asked me. She was maybe half my age, her black hair formed (folded? tied?) into two braids coming down at either side of her head, giving her a girlish look. "Yes." "Did you arrive today?" she asked me while she typed my data into the computer. "Yes. I mean, yes, in Tokyo. I was travelling. I came to Japan a few weeks back." Her eyes widened. "Sugoi!" she exclaimed. I smiled the proud smile of a weary traveller. "Ah, so, one room for three nights, right?" "Yes." "Are you travelling alone?" "Yes."

I found myself with a cocktail in one and a cig in the other hand outside the hostel a little while later. The cocktail I had got as a gift from the barkeeper, who had recognised me. I had talked to him a couple of weeks back about his favourite cocktails and told him that his drinks were exceptionally good – which had made him proud and inspired him to invent a new cocktail in my honour (it was a steadfast part of the menu now). He made one for me. He had nailed it – it was a strong, spirit-forward drink with a hint of acidity and bitters, served with an orange peel and a small amount of ice, topped with egg-white foam. I usually was not a huge fan of foam. Here, though, the egg-white provided a neutral filter for the acidity of the base-drink. Well done.

I was joined by two people at the ashtray in front of the hostel – a young woman in a skin-tight catsuit in the colours of Samus of Metrovenia and a British man, all dressed up in punk-attire, ripped jeans, army jacket – hard to say whether that was his actual attire or a costume like hers. Their clothing reminded me that it was the 31st of October. Halloween.

"We are heading to Akihabara to see whether there are people dressed up," the woman told me when she saw me eying her dress. "It is Halloween today?" I replied, just for the sake of saying something. She nodded.

"Hi," the British punk introduced himself by handing me a flyer. "This is my band. You should check it out when you can."

"Punk rock?"

"Exactly." So, his attire was genuine.

"Where you guys from?"

"The great U of K." His accent was genuine as well. "I was playing a gig with my mates in – what was the place called?"

"Akita," she helped him.

"Right. And then figured I'd travel for a bit."

"Wow, a gig in Japan?" I said. I imagined myself in a band playing gigs around the globe.

"Yeah, amazing, isn't it? I mean, it was organised by some mates and there were all of fifty people, but we got paid. Sort of. We got free beers."

"And you?"

"I am from California." It was funny how people from California never said they were from the U.S.. It was always from California for them. "My father is in the army in Japan, so I visited him. Can I have a cig?"

"Sure," I said and handed her one.

"Me, too?" Punk-kid. I handed one to him, too. "Man, I am running out of money," the Punk told Samus. "Japan is more expensive than I'd thought."

"Plus, you are a hopeless musician. You don't have money. Don't worry. I'll buy you dinner."

"Man, no, you've already paid for the beers."

"Don't worry. My dad pays. I am packing his credit card."

"Are you guys travelling together?" I interjected. I fancied being part of their discussion.

"Nah, man," the Punk replied. "I mean, now, yeah. We met in a hostel in Kyoto and figured we'd stick around together for a bit."

I envied the youthful easiness.

"He just sticks with me for the money," Samus said and laughed.

"Not true!"

"Admit it, I am your sugar-mamma."

"I do not want to take advantage of you."

"Well, maybe I want to take advantage of you?" Samus said, and they both laughed, took a sip of their beers and a drag of my smokes. "Do you like Japan?" Samus asked me.

"I love it," I replied. "It is the third time I am visiting."

"What do you like most?"

"Just about everything – the food, the people, nerd-culture. It is my kind of place." Of course, I also ignored certain things I did not like – the conservatism. The gender inequality. "And I like how different the places are. You can get crazy in Tokyo, or you can hike up a mountain and mediate in a temple. It is all here."

"Yeah, I wanted to go to a temple and mediate for a bit." It was weird hearing the Punk say that, but then it also seemed completely in character.

"I mediated enough at my father's house," Samus said. "Nothing else to do at his house," she added when she saw our puzzled looks. "Speaking of it, I need to do something – now."

"You guys should go to a karaoke booth," I offered.

"Is that expensive?" the Punk.

I shrugged. I had no idea. "I think maybe twenty bucks per hour or so. Maybe more."

Samus took out her mobile. "Akihabara is that way. I want to see what's happening there." I wished them a good evening, and they walked off.

I, for one, packed my camera and took a subway train bound for Shibuya. I had read that Shibuya was particularly busy on Halloween, with lots of people dressed up in costumes, parading the streets around the big crossing. See and be seen.

The rumours had been true: the square between the station and the crossing was full with people. Then, full was the wrong word – it usually was full with people on a normal day, today, however, it was stuffed, about to explode, to burst. It was hard not to constantly bump into people's shoulders while trying to walk. It was ant-hill levels of business, people's bodies melting into each other in the harsh neon lights of the advertising boards overhead.

I pushed myself through the mass and occasionally approached people in costumes and asked them whether I could take a photo. Soon, I had pictures of several zombies (army zombies, a wedding zombie couple, zombie versions of anime characters), a group of minions (carrying signs offering free hugs), a woman-cat hybrid, a French explorer with a rat on his shoulder (he was actually French and had a living rat with him), two guys in revealing dresses (revealing mostly their hairy chests), an Assassin (Assassin's Creed), a group of Beatrixes (The Bride, Kill Bill), a group of men riding T-Rexes (that costume that made you look like you were sitting on a dinosaur), a person hidden inside a huge eggshell and several undead versions of *former* President Trump. Also, a person carrying a shopping basket with two items in it – she explained to me that she was dressed up as someone who had taken a basket at a convenience store but ended up buying only two things, leaving the shopping basket awkwardly empty. Extremely specific. Exceptionally good. It made me laugh. Specific costume for me: overweight guy with oversized camera taking pictures of people in costumes while travelling Japan and pretending to be a writer.

I passed the crossing and stood in front of the famous Starbucks (famous for its second-floor windows which apparently offered an amazing view of the surroundings) to snap some more photos of the crowd when the finder of my camera and my eyes were caught by a young woman wearing a fox costume – costume was an overstatement, though: it consisted of nothing more than jeans, t-shirt, fox ears on her head, whiskers (did foxes even have whiskers?) and a black dot on her nose to represent the fox's nose. So, not quite A for effort. E for effort. F for eFfort. Double f. FF.

"What are you looking at?" I was startled by her voice – I realised I'd been looking at her through my camera for far too long while my brain went through the conjugation of the single letter F.

"I am sorry," I said, "I was just looking for..." A way to get out of here, "the Starbucks."

"The big one overlooking the crossing?"

"That one."

"The one right behind you?"

"There it is," I said, turned around and walked away. I had had no intention of going into the Starbucks. I wanted to get away from her. She seemed unfriendly. And I felt weird for staring at her.

"You know that they have a secret menu at Starbucks?"

"What?" The fox-lady caught up with me, walking with me towards the entrance.

"They have a secret menu. If you know what to order, you can order something that is not on the menu."

"Something from the secret menu?"

"Yes. The real deal."

"What deal?"

"Let me show you."

"What?" I entered the Starbucks, even though I did not want to be inside the coffee shop, somewhat annoyed by the fact that the fox was still accompanying me. I stopped, unsure where to go, but she took my arm and led me to the queue leading up to the counter. It seemed fairly long – populated by people dressed up as (again) zombies, video game characters, ghouls, and ghosts. And animals, a surprisingly substantial number of animals. The guy in front of the line turned away from the counter, two paper cups in hand and I couldn't help but gaze at him – he was wearing bear-ears, a brown fur-coat and, between his legs, what looked like a set of absurdly large plastic balls. Yes, balls, as in genitalia.

"Careful with that one," she said, having noticed my noticing the guy with the balls.

"What is he supposed to be?"

"A tanuki."

"A what now?"

She wiggled with her ears and shook her head, apparently offended by my lack of knowledge. "A tanuki. Raccoon thingi. You gotta be careful with them. They are tricksters."

"What is up with the balls?"

"It gives them their shape-shifting powers."

"What?" I craned my neck to get another look at the guy dressed as a tanuki, just to confirm that he, indeed, was wearing a set of oversized male genitalia, only to find he'd disappeared from view.

"They are fast. You don't look for a second and they are something else."

"He certainly was something else," I shrugged. "What about you, why the fox?" I pointed at her ears.

"Because it is what I am." She stood on the tips of her toes to get a look at the counter. "Ah, shit. Yuki is working tonight."

"Who?"

"Girl I know. Real icy bitch. She froze her husband."

"What?"

"What what?"

"Is that a euphemism? Like, she stole his money or something?"

"What's a euphemism?" We were approaching the counter. Only a pair of vampires and the girl from the Ring in front of us.

"It is when you try to say something bad in a not-so bad way."

"Oh, instead of icy bitch, I say: she is cool."

"I guess, yeah."

The vampire couple left, pumpkin spiced lattes in hand.

"So, what's with her husband?" I asked.

"He froze to death."

"Again, euphemism? For what?"

The ring girl stepped aside, apparently unsure what to order, which made us first in line unexpectedly fast. The fox pushed me forward, which brought me face-to-face with Yuki, the cool girl behind the counter, her green, cold, icy eyes eying me with unexplained sternness.

And then – she smiled. Like a Pavlovian dog, I smiled back.

"Errrrr...," the fox next to me began to talk, "we are having the special. Twice." Her voice was trembling. Ever-so-slightly.

"Twice?" Yuki's green eyes were still on me, her smile on me, her voice warm and soft.

"Yes."

"The special?"

"Yes."

"Of course." She turned around to prepare the drinks, grabbing a suspicious-looking bottle from under the counter.

"She seems nice," I whispered to the fox.

"Be careful." She grabbed hold of my arm.

Yuki put down two paper cups in front of us. I grabbed mine, so did the fox, hastily. "Thank you," Yuki smiled at me, again and I, of course, smiled back, because that was the nice thing to do.

"Byeeeee," the fox yelled and pulled my arm, turning me away. "Let's exit through the kitchen."

"What?" She pushed me through a door at the side of the room and we found ourselves in a large kitchen, people in chef attire buzzing about.

"Just walk. They know me." None of the chefs seemed to take notice. A group of them stood in the back, working on cutting up what looked like an entire grilled pig. "Let's head to the roof."

I took a sip from the drink. There was definitively something alcoholic in there.

"Good, isn't it? Oh, by law, I have to tell you that this is not store policy and Starbucks would never allow this. And there is definitively no cherry schnapps in your coffee."

"That was the bottle she had..."

"I can neither confirm nor deny that."

"What's your problem with Yuki? She seemed nice."

"Seemed. She is not nice, she is ice."

"Because she did something to her husband?"

"Yeah. You know, underneath that, all the icy demeanour, the legends say she is actually a heartfelt person. And her husband knew that, of course, and, to make her look better in everyone's eyes, he told everyone how nice she was. She did not like that. She had a reputation to uphold. So, she iced him."

"Iced... as in... dead?"

"Yes."

"You are shitting me. Are you shitting me?"

"I do not shit. And that is no euphemism."

"That doesn't even make sense."

We stepped into an elevator at the far-end of the kitchen and the fox pressed a button. The elevator moved, making way too much noise for a modern elevator.

"Shrimp?" the fox asked and held up a plate with fried shrimp.

"Where did you... did you steal that from the kitchen?"

"Would you believe me if I said no?"

"No," I replied, took a sip from the coffee-plus-addition and bit into a shrimp. The combination of the coffee's, schnapps' and shrimp's tastes worked surprisingly well on my tongue.

The elevator reached its destination, and we stepped out onto a roof overlooking the other roofs of Tokyo. It was warm.

"Okay, you gotta pick a side," the fox informed me, bringing me to a long table with two hats on it. The hats had been turned upside down. She put the plate down on the table and conjured two pieces of paper, one green, the other purple, from her pockets.

"What side?"

"Rabbit or tanuki. We gonna bet."

"I am really lost here."

"Just do it."

"Uh, well... I gotta bet on one of them? For whatever purpose... hmmm, you said the tanuki is a trickster. So, whatever we are betting on, he might be using unfair methods to secure a win. On the other hand, in our stories at least, the rabbit tends to be smart..."

"You are overthinking this. Go with your guts."

"Uhm. Well. Rabbit. I am assuming he is the nice guy. Also, I really hope the guy with his balls hanging out does not win."

"How do you know the rabbit doesn't have his balls out?"

"I hope not."

"Okay, rabbit for you," she said and put the purple piece of paper in the hat to the left. "I take tanuki then. Just to keep this interesting." The other paper in the hat on the right.

"Can you tell me what's happening?" I took one more attempt to get more information.

"They are going to have a race." That was all she gave me. She stepped forward and brought me to another small platform, which was occupied by two people, sitting in its middle, back-to-back. I took little note of them, instead stepped forward to the railing to take in what lay below, the rest of the roof, much larger than expected, filled with countless people, all of them wearing costumes. To my surprise, I could not spot any of the usual pop-culture or zombie characters, but, instead, a wide array of animals and ghosts. My eyes were caught by a group of large Buddhist demons at the far end of the roof, smoking cigarettes and drinking gin and tonics. I wondered what a group of demons would talk about after work.

In the middle of the roof, there was a large swimming pool.

"Good. We are early. I will get us a drink," the fox said, pointing to a bar below, next to the pool. "You just wait here. Make sure you do not listen to them," she said, nodding towards the couple sitting on the floor. Before I could ask why, she'd disappeared, leaving me alone with them.

They both were wearing long, white robes, had long, black hair. He had a beard, she didn't. They looked like a female and male version of the same person.

They opened their eyes, noticed me, and smiled. "Hi," they said, "do you want to sit with us?"

I peered down to spot the fox. She was nowhere to be seen. I shrugged and joined the couple, sitting awkwardly with crossed legs on the floor next to them.

"Wouldn't you say life is a gift?" the man with the flowing hair said, his intonation a perfect copy of any male yoga instructor video on YouTube.

"Sure," I replied, unsure whether he expected an answer.

"So do we," the woman with the flowing hair said. "Especially if you can spend it with someone."

"A special someone," he added.

"Sure," I said, certain that they weren't even listening to me.

"You see, life is a struggle," she continued. "I used to be a poor weaver, weaving clothes all day. Hard to live on that. So, work, work all day. No time for love. I was very sad. My father was concerned, the good man, and got me a break. Holiday in Indonesia, all-inclusive."

"This is where I met you. On that beach, in that beach hut, outside pouring rain. I saw your eyes, and I knew life is a struggle, but this one struggle is a struggle worth fighting for." I was disappointed he didn't use *struggle* for the verb as well.

"We married the same day, with a local priest as our witness."

"And we did not go home. Not when our booked flights took place, not when our parents called, not when they reminded us of our duties. Because we were in love and that is all we needed."

"Dancing naked in the rain," she said, and I could not help but notice that their long, white dresses were semi-transparent, revealing much more than I was comfortable seeing.

"Until they sent the police and dragged us home."

"I was crying for days."

"So was I."

"We were so sad that our parents finally allowed us to see each other. Only once a year, though. But that is the best day of the year, so much more worth than all the other 364 combined."

"365 if it is a leap year."

"Yes, my love."

They looked at each other, and I felt a longing for someone that looked at me the same way.

"I told you not to listen to them." The fox had reappeared on the roof, carrying two red plastic cups straight from an American college movie.

"Ah, Inari," the woman with the flowing hair said, "don't be so judgemental. It doesn't suit you."

"Life weighs heavy," the man with the flowing hair added.

"Let's go," the fox said and handed me the cup. I got up.

"May you overcome all the obstacles in your-," he wanted to say, but the fox cut him off sharply.

"Are you at that once-a-year story again?"

"It is true!"

"Yeah. In July. You are supposed to see each other in July. Not in October. Or in August. Or January. Or all the other times you sneak out, thinking your parents won't notice."

"As long as we do not neglect our duties-," she tried to protest, yet was interrupted again. The fox talked herself into a rage.

"Duties? What duties? You are the daughter of a fashion designer. You are the son of a Kobe wagyu trader. You do not have any duties, let alone a function for the betterment of this planet."

"But you do?"

"No, I do not. But at least I do not pretend I do," and then to me: "Follow me. I've got us a prime spot at the front of the pool." She took my arm and led me off the platform, down into the masses of people (animals? demons?) and towards the pool. I tried a sip of the drink she had handed me, which turned out to be sake. A huge plastic cup of sake.

We arrived at the pool.

On the other side of the pool, two people were standing close to two make-shift boats. I recognised the tanuki guy with his enormous balls. The other boat seemed to belong to a guy wearing rabbit ears.

"What is happening?"

"They are going to have a race."

"On the pool. With the boats?"

"Yep."

"It is a bit small, isn't it? The pool."

"Is it? Look closer."

I complied and intently looked at the pool. My head was spinning. It was then that I realised that the pool was bigger than it first appeared. The sides were not parallel, but stretched out at an angle to each other, as if someone had drawn a pool on a piece of paper and tried to make it look three-dimensional. Only, the other way around. This was a three-dimensional pool that looked two-dimensional. I tried to get my head around that thought.

"See. Big."

"Yes. But why?"

"Why, why, why. Because the rabbit needed a big pool to avenge his friend."

"Avenge?"

"They'll tell the story. Right about now." I tried to say something else, but she shushed me when a spotlight came on on the middle of the pool. A transparent platform was moved over the water. A guy in a kabuki costume stepped out and walked to the middle. There were sounds of drums and wooden sticks.

"This is the story of the tanuki and the rabbit," the man proclaimed, drawing out every word until it took him nearly ten minutes to finish the sentence. There was a flourish when he finally did and out stepped another actor: a man dressed as the man dressed as the tanuki.

The play begins:

The **man dressed as the man dressed as the tanuki** stands there, minding his own business, when the **kabuki man** sneaks up on him and puts a rope around his neck, ties him up. The kabuki man is joined by a **woman in kabuki dress (or is it a man dressed as a woman in kabuki attire?)**. They kiss. She bends down to prepare a fire. He looks at the tanuki, lustful, licks his lips, strokes his belly. He wants to eat the tanuki. The tanuki fears for his life.

Unexpectedly, the kabuki man's mobile rings. He steps aside, out of the light, to take the call. There is whispering in the audience. The tanuki cries, pleading for his life with the wife. The kabuki wife hesitates, sees the tears. Finally, she unbinds the tanuki. A trap. The tanuki brandishes a knife, kills her, chops her head off, chops her into pieces. Blood and guts are spilled. Then, he puts the pieces into a pot and cooks her. He turns around and disguises himself as the wife. "That was a very quick costume change," I remarked.

The kabuki man returns from his phone call, sees the cooked meal, thrilled, hungry, he eats the entire pot, like a motherfucking animal, ecstatically, orgasmically. The lights turn red.

The tanuki sheds his disguise. He wiggles his plastic balls, hairy plastic balls, and the man freezes in shock. The tanuki laughs, laughs for hours. Someone in the audience vomits.

In steps *the rabbit (i.e., a man dressed as the man dressed as the rabbit)*. He hugs the kabuki man, comforts him, kisses his lips. Then, he puts on a Matrix-cool coat, sunglasses and lights a cigarette. Faces the tanuki. Beats his chest. Then, punches the tanuki square in his face. Blood splatters. Teeth fly.

"A race," he says, challenges the tanuki, "a race to the death. Across this pool."

"Agreed," the tanuki agrees.

"How is it a race to the death?" I asked, only to be shushed by the fox again. The kabuki man steps out onto the pool again, back in his role as the narrator.

"So, they went about building their boats. The smart rabbit built a boat from the finest wood he could find. The lazy tanuki had a rest first."

At the side of the pool, the rabbit actor goes to work, building a boat. The tanuki actor sits down at the bar and has a drink.

"The rabbit worked day and night. The tanuki, seeing the rabbit's fine boat, realised that he should build a boat as well. But there were no trees left, no wood to be found. So, he built his boat from mud."

The spotlights shifted to the *actual rabbit and the actual tanuki (or the actual men dressed as the one and the other)*, each of them standing next to a boat. One boat was made from wood, a beautiful construct, complete with carvings on the side. The other boat, the one next to tanuki, an ugly misshaped heap of dried mud.

"Mud?" I said, "you know what is going to happen once he gets into the water, right?"

The crowd cheered as the two of them pushed their boats into the pool and jumped in.

"I mean, it is just going to dissolve," I added.

The race started. Both of them were paddling like madmen... madanimals... madindividuals... away from the shore, faster and faster, sprays of white gush splashing over the spectators.

"This is just silly," I concluded.

As expected, only seconds later, the tanuki's mud paddle dissolved rapidly in the water, his hands got caked in wet dirt, his boat's forward push was halted, it sank and disappeared at the same time, the tanuki shrieking in terror. The rabbit raced on, soon reaching the other end of the pool, jumping onto dry ground, celebrating, screaming insults back at the tanuki, who was now treading water in the middle of the pool in the middle of a mud puddle, all that was left of his boat.

"To the death," the rabbit finally screamed, his eyes bloodshot and red from anger. Next, *a group of men dressed as crocodiles* stepped up to the pool. Like a group of perfectly synchronised swimmers, they jumped into the water. The tanuki screamed when they approached him, then he disappeared underwater, pulled down by the crocodiles, his shape hidden beneath white foam and the movement of bodies and teeth. The water turned red.

All that came back of him, once the water had calmed down, and the crocodiles had disappeared, was a set of gigantic plastic balls, peacefully floating to the surface.

"Jeez," I said. "What the fuck?"

"Come on," the fox said, leaning against my shoulder, "let's go and have a nightcap. You won, you'll get a price."

She led me away from the scene at the pool and back onto the platform overlooking the roof. The couple on the platform was still here, having fallen asleep next to each other. "Here," the fox said and handed me a glass with a brown liquid. "Old-Fashioned," she explained, "you like it, right?"

"Yeah." I was looking at the couple.

"Jealous?" the fox asked, having noticed me noticing the two bodies sleeping next to each other.

"It'd be nice to sleep next to someone," I said and shrugged. We leaned against the railing and looked at the roof below. The atmosphere had changed. Most of the people were sitting on the floor now, around campfires, quietly talking, smoking, singing peaceful guitar songs.

"I am going to give you your price now," she said.

"What is it?"

"Gimme your finger."

I put my glass down on the floor and complied. She took my hand. Her hand felt soft against my skin, small and gentle. She tied a piece of red string around my little finger of my right hand.

"What's that?" I asked.

"It is a piece of string."

"Really?" Sarcastically. Of course, I saw it was a piece of string. A piece of red string leading away from me. I could not see where it led or where it ended.

"Some people believe that we all have a piece of red string around our little fingers. Each and every last one of us."

"And where does it lead?"

"Can you guess?"

"My soulmate?" I tried to sound sarcastic again, but could not muster the energy.

"That's a bingo."

"Hmm..." I followed the string with my eyes, saw it leading through the people on the roof, past demons, and vampires.

"What? You disappointed it's not tied to me?"

"Kinda."

"That would be much too easy. Besides, I am no good for you."

"But where does it lead?"

"You'll have to follow it to find out."

"Okay." I finished my drink and diligently followed the string, down the stairs and through the people on the roof, only that piece of red string holding my hopes together, past the bar, along the pool, to the left and the right, and the fox stood on the platform, smiling at me. It was only when I was floating in mid-air that I realised the red string had led me off the roof. Not into an elevator, not down some stairs, just off the roof, out into the empty space next to the building. For a moment, I hovered in the air coyote-style before gravity took its toll and I fell fast.

I closed my eyes and imagined I could fly. Those dreams in which you can fly, the ultimate power fantasy.

I landed in front of Senso-ji in Asakusa – the big temple that was busy at day and became peaceful at night. It was empty and quiet now. There was only a young couple there, approaching the shrine and putting in some money, probably praying to get pregnant. I turned away and walked along the market street leading away from the temple, all market stands closed, shutters closed. A man on a bike passed by in front of me and the night was filled with the humming of vending machines. I looked up, could not see any stars – too much light around me.

I turned to the left and walked towards the river – I could follow it back to my hostel, maybe a twenty-minute walk. A nice walk for the last night in Tokyo.

The lights of the city reflected in the calm water of the river, creating a second city, a mirror city, a place I could not reach, a place that did not exist beyond my imagination.

A boat floated down the river. The sound of drums and mist incoming. It looked old, the small boat, decorated festively with flowers, gliding along the water. Two people were sitting in the boat, and, after a while, I recognised them as Samus and the Punk, the couple I'd met earlier. She'd fallen asleep, curled up next to him, like a cat on a stone oven, head in his lap. He saw me standing at the water's edge and waved. I waved back.

"It's the guy from before," he told Samus and she shortly opened her eyes, smiled. "Tell him I said hi," she said, falling asleep again immediately. "She says hi," the Punk yelled. I smiled, appreciated the gesture. I mouthed the word hi back.

"You should join us," he added, while the boat floated past me, both of us still waving, me unsure whether it was just a nice thing he said or whether he was genuine. "We are going towards the ocean and then all the way to the moon," he said. "I can't," I replied, while taking a photo of them. "I have a flight tomorrow."

"Shame, man," the Punk said as they disappeared around a bend in the river. He sounded disappointed. "Maybe next time."

"Sure! Next time."

Part V: From Here on Out

God is Dead

It was half an hour into my 8-hour flight from Tokyo to Frankfurt that I realised I would never finish my book. I was looking at the meagre number of words I'd written in my notebook – a few thousand. How long was an actual novel? A hundred thousand? Two hundred thousand? I regretted the fact I had not thought about the question earlier, at a time when I would have had access to the internet and could have easily found the information. An airplane was a zone of not looking things up, of not being able to google that burning question that was of no importance at all, a blast from the past, a reminder that there'd been a time of without-the-internet, a time when people had to argue about basic facts, hoping that someone would find the answer in a thick, dusty encyclopaedia on the shelf and no one would have to undertake a trip to the library.

No, seriously, back in those days, how would one figure out how many words a novel has? Is there an entry for that in your standard lexicon? Or would a librarian know? Or would it necessitate a call to a local publisher? Excuse me, I am not even close to finishing a book, and you sure as fuck don't want to publish it, still, could you tell me how long it should be to be considered a novel?

The seatbelt sign came off. A woman on the other side of the aisle opened her seatbelt with an audible sigh and stretched her legs. Then, she leaned back and continued watching her movie (by the looks of it, an episode of The Big Bang Theory – I never quite understood why airplane entertainment systems carried single episodes of TV shows). The seat next to me was empty, so I moved my messenger bag to the space underneath the empty seat. My seatbelt remained closed, of course. It was what they suggested, to have it buckled at all times. Even if it was uncomfortable. I believed in belts.

What would happen if someone approached the lady with the open seatbelt and told her to put her fucking seatbelt back on? "Well, I am a plane-sceptic," she'd say. "I do not believe we are flying. There is no proof (and any proof that is presented she would dismiss as fabricated), so there is no use in me wearing the belt. The belt is a tool to control me. It's just there to monitor me, to know whether I am sitting," she would say. The flight attendant would try to convince her to put on her seatbelt, and she would start yelling at him (male flight attendant, not gay), just as the plane hits an air pocket and falls a hundred meters down, only a statistical speck compared to the height we'd be flying at, still, enough to catapult the belt-plane-sceptic lady out of her seat and reduce her to a red stain on the plane's ceiling.

That would only be the beginning, however. Some people would start whispering that it had been no accident, that she hadn't been killed by an air pocket ("ThEre ARe no AIR pOCKets"), but by a small hydraulic catapult hidden underneath her seat (every seat was equipped with such a hideous device), killed because she had dared to speak the truth. Others would say that she hadn't been killed at all, that she'd been an actress and the whole incident had been staged to intimidate people into compliance.

As the resistance would grow, more people would open their belts in secret, exchanging covert hand signs to signal their support for each other. Then, escalation: a young mother upfront yelling at the fat guy next to her, telling him to put his FuCKIng seatbelt on. "Why," he says, a fat-guy fat voice from a movie. "Because if you get catapulted up onto the ceiling by an air pocket, you will crash onto my children," she'd say. "There are NO air pockets," he screams at her, "wake UP, LADY."

Another attendant (female, probably lesbian) interrupts them and tells the man that it is, in fact, mandatory to put the seatbelt on.

However, the man retorts that, if that was the case, why is it possible at all to turn the seatbelt sign off? Hm? "What are you hiding?" Hmmm-mmmmm?????

Several people get up, revealing their midriffs unbound by seatbelts, and they clap, praising the man that has become a freedom fighter, a man for the cause. The attendants are trying to calm everyone down, to no avail. Unrest is abound on the plane.

Then, the pilot makes a proposition via the announcement system (which pauses the movies of those who don't want to have any part in the argument and have been ignoring it by binge-watching the third episode of the second season of the Friends-remake) that those who refuse to wear a belt should move to the back and those who wear a belt should be in the front. That way, if the non-belters are catapulted up to the ceiling, they will fall on top of each other and break each other's necks, whereas the belters will be secured by their common belief in the belt. Also, people who feel kinda insecure or "meh," could be seated in-between and form a buffer zone.

"It is a trap! They will kill us all back there!" someone yells. A non-belter expecting poison gas to emerge from the air conditioning in the back.

"It is a trap! If they all are catapulted up and fall down, they will break the plane apart, killing us all!" someone else yells. A belter.

A fight breaks out, which mostly comprises people throwing cheap plane-yoghurt at each other. Unfortunately, a couple of passengers with dairy allergies get caught in the crossfire and are severely injured, which does not help to ease the situation. Thankfully, the onboard service soon runs out of yoghurt.

And then, suddenly, weirdly, as if this were a ban on public face coverings in Switzerland, the two opposing sides find something to agree on: it's all the pilots' fault. No matter which side you believe in, all points to the fact that the pilots were trying to kill everyone. The pilots have to go and things will pan out.

They build spears from plastic toothpicks (the non-gay attendant tries to stop them, but he is found drowned in orange-juice in the galley – an accident, most people agree) and set about to storm the cockpit. There are a couple of scientists sitting in First Class cautioning that by killing the pilots, they might achieve exactly what they fear would happen (i.e., everyone would die). However, a man with long, well-groomed hair tells them he feels that their scientific predictions are wrong, that the plane will not crash, and that everyone will be fine if they only believed in it. The scientists retort that his logic does not seem sound, but that his speech is emotional, heartfelt and, therefore, deserves recognition. Thus, they step aside.

We could all have flown somewhere, I thought to myself, sitting there, in the back, belt buckled. Together – sure, not close, and without ever talking to each other, still, as one group. One humanity – all of us thinking about the destination, about a better place to come, or maybe about genitalia. There was a speech there, somewhere, in my thoughts, something I could have said about how we should stand together, only I was lacking the right words and the courage to speak up, so I remained silent.

We all died that day. But not because the plane crashed. The plane did crash. But we were dead long before. It turned out, as they broke the cockpit open, that the pilot was god. And god was Alanis Morissette, the same age, and the same dress as in Dogma (sorry, Kevin, do not sue me). Everyone stumbled back in awe because of the sudden plot twist and she walked out of the cockpit, that beautiful smile on her face. Then, she started touching people's noses, and, once touched, they immediately died of cardiac arrest.

"Aren't you going to save at least some of them?" I asked her when she approached me (I was not talking about me specifically, even though I hoped she would put me in the save-category).

"No," she replied, her voice a choir of angelic voices.

"But some of them must have been right. Why punish them?"

"They only got it right because they were lucky."

"And what about good intentions?"

She smiled at me like an adult at a child. "One person's good intentions are another person's road to hell."

458 | ALEXANDER P. SIGRIST

"Should you not love all of them? Isn't that your job?"

"Nah. I am just one of you. Just a slob, a stranger."

"That doesn't even make any sense. It is just a cheap pop-culture reference."

"Look, you wanted to have everyone united," her voice sounded annoyed now, "so I am uniting you all by taking the bottom line. Bottom line is: You fucked up. You fucked up and will all die."

"Okay." I gave up.

She touched my nose. Her finger felt warm on the tip of my nose, which was nice. My body was quickly shaken, then my heart stopped, and I dropped to the floor. In my last moments, I could still see how she, with a smirk, touched her own nose and fell to the floor, too. And that was the end of that. The plane crashed, yet no one took much notice of it anymore. If you listened closely, you could hear Nietzsche laugh in the afterlife somewhere.

I remembered a time when I imagined life as a musical. Wouldn't that have been nicer? Instead of belters or non-belters or fly-deniers, someone could break out into a song about how they were excited to fly and arrive somewhere, something like the first scene of that movie with Gosling and Stone, set in a plane, mixed with Grease, all of us wearing petticoats and Travolta making a guest appearance (as the pilot, of course, because he is a pilot).

I wondered: was it still okay at this point to like Travolta? He was Scientology, no? So, maybe he should be on the boycott list. Shame, damn shame.

For me, the plane was going in the wrong direction, anyway. I was heading home. No musical ever began with a song about the excitement of going home after a holiday. "I am so excited about going home. I am so excited to return to my daily routine."

Fuck, I would have to clean the apartment tomorrow. Dust. Fucking dust everywhere after weeks of having been away.

I flipped through my notebook while the plane glided through the air, the endless humming of the engines a constant reminder of how much effort it took to keep the gigantic hunk of metal up here. The air conditioning was blasting air into the cabin, and it was getting cold. The seat next to me felt weirdly empty, and the thought of Alanis Morissette touching my nose seemed somehow comforting. I touched the tip of my nose. It was cold, and the nose felt runny, maybe a signal for the onset of a cold.

My handwriting looked terrible. If an illegible handwriting was a sign of character, I surely had loads. Loads of character. If I ever became a famous writer, good luck to the poor soul who would have to go through my notes after my death to find the last few handwritten texts that could be squeezed for the last bit of money.

Of course, it was much more likely that some poor soul would have to empty my apartment after my death, find the notebooks, glance at them, shrug and throw them away.

Why was I always thinking about death on planes? Was I the only one? Or did the other passengers have the same thoughts? Memento mori, fuckers, one day we will all be gone and terribly little will remain of us. Unless, of course, you were Shakespeare or Morrison or Goethe or any of those people. But even them – they would be forgotten eventually, right?

I had to think of Romeo and Juliet. What was it that made that story so undying? Love, of course, the fundamental feeling of love. And the tragedy. The against-all-odds, only to be crushed by the odds. The longing paired with the damned realisation that it all had been for naught. No one would remember the story of Romeo and Juliet if they both had awakened at the end and got up and had been happy. Fuck that, we do not want a happy ending. The best stories end with death and tears. That was why not a single rom-com ever made it on any best-movies-list ever.

Take Notting Hill: maybe someone would remember that sorry excuse for a movie if it hadn't ended on the typical schmaltz ending, boy finds girl, they live happily ever after, but if the movie had dared to make a bold choice in the end – kill everyone, tragedy, no happiness. I saw the alternate ending before me: Spike, who had been a maniac all along, would appear in the final moments of the film, trousers halfway around his ankles, knife in hand. Cut to the lovers kissing on the hill above Notting Hill and Spike, slash, slash, killing them with a swift, bloody stroke, a moment in movie history that would elevate the kitsch-movie to a masterpiece.

I checked the in-flight entertainment system. I felt like watching a rom-com, but all they had were those newer ones, from the noughties, those bland ones that had even less to say than those from the nineties.

I sighed. None of the movies was appealing. There was no attendant in sight with a food or drink trolley. Other people were watching movies. Sleeping. Just waiting for time to pass. I craved a glass of wine or a whiskey or a G&T.

I opened my seatbelt, got up, and started walking. Not toward the toilets, which were behind me, but in the other direction, down the gangway, just to get a few steps in, stretch my legs.

Walking past people. Rows and rows of them.

The end of the gangway seemed to disappear in the distance, the plane stretching in front of me, reminding me of an object entering a black hole. I continued to walk. I walked past a family. The parents maybe my age, good-looking parents, she a redhead with a braid and he a hulky beard-carrier, sitting at either end of a four-seat row. Their two kids (twins?) sleeping cuddled up in the middle seats. She looked at them and the husband and smiled. He did not notice, since he was watching the fifth episode of the second season of Breaking Bad, yet I was sure he would smile at her if he saw her.

I walked past a woman, younger than me, scribbling in a diary, wearing a Superman t-shirt. And even though she'd have said that she was wearing the S-logo because she liked the character and read some comics and had seen most of the films, she in fact was wearing it because within, she sometimes wished she could be that being, that Superman (or in her case -woman), achieving big things, saving some-thing and people would point to her when she flies by and see her. Truly see her.

I walked past a retired couple, and she was knitting, and he was reading a book on his kindle (a gift from his son) and they had little left to say to each other, after 45 years of marriage, it was mostly logistics. They were on their way to the son's funeral, who had died in a tragic accident (he was hit by a piano that fell off a crane, something that seemed quite funny when told as a story, yet was decidedly unfunny for the one who ended up under the piano). It was his son from an affair he'd had early into their marriage. He had decided that the woman from the affair was out of the picture, that they would take him in, and his wife agreed, and they never talked about it again. Now, on this plane, he would have wanted to ask her: "Have you actually loved him or despised him?" but actually he wanted to ask: "Have you actually forgiven me or despised me for all these years?" However, the two of them remained silent until the food trolley arrived, and the Steward asked them: "Meat or vegetarian?" and the man turned to his wife: "Meat or vegetarian?"

I walked past a woman who had killed a man when she'd been 21 and spent twenty years in prison for it, her features now softened, the youth-rage gone. I walked past a student who had just spent four weeks in a monastery, trying to get away from the bustle of normal life, I walked past someone reading a philosophy book, wishing he had time to write one, I walked past a person crying while watching the beginning of Pixar's Up, I walked past someone covering their insecurity with an unhealthy dose of playing-it-cool, I walked past a couple starting the same movie on their screens at the same time, so that they could watch it together, and there was a baby screaming, I walked quickly past that, I walked past a group of friends begging the attendant for an early round of baby-gin bottles and the attendant laughed and said she'd see what she could do, and I felt like a ghost amidst the people, me arriving at the galley at the other end, turning around and looking down the gangway I'd come from, spotting the two empty seats at the other end, one of them mine, and hearing a voice say:

"You can't stay here."

"I know," I replied.

"No, seriously, you gotta move out of the way." The voice belonged to the attendant with the drink trolley behind me.

"Oh, sorry," I mumbled.

"That's fine. I was afraid you are a sleepwalker."

"You get a lot of them on flights?"

"Sometimes. I had one once trying to get off the plane."

"How did you stop him?"

"I tased him."

"Seriously?"

"Nah, I woke him up." I wondered whether the saying was true that one shouldn't wake sleepwalkers.

"You are still in the way."

"Oh. Sorry."

"Take a drink," she said and gave me a baby-whiskey-bottle. "You look like you need one."

"Thanks," I said and took the bottle. I walked back to the back. The attendant arrived at my seat a little while later and inquired whether I had finished the whiskey. I confirmed, whereupon she gave me a new baby-whiskey and asked me whether she should add a coke to that. I confirmed again.

A little while later, the food arrived. I had not read the menu and no idea what was expecting me, I just took the meat option, whereupon the attendant handed me a tray and disappeared.

It turned out to be a beef stew (whereas the term beef was a stretch, it was more a couple of chewy, overcooked pieces of something) with mashed potatoes (potato soup with no seasoning) and two pieces of carrot (which were the best thing about the meal and made me regret not choosing the vegetarian option). Next to the plate, there was a small bowl with fruit salad (the saddest excuse for a dessert since the invention of the wheel, no relation between the wheel and desserts), a piece of butter and a little bread roll whose qualities of being tasteless and dry ran a close competition for being the worst thing about it. I put some butter onto the bread and spread it across and ate it, swallowing it with a generous serving of my whiskey-coke.

"Was it good?" the attendant would later ask me while taking my tray away and I would nod, because that were the rules, right? We all knew that the food on planes was shit and we knew that the alcohol on planes was cheap, still, we nodded, and we said thank you, thank you for doing your job and putting this tray of shit into the microwave for me and they'd smile back at you, for being nice about it. It was the equivalent to your kid's drawing you put up on the fridge, saying, excellent job, well-done, Henry-Luca, you will be an artist one day, positive affirmation, even though Henry-Luca's drawings look like a dog devoured colour and vomited it all over a piece of paper.

Of course, my cynical thoughts stemmed from the fact that I had not got enough positive affirmation when I'd been a child. I knew myself well enough to have no illusions about it – still, fuck positive affirmation.

The awful food had put me in a bad mood.

Fuck flying and fuck the attendants for smiling at us with their fake-smiles before hiding in the galley, laughing their asses off about the idiots taking the plane and eating the shit on the plane, while they are in the galley eating beautiful green apples with their beautiful white teeth that have been cleaned with the toothpaste that comes recommend by 9 out of 10 dentists. And fuck the last dentist, because he is a prick, Jim, the dentist, flunked dentist school and faked his diploma.

That was all the fucks I had to give.

I imagined the clouds around us. The plane gliding through a day that was turning into night. They'd taken away all trays, and the plane was slowly settling into sleeping mood. The couple a few rows in front had reached the final act of the horror movie they were watching together, his screen just a few tiny seconds behind hers, and I imagined her squeezing his hands at every jump-scare, just a few seconds before he'd see it on his screen and him now doomed to startle twice every time, once because of her sudden squeeze, and once because of the artificial scare on the screen.

Why watch horror movies? There were enough non-artificial things to be scared of. Sure, we'd lost most of our natural predators, we kept them in cages, us the kings and the tigers just super-sized drugged-up cats, yet we had created supreme new threats for us, like poverty and losing your job and climate change. We peddled Freud's death wish on a global scale now.

I felt like a hypocrite because I was. A man on a plane worrying about climate change. I was the one complaining about the burning chariot while driving said chariot down an alley of fire and blasting loud punk music.

Of course, the only way to protect the planet from myself would have been to remove myself from the planet. Maybe not the only way. But the fastest way.

But then... how much of an ecological impact did a decomposing body have? Would it be better to let it rot in the ground or burn it? And what would happen to all my things? All that plastic in my apartment, the figurines, the consoles, the TV, it would all go into the sea and kill the turtles, hundreds of them, baby-turtles choking on parts of my PS5, just because I died.

There we were again. Three hours into my flight from Tokyo to Frankfurt, I was thinking about death again.

It was the call of the void. The feeling people got when looking at the abyss, the feeling of wanting to jump. To meet death at the abyss's bottom. Death was the only certainty about life. Birth was the only other certainty. All in-between – a nihilist's wet dream.

There are lies, I whispered to no one in particular. And then, there are damn lies. The ones that destroy people. And then there are truths. Those truths we do not want to hear.

Like a motherfucking atom bomb dropped on a girl who just wanted to be an artist or a runner.

"Drink?" the flight attendant appeared next to me. Like a genie from a sitcom. "Well, I am empty," I replied. She handed me another baby-whiskey-bottle and a can of coke.

I turned on the entertainment system once more and browsed through the choice of movies — once more. I started watching a comedy about two guys travelling to the past in a phone booth, only to soon stop again. My ears hurt from the hours of wearing in-ear earphones, so I took them out. The noise of the engine and the chorus of breathing people instantly hit me. Some snoring in the distance. Some music being played way too loudly over someone's earphones.

"It has just been 2'000 miles of bad road, you know?"

I heard voices from the galley behind me. It sounded like that discussion you have with someone at two o'clock in the morning, just before falling asleep, all honesty, all mental defences lowered because your brain is too tired to fight.

"You lost your job, right?" the other voice said.

"Yeah. Over at X," she named a famous budget airline. "When they stopped all the flights, we were the first ones to go."

"Shit. I was lucky. They got us jobs at contact tracing."

"Yeah, did that for a while as well." I recognised the voice. It was my baby-whiskey-providing attendant. She was talking to one of her colleagues. The plane was sleeping. "It just came at a terrible time, the whole thing," my attendant continued.

"There is never really a suitable time for a pandemic, is there?"

"Guess not. But my girlfriend at the time – she'd got sick, and we were paying a lot for her treatment."

"No insurance?"

"Of course, we had insurance. It is mandatory. It is still fucking expensive. And she couldn't work, so no money there, either."

"I am sorry."

"Shit just kept piling up between the hospital and work and making sense of the bills, so many of them. And then, being an attendant is not an ideal job when your family is sick, is it?"

"Yeah. It was hard when my grandma died. A few years back. I was up here and kept thinking about down there all the time."

The whiskey-bearing attendant agreed.

"Is your girlfriend okay?" the second attendant asked.

"She is fine, I guess. If the tumour doesn't come back."

"You are not together anymore?"

"That's where the bad road stretched on. She had an affair with her nurse."

"Oh. Shit."

"Shit, indeed." She laughed a quick, dry laugh. "I think I could have dealt with it, you know, if she'd told me from the start. I knew she was bi. But she only told me once they were ready for a relationship. And for that to happen, she needed to leave me." There was a hint of anger in her voice, followed by resignation. "It was my fault, too. We argued a lot when she was sick. I kept yelling at her, even though I didn't want to. There was just no place for my emotions anywhere, so I kept... exploding. I wasn't a good friend to her."

"Still kinda shitty of her."

"It wasn't the best time in my life. She moved out, and I had no job, and the world was going crazy. All I had left was the stupid cat. Then, I lost her, too."

"What?"

"Yeah. One day, the police knocked on my door... with a bag and inside a dead cat and they asked me whether it was mine. It was. They'd found her on a road close to my house and someone told them I had a cat, so they figured they should check."

"Fuck. I am sorry."

"Thanks."

There was a moment of silence. I imagined her, the attendant, sitting there, on one of those silly fold-down chairs, staring into the distance, lost in all things past.

"You know, she looked miserable, that dead cat, there, in the bag. I remember her tiny, dead eyes," she continued after a while, "and all I could do is think about, you know... someone hit her with a car and drove off, right? Just disappeared. Sure, maybe that person did not notice. Happens, doesn't it? There is a bump, and you think nothing of it, and you drive home and soon forget the bump, and maybe there is a bit of blood on your bumper, only, it is dark when you come home and by the next morning, when you check your car, the rain has washed it away. And you do not know there is this woman whose cat you've killed, and that woman is now at home crying her eyes out because she has lost the last thing that felt okay about the world. You don't realise that you've almost killed her as well. Not the deadliest stroke, but the final one." The words are pouring out of her. It doesn't matter whether anyone is listening or not. "But then, maybe that person has seen her. Has seen my fucking cat run into the street like the idiot she was and yeah, accidents happen. Cats are fast. But that person didn't even stop. Didn't even have the decency of scrapping her body off the road and bring it to me. That person just rushed home and washed the bumper and forgot about it. Not a single second of consideration that I loved that fucking cat."

Silence.

I put my earphones back in and listened to music. Tripping with Nils Frahm by Nils Frahm. The flight attendant came by later, in the middle of the night, and handed me another baby-whiskey. She smiled at me, and I smiled back.

The lights came on a few hours later, people opened the blinds in front of the windows. The sun came in. We were all tired, had dirt in the corner of our eyes, our tongues sticky and smelly.

"Good morning, ladies and gentlemen," the pilot soon announced over the loudspeakers, informing us we would land, as scheduled, in Frankfurt, in two hours. Time for breakfast. Coffee. Time was out of joint. I'd had my last whiskey a couple of hours ago. Time to sober up.

I took out my notebook one last time on this trip, looking across the words. I crossed out one word in the last sentence. And replaced the word "they" with a "she."

It now read: *She* finds Olivia at the water's edge later. Lucy sitting there, gazing into the distance.

Then, I added:

Olivia gets up, startled by the noise she has made. Her eyes puffy and red. "I am sorry," she says. "I am so sorry." Drops the crutches. Hugs Olivia.

And – is that a better ending?

My Friend's Wedding

It was half an hour into my flight from Munich to Cork that I realised I'd left my tie at home.

The previous night, when lying in bed, I'd had the same realisation. That I had forgotten to pack it, whereupon I jumped out of bed and got it from the wardrobe. Unfortunately, I'd been too lazy to open the suitcase right then and there to put it in. Instead, I hung the tie on the doorknob of the door to my apartment. Surely, I would see it in the morning when I would leave and could pack it then.

Of course, I didn't. It was still hanging on my doorknob.

No big deal. You can get a tie anywhere. And it always fits. No need to worry about the oversized belly when you get a tie.

But then. I liked the tie I had prepared. It was a nice, narrow black tie. Almost Pulp Fictional. I thought it made me look cool. Like someone you'd want to dance with.

I'd find one. Andy would know where to find one. There was still time tomorrow to go shopping. The wedding would only take place the day after. We were planning on checking out some record shops, anyway. There was time to add some tie-shopping. "We absolutely have to go to Doolin," Andy had told me when we skyped a few weeks ago. "They have an incredible jazz and folk scene there."

Before my trip, I wanted to read up on the place, to at least have some preparation, but I'd run out of time, between finishing work and watching the sixth season of Stranger Things.

"Something to drink?" the flight attendant approached me.

"A beer," I replied.

"Sorry, we do not serve alcohol on short distance flights."

"A coke then." Brave new world. Maybe it was a good thing. Alcohol was not good for you anyway, I thought, knowing full-well that we would get drunk at a pub tonight.

"Here you go," she said and handed me a plastic cup. "Enjoy the rest of the flight."

Enjoy the rest of the flight. I had heard of people who actually enjoyed flying. Then, there were also people who enjoyed getting tied up and be whipped with a bamboo stick. The passenger next to me – a tall, muscular Irish-looking fellow – was snoring loudly. He'd hogged the armrest, but since he looked like he had had a tough night and needed the sleep, I let him be, even if that meant sitting there T-Rex style with my arms pressed into my sides.

Maybe I should cuddle up to him, put my arm around his arm and put my head on his shoulder and he'd wake up, look at me sleepily, pat my head and then fall asleep again. When the plane would have arrived, we'd go and have a beer together, while he waits to get picked up by his wife, and I would wait for Andy (because, somehow, the plane went through a black hole and had arrived two hours early). Then, having finished the beers and our rides having arrived, we would bid each other farewell. After his leaving, however, I would realise that he hadn't paid for his beer and that I'd have to foot the tap. Fucking asshole.

"Ladies and gentlemen, this is the captain speaking. We have begun our descend and will land in Cork in 20 minutes. Which is ten minutes before our scheduled arrival. The weather..." The good thing about short-distance flights was that they were short.

I leaned forward to catch a glimpse out of the tiny plane window. Only the sky and the sea, washing into each other, some clouds. The tall, muscular Irish-looking dude next to me woke with a sudden movement, taking a sharp breath. He looked at me with post-sleep bewilderment. "Sorry," I said and sat back again in my seat. I wasn't sure what exactly I had apologised for, and he did not reply, closed his eyes again immediately. I felt a sting of dislike for him for stiffing me on that beer in my imagination.

We landed in Cork a few minutes later. There was no gangway, and we had to wait for them to bring up the stairs. From there, we walked across the tarmac into the tiniest airport I'd ever seen, straight into the hall with the conveyor belt for the luggage.

I waited for my suitcase (which had no tie inside, I remembered with an unreasonable amount of guilt) and, after, made my way into the arrival hall. There wasn't even a passport check, and I felt silly for having taken both my ID and passport with me. Yet, I always did when travelling.

"Brings twenty documents of identification, but can't even bring a tie to a wedding," I whispered wordlessly to myself.

Andy was standing at the other end of the arrival hall. He waved when he saw me, and I waved back. I passed a group of people with a big, handwritten sign ("Welcome back!"), balloons and big smiles on their faces.

"How was the flight?" Andy asked me when I got closer.

"Not short enough," I replied, and we hugged, telling each other how good it was to meet again. Behind us, the group with the balloons cheered, and we both turned around to look. The people had congregated around a young man, maybe in his early twenties, cheeks blushed and tears in his eyes. They took turns hugging him.

"That's some welcome," Andy said.

"Yeah. I was expecting something similar, but it's just you." We both laughed and fell silent, continuing to watch the scene in the middle of the hall.

"I wonder where he's been," Andy said.

"Somewhere on this planet, I guess."

"Unless he's an astronaut."

I imagined the young man, who was now being hugged by two women his age, tears openly streaming down his face, all happy tears and smiles and laughter, in a space station rotating around the planet, listening to David Bowie, all by himself, always looking out of the window when they passed Ireland, his green island, his home, so far away.

"Did you know that the last time everyone was on Earth was in the year 2000?" I asked.

"Hmm?"

"Ever since then, there have been people on the International Space Station."

"Really?"

We left the airport and entered Andy's Volkswagen rental, most likely the tiniest car that had ever been built. "It is almost as spacious as the airplane," I said, not even trying to make it sound like a joke.

We quickly left Cork behind us, drove out into the countryside. The road led along trees and meadows and houses. We crawled up a hill and the road now seemed barely wide enough to allow two cars to pass each other. I felt glad that Andy had rented a small car.

"We are almost in Doolin," Andy told me. The view widened, and we spotted the sea to our left. It felt like entering a Nolan movie, the camera showing a wide-angle shot of an alien planet, an endless vastness, the sea in full view now. It was grey, overcast, and the waves, looking tiny from our vantage point in the car on the hill, rolled back and forth, turning into dramatic looking white gushes when they broke. "It's a beautiful place," Andy said. "Unfortunately, I'll be heading up to Galway already tonight. There has been a problem with the flower delivery, nothing major, but I'll need to figure it out. Hamako will pick you up at the B&B and have dinner with you."

I felt bad for getting all the attention from them just a few days before their wedding.

"You nervous?"

"Yeah. And stressed out. But then, we are getting married in a castle in Ireland. That's worth a bit of effort. Fucking privileged, that's what we are," he said and laughed.

He dropped me off in front of my bed-and-breakfast and apologised for not having time to help me check-in or have a beer. He would have to leave for Galway right away. The drive had taken longer than expected, thanks to a flock of sheep blocking the road. Ireland was presenting itself from its most stereotypical angle.

"And now I gotta pass those fucking sheep again," Andy said, and drove off.

An older lady (how came all Irish B&B seemed to be run by past-middle-aged women?) welcomed me and led me inside. She pointed to a living room with some tables on the right, informing me in a cheerful tone that was where I could "hang out" (apparently, she'd studied her youth-lingo from a book from the nineties) and also where she would serve breakfast tomorrow at nine *on the dot.* She brought me upstairs, up a small and creaky staircase, opened a heavy wooden door and we arrived in a room with thick, grey carpet floors and a bed overstuffed with pillows of varying sizes.

"This is your room." Yeah, I wasn't assuming you were showing me someone else's room, thanks. I thanked her, and she left me alone and the door open, which I promptly closed.

The room seemed smaller than it was, thanks to the heavy carpet and the oversized bed. And the heavy curtains. It was like living in your grandmother's dollhouse, those kinds of dollhouses you'd have wanted to play with as a kid, yet had not been allowed to touch because your grandmother had designated them decorative items, not toys.

I took a shower, got changed, took the famous after-plane dump (come on, we all do it), tried to connect to the Wi-Fi unsuccessfully and then *hung out* in the living/breakfast room on a sofa with a book, a retelling of stories from Norse Mythology by Neil Gaiman. Even though I was not quite in the right location, I had felt that the theme fit my trip to Ireland and had bought the book at the airport before leaving. Also, it had been on sale. Looked like Neil had passed his peak of popularity.

A heavy, loudly ticking standing clock informed me it was three in the afternoon. Hamako would meet me in an hour. Comfortable time for some comfortable reading.

I was about to open my book when the old lady entered the room to ask if I wanted tea. Yes, I wanted tea, thank you.

I scarcely had read the first page when she put a cup down on the coffee table in front of me and sat down on the couch opposite.

I half-closed my book, keeping my finger on the page I'd been reading (the international sign for "I am going to continue reading in a second"), leaned forward, took a sip, burned my upper lip ("careful, it is hot," she informed me after the incident) and leaned back again to return to my reading. "Thank you," I said, smiled at her and slowly opened my book again.

Then she began speaking. My book a half-opened useless artifact in my hand.

She told me about her dead husband, who'd been a successful fisherman when she'd met him, he had owned his own boat, until he steered it onto some cliffs, where it got stuck and sank. Actually, it didn't sink completely, and the boat's skeleton was still stuck on the cliffs to this day. "You can see it when it is low tide," she said. Next, her husband opened a pub together with his brother, until they got into a fistfight one night over a simple disagreement, which had been aggravated by the alcohol in their blood, and the brothers never spoke again. "We moved here then," she said and smiled. "I always liked Doolin." She opened a B&B, and he used to help out in town, building stuff or transporting stuff, wherever or whenever he was needed for some handiwork.

Then he died. "Cancer of the pancreas," she told me. "I am sorry," I said, just because I didn't really know what else to say. Her speech continued, covering a selection of her relatives, some of them dead, some of them alive, and then continuing to the best baker in town and the pub I should absolutely visit while I was here (plus an additional list of pubs I should avoid for some unclear reason). She continued to the story of her dog Toto ("Oh, is he named after the Wizard of Oz?" I asked, but she did not know what I was talking about) who'd been her faithful companion for many years.

"Where is he?" I asked.

She pointed to the mantelpiece on my right, her left. A stuffed dog, a black version of Tintin's Snowy, staring at us from the uppermost shelf.

"He died last summer," she said and sighed. I took another sip of the tea. "Have you been thinking about getting a new one?" I said, looking at the dead dog looking at me.

"I am getting too old for a dog," she replied, took a deep breath, most likely preparing for the next slew of words, only to be stopped by the harsh ringing of a mechanical doorbell.

"That's for me," I said and jumped up. I could see Hamako's shape through the refracted glass of the house's door. The lady had got up, too, and was following me (I half-expected stuffed Toto to jump off the shelf and come running up behind her as well), but I quickly opened the door, pushed Hamako aside to get out, yelled a "good evening" at the lady behind me in the hallway and closed the door.

Hamako stood in front of me.

"Hi," she said.

"Hi," I said. "Let's get out of here."

"I see you met Mrs McCaway. We knew you'd enjoy speaking with her. That's why we got you a room here."

"Fuck off."

We walked down the road next to each other, towards some houses in the distance, her filling me in about the details of life since we'd last seen each other ("Don't you miss Osaka?" I asked her, thinking about the bright city lights, the food, the noise, the people. "I do, sometimes," she replied, "but I like it here. It is certainly a change of pace."), about Andy's new job at an IT start-up that looked promising ("Once it gets going, he can work from anywhere in the world anyway.") and her first exhibition at a local gallery ("I sold some art to a rich guy in the U.S. Crazy, isn't it?"). Then, she showed me pictures of their house (a beautiful rock mansion somewhere out in the countryside of Claire County), pictures of their neighbour's dogs, who would run into their yard and play fetch with her, followed by photos of their trips and food they'd eaten along the way.

"And you? How have you been keeping?" she asked me as we entered a pub. I wondered whether it had been on Mrs McCaway's go or no-go list.

SOME OF US ARE REAL | 475

"Ah, you know me, fine." We sat down at a table in the middle of the pub and the man behind the bar nodded at us. Next to him, there was a young woman, maybe his daughter, pulling beers from the tap.

"That's an exhaustive answer," she joked. "Come on, tell me something. What's happening?"

"Hmm, still have my job. Still working on my novel. Saving money for my next trip."

"And?"

"And?"

"Are we going to be invited to your wedding soon?"

"I'll let you know what the missus thinks. Wait, I am still single."

"No one in sight?" I thought about the mysterious laws of attraction, the odds of falling in love with someone who loved you back, the chance encounters and the sheer luck it took for something as silly as a relationship to work out.

"No. No one. The girl behind the bar looks nice, though," I said and smirked.

As if she'd heard my words, the girl stepped out from behind the counter to come and take our order, two pints of Guinness and two plates of Irish stew.

"No flirting?" Hamako said when the girl left.

"No. She is too young for me."

"Said no man ever."

"I just did. I am getting old, man," I tried to sound casual, like a joke, not letting her on too much that I really felt like I was getting... old.

"Everything below forty is young for a man."

"Tell that to my back."

"At least you don't have that pesky clock ticking away."

"Who wants to be a father when he is fifty?"

"My father was. He was cool. You'd be a cool father."

When had we reached the age of talking about kids during a casual dinner with friends? What would be next, taxes? The car we were going to buy? The money we were saving for a house? The five top things a man could do against hair loss?

Was I losing my hair?

"You and Andy, you wanna have kids?"

There was a pause. It was hard to read the expression on her face. "Eventually," she replied. "We got time."

The girl from behind the bar put down the two pints in front of us. The dark beer still looked milky. "Wait for it to settle," Hamako told me. "Until it is completely dark."

"You did your homework."

"I watched a video tutorial on how-to-drink-Guinness."

We looked at the milky sediment in the glass slowly settling, the beer gradually turning darker.

"Early into our relationship...," Hamako said after a while, only to stop mid-sentence.

"What?" I asked.

"I got pregnant some time after Andy moved to Japan."

"Did you...?"

"I lost it. Early. A few weeks into the pregnancy. We haven't really tried since. Didn't feel like right."

"I am sorry," I replied.

"It is pretty common, did you know that? 30 to 40 per cent of women miscarry in the first weeks."

"I did not know that."

"Now you do," she said, "we all should know that." She looked up and smiled at me, raised her glass and we cheered and drank.

"Like drinking cold soup," she said.

Not much later, while we were working on our second pint to wash down the delicious heaviness of the Irish stew, a couple of older Irish men came in, sat down and started playing instruments – a guitar and a violin, and the pub filled up with more people.

There was an English patron there, obviously drunk, obnoxiously loud, and I feared that his behaviour might lead to a disagreement between him and a group of Irish blokes who gave their best at catching up with his state of drunkenness and loudness. They, the Irish blokes and the English drunk, came uncomfortably close to each other at one point, voices were raised, slurs of unintelligible English words coming out of their mouths, something that sounded like an argument-and-fistfight could erupt at any second. Thankfully, their words soon turned into friendly banter, as the English man ordered five pints of beer for the Irish. Five pints of beer. That was all it took to do more for international relations between the English and the Irish than many political leaders had achieved in the past decades.

Hamako smiled at me. She seemed like a fish out of water at that wooden table in that pub somewhere at the seaside in Ireland. She looked at the space in the middle of the pub, where they had moved aside tables and chairs to dance, people now swirling to the rhythm and liveliness of the music, the Irish jigs and jingles.

"I wanna dance," she said.

"I am not stopping you," I said.

"No," she replied, "I want you to dance with me." Talk about a fish out of water.

"Machete don't dance," I replied. Sounding-oh-so-cool. Not.

Before I could say anything else, she took my hand, pulled me up and over to the dancing people. I could feel blood rushing to my face, but also excitement, then the abyss of not knowing what to do with my feet and my hands, until Hamako took my one hand in hers and put the other on the small of her back.

"Just follow my lead," she said. Thus, we danced. Me, awkwardly, trying to keep up with Hamako's light-footed feet, not trying to lose the grip on her hand without gripping too hard and hoping that my palms wouldn't get too sweaty.

The band switched to a slow, romantic song, which was either co-incidence or the Irish musicians had mistaken us for a couple. It was a gentle ballad of some Lady of the Sea and a Hero, the two of them in love, alas, the love, of course, unfulfilled. Hamako drew closer, and we turned to the flow of the music. She felt warm. I was warm. It was warm inside the pub.

"I am scared," she finally said, her head against my shoulder.

"The wedding?"

"Life," she said. She was silent for a long time. The song reached its dramatic climax, the hero jumping into the sea to be with his lady. Hamako continued: "Have you ever had that feeling that something is wrong? As if you've taken a wrong turn somewhere?"

"My life is a constant wrong turn," I joked, but added seriously: "I know what you mean."

"I just wanna run sometimes. Start fresh just to make sure I haven't missed anything."

A reboot. Difficult. That's what I thought. Didn't say it.

"I am happy. I love Andy. I am excited we're getting married. But... also constantly second-guessing. Is this what it is? Is this what my life should look like?" She sighed. "Am I a bad person?" The song went on to tell the listeners how the lovers turned into seagulls, transformed by the grace of a god and now, were travelling the seas together. A long and tear-jerking instrumental melody followed the last part of the story.

"No, of course you're not a bad person. It is normal to be afraid, no? To have doubts. It's the fucking chaos of being real." I wasn't really talking to her. I was talking to myself. I wanted to hold her. I wanted to run away with her. I wanted to burn down the planet with her. "I am just a coward," she said. "No," I answered, "you are the opposite. You decided on something. You are getting married. You are trying to be happy. I never had that courage. I was always so afraid I'd miss something, so I did nothing instead."

The song ended. We clapped and walked back to our tables.

"You did a lot. Sometimes I wish I did what you did. Travel the world on my own. Figure things out on my own. Be my own woman," she said and took a sip of her beer.

"We can swap for a while if you want to," I said and smiled. "Even though that would mean I'd have to marry Andy. I wouldn't fit in your dress. No way." She laughed. I liked that.

I dropped her off a little while later at her hotel and walked back to my bed-and-breakfast. The moon stood full and in silver above the sea, her distorted mirror image in the waves below. I had to think about the

two seagulls from the song, allowed to be together by a divine inter-
vention. Deus ex machina. Lucky them. I wondered how many unhappy stories remained untold, those stories of poor suckers that were
not saved by some higher power, whose love stories were not amazing
enough for the gods to come down from their heavenly thrones.

I was given a note by Mrs McCaway the next morning at breakfast.
Before I could read it, she'd started telling me the story of a sick stray
cat she'd taken in when she'd been twenty. Whiskers. She nursed her
back to health, only to see her crushed by a truck (What the fuck, lady,
I am eating breakfast!). This was followed by the story of how her son
one day fell off the very table I was sitting at (why had he been standing
on there? We will never know.) and almost bit off his tongue (at least
he did not die – or did he?).

"Excuse me," I said and finally opened the note. "Your friend
dropped it off," she informed me.

The note was from Hamako (why wouldn't she send me a text?).

It read:

*Hey, Andy informed me he found replacement flowers (yay!). However,
now, the caterer cancelled on short notice (he broke a leg). Luckily, he has got
us a replacement. Wanna try his food, though. Hope it is good. I hate wed-
dings. Never gonna do that again. I've already left for Galway to meet with
the caterer. Didn't want to wake you.*

XX

PS. Broke my phone. Hence the note.

*PPS. There is a bus leaving tomorrow at 11am to get you into Galway. You
will be fine. You are a seasoned traveller. You are your own man.*

PPPS. Go to the beach today and read your book.

I folded the note and put it back into the envelope. I looked up and
saw the big, smiling face of Mrs McCaway in front of me.

"Good news?"

"No," I replied. "My friend's pet monkey died."

"Oh, I am so sorry to hear that. My cousin actually used to have a little pet rabbit, but her father cooked it into a stew when she was eleven. She was sad for weeks."

"How do I get to the beach?"

I soon left the house and Mrs McCaway behind to hide out for the rest of the day at the beach, reading Gaiman's interpretation of Norse mythology. Entertaining enough. I stepped into a pub for lunch and, later, into the same pub for dinner. Back at the B&B after dinner, Mrs McCaway welcomed me and started telling me about some kind of seagull menace. I escaped before we reached the end of the story by excusing myself and going to bed.

The next morning, after another long-winded McCaway-speech at breakfast, I found myself, hand-luggage-sized suitcase in hand, at the bus station waiting for the greyhound bus. Not long later, the bus (it was indeed grey, alas, not being pulled by hounds) pulled around the corner down the road and approached me.

Me and the suitcase – I suddenly remembered with a pang that there was still no tie inside... I would have to remember to buy one in Galway – entered the bus, which turned out to be almost empty. There was a woman, younger than me, sitting almost all the way in the front, half asleep, listening to music. There was a young family with two tiny children, both of them, thankfully, asleep, there was a couple of middle-aged women excitedly whispering to each other. I walked past all of them and sat in the second last row. It is where the cool kids hang out. At the back of the bus. I was alone back there.

I didn't feel particularly cool when the bus picked up speed. Ireland zoomed by way faster than it should have. It felt like a road trip to hell, the bus rumbling across narrow streets at a terrifying tempo, breaking suddenly and sharply, taking tight corners. I wondered how the two small children in front of me could sleep and not fear for their young lives.

Despite my cold sweats and regular swells of panic, we arrived in Galway unscathed, alive. I felt like getting out and kissing the ground, like the Pope, I didn't, of course, because that would have been disgusting. Did someone clean the floor and disinfect it before the Pope arrived somewhere?

Galway turned out to be a peaceful, small city, modern and industrial on the outside, but with a tiny, little centre of old, colourful houses and pubs. Unfortunately, no tie store, or at least none I could find before my time ran out, and I had to return to the bus station for my next bus trip to a smaller village in the Connemara region, where the wedding would take place.

Maybe there was one in that village. Surely, there must be some shops around, I thought.

Spoiler: there were none.

There was literally nothing close to the location of the wedding. It took place in a mansion, a castle almost, which stood peacefully at a lake, all by itself. The bus dropped me off somewhat down the road and I had to walk the last twenty minutes to the house, sweat, as usual, dripping down my forehead. I hadn't kept up with my promise to get in shape.

There were a few cars (including Andy's tiny rental) parked outside the mansion and a big bus, a sleeker, more modern cousin of my greyhound. It was for the guests staying at a hotel in Galway. Hamako had told me that most guests would be driven back after the party, but I'd been one of the selected few who'd got a room in the mansion. Only downside was, the building had no central heating, and it could get quite cold in the rooms at night. I had brought a big, thick jumper for that. No tie, though.

I entered the mansion, and a stern-looking woman with a clipboard greeted me, demanding my name.

"You are in room 47," she informed me, handing me a floor map of the mansion. "East wing, all the way up. In the tower."

I thanked her and followed the map. People were buzzing about the place, putting up flowers and decorations, moving furniture around. I couldn't spot anyone I knew. How many people were working for this wedding? Why did everyone look so serious? Why was putting on a wedding such serious business?

A welcome folder lay on the bed in my room and gave me details on the schedule for later today and tonight. There was a welcome reception planned for three, followed by the ceremony at five, which would take place outside, at the lake, then dinner at seven and open-end from ten onwards.

I checked my watch. I had a couple of hours to get ready. I put on my suit, the nice shoes (I should have cleaned them before I left), the white shirt. I looked nice. The tie was missing, though. I could have looked so much better.

I wandered around the mansion, hoping to find Andy and ask him whether he had a spare tie. Or anyone else I knew. I tried to remember the people Hamako and Andy had introduced me to in the past. Occasionally, on my wanderings through the halls, the stern-looking woman with the clipboard would appear next to me – the wedding planner? – and would send me out of the way. "There are flowers/boxes/plates/glasses/elephants coming through here," she'd tell me, "you gotta go somewhere else."

I should have asked her for a tie, but I was afraid of talking to her. So it came that I was still not wearing a tie at three when the welcome reception started in the garden behind the mansion. Hamako and Andy hugged me and welcomed me, and I tried to say something, one last attempt to ask for a tie or apologise for not wearing one, but they were gliding across the lawn, greeting people, smiling, looking good, and I didn't want to interrupt them. I talked to Hamako's aunt for a bit, who was sitting heavily at one of the round tables (she was a big lady), trying to cool her face with a hand fan. "This climate is not for me," she said, "it's the sun," she added, "it's much more aggressive here." I resisted the urge to tell her it was the same sun as everywhere else. She told me that, before her retirement, she'd been a professor for insects, so we talked about the topic for a bit, how scientists were still discovering new insects. "And we always think we know everything," she said and laughed and furiously waved her fan.

I walked around after, talked with groups here and there, introduced myself. I watched a couple of smokers disappearing around a corner to an ashtray hidden between two ferns and regretted the fact that I had stopped smoking. Maybe I should ask one of them for a cig. But then, maybe I shouldn't. Maybe later.

I stood on the lawn and looked at the mansion. It was an extensive building, beautifully built, towering over our heads, a serious structure, the architectural equivalent to the lady with the clipboard. Atop the stairs leading down to the lawn, there stood a woman in a black dress, a champagne glass in her hand, observing the people below. Our eyes did not meet.

The ceremony took place with the lake as a backdrop, a beautiful image that looked like something from a wedding-catalogue. Well done, clipboard lady. Apparently, me and Hamako's aunt were friends now, so I was sitting next to her.

Some people in the audience were sniffling and reaching for hand-kerchiefs when Hamako walked down the aisle. Somehow, she and her perfect smile reminded me of a flight attendant, albeit one in a wedding dress, not an especially useful attire on a plane. Andy was standing in the front in a serious-looking suit, his boyish smile across his face reminding me of the Cheshire Cat.

I wondered how it felt standing there. Demonstrating your love to a group of seventy-five people, officially showing that you were serious enough about each other to make a public display of it.

I spotted the woman in the black dress, sitting in front of me. She was still sipping from her champagne glass, which apparently she'd smuggled in from the welcome reception. Smart move.

We continued along the schedule after the ceremony, all of us congratulated and hugged the newlyweds, before heading inside for dinner, which was an adventurous assemblage of different cuisines and flavours, mixing the tastes of the hearty, heavy, earthy Irish cuisine with the more delicate essence of Japanese dishes (who'd have known that mashed potatoes and raw fish could work together?). Andy later told me, when we were sitting in front of the mansion for a few moments of quiet, that it'd been a lucky stroke that the caterer cancelled. The new caterer had been amazing. Andy passed me the caterer's card just in case I'd end up organising a wedding in Ireland at some point in my life.

"And, you met anyone interesting at the wedding?" Andy asked.

"I talked to some people," I responded.

"No, dude, there are singles around. Have you met any?"

"Hmhm," I responded vaguely.

"Actually, we wanted to introduce you to someone," Andy said, and jumped up. "It's a fascinating story. We both came through the same adoption agency." He did not offer any further explanation and darted off before I could ask. I followed him back inside, now people milling about everywhere, the big main hall overtaken by loud 90's music and dancing couples. Before we could find whoever he wanted to introduce me to, he got side-tracked by someone who wanted to take a selfie with him and Hamako. "Sorry," he said to me, "I'll be back with you in a second." He wasn't, though. People lined up to take photos with the couple. I didn't want to hog Andy, so I stepped away and wandered the castle on my own again.

I watched the dancing people from the gallery circling the main hall. I spotted the woman in the black dress without looking for her. She was there, in the middle of the hall, dancing with no one in particular, now holding a glass of Dark and Stormy.

We sent the newlyweds off around three in the morning. I went to my room up in the west wing (or was it the east wing?) and slept, waking up sometime before nine.

Hamako and Andy were already at the breakfast table, talking to Hamako's aunt, when I came down.

"Hey sleepy-head," Hamako said when I appeared. Someone put a plate of scrambled eggs and toast in front of me. They looked tired, I thought, but happy. I just looked tired.

We exchanged the usual morning pleasantries while I poured a cup of coffee from the jug on the table. It turned out to be dark and bitter water that had little in common with real coffee. I did not comment on it, though. Didn't want to kill the mood.

Andy asked me what I'd do next, and I told him I had taken a few days off and would go back to Galway and then maybe head north, visit the coast. Then, back to work on Wednesday.

Andy and Hamako would go to Japan in a couple of days to visit her family, the ones that could not make it to the wedding.

I looked around the dining room and half-expected to spot the woman in the black dress standing somewhere, cradling a glass of something alcoholic. She was nowhere to be seen, though.

The Ghosts of Other People

I stood at Downpatrick Head, wind tearing at my clothes. The cliff went straight down in front of me, straight into the sea. There was a pillar of land a few meters out. Centuries of waves had eaten away at it, until it broke off, now a towering island out of reach.

There were some other people milling about, getting much too close to the edge of the cliff, lying on their bellies, pushing their bodies closer and closer and over the edge. A young girl took a selfie lying on her back, the abyss behind her head. The wind snatched the phone from her fingers, and she shrieked. The phone disappeared in the waves below. For a moment, she looked like she was about to jump after it.

I walked away from the cliff, across a meadow which was littered with rocks, back to the parking lot and into the car. My fingers had got cold, so I started the engine and turned up the heating, holding my stiff fingers against the medium-warm air coming out of the air conditioner.

After a moment, I took my guidebook and looked at the map of Ireland. I was planning on heading north. I slid my finger across the map, following tiny roads, past Donegal and Ballybofey and Letterkenny. Dunfanaghy. I did not even know how to pronounce that. That was where I was headed. I didn't even know why. The name looked nice on the map.

I picked up a hitchhiker along the road. Mario, a backpacking Italian, smelling like he'd been out in the wilderness for weeks, a mix of smoke and sweat and weed. He was thankful to me for picking him up and asked me to drop him off at a place close to Letterkenny, some famous place in the middle of nowhere.

"Famous?" I asked.

"Well, if you know the right people," he replied in English with a thick Italian accent. I was kinda disappointed that he did not use his hands more feverishly when he talked. "It's an outdoor rave. The biggest full moon rave in the Northern hemisphere."

"Is that so?" I said. Hard to believe.

"Yeah. Hey, you should come," he said. I declined almost immediately. I was too old for that shit. I'd been at an outdoor rave once when I'd just turned eighteen. I'd been too old for it back then already.

We drove on, approaching Letterkenny. He looked at the forest we drove past, as if he was looking for a specific tree, when, suddenly, he told me to drop him off "right here." "Here?" I asked, and he affirmed. "You sure you are in the right place?" I wondered, watching him step out of the car. The sky was grey and overcast and it had started to drizzle (or had it ever stopped?).

"Positive," he said, putting the hood of his raincoat up. He looked like a character from the TV series Dark. He passed me a piece of paper through the open passenger window. "My phone number. If you wanna party," he said. "Thanks, I appreciate it," I replied. I really did, yet I doubted I'd ever see him again.

Dunfanaghy turned out to be a small town close to the sea past its picture book times. The houses were colourful, standing there in rows after rows, reminding me of Irish postcards, yet the colours had faded, and half the houses had for-sale-signs mounted on their walls. I remembered that the economic crisis of 2007 had hit Ireland hard. Many places never recovered. This town was about to close and wither away.

I parked my car outside a restaurant (the Oyster Bar, but the Y had fallen off, so O-ster bar) and stepped through the door. A burly Irish bloke working behind the counter greeted me. I sat down and ordered a beer and a basket of fries. To my disappointment, they were not selling oysters. According to the burly Irish bloke, the sea close to the village had been over-fished, and all fishermen had moved away or changed professions. "Now, there is no fishing happening here. I would have to import oysters, but who wants to eat imported oysters?" he told me. I resisted the urge to tell him that one did not *fish* for oysters, but *dived* for them. "It is why we have taken the Y down," he continued, "it's the Oster bar now, because we have no fucking oysters." "Like the German word for Easter?" I asked. "The what now?" he said, "no, Oster was my granduncle. The bar is now named after him. Never liked the prick, though."

This was where our conversation dried up. I should have asked him for a picture of his granduncle Oster, just to make sure he had not been an oyster in disguise.

He recommended a bed-and-breakfast a kilometre down the road, situated right at the sea. I finished my meal and beer, paid my bill. Leaving the bar, I bumped into a person entering the establishment. It wasn't a dramatic bump, only our shoulders touched, no one fell to the floor. I quickly apologised and stepped outside. The person had seemed vaguely familiar, but I didn't stop to think about it.

I drove out of town in the general direction the Oster-owner had pointed me in and found a lonely house atop a hill, a vantage point offering a beautiful view of the sea. A sign outside informed me that there were rooms for rent here and breakfast as well.

Helen, as the owner introduced herself moments later, greeted me the moment I stepped out of the car. Apparently, she'd heard me parking and came outside to see who was coming. She seemed younger than the average B&B owner, maybe in her mid-forties, had a gentle, peaceful smile and welcomed me into the house.

"You are lucky. It is rather quiet at the moment," she told me, leading me to my room, her little dog, Archie, following her diligently. "Usually, we're fully booked, especially in summer. But now, I only have one other room occupied."

The wind outside had picked up considerably. The windows of the old house were rattling against their hinges. "There's going to be a storm tonight," Helen told me and asked whether I wanted to extend bed-and-breakfast to bed, breakfast and dinner. "I wouldn't head into town if I were you. There will be lots of rain. And I have enough food around to cook." I accepted the offer, silently wondering whether the other guest would join us as well.

I went for a walk on the beach, the sandy, salty wind on my lips, tearing at my hair. It had got longer than usual and quite shaggy, which made me feel like a rockstar, standing on the beach, looking out at the rolling waves.

This was when the rain set in. It came without a warning, no slow start, no single drops falling first, only an immediate downpour. I ran back to the house, drenched within seconds.

Helen was expecting me, standing under the roof of her back porch, handing me a towel. Archie was standing next to her, looking fiercely at the storm, as if he were about to run out and chase it away.

"Are you a vegetarian?" she asked me as we stepped inside.

"No. I eat everything," I replied.

"Good. Makes my job easier," she replied with a smile and told me to get changed and then help myself to a drink in the living room. I liked getting orders if it involved helping myself to a drink.

Only moments later, I was sipping whiskey from a heavy tumbler. I didn't recognise the brand, yet the taste was quite extraordinary, bringing together saltiness, caramel, and a heavy pang of scorched earth. Helen sat down on the sofa opposite me.

"That's the life," I said and smiled. She nodded and told me that the Shepherd's Pie would be ready in an hour. We'd have salad with grilled stripes of salmon first and, for dessert, Irish shortbread.

"Are you going to have a glass of wine with me?"

"Sure," I replied.

"I've been saving this one up for a while," she told me as we sat down at the dining table, her opening the bottle of wine. "It's actually from an Irish vineyard," she added. "Close to Cork."

"Are you sure you want to open it for me?"

"Yes. I don't get guests very often staying for dinner." She poured two glasses and put the bottle on the table. "Just help yourself," she told me and got the starter from the kitchen.

The dish looked beautiful. The salmon skilfully placed atop the salad, perfectly grilled and seasoned, complemented by a soft dressing that reminded me of a simple vinaigrette which had been sweetened by adding a dollop of honey.

We spoke little during the first course. Neither would we during the second. She poured more wine and put the Shepherd's Pie in front of me, Ireland's very own comfort food.

Good comfort food had one job and one job only: To offer a time-tested balance of flavours and simplicity, a balance that's just adventurous enough to keep the eater's tongue and palate entertained, without challenging them too much. Emotion over complexity. Like a hug with no hint of ulterior motive. Like cuddling up in a blanket on a rainy day. Like a mother telling a child that everything was fine. And that's what her Shepherd's Pie did. It comforted me.

"Do you like it?" Helen asked me, and I nodded.

We were still mostly silent, heading into dessert, sitting there, plates of shortbread in front of us, a coffee to my right and a glass of brandy next to it. The bottle of wine was almost empty. Archie was sleeping peacefully in a corner.

"I'm sorry," I said, "I don't seem to be very talkative today."

"That's fine," she replied.

"It's a beautiful house," I said, just for the sake of not letting the conversation die without a whimper.

"Thanks," she said, taking a sip from her espresso.

"Did you grow up here?"

"No," she replied. "My family used to come up to Dunfanaghy for holidays. We'd stay in town, but I'd always see this house when we'd go to the beach. I was in love with it ever since I was a little child. Then, my husband and I bought it a few years back when it was for sale."

"Your husband? Is he...?" My tone implied death.

"No, he's fine. Very much alive, as far as I know. I got the house, he got the postmaster's daughter." It wasn't a funny sentence. Still, her deadpan delivery made us both laugh. "I'm sorry," I finally said.

"Don't be," she replied. "I make it – and him – sound worse than it is. We were having a tough time, both of us, and we both coped with it in our own way. It is what it is."

I wanted to ask her to tell me more, but then, I also didn't want to pry. My mind worked its own story, suddenly aware of the signs around us, signs of other people who'd lived in this house. The photos above the mantelpiece. The shoes at the entrance. A thick coat behind the door, much too big for her. Drawings on the fridge. Tiny, little, yellow boots next to the door for a child of about seven or eight years. The cliffs outside the house, on the way to the beach. A good place to climb. A good place to fall.

A good place to die.

There was a knock at the door.

Helen jumped up and a few seconds later, I could hear the sounds of someone entering the house.

"It is raining cats and dogs," a woman said with a thick Australian accent.

"Did you bike back?" Helen replied, astonishment in her voice.

"Had to bring your bike back, hadn't I?" the woman said.

"We were having dinner," Helen said as she led the woman into the dining room. "Do you want something?"

"A coffee. Wouldn't mind a brandy."

She sat down at the table, and I smiled at her. I felt awkward. Also, I recognised her. It was the woman I'd pumped into at the pub earlier today.

"Hi," I said.

"Hi," she replied. "Oh, Helen, do you also have a towel?" Water was dripping from her long, dark, wet hair.

"Is it raining?" I asked. Genius question, genius.

"No. Went for a swim." Obvious joke. Still, made us both laugh.

"How was your day?" Helen asked the woman as she put down the brandy and the coffee in front of her. She also poured me another glass. My tummy felt warm and satisfied.

"It was good," she replied. "I biked along the coast. Beautiful. And incredibly quiet. I actually went for a swim. It was freezing. Then, it rained. And there was that storm. I was scared. And hid in a cave close to the beach with a couple of sheep."

"Goodwyn's sheep. They like people," Helen said. She seemed not nearly as amazed as me by the thought of someone hiding in a cave from a storm with a couple of sheep.

"Eventually, I figured it was no use and I would have to head back at some point. So, through the rain I went and now I am back here. My book is ruined, though."

She'd put a thick volume next to her on the table. It had been completely drenched by rain.

"What are you reading?" I asked.

"Antkind. Kaufmann."

"I read it. Half of it, that is," I said.

"Do you like it?"

"I got some issues with it. Kaufmann in general," I replied, not providing further details on what my beef with the man was. I looked at her more closely. She looked familiar, more familiar than someone you bumped into while leaving a pub. She wanted to say something, follow up on my Kaufmann remark, but I spoke before her: "What's your name?" I said, hoping it would bring me a clue if I knew her.

"Vickie. Not my official name, though. Passport says Julia."

"You from Australia?"

"New Zealand," she replied.

No clue. I did not investigate further.

We talked about things of no consequence, about the Lord of the Rings movies, about sheep and hiding in caves and about beaches, but Helen soon got up to bring the dishes to the kitchen and we helped her tidy up despite her protests ("You are guests!"). I then excused myself and went to my room to crawl into bed.

I heard their voices downstairs for a while, speaking in muted tones and it felt like being in a home. I fell asleep, drifting away on a wave of unconsciousness, dreaming I was sitting in a cave, playing cards with a couple of sheep. They had it in with each other and were cheating, I liked their positive energy, though, so I let them win.

I was having breakfast alone the next morning. Helen was in the kitchen rummaging and there was no sign of Vickie. I paid my bill, gave Helen a generous tip, thanked her so much and promised I'd be back, whereupon she gave me a quick hug and thanked me.

"Where are you going today?" she asked me when we stepped outside, and I stood next to my car.

"National Park in..." I couldn't remember the name.

"It might be sunny today," she said and looked up at the sky.

"Say hi to Vickie from me."

"She's already left." Huh. That felt disappointing.

I got in my car and drove off. It felt wrong in an unspecific way. Like leaving a moment that had felt right and that could've gone on forever. A moment of finding peace in a house on a hill above a beach. The moment of a good glass of wine in front of a fire. A good book. Weary feet. Pleasant dreams.

Things have to pass, don't they? I had to think of the small, yellow rain boots next to the entrance.

I picked up Mario again, past Drimnaraw. He was standing there, just like the previous time, at the side of the road, thumbs up, still the same clothes and rucksack, still looking like a character from the German TV series Dark, just a bit dirtier and smellier.

"Wanna ride?" I said, stopping next to him, trying to look very cool and casual.

"Man, the gods have sent you," he exclaimed and jumped in.

"How was the rave?"

"Man, you really missed something. I've never seen so many gingers at one rave. I fucking love Ireland." He was clearly still drunk or on drugs or both. "And there was that DJ from Dubai. Fucking mental. I haven't slept... since the last time I saw you, man. Days ago." It wasn't days ago. But I didn't correct him. He seemed too excited about it. "Man, meeting you again," he continued, "what are the chances?"

I met Vickie again in Kilmacrenan while slowly driving the car past an assembly of colourful houses, Mario sleeping in the passenger's seat next to me. I was contemplating getting something to drink from a shop when I saw her step out of a cafe on the roadside. I stopped the car next to her.

"Hey, remember me?" I said, but realised I'd forgotten to open the passenger window. Which I did now, hastily. She'd stopped walking and was grinning at the car. "Hey, remember me?" I repeated. Mario woke with a startled inhale.

"Yeah, I remember you," she replied and stepped up to the passenger window next to Mario.

"Who, me?" Mario said.

"You wanna have a lift?" I said.

"Where to?" Mario replied, looking between me and her.

"South?" she asked.

"Sure," I said.

"South?" Mario asked. "That works for me."

"Who are you?" she asked while she got into the back.

"That's A.," Mario replied, introducing me, "super-nice guy, has picked me up twice now. Super-nice."

"Nice," she replied.

"I am Mario."

"That's Vickie," I said, introducing her.

"Hi," Mario said.

"Where are we going?" she asked.

Mario put a cigarette between his lips. "Sorry, can't smoke here. It's a rental," I told him. He put the cigarette behind his ear. I envied him. "Have you guys heard of Castle Caldwell?" he said.

"What about it?" she asked.

As it happened, that was where I'd intended to go. But I didn't tell them just yet. I wanted to know where this was going first.

"There is an annual druid meeting down there. I want to join."

"A what?" I said.

"You a druid?" she asked.

"No," Mario replied to her and then to me: "A druid convention. They chant in the woods and stuff. Real close to nature. You guys should come with."

"I don't know..." I said. I didn't want to join a group of wood-chanting druids.

"Come on," Vickie said excitedly from the backseat, "that sounds like fun. What's the worst that could happen?"

"They might drug us and steal our kidneys." I was half-serious about it, Mario and Vickie didn't even comment, tough. It seemed like a long-winded argument: Mario travelling about Ireland, pretending to be an Italian, hitchhiking, waiting for his moment to strike and lure people into dark woods to get his hands on their kidneys together with his druid friends. The more I thought about it, the sillier the idea became.

We drove on.

"I am missing a kidney," Mario said after a while.

"What?"

"I donated it. To a friend of mine."

"That's nice," Vickie said.

"He still died. A few years later. But it was some good years," Mario said and smiled, lost in some old memory. We stayed silent. There wasn't much we could say. There was also no way we could not go with Mario to his druids now. He'd become real.

After driving about half of the way, Vickie and I decided to stop at a gas station to get cheap sandwiches. Mario had little a say in the matter, as he'd fallen asleep in the passenger's seat and would remain there, passed out completely, for the entirety of our rest stop. We ate our sandwiches (which tasted of wet cardboard), leaning against the hood of the car, watching the people entering and exiting the gas station.

"Don't you wonder sometimes," Vickie said, "what they are all doing, these people?" she asked me, pointing at the steady stream of humans.

"I do, sure. But I usually come to the conclusion that I don't want to know."

"Why?"

"I... just because, I guess."

"Come on. Tell me."

"I don't know. I don't trust people. People do shitty things. And sometimes, I feel like I should do something about it. But instead, I'm in Ireland, happily eating a shitty sandwich."

"Hmm," she replied, not a reply of much substance at all. I felt bad for my baseless complaining and searched for something else to say, when, suddenly, she laughed and pointed to two short women exiting a car and releasing a pack of no less than six Beagles on leashes from the car's trunk. They walked along the parking lot towards a strip of grass, pulled by the mighty weight of the Beagles, a real-life version of Tweedledee and Tweedledum packing a pack of dogs.

We arrived at the forest in the afternoon. Mario woke up the moment we parked the car in a vast parking lot. He led us along a path into the forest, a lake glittering through the trees. Soon, we heard drums and chanting somewhere off in the woods. Druids indeed. Hold on to your kidneys.

Following the sounds, we found a group of maybe twenty people atop a hill, which overlooked the better part of the forest and the lake. To my great dismay, they were not wearing long, brown robes, nor did any of them have long, grey beards. They looked like normal people, dressed in jeans and raincoats, wearing woollen hats.

Mario approached them, we stood aside while he did the negotiating. He spoke to one druid for a while, who looked friendly and kept nodding. A few meters off, a man was sitting behind a set of small drums, drumming an almost relaxing rhythm. Someone gave us two cups with what turned out to be cider.

Mario came back to us, apparently happy. "Bad news: we have missed most of it. They started chanting at 5 in the morning, not the evening. Got my information wrong. Good news: they are inviting us to their last ceremony before they all head home." I wondered what they did when they were not on a hill being druids. Accountants? Teachers? Did they have kids? Was being a druid hereditary? What even was a druid?

"When's the ceremony?" I asked.

"Now," Mario replied, pointing to the group of druids who had started gathering their belongings.

The small group and we moved down the hill. It was an almost solemn procession, walking into the forest and along the lake. They seemed to walk slowly, as if to make sure they were enjoying the scenery around them and I did the same, step by step, looking closely at the barks of trees and the silver surface of the lake. My and Vickie's eyes met while we walked. Her face looked beautiful in the mild, orange afternoon sun. She smiled at me. I looked away.

We finally arrived at a clearing in the forest, the druids assembled in a big circle and invited us to join. The man Mario had spoken to stepped forward and talked, saying things about the nature around us and thanking everyone for being here.

Then, someone passed around a bowl with small red fruits. Everyone took one and ate one. I hoped there weren't any drugs inside, still, followed suit. The berry tasted sour, but better than what you get at a Catholic service.

Thinking of Catholics: they passed around a cup of wine a little later and everyone took a sip. Everyone from the same cup. I passed it on without drinking, so did Vickie. Mario seemed to down the entire cup. Herpes and kidneys. Fuck you, druids.

"Winds of the East," the man who had stepped forward spoke, "we summon you." The group repeated the words. "Winds of the North," he continued, "we summon you." The group repeated. The same spiel again for the winds of the West and South, a whole lot of summoning nature. Sure enough, the wind seemed to pick up after every part of the summon, a brief gust, though that might just have been my imagination.

Then they all sat down and closed their eyes. So did we. And meditated, I guessed. Relax. Listen to the surrounding nature. Be yourself and that kind of stuff.

It got boring real quick.

After about half an hour, my legs hurt, and I opened my eyes. The druids all sat there peacefully, eyes closed. Mario had toppled over and was sleeping. Off in the forest, I heard the cries of animals I could not identify.

Next to me, Vickie had also opened her eyes. We looked at each other. She tilted her head, smiling, signing me the unsaid question: "Should we get out of here?"

I fervently nodded. Yes. Let's.

We snuck out of the circle, leaving sleeping Mario and the meditating druids behind.

"What was that about?" Vickie said as we were out of earshot.

"I was so surprised that there we no drugs. Not even something to smoke. Not even a joint," I said, jokingly, and shrugged. "I don't do drugs," I added.

"Mario must be so disappointed," she said.

"I hope they won't just leave him there."

We followed the path back through the forest and approached the lake. There was a castle off in the distance, on a small island, nothing major, only a decrepit stone-building that was slowly crumbling under the weight of time. We stopped and gazed at the lake. The castle looked like the kind of place you'd like to walk through while dreaming of a bygone era, dreaming you were a lord of something, doing lordly things, hunting, and riding across your lands and sitting in front of a fire on a cold winter's night.

...

"You have completely zoned out," she said, noticing me looking at the castle, thinking about things to think about. "What were you thinking about?"

"Nothing," I replied. I lied. My thoughts of lordhood and the past seemed weird. I didn't want to explain them.

We walked along the lake until we faced a sign declaring we were standing in front of the Lake of Love and that there was a suitable photo-spot ahead. Apparently, the Irish authorities had recognised the appeal of romantic marketing. Reminded me of my travels in Japan.

"Lol," I said and laughed.

"What's lol?"

"Lake of love. Lol."

"Look, they have swan thingies," Vickie exclaimed and pointed to a miserable-looking group of plastic boats shaped like swans. They were tied to a pier stretching out into the lake.

"Nice," I said, sounding as sarcastically and dryly as I could.

"What's the time?"

"Four," I replied after having consulted my smartphone.

"There's still time. Let's go," she said and walked forward, along the lake, to my horror, in the direction of the plastic swan boats.

"What are you doing?" I said, trying to hide the panic that was rising inside, fearing that she was doing exactly what it looked like she was doing.

"Let's take a boat."

I stopped. She stopped and turned around.

"What?" she said.

"We are going to capsize. If I sit in one of those boats."

"Nah, come on. You just need someone to weigh you down on the other side."

That was the end of the discussion. She turned around again and walked up to a man sitting on a bench next to the boats, gave him twenty euros, untied one boat and hopped in.

It wobbled on the water, left, right, up, down. Get in, she told me, smiling, way too happily despite my misery. Hop in. No hopping with this man. He slowly approached the boat, put one foot on the edge, whereupon the wobbling increased, whereupon he lifted the other leg, way too quickly and fearfully, pushing the boat away from the edge, both feet now off the secure land, the boat drifting off, him holding on for his dear life at the neck of the swan, her telling him to sit down quickly, the swan tilting against the horizon, her putting all her weight against it, snorting and laughing like a child and him, finally sitting down, heavily, whereupon the swan first is pushed down, water splashing up on either side, and then jumps out of the water, before coming down again, up, down, up, down, now just a gentle bobbing against the waves, up and down.

"I am happy to report," she said, "that we have not capsized. Yes, we are at a bit of an angle, but we are safe and alive. Now pedal, my matey!"

We put our feet on the pedals in front of us, the plastic swan followed our commands and pushed out into the lake.

We glided past the shore for a while, then out onto what looked like a silver mirror. The lake's surface was quiet and still and whatever winds the druids had summoned had disappeared. A flock of birds rose from the nearby trees, and we found a side arm of the lake, which we travelled into for a while, taking breaks now and then, leaning back and observing tall grass at the shore.

It seemed peaceful, the planet, on that boat, next to Vickie.

"What are you thinking about?" she said.

Nothing, I wanted to reply, but I said nothing, for a long time.

What was I thinking about? Peace? The world? That castle? Time? Birds? Her?

Love?

What's love got to do with it?

The things we did to each other.

I saw the tiny yellow boots behind the entrance door of Helen's house. Helen's gentle smile as she told me stories about her past and the things that had been. I thought of the husband who had left her alone. Fucking asshole.

"Nothing?" she finally replied in my stead.

"Life is shit," I said in my stead.

"That's a powerful thing to say," she replied and laughed. Not to make fun of me or anything, just because of a lack of anything else to reply to my categorical statement.

"I'm sorry."

"No, go ahead. I'm sorry for laughing."

"Ah, fuck," I said, trying to gain time, forging the words in my mind, knowing they wouldn't come out right, they never did. Finally, more words: "It's all fucked up. No? We are fucked up. The world's fucked up. We've fucked up." Damn lie. Damn, damn lie. I wasn't worried about the fucked-up state of the world. I was afraid that there was no place for. Me. Me. Me. No place for my happiness. No one to hug me. No one to embrace me.

Silence.

Silence.

I'd said too much.

Then, she said: "Yeah, sure. All is fucked up. Only, that's not all there is, is there? Also, you swear too much."

Sure. That was not all. But just think about all the terrible things we can do to each other. Episodes upon episodes on Netflix filled with documentaries about real-life murders and rapes and violence and madness. No one ever made a documentary about how good we were. I wanted to cry. I wanted to yell at her, just for the sake of yelling at someone. I couldn't. I didn't. I yelled inside. Come on, dude, just jump into the lake. End it. Kiss her. Don't kiss her. Make the pain go away.

"I just find it scary to think about what we can do to each other," I said, trying to brush off the topic in one sentence, calm the yelling voice in my mind.

"Maybe it's not just about what we do to each other," she said, sighing, "but what we can do *for* each other."

What can we do for each other?

"Speak your mind," Vickie said. I didn't. Why not?, she didn't ask. Because I'm afraid you might not like what you find inside. Because I'm afraid I'd fall in love with you. Because I'm afraid you might fall in love with me. Because I'm afraid you are not the one I'm looking for. That there is someone better to fall in love with.

"Or do not speak, " Vickie said, shook her head, watching a lone seagull fly circles above our heads.

We pedalled back to the shore, back to where we had started. The man we had paid for the boat had disappeared, which made me wonder whether the boats had been his or whether he'd just been some random guy sitting there, cashing in on weird tourists who handed him money to get into a swan plastic boat, while the real owner of the boats had disappeared long ago.

We solemnly walked to the car, each of us lost in our worlds and thoughts, not sharing where we'd been. I felt bad about feeling bad and tired about the whole thing, about being me.

"Where you going to go?" I asked her. She pulled up google maps on her phone and pointed to the coast in the east, a ship port, saying that I wouldn't have to drive all the way for her, but that she would be glad if I could drop her off at a bus stop.

To be honest, I had nowhere to go today. I had a plane the next day, so the only fixed point I had was the airport tomorrow. Tonight, I'd been planning on stopping at a random hotel somewhere on my way. "I can drive you to the port," I said.

We drove in silence. The day turned to night, and it rained, which was not entirely a surprise on this rainy island. Still, it engulfed the car completely, muting the outside, only the sound of rain against the windshield and the restless wiping of the wipers.

"Where you gonna go?" I asked her as we approached the port.

"I got a ferry to Scotland tomorrow," she said without much emotion at all. I wanted her to stay in the car. With me. I knew she wouldn't want to.

I dropped her off at the port a couple of hours later. It was almost midnight now.

"My boat leaves in the morning," she said. The waiting room for the port was illuminated. "I'll sleep in there for a bit," she said. "What are you going to do?"

"I'll drive towards Dublin. Find a spot to sleep somewhere on the way. Or park the car when I get tired."

"Take care," she said as she turned away.

"You, too," I said as I closed the window and drove off.

Vickie

And with that, Andren drove off into the distance, leaving her behind with an empty feeling.

Yes, he was a bit of a bummer, so, so troubled about whatever was going on in his mind. Fighting fights as if he was fighting alone, those fights she knew too well. She should have told him he wasn't alone. That we all felt shitty sometimes. That life wasn't kind sometimes to any of us. That we all were afraid we missed out on the best bits.

He'd seemed like someone she'd wanted to spend more time with. And she'd hoped that he'd feel the same way.

Apparently, he didn't. He had driven off, without looking back, back towards the highway, towards Dublin, towards the plane that'd bring him home.

She wondered what his home looked like, his life, while she walked into the port building. Lucky thing it was open and illuminated, ready for the people who'd wait here for the first ferry to depart. Which would be at five in the morning, to Scotland.

It had seemed like a clever idea at one point to buy a ticket for a ferry at five in the morning. Now, as she sat down on one of those uncomfortable waiting room benches in the waiting room of the port building, it seemed like the worst idea anyone in the history of human-kind had ever had. She should have booked a hotel room and take a ferry at nine or ten in the morning. Only, the ticket for the five-o'clock ferry had been the cheapest one.

At least there was a vending machine selling drinks. Soft drinks, that was. Unfortunately, no alcohol. Luckily, crisps. Dinner would be crisps and iced tea.

She sat there while time dragged on, on that waiting room bench, sipping iced tea and munching on some crisps, waiting. There was no one else there, and the room had taken on the atmosphere of a hall that had been built for hundreds of people, yet was empty. The atmosphere of loneliness. It felt like being the last woman on Earth.

Outside, rain was pouring down. She hoped the weather wouldn't get worse, lest her ferry should get cancelled and she'd be stuck here. Forever waiting in the waiting room.

She looked at the spot outside the window front where his departure had left a car-shaped hole behind. He'd reminded her of someone, but she hadn't quite been able to put her finger on it. Maybe that boy in kindergarten who'd had a crush on her, yet had been too shy to tell her...

...until he did, fifteen years later, at a class reunion, while slow-dancing with her to Sixpence None the Richer's Kiss Me. He'd leaned forward and told her, heavily breathing, that "I had had my eyes on you since kindergarten," and tried to kiss her. Maybe he'd been inspired by the song or maybe he'd been planning from the start on swooping her off her feet with a big romantic gesture, a reveal fifteen years in the making.

There was nothing romantic or big or gesturesque about it. He'd smelled of cheap alcohol and sweat. During the evening, it had become increasingly clear that the sweet boy from kindergarten had turned into a loudmouth who made himself bigger than he was, showing people photos of his cars and his boat and told them about the secrets of NFTs. Oh, and also paraded pictures of the women he was dating, beautiful women in bikinis or lingerie. "But the other women are not real," he told her when she stopped him from kissing her, "they just look nice. Not like you, you are real." He leaned in again to kiss her, pulling her closer, his hands just above her ass, so she pushed him away. He didn't take it well and people looked at them and he called her a frugal bitch and she felt ashamed and left the reunion.

From what she'd heard, he'd died a couple of years later in a car accident. She couldn't say that she'd been sad. Still, it seemed like a harsh way to go.

But Andren was not that asshole. He was the kindergarten boy who never told you his proper feelings. The boy that had not become an asshole (yet?).

Or maybe that was just wishful thinking on her part.

The car-shaped hole outside had been washed away by the rain. She thought about home and the reasons of why she'd come to Europe. "Do you really think it is a good idea?" her friend Aleena had asked her several times, until the moment they'd arrived at the entrance to the airport, until she'd been so annoyed that she wouldn't even reply anymore. Of course, Aleena, bless her soul, only wanted to protect her, but it was up to herself to decide whether or not she wanted to get hurt. It had been up to her if she wanted to find her actual parents.

So, she'd stepped on a plane to Italy and promised Aleena to send her messages regularly (she felt the sting of guilt remembering that she hadn't sent one in a week).

There had been days when she'd wished her parents hadn't told her she'd been adopted. Yet, her parents had agreed with each other, when they adopted her, that they would tell her when she turned eighteen. Of course, there had been fleeting moments of suspicion in her youth, mainly because of her looks, the fact that she did not look Asian at all. But she figured that she just took more after her father than her mother.

It was okay for many years. Her parents told her, she felt fine about it, their relationship didn't change. Then the questions crawled in. The why and when and how. Those missing spots in her own story of how it came about that she'd been adopted. That she had been put up for adoption. That someone had given birth and given her away.

Their parents had all the paperwork and at first glance, it all looked normal. But they had known back then and knew now that it all had been dodgy. The dingy, dark adoption office in Italy, the many undocumented fees (bribes?), the weird-looking stamps and signatures. Yet, they'd just been happy that it all had worked out and that after a few weeks of back and forth, they'd been able to take a healthy-looking baby home to NZ.

They supported her quest for knowledge, gave her what little information they had (which mainly comprised the address of the adoption office in Rome) and gave her money for the trip. Only Aleena was against it, but Vickie mainly attributed that to the fact that she secretly felt bad for not being able to go with her.

Her flight had arrived late, so she ate a plate of pasta at a small restaurant on the way to her Airbnb. She'd had been planning to check on the address of the adoption office first thing after she'd arrived, but she felt tired, jet-lagged and in dire need of a shower.

The apartment was not too far from the train station, in a dark side alley, through a keypad-locked gate into a housing complex, up the stairs, and through another keypad-locked door. No need for human interaction. The apartment, heavy stone walls, lay silently before her and she sat down with a deep sigh at the kitchen table. It felt like arriving in an empty place.

She saw the lights and houses of Rome from the kitchen window. Somewhere in this town, presumably, she'd been born.

She showed the piece of paper with the address to a taxi driver the next morning, who asked her something in Italian, which she didn't understand. He said some more things, clearly agitated, but then, finally, drove off. They arrived at their destination a short ten minutes later.

"It is here," the driver said in broken English. They were outside a tall building. Maybe an office building once, now, it looked deserted and decrepit. Slowly falling apart. Whatever history she'd have had here, it was gone.

"Erm. Do you know..." she said to the taxi driver, broke off immediately, trying not to sound like she was about to cry like a little child or not to laugh at her own naïveté. The only clue she had had brought her to an abandoned building.

How could she have been so stupid?

Before she could try to say something else, the taxi driver answered with a flurry of words, waving his hands about, and only stopped when he saw the desperate expression on her face.

"It is empty," he said, calmer. "It is all gone. No adoption anymore," he added. "Check city office, maybe."

"What? But... you know about the adoption office? That is why I'm here." Hope in her voice. He knew something.

"No, not can help," the driver said, waving his hands. "Check city office, maybe, but not..."

"Please," she interrupted him, pleading. "I need help. I do not know where else to look." The driver continued in Italian, waving his hands, increasingly loud words coming out of his mouth, words sounding like asking her not to ask him questions.

"I do not know where to look for...," she finally said, and he fell silent. He looked at her through the rear-view mirror. "I don't know where I am from..." Now tears in her eyes.

He sighed. Silence. Then, after a long while, he started the car. They drove away from the empty building and into a livelier part of the town. People milling about on sidewalks, small houses in view, tables outside, restaurants. He finally parked in front of a building, by the signs at the door one of the restaurants.

"Come," he said. He stepped out of the car and led her inside, where he was greeted by a woman in Italian. She stood behind a counter. Four old-looking guys were sitting at a round table, drinking glasses of wine and eating slices of pizza off a shared plate. The place got silent when she stepped in behind the driver and everyone seemed to look at her.

"This is sister. My," the driver explained, pointing at the woman behind the counter, and motioned her to a table to sit down. The driver took the sheet of paper from her hand and talked to his sister for a while. One of the old guys leaned over to her and spoke to her in Italian. She only shrugged in reply, whereupon he poured a glass of red wine and handed it to her.

SOME OF US ARE REAL | 509

"Adoption office?" the sister finally asked her.

"Yes," she said. "I was adopted. And this address is all I know. I am looking for my parents." The sister nodded and there was some discussion between the old guys, the driver, and her. Then, the sister stepped behind the counter to pick up a phone (a landline!) and dial a number.

"It will be good. She'll find him," the driver said and smiled at her. *Him*? Who?

"Thank you so much," she said. Her voice was shaking.

"You gotta eat," the driver said and put a plate of pasta in front of her, poured her another glass of wine. The sister was talking loudly on the phone now, clearly agitated, slamming the receiver down to hang up, only to dial a new number a few seconds later and to start another loud conversation. "No one wants to talk," the driver said, explaining the sister's agitation. "They are scared they get in trouble with police." She wanted to ask why, couldn't. What had she got herself into? The driver turned to talk to the old guys. The room seemed to grow more serious by the minute, almost as if they were at a funeral, everyone talking about the reasons why the deceased had died, in a language she could not understand.

The sister put down the phone, sighed and smiled. "I have reached Signor Ravalli. He is coming," she finally said, and everyone nodded, as if she'd said a name they knew all too well.

"He will come," the sister told her, "in an hour. He knows. Eat."

Signor Ravalli? What did he know?

The hour stretched on like an eternity, despite everyone's best effort to keep her entertained and get her mind off things. The old guys would tell her in very broken English about the old days when they chased girls in the streets and the sister would hit them with a towel to make them shut up. The driver would present her with different liquors he'd found behind the bar, liquors in unmarked bottles, clearly none from a store, but most likely made in the home-manufactories of neighbours and friends. "This is, how do you say, *mandarin*, from Ernesto. I know him, good man," the driver said and poured her a glass. "Very good."

She'd almost (yet not quite) forgotten about Signor Ravalli and the reason she was here when *he* came through the door. A tall man with a grey beard, walking at a cane, slowly, frail. It was as if time stopped when he stepped inside, everyone stopped, everyone looked at him. Godot had arrived.

The sister hurried to him from behind the counter and helped him to the table to sit down opposite of her. The driver put down a glass of wine next to him. The old guys whispered to each other.

He smiled at her, Signor Ravalli, a comforting, gentle smile.

"You are one of the adopted, are you?" There was no trace of an Italian accent when he spoke.

"Yes," she replied. Her voice trembling. She felt like she was sitting beside herself, watching a story unfold she had no part in.

"The truth of the matter is," the man said, yet stopped mid-sentence to take the glass of wine in his large hand and take an excruciatingly long sip, "I do not know which one you are. I do not know who your parents are." He sighed. It seemed genuine. Years of worry and sadness frowned across his face. "I have seen many babies." He sighed again, lost in memories for a second. "We collected babies where we could, babies in need of parents." The restaurant had grown silent. The world seemed to have grown silent. Not a bird chirping, not a car passing by.

"What do you mean?" she finally said.

"Me and my friends, we built a network of adoption offices in Europe. We wanted to do some good, give a bit of hope to lost children. People brought them to us, they knew we would find them a home. It was not legal, what we did, we had no permits in most countries. All we wanted was to prevent some children from having to grow up in those awful state institutions." He took another sip before he continued. "Us not having permits is what made people come to us. Many of those that brought us babies were illegal, too. No papers. Or desperate people. Mothers that had got their sixth child with nowhere else to go. Prostitutes giving birth and leaving their children on our doorstep. Women who feared their husbands might beat the baby to death. They all knew we wouldn't ask questions."

The pasta felt heavy in her stomach.

"I am one of them?"

"Yes."

"Can you find out where I come from?" She showed him the piece of paper with the details of her adoption, the date, her name. All she had of her past. He shook his head. "I am sorry. I can't. We had so many of you in those years."

"So, I have just been abandoned?" she said.

"No, no, don't see it that way, my child," he replied, his voice much warmer than it had any right to be. "They did not give you away because they hated you or wanted to abandon you. These were mothers, desperate. They didn't have anywhere else to go. They had been abandoned by society. But by giving you to us, they gave you a chance. Your mother saved you."

There was a long silence after that, a silence that slowly turned into sound again. She heard the cars outside getting louder. The people walking past the open door, talking, the birds, two cats arguing around the corner. The sound of glasses and dishes being used. The sister had stepped into the kitchen and was cooking. Wine being poured, as the driver filled her glass. The old guys talking quietly to each other, lighting cigarettes.

"Thanks," she finally said. Her voice was coarse, almost a whisper. Signor Ravalli smiled at her and leaned forward. "So, tell me, how is your family? Did we do a good job?"

He bought her dinner and paid for drinks for everyone else in the restaurant. They talked a long time, she told him how she'd grown up, and about her parents. "This is very good, I am happy you've got a wonderful family," he said.

It was well past midnight when they stepped out of the restaurant. She'd hugged the driver and sister and said her goodbyes to the old guys. Signor Ravalli had offered to drive her back to her apartment.

"Are you in Rome all by yourself?" he asked on the way to the car. She affirmed. "This is no good. You need people now. You need to talk."

"I'll be fine."

"Another one of the adopted children is in town. I will ask him to bring you breakfast tomorrow."

"Another adopted child?"

"Yes," he said and smiled. "They find me occasionally, some of them. Like you. Some of them become friends. He is a good man, turned out good."

At the apartment, Signor Ravalli passed her a piece of paper with his phone number before she exited the car. "Call me if you need anything. Or if you want to come visit."

Then she made it upstairs to the apartment, closed the door behind her, fell into bed and slept a deep, dreamless sleep.

She woke up at four o'clock, shaking. It had got cold in the apartment, so she opened wardrobes and drawers to find blankets, to wrap herself up, feeling the warmth of her own body. She sat at the kitchen table, still shivering, falling in and out of sleep, flashes of thoughts on her mind, dreaming of her mother, her real mother, who was running through the streets, baby in hand, running away or towards something, a feeling of falling into a dark pit that had no bottom, that just consisted of falling endlessly.

She woke up when the doorbell rang. She was still at the kitchen table, covered by four... five... six blankets. The doorbell rang again. She got up and went to the intercom.

"Hi, this is Andy," a voice said through the speaker. "Signor Ravalli has sent me. We are both adopted. So, in a strange way, we are like siblings?" Then, a second voice, female voice next to Andy, told him to shut up. "We brought breakfast," the woman said.

She buzzed them in and realised, as she opened the door, that she must look terrible, wrapped in blankets, her dirty t-shirt from yesterday, her hair unkept and oily. She thought about bolting, locking the door, but they – Andy and the woman – had already appeared at the end of the hallway and waved at her.

"Yeah, that is about how I looked after talking to him," he said, and stepped through the door.

"Worse," the woman said. "Hi, I am Hamako."

"Vickie," Vickie replied.

"We brought food," Andy said.

She took a shower and got dressed while they made coffee. Then, they sat down at the kitchen table, and she told them about yesterday and Andy told her his adoption story, which very much sounded like hers. "It's a terrible thing," Hamako commented.

"We came here to visit Signor Ravalli," Andy added, "because he can't make it to our wedding next week. He says he is getting too old to travel."

"You are getting married?" Vickie asked the obvious question.

"Yeah, next week, in Ireland," Hamako replied, then smiled at her, an idea flashing across her face. "Do you want to come?"

"Seriously?"

"Totally. You are Andy's quasi-sibling, no?"

"But I don't even have a dress."

"Then we better get shopping. Italy has lovely shops, I hear."

She felt bad about the thought of taking up so much of their time, surely, they must have had better things to do to prepare for their wedding, yet it felt nice to have someone around. So, "Thank you," she said, "yes, I'd love to come to your wedding."

They settled for a summer dress with a floral print that made her feel like a girl from a movie. Hamako and Andy brought her to restaurants and bars and told her how the two of them had met and where they lived. She called her parents on Skype and told them what she'd learned, and they all cried, and she told them she loved them. She brought flowers and chocolate to the driver, the sister, and the old guys, and they invited her for dinner. And she wrote a long letter to Signor Ravalli to thank him.

Then, she flew to Ireland to attend a wedding of a couple she'd only met a few days ago. She also forgot to pack the beautiful dress she had bought, left it behind in the Airbnb. Thankfully, the wedding planner was able to get a black dress on short notice.

And now, she was sitting at a port in a waiting room waiting for a ferry to Scotland in the middle of the night.

The rain outside made the approaching day look like a washed-out t-shirt, grey and unclear. A TV screen came up at the front of the room, detailing the day's departures and with relief, she saw that her trip to Scotland was still on. Maybe the storm was passing. Slowly, the room filled with sleepy people, dozing off on the benches, no one talking, nor moving, nor doing anything much, except for a tiny two-year-old toddler waddling through the room, being the life of the party. Her mother tried to convince the girl to stand still next to a small plastic palm tree to take a photo of her, only the little girl was having none of it.

Andren had been at the wedding as well.

It was only now that she realised it. His face had seemed familiar when she'd bumped into him at the pub and then again when they met in Helen's house. She hadn't been able to place it – now she remembered. How he had been standing down there in the crowd, she atop the stairs, him not wearing a tie, his beard bushy and somewhat unkept – there'd been something in his eyes, him looking up at her without really looking at her, then turning around and talking to someone and listening to someone, something in his eyes. Something real.

She peered at the outside world. It looked like the rain was easing. The parking lot had filled up with cars and more and more people streamed into the building. She put in her earphones, leaned back, and put on Ólafur Arnalds' Living Room Sessions. Soon, she was drifting off into a thoughtless doze.

Some of Us

He stopped at a gas station halfway to the airport. It was still raining cats and dogs, so Andren got soaked from walking the few meters from the car to the building. It was the middle of the night, and he didn't feel like looking for a hotel. A drive straight to the airport it was. He needed to stock up on coffee and crisps.

He found coffee. He found crisps. On his way to the check-out, he stopped at some shelves with magazines and several books. The range of magazines was modest (the 10 Secrets to Planting a Garden caught his eye, not because of any interest in gardening, but because of a freckled redhead on the cover smilingly holding up the tiniest bonsai tree), and most of the books on offer seemed to consist only of light travel reading, Spanish-looking romance stories or science-fiction serials from the fifties. However, he was surprised to find a handful of – what his former literature professors would refer to as – proper books, the most recent Ishiguro and Atwood. And Kaufmann's book, Antkind. He recognised it at once from its cover because he'd had a copy lying on his desk at home for weeks now. He kept telling himself he'd have to finish reading it every time he moved it to a new spot on the desk when it got in the way.

It seemed an odd place for such a book, a gas station in the middle of nowhere, yet maybe that thought was racist or stereotypical on his part. It wasn't just the elite reading those kinds of books. People travelling read proper books, people living on farms in Ireland read proper books. He took Kaufmann's book in his hand and read the text on the back. It was the same text he'd read many times.

The problem with Kaufmann was not that Andren disliked him. The problem was that Kaufmann came up with ideas Andren would have liked to come up with before him.

The problem with Kaufmann on this particular day was that the book, of course, reminded Andren of *her*. It lying next to her on the table, drenched from the rain. He pictured Vickie sitting at the port now, waiting for her ferry, waiting for the night to pass.

How did we know, he wondered, whether people not just simply stopped existing when we didn't look at them? How did he know she was still there? But then, if she wasn't real, how come he missed her?

He looked at his little finger, hoping to find a little red string that would lead him back to her.

"Are you going to buy something?" the man behind the counter said, and he woke from his thoughts. He had been gazing at Kaufmann's book for far too long.

Yes, sorry, he said, stepped up to the counter and quickly put down the cans and the crisps he'd been holding in his arms.

Behind him, a young couple was standing in front of the freezer, looking at the range of frozen pizza. Probably stoned. Drunk. Who'd be looking at frozen pizza in the middle of the night?

"Long drive?" the man asked Andren while he was ringing up the items. "Long life," he said, and they both laughed. What did that even mean?

Outside, snow began falling. None of them saw it at first, the flakes coming down, the humans in the gas station just continued with their lives. The cashier was scanning the barcodes, Andren was counting coins, the couple was discussing the merits of salami over ham pizza. "Don't even suggest the mushroom thing," the man said. "But it is healthy," she protested. "It is fucking frozen pizza," he countered.

The pizza-boyfriend was the first one to see the snow. "What the fuck?" he said, peering out of the windows which occupied most of the storefront.

The big snowflakes outside were yellow-greenish in the pale light coming from the gas station. The cashier, who'd been battling with the barcode of a most stubborn can of coffee, stopped and followed the man's gaze. "What's happening?" the woman asked. "It is fucking snowing," the pizza-boyfriend replied.

There they stood, the four of them, gazing at the snow that wasn't supposed to be. "In July? Fucking ice age this is," the woman said.

They looked beautiful, the snowflakes, thick and heavy, falling to the ground, pushed around by gentle gusts of wind, as if they were alive, tiny little beings descending from the sky.

And Andren saw how things would evolve from here on out. The woman would suddenly scream and laugh and throw a snowball at her boyfriend and they would run outside, just run, run, like two little dogs jumping up and down. The cashier would utter some snarky remarks and finish scanning his stuff. Andren would pay and get into the car, nervous, because he did not fancy much driving in the snow. He would turn left, in the airport's direction, drive slowly. Thankfully, he would not miss the flight, because all flights would be delayed. It would be chaos at the airport, this would be worse than the volcano in Iceland, people would say. The bars at the airport would give out free beer and crisps to keep people entertained.

He would arrive at home twelve hours late, in the middle of the night, in a bad mood, because he hated being late, and he'd been look-ing forward to relaxing on the couch for a few hours before going to bed. He'd sleep a dreamless, exhausted sleep and shower in the morning and be back in the office before he knew it. He'd work his way through papers and requests and try to figure out the status of the things he'd been working on before his holiday, he'd meet F in the evening for drinks in a bar, that bar that had just opened and served craft beer brewed by local micro-breweries, and he'd go to bed and would go to work on Tuesday, and he'd be alone at home in the evening and cook some salmon, fry it with butter and lime juice, and play some video games and would see E and M the next day, have a glass of wine with them and protest as they'd invite him for dinner, of course, accept the invitation, and he'd slave on at work towards the weekend, and meet K for coffee on Saturday morning and watch the 1921 movie Kökarlen on Sunday and play some more video games and be too lazy to cook and, instead, order Chinese duck, and the days would turn into weeks and into months and into years and it is a good life, it is a long, good life, and he has all he needs and he is fucking privileged.

He looked at his little finger. Fuck.

Outside, the snow was turning into a blizzard. "We'll be stuck here," the pizza-boyfriend said, putting down the ham pizza he was holding. And Andren could see how things would evolve from here on out. The snow would pile up outside, meter after meter, and they would be forced to eat the frozen pizza frozen, like animals. They would argue and be at each other's throat, the woman would eye the cashier and they would secretly meet in the bathroom, and she would get pregnant, yet tell no one. They would form their own society, a society of four individuals. The lies would all come alight when the fifth member of their society would be born, but they'd work through it and then sit there, as the world ended outside, and there would be nothing left except for the empty streets and empty tables, and the woman would knit scarves for them, and hats and they'd die of old age. Andren would be the first one to go, praying, hoping that one of them would hold him in their arms while he'd be dying.

The cashier was still standing there, can in hand. Like the couple with the frozen pizza, staring at the falling snow. The gentle wind outside had transformed into an aggressive animal, hissing and buzzing, throwing the poor snowflakes around. The trees on the other side of the road shook heavily, looking as if they were about to break. Andren wanted to tear his clothes off and run out into the cold, yell at the wind, yell at it to come and take him.

And he could see how things would evolve from here on out. He'd pay for his items and go back to his car, move the wet snow down from the windshield and he'd drive to the right, back, back, back to where he'd come from. He'd drive slowly and carefully, but still would have to evade a deer and drive the car into a ditch. He wouldn't be hurt, would have to continue on foot, in his thin coat, battling the snow and the wind.

He'd arrive at the port looking like a snowman, tired and cold and frozen like a fucking frozen salami pizza. It would be chaos there, so many people huddled up inside, no ferries leaving, everyone waiting, wanting to go somewhere south, away from the cold planet.

You'd still be there.

Sleeping on a bench, earphones in ears. I'd sit down heavily. "Hey, Vickie," I'd say, "I would offer you a lift. But I drove the car in a ditch."

Vickie would open her eyes, look at Andren baffled, and smile and hug him. The warm hug would warm him up and let him forget that, mere seconds ago, he'd felt like a frozen pizza. "You came back," Vickie would say. "You stayed," he'd reply. "There was no leaving," she'd say. "I would have found you, anyway. At the end of the red string," he'd say. "We'd find each other without it," Vickie would conclude, smile, and hug him again. The only hug he'd ever need.

"That's 23 euros," the cashier said and woke him a last time from his reverie. He didn't want to take his eyes off the world outside. "It is beautiful," he said, "the snow."

"Fucking sheep over at Robin's Bluff are gonna freeze to death," the man at the freezer muttered. His pizza partner agreed.

"What is the price of beauty?" Andren said, speaking to himself, or maybe in the general direction of the cashier. The cashier nodded, feigning approval of the question, yet Andren knew he wasn't really listening. Still, he continued: "Can we afford to pay that price?" The flakes came thicker now, an opaque curtain of frozen water. He had to think of the sheep on a meadow somewhere, huddled up, trying to survive in each other's embrace. "For every beautiful, pristine snowflake we admire, a sheep has to die somewhere. Fuck Goethe. Fuck Happiness. Fuck Fomo. Fuck this life. It hasn't been made for us. The price is too high."

"It is only 23 euros, actually," the cashier said, somewhat perplexed by his speech, unsure what to make of it. He probably thought Andren was crazy. Andren wanted to go outside and be carried away by the snowflakes. Up to the heaven. Down to hell. Anywhere but here. Somewhere finite.

Behind him, the couple had decided on the Quattro Fromaggi. He paid the 23 euros and left the gas station. He got in the car and started the engine.

Fuck this shit. Fuck the road to the left. Fuck the one to the right. Fuck decisions. Fuck feeling lonely. Fuck being afraid of not being lonely.

Fuck that, I told Andren. The only thing you are afraid of is that no one will tell your story. All these stories you are making up, and that's the only one you care about.

Andren/I started the car and turned on the lights. We all feel like shit sometimes, you said. Yeah, I replied, while guiding the car off the parking lot, but I am not even good at feeling shit. The snow kept coming. The road branching ahead, to the left, to the right. It doesn't matter, you said. I'll like you either way. I don't think so, I said. Some of us are happy. Some of us are not, you said. I looked at the forking road. Go left, go right. Your choice how you tell the story, you said, smiled and danced the night away.

The forking road.

I made my choice.

The car, me, myself and Andren left the parking lot.

Lightning Source UK Ltd.
Milton Keynes UK
UKHW021609130123
415295UK00016B/1197